PRAISE FOR <u>ALTERNATIVE ATLANTA</u>

"Reminiscent of writers like Nick Hornby and Kelly Cherry, while remaining wholly original, Boswell is as thoughtful on the page as he is entertaining, and he's always a pleasure to read."
—Michael Knight, author of *Goodnight, Nobody*

"A heartfelt and kick-ass-funny story that is at its essence about the pain of growing up—especially when you put it off for a decade or two. Smart and highly readable at the same time, keenly observed in refreshingly original style by Marshall Boswell, the promise of his collection *Trouble with Girls* is equaled and then some."
—Elizabeth Crane, author of *When the Messenger Is Hot*

"Amusing... charming."—*Kirkus Reviews*

"Fans of Nick Hornby will want to check it out."
—*Greenville News*

"I'm not sure whether *Alternative Atlanta* falls into the category of 'great rock-and-roll novels' or 'great father-son novels.' Probably both. Marshall Boswell is the voice the new South has been waiting for."—Dan Pope, author of *In the Cherry Tree*

"[Boswell] has written a charmingly quirky first novel with amazing skill and wisdom."—*Booklist*

PRAISE FOR <u>TROUBLE WITH GIRLS</u>

"Boswell [is] a fine, expressive writer... with a light hand and a virtuoso touch.... The momentum of the book is so strong that the [final] story seems... even mythic in the end."
—*Washington Post Book World*

"It's Parker Hayes's world, though Boswell's sneaky skill is such that, every time I stopped laughing long enough to wipe my eyes, I began to wonder with growing dread if it might be my world too.... Charming."—*Atlanta Journal-Constitution*

ALTERNATIVE
ATLANTA

A Novel

MARSHALL BOSWELL

DIAL PRESS TRADE PAPERBACKS

ALTERNATIVE ATLANTA
A Dial Press Trade Paperback Book

PUBLISHING HISTORY
Delacorte Press hardcover edition published February 2005
Dial Press Trade Paperback edition / April 2006

Published by
The Dial Press
A Division of Random House, Inc.
New York, New York

Book design by Lynn Newmark

The Dial Press and Dial Press Trade Paperbacks are registered
trademarks of Random House, Inc., and the colophon is a trademark of
Random House, Inc.

Library of Congress Catalog Card Number: 2004055274

ISBN-10: 0-385-33864-3
ISBN-13: 978-0-385-33864-6

Printed in the United States of America
Published simultaneously in Canada

www.dialpress.com

10 9 8 7 6 5 4 3 2 1
BVG

For Graham and Evan

If I am able to apprehend God objectively, I do not have faith; but because I cannot do this, I must have faith.

—Søren Kierkegaard
Concluding Unscientific Postscript to Philosophical Fragments

Christianity will go. It will vanish and shrink. I needn't argue with that, I'm right and I will be proved right. We're more popular than Jesus now.

—John Lennon

1

ONE

STEPPING OUTSIDE the church, Gerald Brinkman shakes loose a cigarette and looks to the sky in search of his father's incoming plane. His father: that duffel bag of dread. In a dim sort of way he even imagines that the ghostly crucifix he's looking for *is* his dad, a onetime Methodist minister now returned to heaven and trailing clouds of glory. But the sky is silent and blank, not a single cloud in sight.

With mounting impatience he snaps off the lighter's child-protective switch. Behind him in the church, ushers and elderly matrons shuffle and whisper amid pews and brochures and flower arrangements. Before him, the late-Saturday shopping traffic of summertime Atlanta sweeps noisily along Peachtree. The Olympic Games start Friday, so chaos is the rule. Gerald's father, meanwhile, is chaos personified. For the last six weeks he's been calling and e-mailing at an alarming rate, sometimes as often as four times a day. The e-mails offer little more than detailed descriptions of the man's numbing everyday ennui, while the phone calls consist entirely of monologue recitations from *The American Spectator* or

The Village Voice. One morning three weeks ago, while listening to his father read aloud a George Will piece from *Newsweek* about the recent epidemic of black church burnings, Gerald coughed loudly and asked his father if he'd maybe like to come for a visit or something. His father hung up immediately and called back ten minutes later with plane reservations. Gerald now tries to picture his father stepping off the plane and into the United Nations sprawl of the Hartsfield International Airport. The image snags at his heart.

He shakes the lighter in frustration, readjusts the unlit cigarette between his lips, cups his hands against the slight breeze. The lighter catches this time. Before he can bring the darting flame to the end of his cigarette an elderly woman in a shimmering red polyester dress pokes her head out the door and whispers, *"It's time!"* The flame dies. Vaguely relieved, he tosses the unlit cigarette into the bushes and steps inside.

An usher directs him to a seat near the back, an empty pew. Gerald doesn't know the guy: some friend of the groom, whom Gerald also barely knows. The usher's barrel chest strains at his starched tuxedo shirt, his plump cheeks made even plumper by a tidy, bisecting goatee.

No sooner does Gerald sit down than the processional music commences. The congregation rustles, settles, squirms. First up come the bridesmaids, all of them uniformed in the same slate-gray sleeveless dress that hovers just an inch above the ground and features, as its one and only concession to female anatomy, a lateral crease just beneath the breasts. The girls sashay down the aisle in waltz time with a cluster of flowers held before them like muffs. Each one as she passes wears a self-conscious Mona Lisa smile.

As the third bridesmaid enters Gerald's scope of vision he strains to keep his head forward, though his neck itches with an impulse to turn. This is the bridesmaid he's been waiting for:

Sasha Mantrivadi, a simian-eyed Bombay-born drug rep and wife of the bride's college boyfriend. Here amid the church's murky watercolor light her skin looks as translucent as cognac; faint blue highlights glow beneath the surface of her glossy black hair. For the last two years Gerald's harbored an innocent but also sort of pathetic crush on Sasha, partly in response to her lavish exoticism—this despite the rather bland fact that she was raised in Ohio—and mostly due to her regal unattainability. She acknowledges his gaze, however quickly, her eyes brushing his and her mouth tugged into the faintest possible smile of recognition, but she quickly jerks her eyes forward and continues down the aisle, bathed in Vivaldi and the kaleidoscopic play of colored light filtering through the stained-glass windows.

After the remaining two bridesmaids make their way to the front, the Vivaldi all at once comes to a halt. Silence echoes through the sanctuary. Coughs, shuffling feet. An organ blast jolts the congregation to attention. Like a battalion of soldiers in parade, everyone in the pews simultaneously stands and pivots to the back of the church. At the threshold of the entranceway, flanked on both sides by a fulsome funereal arrangement of flowers, stands Gerald's former girlfriend Nora Reynolds, one hand draped on the cocked arm of her silver-haired daddy and the other pinching the smooth skirt of her wedding gown. The organ blasts continue, and even Gerald's cynical heart registers a stir. Something grand is about to happen: the bride has arrived. And here she comes, right down the aisle, walking in time to her very own theme song, by Wagner, of all people. And she does look spectacular, even he has to admit. Her wispy blond hair, topped by a tiara of pearls, hangs loose along her tan shoulders, while her face, with its narrow tapering chin and high cheekbones lightly dusted with honey-brown freckles, now radiates a screen star's enameled glamour. It dawns on him that, until this moment, he's never seen her in full makeup. Most surprising of all, the neckline of her tastefully simple wedding dress dips just low enough to reveal the center crease of her breasts, which look more abundant than usual. Nora in a Wonderbra? A wonder in itself.

Sitting down with the rest of the congregation, Gerald tries to recall how many of these things he's attended in the last couple of years. Five? Seven? He's lost count. And in each one, this procession, this daughter-and-dad show. Also the dress. The beautiful wedding dress. For Nora does look beautiful, as beautiful as she's ever looked. She just doesn't look like Nora. In many respects the girl now standing at the altar looks more like a near approximation of Nora than Nora herself, like some slightly more beautiful and less convincing doppelgänger of his beloved old friend. Back when they were both still graduate students and self-absorbed lovers, Nora tended to bury her body beneath floppy thrift-store outfits composed of soccer jerseys and cut-off army fatigues, thereby making her beauty both a challenge and a source of tension, less an advertisement than a tantalizing possibility that, like the trailer for a movie you haven't seen yet, promised an originality that might dissolve under the penetrating gaze of a full viewing. But now, as she stands at the front of the church saturated in everyone's objectifying gaze, she seems to have tossed aside all that confrontational aggression. But this has always been Nora's way. Even amid the charged political atmosphere of the graduate department she proudly proclaimed how much she liked being a *girl*, giving that last word the same degree of unironic emphasis gay men give to *queer*. And she's never been shy about wanting to get married—as Gerald grimly remembers from their own fractious relationship.

At the altar Mr. Reynolds withdraws his arm and steps aside, thereby *giving her away*, as the saying goes. Nora moves closer to the groom, a computer technician named Brent Einhorn whom Nora started dating about a year ago. Brent has a sensitive guy's shaved head, sensitive-guy wire-frame John Lennon glasses, and a stubble-goatee. Here in the church, amid the incessant play of candy-colored light streaming through the stained glass, Brent's globular head juts from the cardboard collar of his tuxedo shirt like a finial on a staircase banister. An earnest, soft-spoken, likable enough guy, Brent is something of a techno-hippie, with all the attendant Pacific Northwest idealism, so Gerald can sort of see the appeal, even if he can't quite square how that appeal applies to a sharp-tongued cynic like Nora. But that's love. Or whatever it is she feels for him.

Up front, the youngish, smiling minister—more a guidance counselor than a man of the cloth, from the looks of him, his mere presence here one of the many concessions Nora made to her parents, bourgeois believers the both of them—reads a bit from I Corinthians 7 (that old chestnut) before deftly moving on to a more secular sermonette on "relationships" generally understood, which is more in keeping with Nora's style. Gerald is somewhat surprised this thing is taking place in a church at all; it's almost as surprising as the speed with which Nora and Brent decided to get hitched. Had Nora given the thing more thought, she probably would have fought for something less traditional, something more along the lines of a civil union, with music by Joni Mitchell. But she was ready, she'd told Gerald, and doing it this way was just easier, all things considered, particularly since Brent's parents attended this church, and there was a surprise July opening in the bargain.

Nevertheless, Gerald can't help but recall that sunny spring day four months ago when an exuberant Nora appeared at his little apartment all abristle with the news that she and Brent were kaput. "It just wasn't right," she told him, sitting Indian-style on his crappy thrift-store couch and nursing both a beer and a cigarette, the latter forbidden her the last seven months by health-obsessed Brent. "I just feel so"—she glanced around at his cluttered apartment with a glowing expression equal parts nostalgia and appreciation, as if she'd just returned home from a prolonged visit to a strange land—"*free*. And alive. Like I'm finally myself again." She beamed at him as she settled back along the couch's armrest, the cigarette burning unsmoked in her fist (she never was much of a smoker, anyway).

At the time Gerald hadn't known quite what to make of this sudden development. When she'd first met Brent late the previous summer, she was absolutely gaga for him, which wasn't altogether out of character. Nora loved being in love, as Gerald knew very well. She threw herself into relationships as enthusiastically as a kid executes cannonballs off a high dive. What Gerald had principally felt when he first heard about Brent was a vague sort of relief. If Nora was attached, then he was off the hook. Conversely, when she turned up free again, Gerald panicked. "I'm sure it will all work out," he told her, regretting the words even as they came out of his mouth. "You guys are so good together." Nora's sunny expression instantly turned February gray: she stared at him for a chilling moment or two, then put out her forgotten cigarette and left his apartment. When he contacted her a week later, she told him, "You were right: we're back together. Just a bit of cold feet, I guess." She was engaged within a fortnight.

Sitting here in the back of the church with one arm draped along the back of the pew, Gerald registers a sharp pang in his chest at the memory of all that. To clear his head, he thinks briefly about his father, about the one-in-two divorce statistic, about the bag of dope he has back home in his apartment, and instantly feels depressed again. Now that Nora is officially hitched—or nearly so: she's just turned to Brent, and Brent has turned to her— Gerald is officially all alone in the Singlehood, a sloppy rent-cheap section of life littered with unused condoms and empty fast-food cartons and haunted everywhere by the hollow promise of pure possibility. He's everyone else's fun-loving bachelor pal, a long-haired myopic rock critic with a one-bedroom apartment, a library's worth of compact discs and used paperback books, an overweight but friendly enough cat of indeterminate breed named Lester Bangs, a manageable-for-now smoking addiction perhaps augmented by commensurate marijuana and alcohol addictions (churches still inspire in him such brutal honesty), and a widowed father who, in his twenties, sustained a monthly back-and-forth letter-writing correspondence with Harvard theologian Paul Tillich and who now eats cold soup from the can and scours the virtual space of the Internet for information about paranormal activity and millennial eschatology writ large—a father, in other words, who, at this very moment, is probably sitting contentedly in one of the many clean plastic cars of the Atlanta MARTA mass-transit system, his sneakers untied and a placid Buddha's smile on his face, while the train he is sitting in hurtles not toward but *away* from said one-bedroom apartment. How did Gerald end up here? How did this happen? Somewhere along the road of adolescent development he must have missed a crucial exit, the one marked Adulthood or Responsibility or something. What could he have been doing when he passed it? Changing a tape, more than likely. That's probably it.

Up front, the minister commands Brent to kiss the bride.

Gerald arrives at the country-club clubhouse alone. Unfortunately—though it's also no surprise—the banquet hall is already full of laughing couples picking at plates of finger food. And it's huge, this room. It really gives you a jolt, the high, sculpted ceilings festooned with sparkling chandeliers and the vast hardwood floor half-cleared for the inevitable dancing and half-cluttered with a bewildering maze of tables and chairs. Early as it is, the hired band has already begun the first of its three-to-four contracted sets, a standard Holiday Inn lounge band comprised of variously paradigmatic members, from the blond female singer to the long-haired and mustachioed stereo salesman hunkered behind the drum kit. At present, the band plods through an indifferent rendition of "It Had to Be You," which Gerald knows has something to do with Meg Ryan and Billy Crystal movies. Indifferent though the performance may be, the band's still pretty tight, as these wedding-reception bands tend to be. A Lawrence Welk aesthetic: not necessarily a bad thing.

"So," says a female voice behind him, "what did you think?"

He turns around. Sasha stands resplendent before him in her sexless slate dress, all smiles—creamy maroon lips, chocolate-drop eyes. Because the occasion somehow demands it, he makes a brainless gesture to hug her, but then pulls back, though not before she makes a startled and belated attempt to return the gesture. They end up bumping chests and flapping their arms against each other like seals. His stomach burns with embarrassment.

Quickly, to hide his discomfort, he tells her, "You looked great up there. All of you."

"It's a nice dress, isn't it?" She looks down at herself with robotic deliberation. "I might actually wear this one again."

"Nora's practical if she's anything."

"Her mother picked this out, of course."

"That explains it, then."

"And it wasn't cheap."

"You still look terrific—dazzling, really."

"That's so nice." She smiles. "Thank you." *Always so quick to accept my compliments,* he thinks with satisfaction—compliments that, it generally occurs to him afterward, he starts bestowing upon her the minute the two of them are alone, as if he were a Welcome Wagon hostess and she the latest housewife on the block. For years Nora has gently teased him about his only somewhat ironic crush on Sasha, which always had the curious effect of rendering his feelings all the more innocent. Now that Nora's out of his life, however, Sasha is no longer a tantalizing footnote to another complex friendship but rather someone fully self-contained in her own right. As a result, her beauty abruptly unsettles him in ways it never has before. One good thing: he'll probably be seeing much less of her from now on. Ditto Nora, it occurs to him with a pang of regret.

"Where's Aaron?" he suddenly asks, as he also generally does, once the compliments are over.

"On his way, I think. He worked last night but was supposed to meet me here. I called home on the way over."

Gerald takes in this news. Neck deep in the second year of his medical residency, Sasha's husband, Aaron, sometimes puts in over a hundred hours a week. If you find that hard to believe, just ask him. He'll tell you all about it.

"He'll make it," Gerald assures her.

"Wait: I thought you were supposed to go to New York this weekend."

"Not till Wednesday." His stomach drops. Later this week Gerald is scheduled to fly to New York for a job interview with a rock music bimonthly, and now he's not so sure he wants to go. Standard preinterview jitters, sure, but there's more: now he'll have to leave his father alone in the apartment. All of which he tried to explain to his father last week, to no avail. Maybe he'll cancel. As far as he's concerned, the only compelling reason to go at all is to visit his older sister, Eva, who lives in a third-story brownstone with her husband, Walt. No way in hell he'll get the job. And, after all, rock is dead. "My dad's in town, by the way."

"Really? Why didn't you bring him?"

"He's not here yet. Or maybe he is, I don't know. Just invited himself, even though this is like the worst week in human history to visit Atlanta. The Olympics and all that. Plus, right after this wedding I have to review a band playing at the Star Bar. Then I leave town on Wednesday. None of which fazed him, as you can imagine." Sasha gives him a vacant look. "Actually, you've never met my dad, have you?"

In lieu of an answer, she scans the room. *I'm boring her. No: I'm not Aaron, that's the problem.* "Anyway, this is pretty much par for the course for my old man. Good old Mr. Cryptic himself. This'll give you some idea. Once when I was about thirteen he disappeared for an entire week, just up and went without—"

"What are you talking about, Brinkman?"

Gerald grimaces, but before he can turn around, Sasha is already in the capable arms of the voice's owner—Aaron, of course, freed from the hospital and spit-polish clean, his hair slick with styling gel and his jaw so smoothly shaven it glows. Ditto the suit, a brand-new metallic blue two-piece with a narrow-lapelled three-button jacket and pants that taper neatly at the ankle. Like everything else about Aaron, the suit seems fresh from the cleaners, an establishment the likes of which Gerald has visited exactly three times in his entire life, once to pick up an old girlfriend's dress and twice to get some blue jeans patched up. Blessed with flawless vision, Aaron wears neither glasses nor contacts, though Gerald has once or twice seen Aaron sport some very expensive Ray-Ban sunglasses that probably cost about as much as Gerald spends per month on marijuana. Which is quite a bit, actually, if you add it all up.

"I was just telling your wife how my dad once flew to Washington, D.C., without telling me."

"Right, I heard you." Aaron peels Sasha off his neck and settles her down on the carpet like a mover arranging an end table, his hands huge against her arms. Immediately, Sasha reaches for her hair, all of which is still in place. As if commenting on the weather, he asks, "How's this been so far?"

"Great." She stares at him in wonderment. Stroking a finger

along his shoulder, she says, "I looked all over for this suit this morning. I couldn't find it anywhere."

"Well," Aaron replies, his eyes surveying the room, "it was there."

"But you made it here so *fast*."

"Yeah," Gerald adds, "I thought you were working all night."

"And now I'm here." Aaron flashes and then abruptly retracts an eerie Cheshire grin. The whole thing happens so quickly it's like an errant still shot inserted into a film reel. "Fact is, I've got tons of stuff I need to be doing right now. The only reason I'm here at all is because Nora got so bent out of shape about me missing the rehearsal dinner. She said if I missed the reception I could kiss her ass good-bye forever. And you know what? I seriously thought about it."

Sasha taps his shoulder. "How long have you been off?"

"Ten minutes. Then I came right here." He glances down at her and then away. "I mean twenty minutes, thirty minutes, whatever. I went home and changed and *then* came here."

"When?" Sasha asks.

"When what?"

"When were you home?"

"I just told you. Ten minutes ago. I went home and changed and then came right over."

"But I just called there and got the message you left me."

"Right, I know. I called from the hospital."

"Before you went home?"

"Yes, before I went home. Is that okay? Is there a problem with that?"

"No, of course not. It's just, I don't know. That's kind of weird, isn't it? I mean, why did you call home and leave a message if you were *going* home?"

"So you'd get the message if you called home."

"And if I had called while you were there?"

"I would have answered it." Addressing Gerald, Aaron says, "Bust your ass to do something nice and they give you the third degree."

"So you saw my note?" Sasha persists.

"What note?"

"The one I taped to the bedroom door."

Aaron stares at her for a moment. His eyes blink rapidly. He appears to be considering his next move: even Gerald can sense that much. Aaron is simultaneously reviewing an internal transcript of this conversation and devising a new story for himself. With a happy swelling in his lungs, Gerald realizes Aaron has just been caught lying. And about time: according to Nora, who maintains a morbid interest in such things, Aaron's been sleeping with nurses and other doctors throughout his residency. Though it's really not his business, Gerald has always disliked being in possession of such knowledge, which, on Nora's insistence, he's assiduously kept from Sasha. Deliberately or not, Nora has implicated Gerald in a conspiracy against someone he actually likes quite a bit. But now it looks like Aaron's going to get nailed all by himself.

"I didn't go upstairs," Aaron finally says. "I changed in the living room."

Sasha gives him a deep, long stare before saying, "You did," the last syllable landing as flat as a stomped foot.

Aaron extends his arm and tells Gerald, "Just picked this up from the dry cleaners. Six bucks. And lookee here." He points to a spot on the elbow. Gerald bends closer to see. Everything looks fine to him.

"What am I looking at?"

"The stitching, you idiot. Look at the seam there, some bonehead caught it on something."

"So you picked this up from the dry cleaners," Sasha is saying, "and then you went home and changed in the living room."

"Yes," Aaron hisses.

"But you just told me the suit was at home."

"I did not."

"Yes, you did. I said I couldn't find it in the closet and you said it was there."

"I was just answering you, Sasha. I wasn't paying attention. Look, you need a drink? How about you, Gerald? Your hands look empty. Where's the bar in this place, anyway?"

"So," Sasha continues, "I guess you didn't see my note."

He turns a threatening face to her. "I already told you I didn't go into the bedroom."

"You'll never guess what the note says." Though her lips are creased into a thin, pretend smile, tears rim her dark eyes, while inside his chest Gerald's heart lurches toward her. Absurdly, now that the burden of his knowledge seems about to be lifted from his shoulders, he registers a sudden impulse to protect Sasha. He should say something; he should change the subject, flap his arms, start dancing—anything to get Sasha off Aaron's scent for a moment. But first he has to find out what that note said.

Aaron looks up at the ceiling and sighs. "It said mow the lawn, meet me at the reception, I don't know. Look, Sasha, can we please change the subject? I've been at the goddamned hospital since yesterday morning. I don't need this right now."

Sasha turns her tragic smile on Gerald. "The note said 'Honey, I picked up your suits from the dry cleaners, they're hanging in the closet.' That's what the note said."

"Now, isn't this quite the threesome." The voice belongs to Nora, who clutches a champagne flute in one hand and her husband, Brent, in the other.

Gently, almost imperceptibly, Brent removes the champagne flute from Nora's fingers and sets it on a nearby table as Nora, her arms aloft, floats softly into Sasha's embrace. Turning back, Brent approaches Gerald with his usual monk's serenity—his head slightly lowered, his moist lips creased into a thin smile, his feminine hands held poised at waist level. "It means so much to both of us that you made it."

"Wouldn't have missed it for the world." Brent has this weird nervous thing where he rubs the tip of each finger, one by one, across his thumb, somewhat like a skittish gerbil on its hind legs, but he stops his finger rubbing long enough to return Gerald's handshake. Gerbil or no, Brent gives him a solid grip, which feels like a message of some sort. A committed outdoorsman, Brent has a long-distance runner's long lean build and a rock climber's agile poise, so Gerald knows better than to underestimate Brent's feminine tranquillity. In the year or so that she's dated him, Nora has taken up, in turn, like a girl at summer camp, hiking, biking, camping, as well as rock climbing, activities it never would have occurred to Gerald to propose to her and that Nora has undertaken with the mounting enthusiasm of a fresh convert to some new religion. He had always seen Nora as an indoors type like himself, a proudly pasty-faced archivist of books and rock bands, so it hurts him a bit now to realize he had her wrong all along. Or is it Brent who has her wrong? To hell with it: the guy will be worth millions someday, which pretty much explains everything. "My congrats, to both of you. You've got a great girl there."

"That's right," Brent agrees through his teeth, his smile hardening somewhat, "I do."

"Don't I merit a hug?" Nora interrupts, her arms outstretched. Gerald slides his hands around her waist as she drapes her naked arms across his shoulders. She feels oddly insubstantial in his hands, the smooth satiny surface of her wedding dress stiffer than it had looked from the back of the church. Pressing her cheek against his, Nora does a surprising thing: she kisses him on the neck. Her moist lips linger there for a moment before releasing him. A little demon of desire scampers down his spine.

"As for *you*, mister"—she now turns her attention on Aaron, who rears back as if deflecting a blow—"you came about *this* close to being in the doghouse for good."

"Oh," Sasha interjects, "he might end up there yet."

Nora blanches for the briefest fraction of a second, then recovers enough to ask, "I don't get it."

"Just ask him about his suit."

Nora glares at Aaron for a tense moment. Gerald can't quite determine how much she's figured out yet. As Aaron's most indefatigable court reporter, she's surely realized something's come to light; perhaps she's just worried that her silence these last few years is about to come back to haunt her. Aaron freezes up as well, his jaw tense and his eyes focused on no one. But within moments he's sliding his hands into his pockets and rocking back on his heels: a full recovery. "Girls, please. Enough already."

Seizing this as his moment finally to intervene, Gerald says to Nora, "Listen, I should take off. My dad's waiting for me at home."

With the choreographed ease of a professional actress obeying a stage direction, Nora reclaims her bride's happy face. "I'll follow you out."

They maintain an edgy silence all the way to the front entrance. As Gerald steps out onto the brick patio she gently touches his arm. "What did she mean back there about the suit?"

"Oh, come on, Nora, wasn't it obvious?"

Closing the door behind her, she steps onto the patio and makes a visor of her hand against the July sun, gazing directly at him, her face expressionless. "So," she says after a pause, "Sasha finally caught him."

"Bound to happen eventually." He pats his suit jacket for his smokes. Behind her the front door to the clubhouse opens, out of which tumble two towheaded boys in matching suits. The sound of the band spills onto the driveway and ceases when the door shuts again. Silence slaps them like a rebuke. "For every marriage, a divorce."

"I guess you're right." She lowers her hand and sighs. "Sort of sad, though, don't you think?"

"For Sasha, maybe. But not for that creep."

She gives him a barely perceptible nod, her eyes directed at some vague spot before her, and continues to stare into space as he walks backward down the driveway, a bent cigarette between his lips. He's halfway down the driveway and lighting up before she calls, "Hey, shouldn't it be bad luck to talk about divorce at a girl's wedding?"

TWO

FRESH FROM the wedding, Gerald comes to a reluctant stop in front of his house and crosses his arms along the steering wheel. The stereo and the air conditioner continue to blast away as he braces himself to face his father. His duplex, with its mustard-colored brick, seems to glow amid the liquid blue of oncoming night. A driveway runs along the building's side, leading to Gerald's cramped backyard apartment—less an apartment, really, than an add-on efficiency; Gerald suspects the original owners built it for an old widowed grandmother. But tonight, to his annoyance, a white pickup blocks his path. The pickup belongs to his landlady, a thin, mousy-haired ex-hippie in her mid-forties named Carol Radford. For the last four years Carol has been mismanaging the place from four hours away, via a little town just north of Nashville, where she lives with her two sullen and unkempt children, a boy and a girl whose names Gerald has never managed to remember. Local gossip contends that she was granted ownership of the building when her husband passed away three years ago—from AIDS, so say the local wags, the final testament of a double life whose existence she discovered only after it was too late. The other tenants grumble about her incessantly, while residency in the two front apartments seems to change hands with the regularity of the seasons. Gerald has been here the longest, partly because he's never mustered the energy to move but mostly because he sort of feels for Carol, a schlemiel after his own heart. He also prefers that she's never around. Which means her presence here on a Saturday night can only mean trouble. With a faint defeated moan, he leans back in the seat and closes his eyes.

He pretty much already knows what that trouble's going to be. For the last week or so rumors have been spreading up and down the street that Carol wants to rent out one of the apartments during the Olympics. *Alternative Atlanta*, the free weekly newspaper for which Gerald writes music reviews, has been listing home and apartment rentals for upwards of four thousand dollars a *week*. Carol simply has to convince Gerald to vamoose for two weeks, give him a couple of months' free rent for his trouble, and collect the profits. Gerald isn't exactly in a position to turn her down. Each of the two front apartments currently rents for twice what Gerald pays for his own dreary hovel, and even then his rent still eats up something like half his monthly income. Plus, he missed June's rent, a piece of negligence that Carol, for some reason, let slide: maybe *this* is the reason.

The fact is, he should move. Unfortunately, he can't bring himself to leave the area, this perfectly situated, ragtag neighborhood of winding tree-lined streets and century-old homes and art galleries and ethnic restaurants, the brick housefronts speckled in autumnal orange and brown and the eastern horizon aglow with the white nimbus of downtown city light. He loves that he lives on a street paved with brick, even though he also realizes this quirky detail accounts for about 40 percent of his inflated rent. He's out of his league here in glorious Virginia Highlands, amid all these affluent gay couples with their green Volvos and energetic young professional women in their Lycra jogging tights and Patagonia fleece jackets. From the moment he moved here Gerald's felt as if he were hiding out, just sort of *visiting* until the attractive locals sent him packing south to Little Five Points, where he could finally hunker down with the city's other losers—the tattooed musicians, the pink-haired performance artists, the Goth kids with their pierced tongues and disfigured earlobes. Even his little backyard apartment makes him feel clandestine: the crazy uncle in the basement. Most of his neighbors don't even know where he lives. They just see his piece-of-shit car appear from nowhere and tear-ass down the driveway like the Batmobile bursting from the Batcave. Carol also seems to prefer that Gerald remain hidden, since his backyard efficiency apparently violates local code, which also contributes to Gerald's sense of precariousness, of imminent disruption.

Finally he turns off the car and steps out. All about him cicadas wheedle, crickets chirp. From the murk of the front porch Carol suddenly materializes, her white sneakers precisely defined amid the soft dusk light. Despite the ninety-degree weather, Carol, as usual, wears baggy Wrangler jeans cinched at the waist with a beaded Navajo belt. Also, as usual, she has her brown hair pulled into a ponytail, the center crease of her skull like a chalk line drawn into burlap. Her hands flap at him nervously, her thin mouth with its flesh-colored mole fluttering in preparation for speech.

"The rent's coming," he tells her before she can make it down the stairs.

Shaking her head in a gesture of dismissal—which Gerald reads as bad news: she's going to kick him out now for sure—Carol stops before him and gently touches his arm, takes a deep breath, smiles faintly, then breathes again. She's easily the most frazzled woman he's ever known.

"I've had a rough couple of weeks," he continues, "but I swear to God—"

"There's a man," she interrupts. Her eyes dart about with uncertainty. "Someone's in your apartment. I saw him walk up the driveway and I thought . . . Well, you know."

Gerald's heart drops. Dad. "Was he carrying a duffel bag?"

"No," she replies, shaking her head, as if this were just the thing she wanted him to say. "Nothing like that. It was shopping bags, the little plastic ones, with the handles? They were filled with"—she hesitates, looking for the right word—"*things*. Clothes, bottles, books. And he was wobbling up the driveway as he walked. I was going to call the police but then didn't think I should. Was I right not to do that?"

He now notices music thundering from the back—an orchestra, from the sound of it. As in an *actual orchestra*. "It's fine, Carol. I know him."

"You're sure? I mean, he struck me as somewhat—"

"He's my father." Gerald waits to see how she takes in this information. Even in the dim light he can see her face blanch.

"Oh, Gerald, I am so sorry. I didn't know. I mean, I didn't mean to—"

"I know you didn't," he assures her, and taps her gently on her bare shoulder. Her arms are quite solid, he's surprised to see. She must work out, though he can't really imagine Carol Radford joining a gym. "He's just a little eccentric, that's all. I'm used to it," he lies.

She continues to hurl a barrage of nervous blundering apologies at him as he steps around the pickup and trudges up the driveway, turns a corner at the back of the house, and confronts his ramshackle domicile. The front door hangs wide open, the orchestral music crashing onto the lawn. Lester lounges in the doorway, the cat's big belly hanging off the threshold like one of Dalí's dripping clocks and his tail whipping back and forth, back and forth. Lester looks up at Gerald and meows loudly with worry, or confusion, or something. With a heavy heart, Gerald steps over his cat and into his apartment.

The floor to his front room, carpeted in a sort of khaki fur and stained all over with cat pee and spilled coffee, slants and wobbles under his feet as he works his way through the cigarette smoke and sawing violins. Dirty clothes, empty Taco Bell bags, and un-opened CDs litter the bedroom floor. Now this spontaneous decor has been augmented by no less than six stuffed-to-bursting grocery bags, all of which lay scattered about like detonated land mines in Sarajevo. The music, which seems to be issuing from the small oyster-gray portable stereo Gerald keeps by his bed, thun-ders and pounds against the walls of the contraption's little over-loaded speakers. Against the back wall, hunched over the desk and haloed by the turquoise glow of a computer screen, looms a mas-sive, indiscriminate shape that, on closer inspection, turns out to be a human back. Through the thundering timpani drums and piercing brass Gerald detects the flat, innocent sound of fingers tapping a keyboard. Cords of gray cigarette smoke dance and weave overhead. Dad.

Gerald approaches slowly, on tiptoe, though the music is so loud his father doesn't seem to notice. The furious tapping con-tinues as Gerald leans forward and peers over his father's head at the flickering computer screen. Dad is working in DOS, doing God knows what to the computer's configurations. Dense two-column directories scroll vertically down the black screen so quickly they blur.

"Boo," Gerald says into his father's ear.

No response. From past experience Gerald knows this doesn't necessarily mean anything. Dad reacts to the world according to his own larky caprice. Credit card companies, telemarketers, door-to-door Jehovah's Witnesses—all of them have an equally good chance of being ignored or showered with attention, depending on how Dad feels at that particular moment. Whatever strikes him as the more interesting option is what he does. There's some wisdom in that, Gerald concedes, and pulls up an empty chair.

Computer light flickers across the glinting glass of his father's reading specs, which sit askew on his nose. A cigarette comprised of little more than a wet filter and at least an inch and a half of delicate ash wobbles in Dad's mouth. His father's face, each time he sees it anew, never fails to surprise him—the presence of it, the weird, immutable fact of its existence. Gerald has looked at and examined his own face from every angle hoping, or perhaps dreading, to catch some glancing flash of his dad, but he just can't see the resemblance. When he looks at his father he sees not himself but rather his antiself, his dialectical partner in confusion. Gerald is vain about his long hair, for instance, while his father appears not to have given his hair a single momentary thought in nearly two decades. Then again, there's not much hair left, his bare, smooth skull totally bald except for a lonesome underarm tuft at the top of his forehead that he leaves alone not so much out of vanity as out of neglect. Meanwhile, his doughy, unshaven face, with its sagging jowls and dark droopy eyes, strikes Gerald as a perfect outward manifestation of the man's internal spiritual collapse, and thus represents everything that Gerald would wish to avoid in himself.

Gerald withdraws the cigarette from his father's lips, takes a drag, exhales a solid pipe of smoke directly into his father's face, waits for a response, gets none, and says, "So, how was the flight?" He must bellow to be heard over the music. His father, one eye squinting, continues to tap on the keyboard. "No problems, I trust. No engine malfunctions, no oxygen depletions, no airline food poisoning or rude in-flight staff personnel. Found your way to the MARTA station with minimum fuss, I gather. Easy straight shot to Midtown, just like I said. And the key I left you must have been right where I said it was. So that's good to know. Glad to hear everything worked out. What a relief. Listen, would you mind if I turned that down? I can barely hear myself talk to myself."

Abruptly, Dad raises a hand and shuts both eyes. Behind him the music swells and spirals up and up in an ecstasy of resolution until, after a heart-stopping fermata, the violins and cellos regroup for a cadence of three sharp thunderous chords that bring the piece, whatever it is, to its conclusion. In the ensuing silence Dad opens his eyes again and, for the first time, looks Gerald directly in the face.

"Name it."

"No idea." Gerald gets up from his chair, but before he can get to the stereo, the next piece on the CD starts up with a slow swelling of strings.

"Don't be a brat. Name the piece. We heard it in Boston that one time."

"I told you, Dad, I don't—"

"Eighteen eighty-five. That's your only clue. A dead giveaway."

"Fine. It's Brahms or Chopin or somebody."

"Chopin, my foot."

"Brahms, then. That's the best I can do."

"Now the piece. Including the key."

"C'mon, Dad."

"You're stalling on me, Gerald. I know how you get. You hate being wrong, so you act like you don't care. But that mind of yours is spinning away."

"Oh, it's spinning, all right."

"That big finale, those chunky chords. You know what it is. Think, son."

At the searing sound of that last word, Gerald looks back at his father, who hasn't even turned around yet. He's typing again. Beyond his hunkered form the screen flickers and flashes.

"Okay," Gerald relents. "I'm going with No. 4, Opus 98, key of E-minor, the funeral key, the key of death, the key to end all keys."

"Cute." Dad swivels around in the chair, the keyboard in his lap. He wears a smile, his eyebrows raised impishly above his crooked reading glasses. "But you're misquoting me. A-flat minor is the funeral key, not E-minor. Think Sonata No. 12. Ludwig Van."

"Yeah, yeah, yeah." Gerald punches the eject button. The little lid pops open to reveal the shiny, still-spinning disc within. "You and your gloom music. You make Beethoven sound like Megadeth."

"Good old death," his father retorts. "Where would we be without it?"

Gerald registers a little spine chill of discomfort. His mother's ghost passes through his chest and exits out his back, leaving behind an empty flutter in his stomach. "The wedding was fine, by the way. Since you asked."

"Uh-huh," is the response. The tapping starts up again. "When was the last time you cleaned up this hard drive, boy? You realize how much garbage you've got on this thing?"

"Good old garbage." Gerald fishes around the stereo for another disc to pop in. "More reliable than death."

"First of all, you've got tons of games you never play, plus about six different Internet programs, none of which you seem to be using, not to mention hundreds of temporary files you've never bothered to delete."

"Dad, just leave it alone, please, it works fine the way—"

"And look here, where you've got your Microsoft Word running out of this subdirectory—"

"Yes, yes, I know." Gerald returns to the desk, an old Be-Bop Deluxe song launching into flight behind him. "I put it there deliberately, so I could remember where it was."

"But see here," tapping away, "where I sectioned off all this disc space to serve as RAM, right? Which means—"

"Dad." Gerald waits beside his father, his hands on his hips. After a moment or two, Dad stops typing and looks up over his glasses. The keyboard still sits on his lap, atop his white, almost-hairless old man's legs. Tonight Dad's sporting blue polyester running shorts and a black short-sleeved T-shirt so tight-fitting that a tiny roll of white flesh pokes out of the bottom. He's lost weight. Lots of it. Last time Gerald saw him he was carrying a boiler the size of a beanbag chair. Now he's got the tiniest old man's sag, a stomach rather than a gut. Gerald's own stomach drops at the thought of his father wearing this outfit on the plane—which, he fully knows, the old fart most assuredly did. Don't even glance at the shoes. "Look, I appreciate you fixing up the computer and all but, please, do me a little favor: stop dicking around with it. Just leave it as is."

"No can do, my boy. For one thing, I haven't finished reinstalling your Windows program. For another—"

"Okay, right, I get the message." Yanking at his tie, Gerald looks around the room and starts kicking at the clothes on the floor. "Did you bring any smokes, by the way? I'm all out."

"I never buy those things, and neither should you. The tobacco companies play second fiddle only to the NRA as both the most powerful lobby in Washington and the most ethically degenerate political action group in the entire country."

"So those are my cigarettes, I take it."

"Yes. And you're out."

"Oh, but of course." At the open door of his clothes closet Gerald steps out of his dress pants, smoothes them along his chest, and runs the legs through the rungs of his one and only wooden suit hanger. "On my way home I'll be sure to stop at 7-Eleven and make my own small but significant contribution to the merchants of death. You have any brand preference?"

"Camel Lights if they have them. On your way home from where?"

"I *told* you, Dad. I have to work tonight."

"I thought you had a wedding to go to."

"I did. Why else would I be wearing this idiotic suit?" But in fact Gerald is now standing before his open closet door in nothing but black socks, boxers, and an untucked dress shirt. His father, during a brief pause in his typing, glances at him for a moment, and then turns his attention back to the computer screen. Gerald resumes: "Anyway, I explained all this in that itinerary I sent you. The wedding, this gig, my interview in New York this Wednesday. It's all there. Turn on that light beside the screen, I can't see what I'm doing."

"This is a rock concert, I presume."

"Yes, Dad. It's a 'rock concert,' more or less. Though it's only in a nightclub. And the group is local."

"Will I like them?"

"Who?"

"This group we're going to see."

Gerald stops midway through slipping on a pair of jeans and ponders the full ramifications of the word *we*. All at once Dad commences a flurry of mad typing and just as abruptly stops. Slowly lifting his hands from the keyboard on his lap, he leans forward and gazes intently into the screen, which, for the first time since Gerald walked into the room, has stopped flickering.

"Dad. I said—"

"Well." Gingerly, his father places the keyboard on the desk and scoots away. "I guess I'll just have to fix *that* when we get home."

Gerald hooks on his belt. "Fix what?"

"Nothing." Dad swivels around in his chair and stands up. The shoes, Gerald now sees, are Birkenstocks. They wrap around sky-blue dress socks pulled to the knee. A sliver of Dad's tiny belly pokes out over the elastic band of his shorts, while his pudgy arms fill completely the armholes of his black T-shirt, the front of which, as if in echo of all those scrolling file directories on the computer screen, bears the repeating typescript Cheap Trick logo from the late seventies. The T-shirt hails from Gerald's junior-high days. Judging from the topography of those iridescent shorts, Dad does not appear to be wearing Jockey briefs. "Just a little glitch in the Windows program," he explains.

"Dad." Gerald shakes his head. "What did you do to my computer?"

Walking past him and into the kitchen, his father calls, "Microsoft makes a third-rate product, Gerald. I *told* you to get a Mac."

Gerald steps to the screen and tries to discern the contents therein, but all he sees are lists and lists of unreadable commands. "Will this thing ever work again?"

Dad now stands at the door with a glass of milk. The light from the front room traces an eerie outline along his silhouette, darkening his face and making him seem lit from within. "Too early to tell. I'm still figuring out DOS."

Gerald stands up, puts his hands on his hips, hesitates. "You have no idea what you're doing, do you?"

"What can I tell you, son?" His father tilts his head back and lifts the glass higher and higher until the very last drop of milk falls into his wide-open maw. When he turns back to Gerald, he wears a mustache of milk on his upper lip. "Ultimately, you know, I'm a Mac man."

Like the general public's collective sense of Grace Kelly, Jackie O., and Paul McCartney, Gerald's private and personal recollections of his father split neatly into two distinct phases: a Before and an After. The Before phase represents the world as we wish it; the After phase constitutes the world as it actually is. It's the difference between *To Catch a Thief* and Princess Stephanie, between Camelot and Daryl Hannah, between "Yesterday" and "Silly Love Songs." The Before always wins.

Paul Brinkman's Before phase ran, in Gerald's private and personal estimation, from March 1966 (Gerald's birth) to October 1973 (his mother's death). Eight point five years total: five and a half years longer than Camelot, three years longer than Grace Kelly's Hollywood career, and maybe a full year longer than the Beatles' stint as Capitol Records' most successful recording artists. So there's some reason to feel grateful; it could have been shorter. The After phase, meanwhile, runs from October 1973 to the present. As such, it encompasses most of Gerald's actual, as well as his remembered, existence. It subtends the heartbreaking quotidian world we all inhabit, a world that will never produce a new Beatles album no matter how hard it tries, but must offer instead, as a pale consolation to the ravages of time, the latest Paul McCartney solo record, complete with harmonies by Linda. And for these reasons among others, Gerald prefers the Before.

Before, Paul Brinkman was a Dad. He was a Dad in the sense that he was in partnership with a Mom, e.g., Gerald's Mom. It made sense to Gerald, this partnership; it jibed with the way he understood the world to work. And nothing else has quite jibed for him since. His dad was slim, confident, authoritative, solid, enormously tall, and fully in charge. His dad smelled of cigarette smoke and Hai Karate. His dad's teeth were perfectly straight and stained a faint yellow, a detail Gerald for some reason found fascinating as a child. His dad's eyes were narrow and lidless, his lips thin, his nose slightly flattened, like a tasteful bas relief design on a smooth and narrow vase.

Gerald can still remember his father's bristly crew cut and horn-rimmed glasses. He can still remember Dad's voluptuously elegant preacher's voice, with its precisely pronounced T's and slightly rounded A's (*farther* for *father*, *madonner* for *madonna*). He can still remember the old man's fussy neatness, his immaculate grooming, his efficient cigarette smoking. Gerald can still see, the image so precise in his memory that he wonders if he isn't confusing it with something he's seen recently on television, this neat and handsome thirty-two-year-old father of two sitting at the breakfast table and silently regaling his son and daughter with this wonderful trick he has of making a banana disappear into thin air. He performs this trick with one hand and a butter knife. No scarves, no top hat, no magic wand. Plop plop plop go the banana disks into the sloshing bowl of Cheerios, each disk as perfectly symmetrical as a checker piece. Plop plop plop goes the milk. Before the children can return their gaze to the man he opens his fist to reveal a perfectly empty palm. Not a mirror anywhere.

Dad Before was also a taskmaster, a maker of games, an impresario. He was the guy who invented the Beard Game. The Beard Game took place each night before dinner. After work, Gerald's dad would come home and toss his sportscoat across the vinyl couch in the living room, drop to his knees on the shag carpeting that always looked to him like spilled spaghetti, and crawl with a feral growl toward Gerald, who would be waiting, his bladder quivering with anticipation, in front of the family's enormous Magnavox home entertainment center. Dad would crawl mindlessly over tiny Gerald, growling all the while, and scoop him up in the cave of his arms and legs until Gerald, like a piece of farmland scythed by a plow, toppled onto his side, giggling hysterically. Next came the Beard, which Gerald had to keep at bay however he could. When the beard went for the tummy, Gerald flipped over; when it went for the back, Gerald sat upright; when it went for the face, Gerald dove between the monster's legs and squirmed his way to safety. Laughing uncontrollably throughout. Split wide open with bliss. Dad Before was big enough to crawl through, large enough to scale, massive enough to hide beneath.

Dad After is more or less Dad as he is now.

And Mom? What was Mom Before? Mom remains ever and

always Before. There is no Mom After. Gerald has no Mom After to compare against Mom Before. He knows that behind this idealization lies someone much more complicated and real and irrational, someone as susceptible as himself to doubt and duplicity and failure of nerve, to humiliation and hubris. He's perfectly aware of all this hard-nosed pragmatism. He fully accepts it—in theory, at least. He just can't make himself *feel* any of it.

Mom Before was every kid's Mom Before—young, vibrant, omnipresent; a fount of blessings, an origin of love, a reality principle. She remains for him forever lovely and lean and young, ceaselessly green-eyed and smooth-skinned, eternally brown-haired and healthy, her cheek glazed by a thin down of soft white hair, her skin gleaming with face cream. She still smells of coffee and baby powder and—perhaps this is a specific Christmas memory—gingerbread. She continues to sit at the kitchen table with the other grown-ups, stroking Gerald's hair and firing off these sardonic and mysterious one-liners that the grown-ups all "get" and that Gerald imagines are about him, somehow, a sustained string of sinister jokes at his expense that he does not understand but also doesn't mind all that much, since the jokes keep the attention focused on himself. Mom Before maintains cool mastery of such elusive suburban arts as macramé, ceramics, yoga, and watercolor painting. She continues to smile her toothsome, exuberant smile. Endlessly, timelessly, she drives around town in the Brinkmans' old Chevrolet Caprice station wagon, the first family car Gerald can remember, complete with fake wood paneling, an eight-track player, and khaki-colored vinyl interior imprinted with an intricate and fascinating pattern of pinholes running up and down the padded rows. Vinyl permeates all his childhood memories of Mom, from her oversized purse, a treasure chest of goodies, to her gleaming purple rain slicker, even down to her burgundy cigarette pouch, with its Cricket-lighter holster. Vinyl and plastic and a periodic table's worth of other smooth and disposable polymers surround her in his memory, everything weightless and bright and candy-colored. And Mom in the middle of it all.

What else does Gerald remember from Before? He remembers his toys—dolls mostly, action figures like G.I. Joe and Big Jim and Action Jackson, each figurine equipped with a full array of action outfits and all-terrain vehicles and headquarters and kung fu studios. He remembers his books, piles and piles of thin hardcover books purchased from the Scholastic Book Service. He remembers those twilight Saturday nights at home, a chicken pot pie cooking in the oven and the house shot through with the smell of perfume and cologne. He remembers eating this scalding pot pie in front of *Hee Haw* as his glamorous parents march past him on their way to a neighborhood party, Dad in maroon flares and white shoes and purple scarf, Mom in a long skirt and rubber boots and one of her very own macramé-bead necklaces. He remembers many nights waking up in his room to the sound of Mom and Dad and their friend Dr. Stanley Torrent talking loudly in the kitchen. He has a vague related memory of walking into the kitchen one night and finding Mom and Torrent in an embrace. More than anything else, he clings tenaciously to a foggy memory of sitting in the front seat of the station wagon while his mother, all agleam in her purple vinyl raincoat, drives him all over town. It's a vision without meaning, an image without Dad in it, a moment from Gerald's life that, in all its banality and specificity, absolutely must be true. At the very least, it's something to believe in.

After that, he has only his own life to believe in—*his* life, whatever that means. He also believes in his sister, Eva, married now and living in New York with her husband, Walt, and in his massive collection of vinyl rock 'n' roll LPs and shiny compact discs, the whole of which he keeps prominently displayed in his front room, stacked neatly in alphabetical order. Rock has taught him all he cares to know about integrity, aesthetic form, and love. Don't sell out, don't overstay your welcome, don't grow up: those are the three lessons of rock. Also, turn it up and keep it short. The Clash had more to do with determining his political convictions than any of the presidents elected during his lifetime, while Pete Townshend gave him a better handle on religious experience than any of his former Sunday school teachers, the old man included. He isn't always sure how he feels about all this. Lately, he's begun to feel a little ashamed about it. But it's a fact. Nothing his father ever gave him to read hit him as deeply as *Born to Run* or *Armed Forces* or *Never Mind the Bollocks, Here's the Sex Pistols*. His only consolation these days is that he's probably not alone in this fact.

Given the nature of his job, Gerald has found it professionally useful to maintain, on his home computer, an up-to-the-minute List of Achievements in the Sublime. Such a private inventory helps one maintain perspective. It functions as a long-view reminder of what's worth keeping. One's enthusiasm over a new piece of pop music can be as effervescent and deceptive as lust. He went through a Dan Fogelberg phase, for instance. He championed drum machines for a while. He has made major projections about the "seminal" and "groundbreaking" importance of groups who never made a third album and whose members now work in used-record shops in places like St. Paul, Minnesota, and Manchester, England. A List of Achievements in the Sublime also serves to offset those moments of rapturous overenthusiasm he experiences sometimes when he listens to new music while under the influence of a good bowl or two of high-grade marijuana. Pot knows no taste. While stoned, Gerald has found himself enraptured by those four linear harmonic notes on Rush's

"Red Barchetta," brought to tears by the sentiments expressed in Whitney Houston's "The Greatest Love of All," and sent into or-bits of aesthetic ecstasy by those big, Who-like power chords lodged in the middle of Styx's "Come Sail Away." So you gotta be careful. Especially if you're a rock critic for a hip alternative weekly.

Of course, Gerald could always quit smoking pot. He could make a solemn vow never to get high while listening to new records or while watching a local rock group he has been assigned to review. He knows that. He knows he should quit. In fact, he thinks about quitting every time he gets stoned. The thought of giving up this juvenile habit flits through his brain every time he packs his ceramic Yoda bong, or swivels his stainless-steel, cigarette-shaped one-hitter into a mound of granulated dope, or runs his tongue along a freshly rolled joint. *I should stop doing this,* he tells himself, his hands trembling with excitement. *This is ridiculous.* But the mere anticipation of that glorious transition from flat digital clarity to fuzzy analog bliss always goads him into taking that first long drag, the smoke burning the lining of his throat and swirling around his lungs. And no matter how bad he feels the next morning, or how paranoid he grows an hour or two later as each chime of the telephone sends his heart racing into his mouth with the nameless and wholly irrational panic that every true pothead knows as intimately as a drunkard knows the shakes, he nevertheless feels, the next evening, utterly convinced that such self-lacerating side effects are entirely worth the plea-sure of that first happy moment during which you realize, with a stupid dreamy grin, that you're, like, totally baked.

Still, Gerald should quit. And he will, any day now.

Just not today, he silently declares, and, relieved to have solved this ongoing inner debate for the time being, takes his hand off the gearshift and reaches into his jeans pocket for that stainless-steel one-hitter.

"Hey, Dad," he says, turning down the stereo and pulling open the dashboard ashtray, "do me a favor and reach in the glove compartment for that little plastic film canister rolling around in there."

His father, slouched into a distorted pile in the passenger seat, his right hand methodically scratching a red patch into the flabby skin of his left biceps, says nothing.

"Jesus," Gerald sighs, and opens the glove compartment himself. After rummaging around for a frantic moment or two—and after barely catching a yellow light—he withdraws his hand. "Listen, I'm trying to drive, okay? Just, um ... It's a little plastic film canister, you know, like for a roll of film?" No response. "*Dad.*"

"What is this music?"

Gerald stops at a red light. On either side glow the shops of Ponce de Leon Avenue, a strange incongruous strip of gas stations and Church's chicken joints and doughnut shops and liquor stores that Gerald secretly adores. While he waits for the light to change, he rummages around some more in the glove compartment.

"I kind of like it," Dad continues, "whatever it is."

Gerald's fingers close triumphantly on the film canister just as the light turns green. "Well, that's good to know." He tosses the canister into his father's lap and rams the car back into gear, all in one unbroken motion. "Because it's the group we're seeing tonight."

"And how would you describe this type of music?" Dad fingers the film canister but does not look at it.

The music is loud and lumbering, with lots of thick, distorted guitar chords arranged without apparent forethought over a steady, walloping, four-four drum beat reminiscent of Led Zeppelin at their most punishing; over the top of all this noise rides the gravelly voice of the lead singer, a guy whom Gerald knows fairly well (he works at a used-record store nearby) and who emits his lyrics in a single sustained melody line located somewhere between B and B-flat. "Oh," Gerald muses, "I'd call it talentless local-band type music."

"And their name?"

"I can't remember." Impatiently, he takes the canister from his father and peels off the lid with his teeth. "The, um, the Susans or something." The plastic lid drops into his lap as he hands back the little canister. The first time he ever got high around his father—this was five years ago, during a visit home—he and his father were nearing the end of a typical three-day sulk during which neither of them could find anything interesting to say to each other. Gerald was partly tired of the effort to make conversation and also half-conscious that what he wanted more than anything else was to provoke some sort of reaction from the guy, a full-blown confrontation that could possibly lead to more substantial issues. But, typically, the old man had said nothing, and Gerald had to admit even at the time that he was somewhat relieved. A precedent had been set, at least. He no longer had to sneak around every time he went home. At another stoplight he takes the one-hitter from the fist of his steering hand and instructs, "Now, just poke this little rodlike thing into the canister there and twist it around a few times, would you please?"

"The Susans," Dad reflects, taking the steel device from his son. "So everyone in the group is named Susan?"

"Of course not. Just listen to that: pure idiot testosterone. These guys have names like Ethan, or Jeff, or, I don't know, Greg."

"No one's named Susan?"

"Not even remotely." Gerald glances at his father, who is absently twisting away like a preoccupied gargantuan with a miniature butter urn. The light turns green. "That's probably enough, Dad."

"But I don't get it."

"Get what?"

"Why they're called the Susans."

"You're not *supposed* to get it."

"Why not?"

"I don't know. There's nothing to get. It's just a name."

"But a name must stand for something."

"Not always."

"Take your name, for instance."

"My name doesn't say anything about me. Look, give me that." Gerald snatches back the one-hitter and reaches beside the gearshift for his lighter. "Hold the wheel for a second, pretty please."

"Right," the old man says, taking the wheel in his left hand. "But your name does refer to something tangible. You. There's its meaning."

"Mm-hmmm." Gerald exhales a fat, almost solid mushroom cloud of smoke and immediately erupts into a volcanic fit of violent coughing. Without comment his father takes the one-hitter and sets it delicately along the base of the gearshift panel. The pungent, citrusy smell of pot fills the car interior. In a guttural croak, Gerald manages to say, "But there's no meaning. To the word. *Gerald*. Is there? I mean"—punching his chest and coughing one last time, for good measure—"you could call me, like, Oldsmobile or whatever, and it would work just as well."

"This is deconstructionism, isn't it?"

"Deconstruction," Gerald gently corrects, "but basically, yeah," though he isn't really sure. Despite four years of undergraduate education and two years of graduate work, he never quite figured out what "deconstruction" actually was. During his brief stint as a graduate student he visited his father one weekend and brought with him a stack of paperback books by Michel Foucault and Jacques Derrida that he had been assigned to read for a seminar he was taking, and his father read through the whole stack. Over the course of that weekend the guy read all of *Discipline and Punish*, in two marathon sittings, and most of *Writing and Différence*, during which time Gerald, who should have been at home bonding with his dad, drove around town by himself, scouring used-book-and-record stores and getting stoned with old friends from high school. The morning before he left, he sat silently at the breakfast table while his father pelted him with questions. "You really believe the West privileges speech over writing? Is this Foucault an anthropologist or what? Are they really still reading Marx in graduate school?" Gerald chewed away at his Frosted Flakes, shrugged, and offered little else by way of response, primarily because he couldn't then, and still can't, answer any of the questions his father was asking, even though he was the one taking the course, even though he was the one in graduate school.

"And this group," his father continues, "the Susans, are they what you'd call a deconstructionist group?"

Gerald smiles. The remark strikes him as extraordinarily insightful, which probably means the pot has kicked in. He arrives at still another stoplight and takes up the one-hitter again. "Not consciously, no. But it's in the air. Most band names nowadays consciously refer to nothing." He lights up, inhales, exhales. The light turns green.

"Let me try some of that," his father murmurs.

Gerald glances right in amazement. "When have you ever smoked pot?"

"Before you were born, my boy. And a little when you were a toddler."

A Joker's smile spreads across Gerald's face. "You're shitting me."

"I shit you not. Your mom and I both did it. Hell, everybody did. It was—as you say—in the air."

Mom. An acid discharge zips through Gerald's veins. He never allows himself to think of his mother while stoned. The faintest.

glimmer of her opens a void inside him so vast his stomach drops. He hands the one-hitter to his father and turns right down Moreland, en route to Little Five Points. "Anyway," Gerald says loudly, sitting upright in his seat and clutching the steering wheel, "the Susans is just a meaningless band name, like Pearl Jam or the Smashing Pumpkins or, I don't know, Belly or whatever. Anything can be a band name nowadays. Look around and say the first thing you see."

His father exhales slowly, sits back in his seat, stares placidly out the windshield. After a pause, he says, "Traffic light."

"See? That could be a band name."

"The Traffic Lights?"

"No. Drop the 'The.' And make it singular."

His father mulls this over for a moment. Slowly, he says, "Traffic Light."

"That's it. That's a good band name. Now do another."

Dad looks around. "Dead Tree."

"Another good one."

"Homeless Man."

"Drop the 'Man.' "

"Homeless? That could be a name?"

"Sure, why not?"

"How about Glove Compartment?"

"I'd go with Glove Box," Gerald says.

"I sense a sexual innuendo there."

"All the better."

"But that suggests meaning."

"Suggests, yes. But doesn't *actually mean*."

"So Glove Box is a band name," his father marvels, shaking his head. "How about Body Box?"

Gerald pulls into a parking lot. They are finally here. "Sounds good to me." A warm stoner's sense of serenity and well-being courses happily through his system, his legs as light as balsa wood, his cheeks sore from smiling.

Beside him, his father takes up a chant: "Body Blow, Body Clock, Body Beautiful—"

Gerald slams the brakes as something thumps the hood. As if conjured from thin air, a bearded homeless man stands stock still in the headlight beams of the rocking car, his eyes blazing and his hands splayed Superman-like across the hood. It takes a moment for Gerald to realize that he, and not this strange man, has just brought the car to a halt. His heart pounds in his chest. You're stoned, a voice in his head scolds him. You could have killed this guy.

In the passenger seat Dad whispers, "Good heavens."

His head dizzy with panic, Gerald yanks the parking brake, shifts into neutral, and climbs out his door, his arms stretched toward the bearded man, who still has not moved. "Hey, mister, listen, I am *so* sorry, I didn't see you, it was like you *materialized* from nowhere . . ." His voice trails off. The man continues to stare through the windshield of the car, his hands firmly pressed on the hood. A faded red sweatshirt and matching sweatpants hang loose on his emaciated frame while his hair, thick and matted with accumulated grime, sits on his head like one of Mom's macramé bags. Gerald, unclear what to do next, follows the man's gaze, which seems to be directed at Dad, who, still sitting in the passenger seat, gazes back. "Sir, did you hear me?"

"I belong here," the man replies, his voice a low, menacing growl.

"Yes sir, I'm sure you do. Like I said—"

"He does not." The man has not taken his eyes off Gerald's father.

The passenger door opens and out steps Dad. Perched in the V of the open door, he asks Gerald, "Is this man all right?"

"I think so." Delicately, Gerald touches the man's shoulder again. "Sir, listen, can we do anything for you?"

Suddenly the man whirls on Gerald, eyes flashing. "This is *my* place."

A little crowd has accumulated. Through the foggy lens of his marijuana buzz, Gerald senses that the whole episode has turned sinister and ominous. In the paranoid logic of pot, he imagines that these people are going to start reprimanding him. He knows that the alternative crowd of Little Five Points, the bohemian faction of Atlanta, and the hippie-punks of nightclubland are all, as a group, pro-homeless. As is Gerald. He wants to do right by this man.

"You're absolutely right," his father agrees, and begins guiding the homeless man away from the car and out of the headlight beam. "We *are* in your place, aren't we? We had no idea."

The man lets Gerald's father lead him away. The crowd cuts a path for this strange couple, both of them hunched over, both of them in kids' clothes, both of them disheveled. Head down, the homeless man mutters, "You don't belong here. You're in my space," while Dad nods and says, "You're certainly right about that, God knows."

"Dad," Gerald calls through the crowd. The car is still running. "Don't take off, I still need to park this thing." The observation strikes Gerald as crass and unfeeling, though he doesn't know why. A couple of crowd members turn on him and glower, though he might be imagining that as well. His throat burns with shame. *That's it*, he tells himself. *No more dope for me. I'm done.*

Dad dismissively waves his hand and leads the bearded man through the parking lot. Both men have their heads down, as if they are talking about something top secret. *Cigarettes*, Gerald suddenly remembers. *I need cigarettes.*

By the time he gets the car parked the crowd has dispersed, his father with it. For about ten minutes—or, for that matter, five seconds: he can't say for sure—Gerald stumbles around the parking lot in a frenzy looking everywhere for his disappearing dad, who finally turns up on the curb out front of the club, crouched into a huddle with his arm around his newfound friend. No one pays them any heed, just a couple of homeless guys muttering homeless-guy gibberish. Gerald crouches down and taps his father on the shoulder. "You okay out here?"

His father, when he turns around, seems utterly beatific, as happy as he has seemed in years. "This is a very interesting gentleman, Gerald. You should hear what he's saying."

"I'll take your word for it." Gerald manages a diluted smile, which his father returns. Something passes between them, some message Gerald cannot decode. "Look, I need to go on in, the group is starting. I'll pay your cover if you want. I know the bouncer, he'll let you in."

"That's fine, Gerald. That'll be just fine. I'll be in shortly."

Gerald nods, pats his dad on the back. The homeless man is still muttering, his head nodding up and down and his matted hair draped across Dad's bare arm. That inarticulate message rises through Gerald's throat as if seeking escape. To stave it off he says, "We need to talk later." His father blinks but does not respond. "About why you're here and all."

"That's what I'm trying to find out from this man," Dad says. "Maybe he can tell me." His father turns away and lowers his head toward the homeless man's muttering mouth. Gerald stands up and rubs his hands on his jeans. Feeling somehow defeated, he approaches the bouncer—an old friend named Thomas: broad shoulders, bald head, goatee—and reaches for his wallet.

As it turns out, the local group is not called the Susans. They're called Sewer Pipe, without the "the." Another thing: they're *fantastic*! Inside the closed, smoky space of the Little Five Points

Star Bar—a kitschy hole-in-the-wall with a dimly lit beer bar, a smattering of Populuxe chairs and tables, a checkered dance floor, and a makeshift stage—Sewer Pipe becomes seminal and ground-breaking. The drummer pounds and pounds while the two guitarists, both bent over at the waist à la the Red Hot Chili Peppers, run their hands back and forth across their fingerboards palming thick, solid bar chords. Center stage Ethan, the band's lead singer, drapes himself all over the microphone stand, his knees collapsed beneath him and his two bony hands clutching the microphone that, held in its cradle by mounds of gray duct tape, points downward, thereby forcing him to sing up, like a man crying for help, like a man drowning in pain. The clutch-and-collapse: a new paradigm for lead singers. Only rappers stalk the stage nowadays with microphones in their fists, whereas country singers opt for those air-traffic-controller headsets, which is a different story entirely. Something to do with Garth Brooks, or maybe—

"So *this* is how you make your living!" The voice rattles in his ear like tin. Bewildered, he turns to see Sasha Mantrivadi standing beside him, beer in hand and an impish smile on her face. Totally from left field. A bridesmaid no more, she's now wearing a snug cream blouse with wide trapezoid collar flaps, black flared slacks, chunky black shoes. Her hair is perfect.

He opens his mouth to respond, but in fact he's so astonished to find her here that he can't think of anything to say. He's also stoned, even from those two hits. Two hours ago he was wondering if he'd lost her as a casual acquaintance, let alone the object of a crush, and now here she is, an unexpected visitant to a part of his life that had never included her. He then recalls with a pang of dread her humiliation at the reception. If Aaron's with her, he doesn't think he'll survive the rest of the evening. For too long he's been covering for Aaron—and Nora, for that matter—and now he just wants to be freed from the whole messy business.

"Too stunned to speak, huh?" Playfully, she elbows him in the arm, then tips her beer bottle to her mouth and somewhat unconvincingly bobs her head to the music. On the rare occasions that he's visited her house, Gerald, as is his habit, has surreptitiously taken stock of her CD collection, which, based on his careful investigation, contains exactly eleven discs, three of them European dance compilations purchased during her junior year abroad in Madrid.

Leaning down, he breathes in the delectable apple-blossom scent of her shampoo and shouts, "Why aren't you at the reception?"

"It's already over," she shouts back, then says something else that sounds like "totally lame" or "Nora's insane," he's not sure which. Onstage, Sewer Pipe pounds away at one chord, over and over again, the singer stomping up and down in perfect four-four time, his long hair whipping back and forth like a flag thwapping in the wind. They've been playing this chord for so long they've achieved a sort of white wall of noise. Gesturing toward the band with her beer bottle, she yells, "What do you think?"

Gerald raises his own beer and nods in the affirmative, though he's no longer sure what he thinks of Sewer Pipe. He's also suddenly concerned about Nora's lame reception. Maybe he should have stayed around a bit longer. They say the first person to leave a party can sometimes start a stampede. Perhaps he *single-handedly* ruined the reception. He and he alone.

Meanwhile the singer stomps up and down as the guitarists saw away at that one chord. All around the bar people stare at the stage as if hypnotized. They've been pounded into submission. The members of Sewer Pipe, Gerald suddenly decides, are complete pricks. His stomach flutters with anxiety. He has absolutely nothing to say to Sasha. She doesn't belong here, for one thing, in this bar and in this facet of his life; at the same time, he feels guilty and ashamed about being stoned. And about Nora. He tries to will himself sober, then decides he should just tell her he's high. Such an admission could serve as both a conversation topic and a preemptive strike in the event that he says or does something regrettable later on: a very likely possibility. Instead he shouts, "Where's Aaron?"

This last word gets shouted into a sudden, unexpected silence. Sewer Pipe, without warning, has concluded its performance. No one moves. A ringing vacuum fills the bar for a moment or two, and then someone in the crowd shouts "Yeah!" and everyone starts clapping. One chord or no, that was pretty impressive, stopping like that all of a sudden, like side one of *Abbey Road*. Gerald cradles his beer against his ribs and applauds; beside him, Sasha elbows him again and points to the left. "We've got a table."

The "we" includes, weirdly enough, an old grad-school chum, and Nora's onetime lover Kira Dunkin, who, like Sasha, has ditched her bridesmaid dress, opting instead for army fatigues and a black tank top. No Aaron, he sees, which is a relief. Still in the doghouse, presumably. Kira stands up when Gerald arrives and extends her hand, a wry smile on her face. Her dyed hair, a chromatic silver that she keeps boyishly short and combed forward, makes her look a bit like Julius Caesar, a comparison she might like or might resent: hard to tell. Everything with Kira is political.

"Didn't get a chance to talk to you at the reception," he tells her, taking an available seat. "Sorry about that."

"No, you're not," she smiles back, and raises her beer bottle for a toast.

"What are we toasting?"

"Nora's big mistake," Kira replies, and just like that it's out there: the thing on everyone's mind. More paranoia races through his veins—gossip spooks him when he's stoned—but it quickly dissolves, principally because he likes Kira, and also because he understands where she's coming from. Though in class they were always on opposing sides—Kira the Theorist, Gerald the Male—he always admired her candor and ferocity, not to mention her sense of humor. He understood why she was the one Nora chose to experiment with, and felt sorry for her, genuinely sorry, when Nora realized, as of course she eventually would, that her sexual feelings for Kira were in fact experimental. Kira wasn't experimenting with her sexual feelings at all, and got hurt. Not that she showed it to anyone.

"Might be a bit too early to say that," he dutifully replies, even though he sort of agrees. "We should give them at least a year."

"What are you guys talking about?" Sasha cries, and settles down on the other side of Gerald, distributing fresh beers for everyone.

How on earth did Sasha and Kira hook up together? Like Gerald, Nora also compartmentalizes her life, separating her grad school existence from her mainstream bourgeois friends. Now that Nora's joined the mainstream, maybe she's seeking a merger. Or maybe Sasha latched onto Kira as a way to get away from Aaron for the evening. Picking up the fresh beer, he explains, "Kira was just telling me how happy she is about Nora's marriage."

"Right. Which reminds me." Sasha puts a hand on Gerald's thigh and gives him a little squeeze. "How are you holding up? You handling this all right?"

Her saying this in front of Kira confirms what Gerald has always suspected: Nora never told Sasha about her brief experiment with permeable sexual identities. With a sly glance to Kira, who is scanning the bar, he replies, "Ancient history, Sasha. I'm happy for her."

"I'll bet." Only now does she withdraw her hand. A faint patch of warmth remains on his thigh. "I still can't believe it happened. Brent's sweet and all, but it was just so sudden. Frankly, I always imagined it would be you."

"Nora and I are much better friends than we were lovers. Trust me."

"That may be," she shrugs. "I never told you this, but back when I first moved here she told me you were"—her fingers form quotation marks in the air—"The One." Lowering her hands, she surveys his expression to see how this news sinks in, though in fact it isn't news at all: Nora told him the same thing right after they broke up. It spooked him, this admission, even though Nora threw it at him as a bitter charge. "I shouldn't have said anything," she adds after a moment.

"It's fine," he assures her. "Water under the bridge. Tell me what else I missed."

"Not much," Kira assures him. "Though you've been invited to a dinner party at Nora and Brent's. This Thursday, I think. Her parents are supposed to be there."

"I might still be in New York," he says, and feels edgy all over again. He suddenly figures out how Sasha knew he would be here: he mentioned something about it at the reception. This realization gives birth to another: his father still hasn't turned up. He also remembers he needs cigarettes. He picks up a random beer bottle, realizes it is empty, and says, "You guys need anything? I'm going to the john."

"I'll go with," Sasha says, and stands up with him.

"I'm cool," Kira says.

With Sasha on his tail and the empty beer bottle absurdly in his fist, he weaves through the crowd trying to figure out how to pull this off. It was stupid of him to lie about going to the bathroom, but for a variety of reasons he's never felt comfortable smoking around Sasha. Healthy, well-adjusted people always make him feel this way, and, of course, Sasha's Sasha. Fortunately, the cigarette machines are in the bathroom lobby, so he can simply dash out while she's in the john and punch in his quarters. But he only has a five, which means he'll have to stop at the bar and get change. Just as he turns around to make some excuse to her he feels someone seize him by the arm. It all happens so quickly he drops the empty beer bottle and is nearly lifted off his feet. What the—

"C'mon," barks a voice, "it's your dad."

Two blinks of an eye later Gerald is halfway through the packed nightclub and walking rapidly behind the bouncer's broad shoulders. At the front door Thomas stops dead in his tracks, and Gerald bumps into his back. Peering around the thick cords of Thomas's neck, Gerald can see a tiny crowd gathered on the sidewalk. Beyond this little mob the Saturday night traffic of Moreland Avenue crawls slowly by, lights aglow, stereos throbbing. Gerald's heart thumps loudly in his throat as he tries to force his way outside. Thomas stops him.

"Just chill for a sec," he tells Gerald, his hand clasped around Gerald's upper arm. "Let me disperse this crowd, and then you can go."

"What do you mean?"

"I've got to disperse the crowd."

"Let go of me, man." With difficulty, Gerald yanks free his arm. "Where's my father?"

"Someone's with him. Now, just wait here and—"

But before Thomas can grab him again Gerald dashes out the door to the crowded sidewalk. Streetlights, voices. The crowd, which stands three people deep, pushes and buffets him about—it's like slam dancing, for Chrissakes—but he finally breaks into the clear, into the crowd's calm core, where all is quiet and still. Directly at his feet his father lies splayed on his back, arms out and legs collapsed to the side, his white belly turgid in the dim light and—here Gerald's stomach leaps—a puddle of blood spilling from his head. Dad's eyes are open. He is talking.

". . . yes, that hurts just a little, right there, *ouch*, that's very tender. The body, you know, a miraculous thing, really, the way it regulates itself, pain of course being, *ouch*, there it is again—"

"Dad, I'm here." Gerald crouches down at his father's shoulder, knee-to-knee with another fellow he's never seen before, a chubby, completely bald character with a neat brown beard and, presumably, some sort of first-aid license, since he's the one who's been poking around the old man's head looking for tender spots.

"Son," his father declares. "How are you, my boy? How are the Susans?"

"Terrible." Gerald tries to laugh, though in fact he wants to cry. "They're awful, Dad, just terrible. Nearly as bad as you right now."

"Oh, heavens, boy, I'm fine."

"Yeah, you look it. Tell me what happened."

"Not a thing. Not one thing worth discussing."

"Someone's called an ambulance," says the amateur paramedic.

"Been ages since I've been in one of those," his father observes. All this time he has kept his gaze focused on the sky above him. "Probably not since your mother died."

"Just relax, Dad."

"Isn't that something?"

"What are you talking about?"

"Isn't it strange I haven't been in an ambulance since your mother died? Don't you find that odd?"

"Not really."

"Why not?"

"I've *never* been in an ambulance." Gerald drops down cross-legged on the concrete, his father's arm in his lap and his back bent low so that he can speak directly into the old man's ear. "Lots of people have never been in an ambulance. Now tell me what happened."

"Oh, just a little misunderstanding with Mr. Mountjoy."

"Who's Mr. Mountjoy?"

"That interesting man we almost ran over."

"Right. I get it now." Gerald squeezes his father's arm as tears well in his eyes. "What happened between you two?"

"Oh, nothing much. We just had a misunderstanding."

The crowd standing above him remains quiet. They are listening closely to this father-son conversation. They are witnessing a spectacle. Real life is happening, right here, right now. Off in the distance Gerald detects the mounting wail of an ambulance siren. His father, also quiet, closes his eyes, a thin smile on his face. Someone taps Gerald on the back. He wipes his face across his shoulder and looks up.

Sasha crouches beside him. In her small hands she clutches a gray cell phone. Streetlights flicker across her liquid black eyes. "I've got a phone if you need to call someone."

Gerald looks at her but says nothing. Why this sudden interest in him? Why now? Particularly since he's no longer at the center of Nora's inner circle, the only place his friendship with Sasha made any sense. "The bouncer already called an ambulance," she tells him after a pause. "I'll go with you, if you want."

"Go where?"

"To the hospital."

"Why would you do that?"

"Because I'm a nice person."

The ambulance has almost arrived, its progress impeded by the one-lane traffic that clogs Moreland every weekend night. The crowd has even created a little path to the street to allow free access to the phantom ambulance. "You don't have to waste your Saturday night on us."

"It's not a waste," she insists. To prove her point, she drops down beside Gerald Indian-style and cradles her phone in her lap.

From out of nowhere, a ghostly voice says, "Let her come." It takes Gerald a couple of heartbeats to figure out the voice belongs to his father.

Gerald and Sasha laugh. "See?" she says, giving Gerald a playful elbow jab in the shoulder. "You should listen to your dad."

The ambulance is here, though Gerald isn't ready to stand up yet. He should introduce them, he realizes, but promptly decides that's a stupid thing to do. He's still a little stoned: the thought depresses him. "I feel like I'm ruining your Saturday night."

"Don't be ridiculous," she assures him. "This is just friends sticking together." Gerald notes an extra throb of emphasis on the word *friends*. Whereas Sasha's always been the principal outsider of Nora's little nexus of friends—Gerald and Nora forming one alliance, Nora and Aaron forming another—Gerald abruptly understands that he's now on the outside as well, right there with Sasha. Apparently she's trying to forge a new alliance. To get back at Aaron, presumably, though who the hell knows? Gerald's always been a colossally bad reader of female motives, from all the way back to dimpled Diana Morris in third grade, a dazzling black-haired beauty in the desk behind him who approached him one afternoon on the playground and, poking a firm finger in his chest, proclaimed, "You had your chance, Gerald Brinkman, and you missed it." He had no idea what she was talking about then, and has even less now. Before he can respond she adds, "You'll pay me back someday."

THREE

"CAN YOU just sit still for a minute, Dad?"

"I don't need any lunch."

"Yes, you do. The doctor said—"

"Forget what he said, Gerald. Forget that snooty know-it-all kid—younger than you, did you notice? Not even thirty years old and thinks he knows more than me about my own body. And here I've been lugging this old carcass around for sixty years. You know what that is, son? *Hubris.* Excessive pride."

"Then will you at least relax?"

"I am relaxed. Never felt more relaxed in my life."

"That's the spirit. And look, here's the remote."

"Please, son. Honestly."

"Okay, forget the TV. What about, look, here's the latest *Newsweek*, how about that? Lots of stuff about O. J., the Gaza Strip, everything. Even better, here's *The New Yorker*, just arrived this morning. The whole *thing's* about O. J. Everywhere you look, Jeffrey Toobin, cat cartoons, and look at this—"

"Where *is* Lester, by the way?"

"Outside, I guess. He'll come if you open the door and make this whistling sound I made up, I don't know what it means but he seems to understand—"

"Son."

Gerald pauses at the kitchen, takes a deep breath, composes his face into a pleasant expression, and turns around. Surprisingly, his father's still sitting on the couch, a wide gauze bandage encircling his skull and an open terry-cloth robe draped across his shoulders. Like a self-satisfied chimp, he scratches his sagging breasts, then the top swell of his stomach, which is as curdled as cottage cheese: all that lost weight. From over the tops of his crooked glasses he sends Gerald a penetrating stare, which Gerald tries to return. "Yes?"

"Now I want *you* to sit down."

"Look, your soup's about ready, Dad, and I need to find the cat, and then—"

"I told you I'm not hungry."

"Yes, I know, but you need to eat something. The doctor said."

"I told you already, screw that arrogant son of a bitch. Just sit here beside me so I can tell you something."

"Dad—"

He pats the couch cushion beside him. "It'll only take a minute."

Gerald clutches the door frame and shuts his eyes. "Listen, I just want to grab your soup before it burns. That's all. Can't I do that for you? Won't you let me do that much?"

His father stops patting the cushion and slowly returns his hand to his lap. "Sure. It can wait a few more minutes."

"Excellent," Gerald sighs and, like a photographer finding a pose, holds his hands out before him and steps backward into the kitchen. "That's all I ask. Just stay right where you are and *don't move.*"

But when he returns to the living room with the soup, his

father is gone. Worse still, and in direct defiance of his many admonitions to the contrary (mostly air-conditioning considerations, though flea and mosquito worries as well), the front door stands wide open. Annoyed but also resigned, he sets the bowl on the coffee table and steps outside. He finds his father crouched on the walkway in his robe, the waist sash hanging on either side of him like the loose ropes of a tent. Lester coils around the robe with his tail upright and a happy kitty smile on his triangular face.

"Atta boy," his father whispers. "That's my kitty."

Fixing his eyes on Gerald, Lester arches his back and pads back and forth on his tiptoes, staggering like a drunk against his father's leg.

"All right, you found him. Are we happy now?"

"Lovely animal," his father says. "A miracle of engineering. Cats in general, I mean. Just think of the complexity of this little organism here—the brain, the nervous system, the musculature. And all it does is sleep and eat."

"Same as us. Now get in here before you pass out. You've got no business being out in this heat. That sun is a killer."

His father squints up at the sky and nods. After a moment, he says, "You know, I still say the sun sets. Don't you? Everybody says it. Even the weathermen. Rises in the morning, sets at night. Sometimes in the mornings I'll walk outside and stand perfectly still and see if I can feel the earth rotating beneath my feet. Seems like something you could feel, like your own blood moving through your veins. You can feel that sometimes, if you're still enough. But I just end up standing there scratching my ass. That's when I know we're just insects stuck to a rock. Comforting in a way."

All day yesterday, while sitting around the apartment, Gerald had to listen to this stuff. Floating blissfully in a Demerol haze, his father talked and talked and talked. About astronomy mostly. About physics and biology. About entropy and death. He told

Gerald that all the basic contents of the physical universe exploded into being in about 10^{-32} seconds some 14 billion years ago. *Exploded,* he added with a raised finger as Gerald sat nearby nursing a cup of coffee and staring out the window, *from essentially nothing. I'm talking about perfect nonexistence here. As in no space and no time. Can you imagine it? I sure can't. Another thing: the existence of carbon-based life requires a universe with a radius exactly fifteen billion light-years in length, no more and no less, a size that happens to be— consider it, Gerald!—precisely the radius of the universe that contains us. Why this immensity? What's the point?*

"Speaking of insects," Gerald says, patting his father's back, "the front door's still open. Come inside before the mosquitoes take over."

"I haven't told you why I'm here" is Dad's response. Only after he says this does he look at his son head-on.

"No," Gerald says, guiding his father upright, "you haven't."

"I've been meaning to tell you, too. All weekend."

"I know, Dad. I know you have. Here, watch your step."

"Mountjoy confused me for a day or so, but I'm coming around again."

"That's good to hear." Gerald closes the door behind him with his foot and leads his father to the couch, though by this point the man hardly needs guiding. The moment he touches the couch his whole body sort of collapses, and before Gerald can make it around to the other end his father is resting peacefully on his side, his legs curled up fetally and his hands forming a flat pillow beneath his bandaged head. His glasses sit on his nose at a ridiculous, haphazard angle. Gerald drops to his haunches and examines his father's face. The expression is calm, content even, a tired man securely at rest. With a bachelor's clumsy delicacy, Gerald slides off his father's glasses and folds the arms and sets them along the couch arm, all the while gazing intently into the man's open eyes.

"That's why I didn't want you to go out," Gerald gently scolds. "I'm only doing what your carcass is telling me to do."

His father closes his eyes and smiles. Wets his lips. "Did I tell you I sold the house?" His eyes remain closed.

"What house?" Gerald stands and heads to the kitchen to fetch a glass of water. "Speak up, I'm just in here."

"The house, Gerald. Our old house."

Gerald surveys the wreck in the kitchen. Dirty cups, soup pans, and plastic hospital containers clutter the sink, while blots of spilled coffee stain the counter and the floor. "Say again?"

"I sold our old house. All the furniture, too. The television, the bicycles, the lawn mowers, all that crap. I've been liquidating all summer. Ever heard of an estate sale? Technically you have to be dead to have one of those, but no one really checks. I just put an ad in the newspaper and the next Saturday morning I walked out to the front porch and found fifty people, maybe more, gathered there in the yard, ready to buy. Sold everything, for cash. Good old Torrent helped me. He misses you, by the way. You should call him."

Gerald shuts off the faucet and holds his breath. Though he's only been half listening, the name *Torrent* comes through loud and clear. Purse-lipped and patrician, with his narrow manicured fingers and his beady little eyes and his annoying Hah-vahd accent—an accent Dad himself once affected but dropped like a bad haircut the minute he left the pulpit—Dr. Torrent was his father's old college roommate and longtime friend, though in fact Dad never seemed to like the guy all that much. Gerald still grimaces when he recalls those painfully dull Christmas visits to the good doctor's library. Torrent, genteelly sipping his Scotch (he took it neat), would needle Gerald with mundane questions about his life at college, his father would provide the occasional sardonic gloss, and when these questions dried up, that was pretty much it. In earlier years, Eva, in her light-handed, easy way, kept the conversations afloat; once she left home for college and a dazzling adulthood, the men were utterly hopeless: not one of them followed sports, Dad's political views over the years had become so outthere and conspiratorial that Gerald and Torrent both learned long ago to stay clear of anything involving governmental figures of whatever political persuasion, and Gerald's one area of encyclopedic expertise—rock—held zero in the way of interest to the other two. The three men would sit there and sip their drinks and listen to the hi-fi and then, all of them barely disguising their relief, enthusiastically part. After Gerald explained all of this to Nora one night several years ago, she advanced the possibility that Torrent was a pederast. For her, this explained everything, though Gerald remains unconvinced.

"I don't have anything to say to him," Gerald calls from the kitchen, and resumes filling the glass.

"You will, trust me. Now guess how much I made."

He returns to the living room with his father's water. Dad remains curled on his side with his hands tucked beneath his cheeks and his eyes closed. Gerald sets the glass down and sits on the coffee table. "I'm sorry, but I'm a little lost here. What are we talking about?"

"The sale. I'm asking you to guess how much I made."

"From Torrent?"

"No, son. Pay attention. I'm talking about the estate sale."

"Look, are you fucking with me?"

"Thirty-four thousand dollars. Actually, that's not strictly true. I sold the car and some of the more valuable stuff separately. Your mother's old jewelry, for instance. Been holding on to that for what? Twenty-three years? Just sitting in that house, dormant matter, totally meaningless."

"Dad." Gerald shakes his father's shoulder. "Look at me. Sit up and look at me."

Dad opens his eyes and stares impassively into the air. With his free arm, he claws at his bare chest. "That's not all that much," he resumes, still scratching. "Thirty-four thousand dollars, I mean. After all those years, you'd think my worldly possessions would be worth more than that, but there you go. A good reminder of our worthlessness, wouldn't you agree? Pretty bleak realization. Now ask me about the house."

"What house, Dad?"

"How much you think it fetched? Keep in mind it was paid for. No realtor fees, either. I'm talking about pure cash profit here."

"You're serious, aren't you? Please, somebody tell me this isn't happening."

"You probably don't even know what I paid for it originally. Any idea? Remember, this was sixty-seven, so you'll have to make a massive adjustment for inflation."

"Dad, why didn't you *tell* me you were going to do this?"

"Oh, I tried, but you seemed so ..."

"*What*, Dad? How did I seem?"

"Forget it, Gerald. Don't sweat it. All your stuff is in storage, by the way. Remember nice Mrs. Ethridge down the road? The one with the cats? Well, she let me keep your and your sister's things in her garage. You can pick them up whenever you want. All that Big Jim and Barbie stuff, tons of kids' books, board games and whatnot. It's all there."

"But, Dad," Gerald whispers, and bends forward so that his nose nearly brushes his father's, "I've talked to you nearly every day for the last three weeks. All you did was read to me from *The Nation*."

"Which, by the way, you should be getting in the next week or so. I had the subscription transferred to this address. It's good for another year, but after that you'll have to renew."

"Hold on a sec, just—"

He is interrupted by a rapid knock at the door. Both he and his father glance around like burglars caught in a searchlight. No one has knocked on this door in days. No one has called, no one has e-mailed. Gerald has forgotten about work, about his job interview this Wednesday in New York, about the Olympics. The knock enters his consciousness like an abrupt summons from the afterlife. Without really thinking what he's doing, or why he's doing it, he brings his index finger to his lips and glares at his father. Within moments the knock sounds again.

"Gerald!" calls a woman's voice. "You in there?"

Nora. Gerald's inner panic slowly subsides. It's only Nora. He lowers his finger and calls, "It's unlocked."

The door beside the couch slowly opens. Through the widening crack pokes Nora's blond head, her complexion radiant. She enters the room on tiptoe, a veritable study in daisies—they're on her dress, in her hair, on her sandals—and closes the door behind her, though not before Lester dashes in and skids across the kitchen linoleum. She cries, "Oh!" at the cat and, turning, exclaims, "Ah!" at the sight of Dad bathrobed and bandaged on the couch.

"The blushing bride," Dad smiles.

"Oh, my God." Her palm pressed against her chest, Nora lowers herself onto the edge of the couch and delicately touches Dad's bandage. "What *happened* to you, Mr. Brinkman?"

"He rammed his head into some homeless guy's beer bottle," Gerald explains. "You know, the usual."

"You what?"

Dad closes his eyes and nods. "It was a piece of cement pipe."

Nora turns to Gerald. Gerald smiles. Shrugs. "Oh, what fun we've been having."

"When did this happen? Why didn't you say anything at the reception?"

"Nothing had happened yet. Isn't that right, Dad? You were here *three* whole hours before you ended up in the hospital."

"Ignore him, honey. He's just sore he has to share a bathroom with an invalid."

"And this happened on Saturday?" Nora glances at both men for confirmation. "On my wedding day?"

"Astonishing, isn't it?" Gerald crosses his arms and smiles. "How is married life, by the way? Haven't had a chance to talk to you since the big event."

Nora glances around the room and into the kitchen where, apparently, her eyes land on the hospital containers and medicine bottles. Her face registers a little heart snag but she quickly recovers, in dramatic proof of which she sinks back on the couch and drapes her elegant arm across Dad's bare knees. "This is a bad time. I shouldn't be here."

"Don't be ridiculous," his father snaps, and takes her in for the first time. *How Dad adored this girl. We really should have stuck it out.* "You're the best thing I've seen in ages."

"He's right," Gerald agrees, marveling. "You look spectacular."

"Yeah, well, it's one of the side effects."

"Marriage'll do that to you," Dad chimes in. "Which leads to my next question: why aren't you on your honeymoon?"

"Brent has to work." She removes her arm from his knees and props her legs on the coffee table. "He's doing this thing for the Olympics, a webcast or whatever. The university's sponsoring it. We're going to Cancún after the games are over."

"Brent's one of the university's computer techs," Gerald explains to his father. "That's how they met. One day Nora's hard disk crashed, the next day Brent's recovered this huge chunk of her dissertation. You could say it was love at first byte."

"A chunk I've since cut," she sighs. She started her dissertation— "Coming Clean: Hygiene and Hysteria in the Victorian Novel"— right around the time she and Gerald first split up; three years later, it's still gestating. "Brent wants me to feel you out about working for him. He's short on writers."

[61]

"I'm kinda busy," Gerald protests, still bitter that no one appreciated his "byte" pun.

"That's what I told him. But I promised I'd ask."

"What's a webcast?" Dad wants to know.

Nora raises her eyebrows at Gerald, to see if he wants to explain; he looks back and shrugs. "It's a Web page where they cover the Olympics," she tells Dad. "Brent says it's the wave of the future."

"Never much cared about the future," Dad opines. "Or the present, for that matter."

Gerald's still staring at Nora, sort of taking her in. It hurts him, in a way, how terrific she looks. Did *he* ever have this effect on her? "Seriously, Nora, you've never looked this happy."

"It ain't happiness, Sherlock." She lets this remark hang just long enough for Gerald to realize he's supposed to figure something out here. Back when they were dating one of her favorite pet names for him was Clueless Joe—a marked improvement, he had to admit, over his loathsome elementary-school nickname, Stinkman, which she also used once in a while, to get his goat. Several more moments pass, during which the only sound in the room is the hollow, jagged crackle of Lester chomping on his Meow Mix. Finally, in a flat, emotionless voice, she declares, "I'm pregnant."

What surprises Gerald most about this information is how unspectacular it turns out to be. Though the announcement is monumental in its way, it is not thoroughly unexpected. It makes sense, all of a sudden. And that's when he recalls a little detail about Nora that he hadn't had occasion to think about in a long time: she refused to be on the Pill. She said it made her bloated and moody and was in any case tantamount to rewiring the natural mechanics of the female body, which she didn't want to do, if she could help it. Always up-to-date on everything from airline safety statistics to the latest research on asbestos poisoning, she reserved a special place in her catalog of obsessions for any and all possible connections between oral contraception and breast cancer, of which her mother, Libby, was a survivor of eight years' standing. "Well, shit. Congratulations, I guess."

"Don't sound so overwhelmed," she sneers.

"Ignore him." His father struggles up to stare Nora squarely in the eye. "I think it's wonderful. And a bride besides. This really is terrific news."

"It's still kind of early. They say you're not supposed tell people till you're past the third month. That's why I've been so mum."

Gerald's stomach, he's surprised to realize, buzzes with discomfort. So that explains the marriage. "How far along are you?"

"I just *told* you." She rolls her eyes in mock disbelief. "Anyway, I'm sorry for barging in like this, totally unannounced—"

"Please," Dad interrupts.

"—and dropping this little bombshell. In fact"—addressing Gerald now—"I was getting ready to call you on the phone, but then realized I was completely bored. I'm still getting used to being in Brent's place, that's part of it. But I also just . . . I don't know. I wanted some company, I guess."

"We're glad you came," Dad assures her. "It really is wonderful news."

She looks away, her eyes rimmed with tears, sniffles, says, "Crying's another side effect," and wipes her nose against her wrist. "Oh, and guess what I'm supposed to be doing right now?"

"Resting," guesses Dad.

"Try *writing* my fucking dissertation."

Gerald tells her, "Forget the diss, Nora. Why don't *you* start writing for Brent?"

"Uh, I don't think so."

"How come?"

"Well, for one thing—"

Someone knocks at the door.

"Unbelievable," Gerald marvels. "Most traffic I've had in months."

Abruptly, Nora stands up. "I should go, really."

"I can come back," a voice calls from the other side of the door. It is a female voice, slightly familiar. He turns to Nora. She arches an eyebrow.

"It's fine," Gerald calls. "Come on in."

Sasha enters the apartment bearing a glass casserole pan covered with tinfoil. She's dressed in khakis and a green polo shirt with the mysterious word *Dazynalin* emblazoned on the left breast. Stomping her white sneakers on the carpet, she cocks a fist on her hip and raises the casserole aloft. "Thought you boys could use some nourishment." Only then does she take note of Nora. Nora, too, takes note of her. Gerald's heart kicks against his rib cage but, unfortunately, she doesn't flinch, not Nora. She just stands where she is, hands behind her back, a soft smile on her face.

Sasha stares at her for a blank moment, glances at Gerald, and then, fully recovered, turns back and cries, "Oh my *God*!" Placing the casserole on the coffee table, she steps forward and opens her arms. "How are you *doing*! I haven't seen you since the *wedding*!"

"Oh, right," Nora replies, and steps into Sasha's open arms, gently returning the hug. Over Sasha's shoulder she raises a meaningful eyebrow at Gerald, who shakes his head in bewildered reply. Seriously: no clue what this is about. "Some big night," Nora says as she steps away. "I had gas and he fell asleep. Whoopee."

"Oh, don't say that," Sasha urges her.

Sasha has only been to Gerald's apartment twice before, both times to gather with a larger group en route to some more interesting outing. In each case he had given the place a thorough cleaning beforehand. Now the apartment's ashy aura of cigarette smoke turns his stomach. Most traffic he's had in years, more like. "Thanks for the food," he tells her. "We'll certainly knock it back."

"Yes, very thoughtful," Nora agrees, crossing her arms. "I'm just amazed you knew about all this."

"Oh, she was there," Gerald explains, then tries to swallow it back.

"Oh?" Nora tilts her head, as if this were sweet, or cute, or something.

"It was very late," Gerald stammers. "Like way after midnight. Or was it later? Do you remember?"

"It was late," Sasha agrees, and sits down on the couch's arm-rest, avoiding Nora's gaze. "How you doing, Mr. Brinkman?"

"Can't complain." His father has resumed his supine position, the robe hanging open just enough to reveal his flabby chest, his marbled belly, his ratty boxers. He looks like Brian Wilson in his bedroom phase. Embarrassment floods Gerald's face. "Right now I feel like a sultan with a harem."

Sasha smiles, pats him on the hip. "How's that head?"

"Pounding something fierce."

"Can I get you anything?"

"You may, indeed." Everyone in the room stays perfectly still, Gerald in particular. Forty-eight hours he's been taking care of the old fart and not once has his father accepted gracefully one of Gerald's offers of help. Now this lovely girl breezes in here and the guy's as docile as a puppy.

"Name it," Sasha coaxes.

"I'd like you to get *him* out of this apartment." The old man's voice is soft and viscous, his eyes closed, his mind already else-where. "Think you can do that for me?"

Sasha looks up at Gerald and shrugs. "You hungry?"

"Count me out," Nora suddenly says, though actually Sasha hadn't included her. "I should have been home hours ago."

"And I've got work to do," Gerald tells her, for some reason. He suddenly remembers that Dazynalin is an antidepressant drug Sasha sells. She suggested once that he get a prescription, to help with his insomnia, but he had politely demurred, secretly worried he'd have to give up pot. "Plus, you've brought us this grub, as you said. Maybe later."

"Sure. What time?"

"Come again?"

"For dinner," Dad chimes in, pulling the robe around his bare chest. "She's asking what time is good for you."

"I heard what she said, Dad," Gerald snaps back. He looks at Nora, to see how she's taking all this, but she's already at the door, waving good-bye. He feels as if he is betraying her somehow, before he realizes that makes no sense. Didn't she just get married two days ago? Isn't she pregnant? Quick enough for Nora to hear, he asks, "What time does Aaron get off?"

"He doesn't," Sasha replies, just as the door slams shut beside her. Into the ensuing silence a hollow echo slowly spreads. Sasha runs her fingers through her lush hair, the thick strands crackling with static. "At least I think so. I'll have to check."

"I see." No getting around it: without Nora around he feels abandoned. Or unfettered. Or frightened. A strange feeling, all right. The old man sinks deeper into the couch, deeper into the cave of himself. Nothing seems particularly sinister here, the entire transaction having taken place in broad daylight, as it were, before several credible witnesses. A blade of sunlight cuts across Sasha's forehead, painting her black hair an electrifying butane blue. "Well, all right then. We can pretend it's a date."

FOUR

IN THE last couple of years Gerald has dated more or less regularly but not any one person consistently. He's remained single, unattached. The reasons for this are complicated, Gerald would submit—and often does submit, to anyone who cares to listen—but even he would also have to admit that Nora probably has something to do with it. Or a lot with it. After all, Nora is the last person Gerald officially dated. He and Nora dated for nearly a year, and since then Gerald has dated no one seriously, despite the myriad women he has escorted to various and sundry one-off dates. Nora was a hard act to follow, is the problem. She's insisted as much. Whenever he finishes describing one of his horrible, disastrous dates to her, she smiles serenely and says, "You can't get over me." She has a point. As violently as he and Nora used to fight, it is nevertheless true that no one else he has taken out in the last three years has quite matched the tremendous force of her personality. No one has quite measured up.

This fact has raised a tricky emotional dilemma. For it was Gerald who officially split up with Nora way back when, and not vice versa. He broke up with her because he was sure there was someone else out there in the world more compatible with him and somehow less difficult to live with than she. Curiously enough, the only woman who has even come close to achieving this ideal is—well, Nora. And she's come awfully damn close. Sometimes she gets so close to becoming that spectacular someone else that he can barely tell the two women apart—the Nora he left and this other Nora: Nora Deluxe. Whenever he finds himself confronted with this sort of realization, he stops and asks himself why he broke up with her in the first place, particularly if the only tangible benefit was a worse romantic life than the one he abandoned. Fortunately, this sort of honest introspection doesn't happen very often. What usually happens is he goes out on a date, tells Nora about it, goes home, gets stoned, and immediately decides to start searching for someone else to ask out.

He met Nora his first year in graduate school. A second-year veteran, she was smart, brash, and radiantly blond. In the previous year she had firmly established herself as a departmental social arbiter, a coiner of phrases ("grad fad," "paper PMS," "the beastie yeasties"), and a master of the witheringly ironic put-down (she preferred the term *ironical*), so by the time Gerald encountered her she was already a fully established personage. She also promoted a comic version of herself as a Serious but Chaste Working Girl, an affectation made all the more striking—i.e., ironical—by the carefully manufactured thrift-store ambience in which she lived. Engagingly combative in matters both intellectual and pop, as frightening as a school principal and as lovely as a ballerina, she was one intimidating little package. She certainly intimidated Gerald, and like magic this air of intimidation quickly turned into desire. He discovered this strange matrix of emotions while watching her perform in the classroom, a milieu in which she was unsurpassed. No one could match her in a seminar setting, that long, gleaming table with its surrounding circle of peers and its

King Arthur professor at the head as tailor-made for her own brand of charmingly sardonic aggression as the gridiron for a football team. She didn't even have to do the reading. In her hands, doing or not doing the reading might suddenly become part of the discussion, just one component in an elaborate, slippery, and cagey argument about institutional power and textual indeterminacy, complete with memorized quotations from Jane Tompkins and Frederic Jameson. What's not to love? For two weeks straight he watched her longingly from across the table of both his nineteenth-century British lit seminar and his seventeenth-century poetry class ("Sexual Metaphysics and the Body Politic"), and one day early in week three of his stint in the English program they finally exchanged words. He told her about his difficulties finding an apartment, and somewhere along the way he revealed to her that he had a cat. Later she would tell him, "That did it."

"That's my big problem right now," he tried to explain. They were standing beside the department's IBM photocopier as Nora smashed the lid over and over again onto the spine of a thick scholarly quarterly. "I keep finding places I like and all, but they keep saying 'No pets.' "

"Oh, but you *have* to keep your cat." With her free hand she gave his forearm a provocative little squeeze. Behind her a rod of green light passed beneath the journal she was mashing down. The photocopier flashed brightly and Gerald felt the floor dissolve beneath him. "You'll just have to keep looking," she insisted.

"I know, I know, you're absolutely right." He looked into her eyes again—olive green, with specks of orange and red, like an apple in an impressionist still life—and felt himself falling, falling. "It's just, I don't know, I feel like I could be looking for*ever*."

At first, everything seemed perfect. She was smart and attractive and popular within the narrow confines of the graduate English Department. Her approval guaranteed his success. They were sexually compatible. They were both cat people. He met her parents and everyone got along. She met and more or less courted Gerald's father, a performance so irresistible even the old man fell in love. All that fall Gerald whiled away his evenings in her apartment, drinking beer and watching her television—she had cable—while she flipped alternately through *Mother Jones* or the latest volume of *Gender Studies Quarterly*. At the end of each semester, while he filed incomplete after incomplete, she gave protracted birth to one of her knotty, exuberantly argued seminar papers on same-sex desire in Charlotte Brontë's *Villette* or anal retentiveness in Dickens's *Our Mutual Friend*. There was nothing wrong between them, not one single thing. Everyone said so. Everyone she knew, anyway. And since he only knew the people she knew—he was still new in town, after all—he took their word for it. They were so compatible, he and Nora. A match made in academia.

Occasionally, they socialized with one or two other couples in the program, the most prominent couple being an unlikely duo named Jeff and Tanya Flibula. A moderately pretty redheaded Midwesterner with a passion for cooking, homemaking, and nineteenth-century women's fiction, Tanya was the theoretician's domestic. In her hands an artichoke-and-hummus hors d'oeuvre became a tool of empowerment. Meanwhile, her husband, Jeff, a six-foot, 138-pound fellow graduate student, remained languorously engaged in a lengthy dissertation, now over eight years in the writing, on Cold War allegories in science-fiction novels from the fifties and sixties. Jeff Flibula had long, stringy black hair and thick wire-rim glasses that sat at a perpetual tilt along his long hawk nose. Outfitted comfortably in blue sweatpants, a black Blue Öyster Cult T-shirt, and a terry-cloth bathrobe, he spent the bulk of his ample free time slumped on the couch in his living room smoking prodigious amounts of marijuana, watching *Star Trek: The Next Generation*, and reading fantasy quest novels, the covers of which featured dragons held at bay by astonishingly muscular, and nearly nude, women in chain-mail string bikinis. These novels and smoking materials were simply the merest tip of an enormous iceberg Gerald referred to as the Jeff Flibula Collection, a massive anthology of labeled and alphabetically arranged pop-culture artifacts including over 450 art-rock and heavy-metal CDs, three shelves' worth of science-fiction videotapes, innumerable paperback books, and a gargoyle menagerie of ceramic bongs and water pipes. The Flibulas' living room was the principal site of the Collection.

Looking back on this period of his life, Gerald would return over and over again to a particular evening at the Flibulas that proved, in retrospect, to mark a decisive turning point in his relationship with Nora. It was late July, a month before classes resumed. As usual, the women had disappeared to the back of the apartment, leaving Gerald and Jeff free to peruse the Collection. That particular evening they were listening to Rush and inhaling Turkish hash through an ingenious ceramic pipe molded into the shape of Yoda, a cherished item of the Collection that Jeff later left at Gerald's apartment one evening and that Gerald still counts among his own possessions. Just as Jeff tapped Gerald on the shoulder with the Yoda pipe and croaked, "You're up, dude," Nora stepped into the room, put her fists on her hips, and declared, "They're trying to have a baby."

Gerald took the Yoda pipe from Jeff and looked up. "Who is?"

"Who do you think?" She pointed an accusing finger at Jeff. "*They* are."

Gerald turned to Jeff and smiled. Jeff smiled back. On the stereo, Rush explained, *If you choose not to decide, you still have made a choice.* "That's great, man. You didn't tell me."

Jeff shrugged. "Didn't think you gave a shit."

Gerald nodded and looked back at Nora, who had not moved from her position in the doorway. Her eyes bore right through his skin. Recoiling, he said, "What? What'd I do?"

"I swear, sometimes I—" The fists on her hips compressed

once before she turned and walked back to the bedroom, where she and Tanya had been consulting all this time.

"Did you follow that?" Gerald asked Jeff.

"Follow what?"

"That, I don't know, that whole exchange? What just happened?"

"When?"

"Just now. When Nora came in here."

"Nora," Jeff said cryptically, repacking the Yoda pipe. "I hear you, dude."

On the drive home—Nora behind the wheel, Gerald loopy and edgy in the passenger seat—they both sat perfectly still as they drifted through the glowing Technicolor landscape of retail Atlanta. They passed three Subways, two Krogers, and four Blockbuster video emporiums before Gerald worked up the nerve to ask, "What are you so pissed off about?"

"You're stoned, Gerald."

"Is that your answer?"

"Can we not talk about this right now?"

"Fine."

He counted to ten, got lost somewhere around seven, conducted a mental inventory of everything he'd said tonight, regretted about 80 percent of it, squirmed uncomfortably in his seat, and finally blurted out, "I'm not *that* stoned, you know."

"If you say so."

"Meaning?"

"Look, didn't I just say I didn't want to talk about this?"

"But I don't understand what we're *not* talking about."

"Exactly. That's precisely my point, honey."

But of course they did end up talking about it. Back at Nora's apartment Gerald ostentatiously poured himself a big glass of ice water—nature's elixir, the innocent liquid—and joined her in the living room. She was curled up on the couch firing the remote at a silent television screen. She had already changed into floppy men's boxer shorts and a ratty T-shirt, her preferred mode of dress for lounging around the house, but also a possible message to Gerald as re: future sexual activity. Not quite sure how to begin, he sat down across from her on the easy chair and gnawed nervously on a piece of ice, drained the glass, and rattled the remains.

"Stop it," she said.

"Only if you tell me why you're so snappish."

"You must have some vague idea."

"Not even a clue. Nor do I know why you embarrassed me like that in front of Flibula."

"I told you already: they're trying to have a baby."

"So what?"

"*So*, you were getting high with him."

"Yes? And that's it? Flibula gets stoned every day, and now I'm the villain? Wake and bake: that's Flibula's idea of Lauds."

"You shouldn't encourage him."

"Fine: I didn't."

"It's bad for the baby."

"Is this what you and Tanya talked about?"

"Yes. That and some other stuff."

"Well, look, Flibula's her problem, not yours, so don't blame me if she's got a pothead for a husband. It's not my fault."

"Nothing's your fault, Gerald. That's *your* idea of Lauds."

"Aha. Now we're getting somewhere."

She turned to him, the remote still poised in the air. Her eyes were concealed behind the glinting discs of her glasses, across which television images flickered and danced. After a moment, she turned back to the screen and asked, "What about you?"

"What about me?"

"Well, what if I were to ..." She stopped here. On the television screen David Letterman rocked back on his heels and grimaced. Paul Shaffer shrugged a weak go-figure. She clicked the remote a few times—Home Shopping Network, TBN, Charlie Rose—and ground her teeth.

"If you were to what?"

"Let's just forget it. You're being very aggressive right now, and I don't like it."

"Well, stop being so dramatic." But she had a point: he was only making matters worse. So he sat back in his chair, shook loose a piece of ice, and gnawed on it for a moment or two. When he figured enough time had passed, he said, "I'm just trying to follow you, Nora. That's all I'm doing."

She turned to him again. He could tell she was considering her next line of attack. She seemed to have several issues she wanted to open right now, but she also seemed unsure how best to begin. His heart raced with anticipation. What would it be? Were they breaking up? Was she sleeping with someone else? In his frazzled condition, both options thrilled and terrified him in more or less equal measure. Without shifting her gaze, she clicked off the television, set down the remote, and took a deep breath. "Okay. Now I don't want you to freak out or anything, but this has been bothering me for a while so I just need to ask it."

"Ask away."

Gentle, self-effacing smile. "Please understand I'm not judging you, Gerald. I just want to know how often, on average, you get high."

His immediate response was totally unexpected. He felt—there was no other word for it—a white-hot bolt of rage. He wasn't even sure where it came from, this anger, but it was there, all right. He was lifting the glass to his mouth as she spoke and the moment she said the word *high* he was seized with an impulse to bite off the rim. But he suppressed this urge, lowered the glass, jiggled it once, and replied, "I don't know. Once in a while."

"I realize that. Like I said, I'm not . . ."

"When I have it around, I smoke it. How's that?"

"But how often? I mean, when you have it around?"

"Look, it helps me relax, all right? I like listening to music this way, always have. That's all it is, Nora. Something to do at night. It's just a ha—" He stopped midword.

"A what, Gerald? A habit?"

"I was going to say a hobby."

"And how often do you have it around?"

"Why are you asking me this? What is up with you?"

"Nothing's up with me. We're just having a conversation."

"Oh, is that what this is?"

"Second question: do you think you could stop?"

"Of *course* I could stop. Christ." He stood up now and went to the kitchen. Self-righteousness had made him bold. To hell with all this ice-water bullshit: where's the Scotch? He crouched down behind the breakfast counter and began rattling around in the cabinet where Nora kept her booze. Vodka, margarita mix, rum—

"Excuse me?" she called. "I was *talking* to you."

Success! He shoved aside all the other stuff and withdrew the squat bottle of Jim Beam he'd bought last week and tilted it into the light. Two good drinks left, maybe three with water. Clutching the bottle by its neck, he dug around in the sink and found his orange-juice glass from earlier in the morning, shook it clean, and ran it under the faucet, all the while ignoring Nora's eyes, which he knew were trained on him. He wasn't going to hide what he was doing, but he wasn't going to look at her, either. Opening the freezer, he felt a cold burst of air strike him in the face, but he ignored this as well; he just barreled through his task, grabbing (and dropping) ice cubes and plinking them loudly into the slippery wet glass. The ice crackled and collapsed as he poured in the brown, translucent liquid. He stood before the refrigerator and took a good solid belt, the ice clacking against his teeth. Then he composed his face and turned around. She was up on her knees, her arms crossed along the back of the couch, her mouth pressed into the merest suggestion of a smile.

"You were saying."

"You heard me," she replied. "Do you think you could quit?"

"Quit what, Nora? What exactly are you getting at? Are you asking me to quit smoking pot? Is that it?"

"No. I'm not asking that. But what if I did?"

"And why would you do a thing like that?"

"Oh, gosh, let me think about that for a second. Hmmm. Well, let's just say for the sake of argument that you and I were trying to have a baby."

Bam. That's the kind of night this was: from rage to panic in less than three minutes, and things were only now getting started. His heart, already thumping at a fairly fast clip, suddenly hit a bump: he almost rocked forward with the force of the internal jerk. The glass rattled in his grip. He took another sip of his drink, did a Letterman grimace, and set the glass back down. "I take it you're speaking hypothetically."

"Of course. But what if I weren't? What if this were a real possibility? Would you quit?"

"But we're not, Nora. We are not in any way trying to have a baby right now."

"You still haven't answered my question."

"Because it's a stupid question. It's one of those idiotic hypotheticals girls are always asking their boyfriends. 'What if I died?' 'What if I got fat?' You're just fishing for some preordained answer. You don't really want to know how I feel. You just want to see if I'll answer correctly."

"Yes or no, Gerald. It's a pretty simple question."

"Yes, speaking hypothetically, I would quit."

"And the cigarettes?"

"Look, what's all this about having a baby all of a sudden? I thought that was the last thing on earth you wanted."

"I never said that."

"Yes, you did. Many times. The glass ceiling, the tenure disparity, the myth of motherhood. I've read your papers, Nora. Motherhood is a trap: isn't that your big argument?"

"Yes, but that's no reason not to have a baby. I was talking about the culture surrounding motherhood. I was saying women shouldn't be punished for having children: I didn't say they shouldn't *do* it."

"So that's what this has been about. You're jealous of Tanya."

"No, I'm not."

"Sure sounds like it to me."

By now the smile had completely left her face. He realized, as he stood there behind the breakfast counter, that she was reconsidering everything she'd just said to him. She was sizing him up. He had given all the wrong answers to her questions and now she was rethinking her ambitions for him. She didn't even seem mad at him anymore, just sort of disappointed.

"Forget it," she finally said, and plopped back down on the couch. The television volume came on, then climbed, all laughter and drum rolls.

But he didn't forget it. All that night he lay in bed beside her and thought about the implications of all that she had opened up. So she wanted a baby. That was apparently now part of the deal. All this time she had been seeing him not simply as a lover and partner, as if those were simple, uncomplicated roles, but as a potential husband as well, perhaps even a potential father for her children. How could he have missed it? How could he have been so blind? Beside him she lay sound asleep, tunneling deeper and deeper into herself and the security she must have been feeling about her own long-range desires, while he tossed and turned. For the last seven or eight months the two of them—good graduate students that they were—had discussed marriage and child-rearing in only the coldest, most theoretical terms. They discussed other couples they knew, analyzed everyone else's bad decisions, out-lined the cultural preconceptions that compelled people to make that drastic and ill-advised gesture toward lifelong commitment and parenthood. But now he realized they had been talking about something else. That is, *Nora* had been talking about something else. They had been speaking not directly but in the elusive, gen-dered code of adult relationships, a multivoiced discourse of signs and double meanings that required constant, on-the-spot inter-pretation and light-speed, simultaneous translation. And he had misread her. Whereas he had been addressing the secondary sources, she had been talking about the primary text. All this time he thought they were talking about one thing when in fact she was talking about that one thing and the other thing as well, all at the same time. He just hadn't been paying attention.

But she had his attention now. As he lay there, hour after hour, trying to locate the source of his unease, he felt like an inept ar-chaeologist on a fruitless dig. He kept coming up with shards and pieces of flint, but nothing solid, nothing complete. Most of what he did uncover he dismissed out of hand. First he rejected the notion, implicit in her opening question, that he couldn't con-trol his marijuana intake. Then he rejected the idea that he was not ready for fatherhood. He *wasn't* ready, as it happened, but he didn't see what that had to do with how he was feeling right now. Next he rejected the supposition, also latent in some of the things she'd said tonight, that they were heading for marriage. Because of course they weren't. The very idea was preposterous. They were old enough for such a thing, to be sure, and certainly the prospect was not altogether unappealing to him, at least in the abstract—marriage here regarded purely as a self-contained con-cept in its own right—but he didn't see how she could possibly be thinking about the two of them actually turning that abstraction into a specific, hard-nosed reality. He was in graduate school, for Chrissakes. He earned nine hundred dollars a month on stipend.

And he wasn't even sure if he wanted to stay in this idiotic profession, with its total absence of jobs and its perpetual learning curve. In fact—he suddenly realized, all at once, from out of nowhere—he wanted to start living another sort of life entirely, a normal life, a mundane and unexamined life without consequences. And he couldn't start doing that if he was dating a woman in graduate school, could he? Why, he was a liability to her now. He'd ruin her career. And he didn't want to do that, did he? No, he did not. So what on earth was she thinking?

Having rejected all of these options, he found solace in an entirely new idea. The thought just popped into his head, one more option among several, and yet this new idea had the magical effect of solving everything. He could break up with her. Of course! That was the answer! How could he not have seen it? It was as obvious as a symbol in Steinbeck. There was no way he could take on responsibility for her life and her career, particularly since he wasn't ready to take on responsibility for himself, so what other choice did he have? And that *was* what she wanted, wasn't it? For the two of them to take on responsibility for each other? A laudable thing for her to want, no question about it; he was just the wrong person for the job. No, the proper thing, the only sensible thing, was to let her go. She wanted marriage, children, all of that, while he wanted … Oh, hell, whatever it was he wanted. Actually, he didn't know what he wanted. Which was *precisely* why he couldn't get married to her. He couldn't get married to her because he didn't know what he wanted. And wasn't that the whole point of marriage, after all? Getting what you wanted? So there: problem solved. He was all wrong for her, that was what it all boiled down to. The only way to make her happy and give her a chance to acquire all the things she longed for was to step aside and let her *move on*. A noble decision, if you stopped and thought about it. An act of altruism. And the only answer to his dilemma. There was simply nothing else he could do.

A month later, he dropped out of graduate school. Two days after that, they split up.

The first thing he did with his newfound freedom was look for a job. As he put it to his friends, it was high time he got his shit together, and to do that he should start selling something. By God, salesmen had their shit together. And it was better than waiting tables and working in record stores, which is what he did throughout those directionless two or three years after college graduation. After less than a month of halfhearted searching he found a job selling ad space for the city's free weekly newspaper, *Alternative Atlanta*, the one that ran Tom Tomorrow cartoons, "News of the Weird," exhaustive nightclub listings, and men-seeking-men personal ads. It wasn't exactly the sort of sales job he'd had in mind, but it was a start. He now made *fifteen hundred* dollars a month—plus more on commission if he just put in the extra hustle and bustle, just gave it his all, just walked that extra mile—and he had a desk and a work phone number and a business card with his name on it. He especially liked the work phone number—or, as it was often referred to on official forms of every stripe, a *day* number. He had a home number and a day number, just like all the other grown-ups out there who had their shit together. He had a home life and work life. He had casual clothes and work clothes and exactly one very cherished ninety-dollar dress shirt he purchased from the J. Crew catalog, on whose elaborate order form he was also asked to list his day number and his home number.

Even more than the day number, he fell head over heels in love with the J. Crew catalog, which, after that one purchase, began appearing in his mailbox about every other day, it seemed like. He loved the way those glossy pages clung together as if connected by a soft adhesive felt, the way the men's shirts were stacked on top of one another like pastel-colored newspapers in a kiosk, the way all those beautiful WASPish models managed to look so comfortable and languorous and just plain *satisfied* in their wool corduroys and plush fishermen sweaters, all of them clutching big coffee mugs or spinning footballs between their shapely palms as they lounged about in Vermont in the fall or at seaside summer homes in Cape Cod or Nantucket, tossing around the old pigskin while Biff and Caroline refueled the Piper Cub, or reading leather-bound Victorian novels by the bay, or prepping the sailboat. Dressed in his beloved J. Crew button-down and a pair of Old Navy khakis, he tooled around town in his old Toyota Corolla listening to the music of the Crows—the Counting Crows, Sheryl Crow, the Black Crowes—while all about him zoomed other young professionals clad in J. Crew outfits and bathed in Crow music. He waved at them as they passed, nodding his head in time to the music, and then he went home alone to his cat and his pot and his albums.

About four months into his stint as an ad salesman, sometime in mid-January, the paper's resident music critic left the paper to enter a film-writing program out west, and Gerald, showing (even he would admit it) uncharacteristic initiative, offered to fill in for a couple of weeks, and that was basically all she wrote for the J. Crew catalog. And he's never really looked back.

At first he loved the job. He attended concerts and hung out at nightclubs and listened to piles of CDs. All those years of compiling data about record producers and obscure b-sides had finally paid off—quite literally, as his new salary, though still less than what he had made as a member of the sales team, was somewhat larger than his old graduate stipend, more than enough for him, particularly since he no longer needed to buy CDs: they just turned up in his mailbox at work. What's more, he discovered early on that a great many local Atlantans religiously read his column. Some even wrote him angry or congratulatory letters. Within a period of six months his weekly fan/hate mail was exceeded only by the newspaper's deliberately volatile right-wing political columnist, a Rush Limbaugh clone who referred to the president as "Swill Blimpton" and the First Lady as "Billary Rodman" and who, in person, was actually a pretty funny guy. Gerald had an audience, for what that was worth. His high-water mark of public praise came in response to what one moved reader called his "clear-eyed" and "unsentimental" eulogy to Nirvana lead singer and suicide victim Kurt Cobain ("Don't confuse chemical addiction with heroism. You don't get to be Samuel Beckett by blowing your head off"). His low-water mark of reader wrath came in response to what one pissed-off reader called his "incredibly stupid" and "unfeeling" eulogy to Grateful Dead lead guitarist and Deadhead guru Jerry Garcia ("Good riddance. Now the rest of you can go get a life"). For a living, Gerald stood around in smoky bars, burned cigarettes, drank bottled beer, and listened to loud music. For a living, he leveled his verdict on cartloads of free compact discs. For a living, he interviewed, often by phone but frequently in person as well, famous, washed-up, and unknown rock musicians. He woke up when he woke up. He sometimes performed his job while drunk. He often performed his job while stoned, and with improved results. If a genie had appeared to him when he was thirteen years old and had asked him to choose any job in the world, any job whatsoever, Gerald would have said, without hesitation, "Lead singer for The Cars." Forced to produce a second choice, he might have said, "Give me a job that will allow me to attend rock concerts, receive all the free albums I'll ever want, and hang out with rock musicians." And that, basically, was the job Gerald somehow ended up with.

For the next two and a half years, which period local Atlantans will forever remember as the Olympic Countdown, Gerald honed his reviewing skills, considerably upped his daily intake of mari-juana, began reading Heidegger and Sartre, and commenced his long night's journey into the Singlehood. There he encountered a vast assortment of strange and baffling creatures. The Singlehood teemed with all variety of desperation. He piled up a number of heartless and awful one- and two-night encounters and contracted a case of insomnia every bit as tenacious as herpes. He went through one whole box of condoms. A six-count box at that: a half gross. It took him a little over two years, but he finished the box. He used the last one, in fact, a year ago last February. And he hasn't bought condoms since.

The first of these half-dozen condoms went to Colleen, his old girlfriend from Rhodes College. A pale, strawberry blond art ma-jor with a Natalie Merchant fixation and a wardrobe full of paisley skirts, Colleen was, up until that part of his life anyway, his last real piece of unfinished business. They dated for three years, from sophomore year to graduation, and on weeknights they would throw a red bandanna over an upright flashlight, smoke pot, and make love to the faraway sounds of Josephine Baker and Edith Piaf. They separated at graduation. Yet their separation, they told each other, was purely geographical. Their love transcended such bland commonalities as time and place. They parted on gradua-tion day serene in the knowledge that they, and they alone, could manage to sustain that most desperate and naive of emotional arrangements, the long-distance relationship. It was over before the summer ended. She came through town the Christmas after he broke up with Nora, right around the time he began writing music reviews. She stayed three days, during which time they managed to use two from the box, though only one successfully. The other ended up dry and wilted beneath his couch, a fitting testament to the whole weekend. As he watched her pull away he realized he was officially out of unfinished business.

The third condom went to Nora, apropos of a phone call she made to him one unspectacular day in May, roughly nine months after they broke up. Her call that afternoon was not without precedent. For the first two months after their breakup, while he sold ads in his J. Crew button-down, she called him more or less daily—angry, difficult calls punctuated by long silences and fleeting moments of clarity and insight. After three months the calls tapered off to one or two every six weeks. In content, these second-period calls were more or less benign. They generally ended with Nora saying, "I'd really like to see you," and Gerald responding, "That's probably not a great idea," and Nora adding, just before slamming down the receiver, "Oh, please, Gerald, get over yourself." The call she made to him on that unspectacular day in May was the first such call in months: not a peep on either end, and now this friendly hello. He had spent the larger part of that day—okay, that entire winter and spring—entirely alone, the crushing truth of which hit him hard when Nora asked, in a chirpy, suddenly welcome voice, "Listen, and don't freak out or anything, but I was just wondering if you maybe wanted to, I don't know, get, like, a beer or something."

"I'd love to," he said without hesitation.

"Really?" She emitted a little chuckle of discomfort. "I mean, gosh, I . . . Are you sure?"

An hour later she appeared at his door in a featherweight red sundress that fluttered lightly along the upper crests of her honey-hued thighs. As she stepped into his apartment his nostrils flared in response to her scent, a complex mixture of coconut and jasmine. Instantly he recalled that period, a little less than two years ago, when he first fell for her. He couldn't believe he had ever considered her anything but irresistible, nor could he remember why, a little less than a year ago, he had suddenly found her so impossible to live with. Everything he had been thinking that winter and spring, all his stoic resolve and hardhearted self-analysis, disappeared into airy nothingness before the overpowering assault of her scent, before the fluttering fact of that sundress and the extraordinary force of her corporeal presence—the arabesque curve of her spine, the thin down of hair on her upper lip, the milky tang of coconut lifting off her freshly washed hair. He was standing before the three-dimensional embodiment of an abstraction he now realized he might have made up all by himself, an abstraction, moreover, that he had been talking to, in solitude, for the last nine months—long, private, one-sided monologues in which he would justify himself, explain himself, exonerate himself. Poof: all that was gone. All that was history.

"Why are you looking at me like that?" she asked, standing in the middle of his living room.

"No reason," he said, rubbing his palms on his thighs. "I just ... I don't know. I guess I'm just really glad to see you."

All through their beer, his desire for her rose and bobbed through his chest like a jaunty fluorescent buoy. At times his voice audibly shook. She, too, fidgeted, laughed at things that weren't funny, scraped frantically at the label on her wet bottle. Their conversation flowed easily, excitedly: they had always been compatible in this way. Yet, Gerald couldn't stop remembering, they had always been compatible that *other* way, as well. He couldn't stop remembering this because he had forced himself, these last nine months, resolutely to forget this.

They drove back to his apartment, where she had left her car. They walked down his driveway, still talking, and when she got to her car door she paused before inserting her key, and then asked him if she could use his bathroom. Sure, sure, he said, and ushered her inside. Without quite articulating to himself what he was doing, he silently programmed about forty minutes of low-throb make-out music on his CD player, the first selection of which kicked in just as she emerged from the bathroom. She stationed herself beside him and picked up the various CD cases scattered about, read the song titles aloud, scanned the spines of the discs in his collection to see what he had picked up since she was last here, pulled out one or two of the new ones, and asked him what he thought. For the next twenty minutes they slid disc after disc into his player and punched buttons. They listened nervously to about forty seconds of each tune before careening off to something else. Throughout, they kept brushing wrists, hips, backsides.

Finally, Nora said, "Close your eyes."

"Why?"

"Just do it. Close your eyes for a second."

He obeyed, standing perfectly still in his living room as she fiddled with the player behind him. After a moment, he heard the opening scream and cymbal crash of an old Prince tune they used to put on for lovemaking. There were no new discs to play: it was nostalgia time.

As the song's sexy, decadent groove locked into place, he felt Nora take him by the wrists and lift his arms, which he took as a cue to open his eyes. In the implicit crescent made by his outstretched arms, Nora danced slowly and languidly in time to the music, her eyes closed and her hips rocking smoothly back and forth, back and forth. When she pulled him closer, he let himself be pulled. Tossing her head back, she pressed against him and opened her eyes. "You know what's about to happen, don't you?"

"Nora," he croaked, his hands already sliding down her back, "we can't."

"We already are," she said, and quickly spun around, leaned her back against him, and wrapped his arms around her waist. Through the dress's flimsy material he could feel the warmth of her skin—specifically, the smooth unblemished skin of her terrific torso, with its tiny pinched navel. They rocked in this position for a moment or two. Gerald's eyes began to water.

"You really should leave."

She turned around in his arms, slithered up his chest, took his face in her hands, said, "You are so full of shit," and pressed her mouth against his.

They said nothing, not one single word, as they stumbled into his bedroom and clawed at each other's clothing. They said nothing as they dug into each other's underwear. And they said nothing as they both removed their watches.

Nora finally broke the silence. Her lips still adhered to his, she mumbled, "Do you. Have. A condom?"

He stopped kissing her. He knew from past experience that Nora wasn't on the Pill, so the condom, for more than the obvious reasons, was absolutely essential. The thought of her fertility terrified him. Raising himself on his arms, he stared into her eyes and said, "No." He figured that would settle the matter once and for all—no condom, no sex—and he actually waited a full second and a half before adding, in the most solemn tone he could manage, given the circumstances, "Actually, I mean yes."

Now it was her turn to hesitate. An uncomfortable smile appeared on her face and her eyes welled up. "Not altogether sure, are we?"

They remained frozen for a moment or two, smiling nervously at each other. The air hung heavy with the weight of what they were about to do. They each needed to stop and ask, Should we do this? and, Isn't this wrong? Those two preliminary questions were a crucial part of the whole experience. Gerald got turned on just uttering them to himself. With this momentary, subjective acknowledgment of possible wrongdoing, he abruptly entered an entirely new world, a place he had not inhabited since high school: the realm of the illicit. Those two questions had put him there. Slowly losing his smile, he stared intently at her, trying to figure out what she was thinking. In answer, she fluttered eyelashes and said, "Well, don't leave a girl hanging. What's your answer?"

"I'm thinking yes."

"You're sure about this?"

"Pretty sure."

"You sound tentative."

"Not at all. I'm giving this a solid roger wilco."

"Oooh," she mock swooned, and rolled her eyes. "Don't get my hopes up."

Unfortunately, this levity proved fatal. Before his very eyes her body lost its beguiling spell. Nora became Nora again. He blinked once in confusion. In seconds flat she went from siren to someone specific, from harpy to human being. Her breasts fell at lopsided angles along her chest, a roll of fat emerged beneath her chin. He could see flakes of deodorant crusted along her armpits. Whereas before she came shrouded in memory and desire, now she appeared stripped and disclosed: he knew exactly what she was thinking, and realized, simultaneously, that she knew the same about him. Now he really *was* confronted with the three-dimensional embodiment of his abstract need for self-justification, and he wasn't sure if sleeping with this embodiment was the smartest thing in the world to do. He also knew he was going to have to run into the bathroom and get that condom, the thought of which utterly terrified him. If he was having thoughts like this now, what was he going to be thinking when he returned? If his desire was this precarious now, how would it withstand a naked run across his apartment?

But he did it. Or she did it for him. When he returned with the condom, he found her stretched out on her back, one leg cocked at an inviting angle and her arms crossed behind her head, a pose he found so instantly alluring—they really *were* compatible that way! he hadn't imagined it!—that he actually became *even more turned on* as he opened that glossy foil package, located right-side-up, and slid it down . . .

Afterward, they stayed up until 3 A.M. talking about everything under the sun—their relationship, books and records, sex in general, Clinton, and, most memorably, a guy named Aaron Vaughn, Nora's old college boyfriend who was planning to move to Atlanta that summer with his Indian wife, Sasha. When, a month later, they tried unsuccessfully to repeat this experience (they never even got to the condom stage), they both agreed to drop the sex but retain the good conversation, and so began a friendship that has run without a hitch for a little over two years.

The fourth condom went to a thirty-six-year-old resident nurse named Linda Trevino. She was the only other single person at a Fourth of July picnic he attended that next summer—a year later!—in the company of his sister, Eva, and her husband, Walt, both of whom had dropped into Atlanta from New York on business. A broad, fleshy brunette with enormous breasts and a throaty laugh, Linda charmed Gerald that afternoon with her running commentary on every other married couple in attendance. "Bulimic, that one," she'd say, pointing across the picnic grounds at a skinny young suburbanite in white shorts and a flowered bikini bra. "Her husband's no good, probably, you can tell from the flat ass and the mustache. Over there, those two, they're big potheads. The complexion gives them away, that and her bead necklace. See that guy over by the keg? Closet homosexual. I happen to know this for a fact. The guy beside him is his lover. The wife, the mousy little redhead, knows it, too, and doesn't care because he's loaded, and she takes lovers. They have the best marriage of anyone here, actually. I've never known them to fight, not once. And see over there . . . ?" He called her the next weekend and they went to see Big Audio Dynamite at the Roxy. They used Gerald's fourth condom that night, at her apartment. After lovemaking, she rolled away from him and he from her, and he proceeded to spend the next six hours staring directly into her stucco ceiling, his heart racing. At 5 A.M. he peeled himself from the covers and tiptoed out of the room with his shoes in his hand. In the hallway he turned back to make sure she was asleep and saw a chilling thing: Linda Trevino on her side, the covers around her waist, her pendulous breasts bare in the early morning light, her eyes wide open. They stared at each other for a moment, then he turned away and left, and never heard from her again.

Condom number five went to a delightfully insane young woman named Karen Middlebury. Karen was a bartender at a taco joint out by the university. Gerald began going there regularly a year ago last fall, mainly because he couldn't stand his apartment any longer, and partially because he was starting to worry he would never find anyone, ever. The biggest problem with being single is that you're wasting your time if you're happily lounging at home. So Gerald started going to the taco joint two or three nights a week, during which time he would sit at the bar, drink draft Pabst Blue Ribbon, and make his slow, ponderous way through *Being and Time*. Each night when he showed up Karen would say, "What chapter you on?" Gerald would take his seat, show her the position of his bookmark, and shake loose a smoke. Karen was a short, curvaceous bundle of bristling nerves. She kept her brown hair tied behind her head in a bun, and every night at work she wore the same pair of tattered cutoff jeans and old Doc Martens. She moved back and forth behind the bar and talked nonstop both to Gerald and to every other desperate barfly the place attracted. She loved to talk about sex. Also men and why they were such creeps. And her old boyfriend, with whom she still lived at the time despite the fact that they were officially split up. Also her old boyfriend's current girlfriend, who sometimes slept over. It took Gerald two full months to muster up the courage to ask her out. She said yes, and proposed they take a jug of wine and a joint out to Tallulah Gorge. They hiked and hiked that evening in the dead of night, stopped midway to get irreparably baked, hiked some more, then found themselves completely lost and utterly terrified with nothing to tide them over but the wine, a couple of soggy Subway sandwiches, a blanket, and a carton of Winston Lights. That night in the woods they had exciting outdoor sex, after which Karen experienced a punishing anxiety attack that resulted in her dashing wildly through the woods in her bra and cutoffs, Gerald in tow, both of them stoned and petrified, and both of them, Gerald had to assume, wishing they were elsewhere, and with someone else. Eventually he found her curled up asleep in a clearing, eerily lit with moonlight, and in the morning they walked less than a mile before they found their car, which meant they had wandered in a perfect circle and stayed out in the woods for nothing. Karen never called him back, and Gerald never again stepped foot in the taco joint out by the university.

The last condom in his box went to a laconic, verbally adept young urban professional named Gloria Wilder. Gerald met Gloria a year ago last New Year's Eve at a swanky uptown party he'd attended with Nora in the capacity of friend and last-minute replacement date. The party took place in the main ballroom of the Ritz-Carlton Hotel in Buckhead, and was sponsored by the Atlanta chapter of the Chamber of Commerce. Nora won her invitation through a raffle organized by the Graduate Student Council at the university, and she asked Gerald to accompany her an hour before she was scheduled to leave. Her date had suddenly canceled on her, and at the moment she called, in tears no less, Gerald was putting the finishing touches on a pinkie-sized joint, which he had rolled in anticipation of a lonely solo New Year's Eve in front of the television. He even had a Blockbuster bag full of ultraviolent and luridly near-pornographic suspense films to help him while away the time. Gratefully, he donned his one and only suit, brushed his long hair, and entered the ballroom with Nora, now beaming and giddily stoned, on his arm. Incredibly enough, Gloria was alone. He first saw her standing beside the hors d'oeuvres table in a red velvet strapless evening gown, with red lipstick to match. Her face was all triangles and trapezoids, an effect made more striking by her retro cat-eye glasses, while her hair, cut close to the skull with jagged bangs and a spear-point neckline, was not blond so much as white. The dress and lipstick set off her pasty skin. Between her long, thin fingers she dangled the stem of a champagne flute. It was she who approached Gerald, technically to bum a smoke. He handed her one and extended his hand in greeting. She took it and said, "You two are the only people I've seen who look as stoned as I am."

As it turned out, she was a creative consultant for an advertising agency. She was there at the behest of her boss, a Chamber member who was out that evening with his mistress. She explained all this on the patio outside in the space of time it took her to smoke her one cigarette, and by the time she had crushed it out against the bottom of her high-heeled shoe, Gerald was hooked. The three of them stayed together throughout the evening and even ended up eating breakfast together at a crowded, rambunctious Waffle House later that morning. The next day, at about three o'clock, Gerald called her up. By way of greeting she said, "Get over here with a jar of Advil and a carton of orange juice."

Within a week Gerald was seeing her regularly. But they weren't dating. They certainly never used that word, nor did they do anything more intimate than kiss and hold hands. They just, you know, farted around (Gloria's phrase). She was thirty-one, consumed two 1.75-liter bottles of Beefeater per week, owned her own home, a 1971 Volvo, a library of classic black-and-white movies on videotape, and five Siamese cats, each one named after a character from the Archie comics series. She made nearly six figures a year, had never been married, and was buried in credit-card debt. By their second week of hanging out together, Gerald began thinking he was falling for her, and when he proposed that they sleep together later that same night, she turned even whiter than usual and asked him to leave. For the next week they talked about sleeping together. They talked about it and talked about it. He spent one night at her place, she spent another at his, and they talked about it some more. She never removed more than her shirt, and even then she protected her chest with her arms. All the while they continued to discuss the prospect of sleeping together. They drank gin and wine and smoked pack after pack of cigarettes and talked and talked about sleeping together, and finally, after ten days of talking about it, they almost pulled it off. At any rate Gerald unwrapped the last condom in his box. But somehow the gin, the cigarettes, and, most of all, the talking had given him the shakes, and he just couldn't pull it off. There was simply nothing for him to put the condom on. Oh, how he tried! But it was like trying to bait an earthworm, and after about three or four such tries he realized it just wasn't going to work. Besides which, Gloria, rigid in the bed with her arms across her tiny breasts, was dry as an unsliced peach. She cried for a good hour and a half, he apologized over and over again, and not too long after that—as in, like, three days after that—she joined Alcoholics Anonymous and told him she needed some time off and that was what? February? Early March?

After Gloria, Gerald took himself out of the Singlehood entirely. Just packed up and moved his emotional baggage elsewhere. In the interim he screened his calls and reviewed lots of records. His insomnia got worse. As did his intake of dope. He went on a date every now and again, but never on more than two dates with the same woman.

He ran into Gloria one day last winter while pushing a cart through Winn Dixie. She had put on weight—which she needed to do anyway—and her hair was now brown, her natural color, she admitted, with a charming, self-effacing laugh. She looked as healthy and robust as a fresh head of iceberg lettuce. She talked frankly about her sobriety and her Higher Power, during which conversation Gerald's heart plummeted to his ankles with a hollow thud. He realized she would never want anything to do with him ever again. He realized his own life was going nowhere. He realized he hadn't been laid in well over a year. And he realized he probably also qualified for AA. He told her she sounded great and good for her and all that and waved good-bye and walked back to his apartment and, typically, got high, very high, so much so that by 2 A.M. he was pacing around his apartment hyperventilating with the absolute rock-hard conviction that his years of sneering unbelief in God and/or a Higher Power had relegated him to an eternity of unimaginable pain in the hottest section of hell. Seeking solace, he listened to record after record, yet every disc he put on, even his favorites—*particularly* his favorites—seemed to be telling him that there was a God after all and that he'd been willfully damning himself to cosmic alienation all these years. The Jam sang approvingly about a church where "all shapes and classes sit and pray together," Bruce Springsteen whispered that "it ain't no sin to be glad you're alive," Beatle Paul testified about finding himself in times of trouble, and so on and so forth. These messages, which had always comforted him in the most ecumenical and Unitarian sort of way, sounded that night like sinister intimations of his own damnation. When he finally crawled out of bed the next morning he had the presence of mind to realize he had simply had a bad pot experience, that's all, and yet he also knew something vital had been communicated to him and therefore vowed to alter his behavior from that moment onward.

He promptly abandoned the idea later that exact same night, and since then his life has been pretty much unchanged in all major aspects, which is to say more or less the same as it was before he ran into Gloria Wilder in the Winn Dixie. And he doesn't know how much longer he can keep it up.

FIVE

GERALD SITS on a kitchen stool and watches Sasha stir pasta and talk about Aaron. She's been talking about him pretty much nonstop for the last fifteen minutes—his gourmet cooking skills, his punishing schedule, his annoying friends from medical school. Though Gerald would rather talk about anything else, he sits quietly and nods with feigned interest. He's not sure if she's invoking Aaron to create a buffer between them, or if she's simply nervous about Gerald's being here all on his own. Gerald's certainly nervous. Until now, he and Sasha have only interacted in groups, with Nora and Aaron always present as a common denominator. But now here he is, on Sasha's invitation, with neither Nora nor Aaron anywhere in sight.

Nevertheless, Aaron sure feels present, and not just because Sasha keeps talking about him. All over their beautifully appointed kitchen—ceramic and granite countertops, gleaming stainless-steel sinks, smooth glass burners on the brand-new cooktop—Gerald confronts depressing evidence of Aaron's culinary pretentions. Copper pots swing suspended from the ceiling; over the stove sits a neatly arranged row of squat glass bottles, each containing a different brand of balsamic vinegar or olive oil; and right beside the massive stainless-steel refrigerator Aaron has a special hook for his white smock and poofy white toque, both of which, Sasha explains, he wears only when guests are around, though not necessarily for laughs.

"It's geeky, I know," she admits, passing Gerald the wine. The bottle bears some sort of flowery French label from some flowery Frog winery: Sasha told him all about it but the information slid through his consciousness like flour through a sieve. He knows nothing about wine, nothing about cooking, nothing about anything really, aside from pop music, about which he knows everything.

"If he's that serious about his cooking, more power to him." Gerald takes the bottle in his hand and reads the label: Saint-Émilion, whatever the hell that means. He's supposed to know French—three years in high school, two more in college—but in fact can't remember anything more complicated than *c'est la vie*, which is the title of an Emerson Lake and Palmer song. And he knows *Michelle, ma belle, sont les mots qui vont très bien ensemble.* That's about it. "Where'd he learn to cook?"

"His dad taught him. A piece of work, his father. Ever met him?" She takes a dainty sip of her wine, closes her eyes, nods. "Hmmm. Tell me what you think."

"I trust your judgment." But he goes ahead and takes a sip anyway. Fuck if I'm closing my eyes. What *merde de cheval*. But in fact the wine is stupendous—warm bodied, rich. Or is it tarty and light? It's wine: that's all it is to him. "I've never tasted anything like it."

"I know. Aaron never misses." She says this last line wearily, as if it were a critique, which maybe it is. A billow of foam flares up from a big pot on the stove; Sasha plucks a pair of oven mitts from the pocket of her apron, slides them on her hands, and lugs the pot off its burner. "You should talk to him about wines sometime. He can give you some great recommendations."

"I'm sure he can." Raptly, he watches her pour the steaming cascade of noodles into a chrome strainer already waiting in the sink. Beneath the madras apron she's wearing cream-colored shorts and a V-necked T-shirt. What he especially likes is that she's barefoot. He's weirdly entranced by the way her skin's dusky brown fades out along the top of her foot, revealing a soft manila underside as pale as his own bottom. She's got sturdy thighs, it surprises him to see. He'd never noticed before. "And no, to answer your question. I've never met his dad. What's he do?" The inevitable male question, the subtext of which is *How much does he make?*

"He's an investor." Sasha tilts her head back and coils a damp noodle into her mouth. The end of the noodle wiggles, then disappears into her pursed lips. "I think we're ready."

"You really didn't have to do all this, Sasha. I feel like *I* owe *you.*"

"It's no trouble, honestly. This is Aaron's recipe, anyway. Piece of cake."

Aaron's recipe, Aaron's wine, Aaron's piece of cake. "Well, if you say so."

"Trust me, Gerald. Re*lax.*"

"I am relaxed," he protests, in unintended imitation of the old man. Dad, alone in the apartment, simmering his little mysteries. An anxious fluttering of dread erupts in his stomach. To calm it, he asks, "What's the big deal about his old man? You two pretty close?"

"Let's just say we tolerate each other."

"I can't believe he doesn't like you."

"He's never said as much, that's true. But just get him going on the Middle East. Boy."

"I take it he's a conservative."

"I don't know about that. He's just got this hate on for Arabs. Has something to do with the companies he works with, I guess."

"But you're not an Arab."

"Sure took him a long time to figure that one out."

In the two years he's known Sasha he has never once heard her utter a negative word about her marriage, which clearly has its share of problems, so it is with a tingle in his stomach that he carts the salad bowl and the pepper shaker to the table and takes his seat. Although Aaron, with his radiant charisma and bellicose charm, would be a handful for any woman, Sasha has been further handicapped by her implacable poise, by her gentle and trusting manner. Gerald used to be annoyed by her blithe ignorance about Aaron, but now that she's opening up to him, he feels once again a keen desire to be free of this awkward friendship, compromised as it is by all that Nora's told him over the years. Gerald can still remember when Aaron first moved to Atlanta: Nora went out of her way—even went a bit overboard, to Gerald's way of thinking—to embrace Aaron's lovely new wife. Still, anyone with eyes to see would have recognized how tenuous, even false, this elaborate air of coziness really was. Even Sasha's participation in the wedding felt rigged. By keeping Sasha safely within her fold, Nora could continue to maintain a friendship with Aaron—a friendship Gerald's never quite understood, aside from Nora's curious tendency to keep old lovers as friends, Gerald himself also falling into this curious liminal category.

"Okay," Sasha calls as she enters the dining room. She comes to a stop directly behind him and peels off the apron, wads it into a ball, and tosses it onto his vacated bar stool with an insouciant flick of the wrist. "We have everything?"

"Looks fabulous," he says, then feels her place a firm palm on his shoulder. Her hip hangs level with his rib cage, and though he's not 100 percent sure—all his sensory attention being focused on Sasha's palm—he thinks she might be leaning against him.

Glancing down at his plate, he sees a fresh wine stain on his shirt, while in the kitchen the freezer discharges a tiny avalanche of ice. With a friendly pat she releases him and whispers "Dig in" directly into his ear.

Not until she's taken her seat opposite him and poured him another glass of wine does the skin along his scalp stop tingling. When it does, he emits a preliminary safety cough and says, "What about your parents? How do they take to Aaron?"

"Oh, God, they adore him. It's sickening, really. Of course, it helps that my dad's also a physician."

"Didn't know that."

"They might have liked it if I'd married an Indian, I don't know. My sister married a boy from Bombay, and that went over pretty well. Here, put some Parmesan on that."

"Looks just great. Seriously." Gerald stares at his plate, admiring Sasha's care in putting together this little repast. Now there's a word he's rarely had occasion to use: *repast*. Hard to call a Wendy's Double-Stack Combo a *repast*. "So it's more under the surface," he prompts her, taking up his fork. "The tension between you and the dad, I mean."

"No, it's right out there in the open—more on my part than on his, probably. What he can't stand is the thought of us having children. I guess he always imagined Aaron would live in New York and work on Wall Street and produce a litter of little Aryan offspring with a skinny little blond wife." She pokes a neatly wound cocoon of pasta into her mouth, withdraws the fork, chews, swallows. "Like Nora, for instance."

From out of nowhere he tells her, "My brother-in-law's black."

Most people, when they learn this fact about Walt—whether secondhand or by way of a direct handshake—try too hard to show that the news slides right off their backs, but in Sasha's case it's actually true: a perfect slide. He reaches for his wineglass. "They live in New York, too. Not on Wall Street, of course, but close, somewhere in Manhattan. She's a filthy rich corporate attorney and he's in publishing. Walt is his name. I'm off to see them this week, in fact. This Wednesday."

"Oh, right. You have an interview or something." She's coiling noodles on her fork again, barely listening.

"The story of Walt's first visit to our house is classic Dad, part of the Brinkman family legend. There we were, sitting around the table, everybody sort of poking at their plates, you know, the way people do at these sorts of things, when from out of nowhere Walt says, 'Excuse me, but can I ask a frank question? I normally wouldn't do this, but I think it's better to get this stuff out in the open. I'm just wondering if anyone here has a problem with our being together.' No one says a word. Total silence. Suddenly the old man sits up and starts punching his chest like Tarzan. He does this for a moment or two, then lets out this massive belch. Eva—that's my sister—sort of groans and goes, *'Daddy.'* And Dad, all innocent, turns to Walt and says, 'No.' And that was it. The subject never came up again."

Sasha gives him a perfunctory laugh and reaches for her wine. "What about your mom?"

"Oh, well, she was dead by this point."

"Oh, God. I'm so sorry."

"Perfectly all right. Wasn't your fault." An old joke of his, and one that has never once succeeded in doing what it is intended to do—that is, put people at ease. Maybe because it's a crummy joke. "I mean, I thought you knew that already."

"No, I guess I did. Or maybe I didn't. When are we talking about?"

"Oh, God, ages ago. Early seventies."

"Still."

"Ancient history, Sasha. Relax." Once again he takes refuge in his wine, which he decides is full bodied after all. Maybe he should say something about it, if only to change the subject. Some conversation we're having. His skin prickles with the totally irrational conviction that Aaron is about to burst through the front door. So what if he does? It *is* his house. We're just sitting here, eating his recipe, drinking his wine, talking smack about his father. "Speaking of moms," Gerald finally says, to say something, "what about Aaron's?"

"What about her?"

"What's her take on you guys? She agree with her husband?"

"Oh, God, they've been divorced for decades. I barely even know her. She's this complete flake who lives in Vermont with her paranoid boyfriend and all these slobbering, smelly dogs. She makes trash-can sculptures or something. The boyfriend's a jazz disc jockey for a public radio station up there. Volunteer, you understand. They live off her alimony. Out of respect for his dad, Aaron refuses to talk to her, and I've only met her once. Went up there by myself, in fact. I've never even told Aaron. There's a lot about me Aaron doesn't know," she says with a little squint of the eye, then adds, "and vice versa, I'm sure."

Gerald smiles through a mouthful of pasta and shrugs. What the hell: they were both at the reception. She knows he knows something. Swallowing with difficulty, he wipes his lips and tries another approach: "Here's a great idea: why don't you guys *really* piss off the old man and have a kid?"

"We've tried that already" is the gloomy answer. She sits back in her chair and slides her wineglass toward her, swiveling it back and forth on its stem and staring intently at the blood-red liquid tipping back and forth in the gleaming globe. "Trust me, we've tried. And *tried*. This is—what? Year number two? Closer to three, actually. You sort of lose track after a while." She smiles sadly into her wine. "It's been kind of rough."

This is news to him, more than he wants or might have expected. She's apparently determined to invite him in enough to secure his allegiance, and he's starting to wonder how he'll get out of here with his independence intact. At the same time his hatred of Aaron is poignantly renewed. To cheat on your wife while she's carrying this anguish. What a son of a bitch. Sasha quietly twirls her fork into her pasta, waiting for him to talk, while Gerald sifts gingerly through his options, looking for a response that will seem commiserating without soliciting more disclosure.

"It can take some time," he finally tells her. "My sister and her husband are in the same boat. Actually, they're just trying to see a fertility doctor, which, according to Eva, is harder than making a baby. In New York at least. I think they're scheduled for spring of 2006 or something."

"Well, we've done that, too. Correction: *I've* done that." Without comment, she passes him the wine.

And what d'ya know, his glass is empty after all. Wonder if she's noticed how fast he's knocking it back? "But Aaron has not," Gerald continues for her, pouring himself a big sloshing glass of good old Saint-Émilion.

"If he has, he hasn't told me anything. We don't really talk about it anymore. It's a touchy subject, very threatening for some reason."

Gerald starts nodding and sipping his wine. Nod and sip, nod and sip. In lieu of a better plan of action, he tries some levity: "Well, hey, speaking as a member of the male species, let's just say it's a touchy subject in general."

"I imagine so."

"It'll work out, Sasha."

"That's what everyone says."

"Well, there you go."

"You don't like Aaron very much, do you?"

He can't help it: he pauses a damning millisecond before lying, "I like him just fine."

"Yes, I'm sure you do. So, still speaking as a member of the male species, what else do you know about him?"

Now the pause is unavoidable. To buy some time he asks, "What do you mean?"

"Oh, c'mon, Gerald. You were there at the wedding. I'm embarrassed enough as it is. Don't make me say it."

He suddenly recalls what Nora had said just before he left the reception: *Sort of sad, though, don't you think?* Measuring his words very carefully, he says, "I'm still not sure what you're asking me."

"Yes, you are." She leans forward, gazing intently at him for several galloping heartbeats. She has overplayed, that much seems certain. Having swept so abruptly into his side of the board she now wants to give him ample opportunity to seize this opening. But Gerald remains perfectly still, matching her heartbeat for heartbeat. Finally she sits back in her chair. "Forget it."

"You know, Sasha, sometimes things look one way and turn out to be something else entirely. You ever thought of that?"

"Meaning what?"

"Meaning," he says slowly, treading carefully now that he realizes, perhaps a bit too late, that he's just admitted, indirectly, that he does know what Aaron's been up to all these years, "sometimes things are a lot less complicated than they seem."

"That's exactly what I'm trying to tell you," she earnestly replies, her eyes level with his.

"Or maybe they're *more*, I don't know. You were asking about my mom before." He pauses here, to let her adjust fully to the seismic shift he's trying to effect here. He registers some guilt about using his mom to protect Nora, but decides it's too late now.

Sitting back in her chair, Sasha slides her wine toward her and lets her shoulders sag in surrender. "Sure. Go ahead."

"This is just an example of what I'm talking about. It applies, trust me. It's the fall of 1973. I'm seven years old. For months my mom and dad have been in this fight where they don't talk to each other, they just sit there and generate this eerie, ominous silence. My dad would say, Tell your mother this, tell your mother that, and my mom would be sitting right there in the room with us. I'd relay the message and she'd say, Tell your father blah blah blah. Creepy. So anyway, one day my mom doesn't come home from church."

"This was a Sunday?"

"No, a weekday. Sorry. She taught preschool there. My dad was the minister."

"I knew that."

"Right, but still hard to believe, isn't it? Anyway, Dad comes home and asks me where she is. I'm sitting there watching *Speed Racer* wondering the same thing. Then he tells me to stay where I am and takes off in the car to go track her down, and about three hours later Eva and I get this call from the police station telling us our parents have been in a massive automobile accident. Dad rammed the car into a tree. He survived, and my mom did not."

Her eyes waver with concern. "Oh, Gerald, that's so awful."

"Yeah, well, wait, it gets worse. When he went after her that afternoon he found her at a friend's house, where she'd gone to unload. We only had the one car, since they both worked at the church, so she'd walked. Instead of just coming home they drove around and hashed out whatever it was they'd been fighting about, and at one point my mom says something like 'Okay, then, if you really want to know the truth, then I'll tell it to you,' and he turns to her, takes his eye off the road, and that's when he hit that tree."

Sasha sits silently and stares at him, her mouth slack. "Wow."

"Some story, huh?"

"I mean, that's so ... I had no idea you were ..." She blinks a couple of times, looks away, then faces him again. "So what did she tell him?"

"That's just it. He never found out. None of us did. I guess we'll probably never know. But see, here's the thing." Gerald pauses, leans forward. His voice has been quivering. This story, the whole of it anyway, he's only told to a few people—Nora, a few close friends from boyhood. It's a narrative that for the last twenty-three years has been throbbing incessantly in the back of his mind like the faint trace of an old track he's unsuccessfully tried to tape over. But now that his dad has set up shop in the apartment, now that the old man has arrived with a bag full of secrets he seems poised to open once and for all, the narrative has pushed its way to the front of his interior soundscape. Gerald's needed to get into this for days. And Sasha is as good an audience as any. "For a number of reasons, I think my dad's been lying to me all these years."

"Lying? About what?"

"About what he knows. About that wreck and what Mom did or did not say to him. I think he's been protecting me, is what I'm getting at. Or protecting my mom, which amounts to the same thing. I mean, I'm not sure, and I don't have any proof. Not yet, anyway. But I've always wondered if she maybe actually *did* tell him whatever it was she needed to tell him, and *that's* when he wrecked the car."

"You can't believe that." Sasha's irises are as big and bright as two marbles. "You think he *purposely* wrecked the car?"

Gerald's lungs go empty for a moment. "God, no. I didn't mean that at all." But a wave of unease swells within him, nevertheless. Is that what he's always suspected? He shakes his head, as if to shed the thought from his mind. "The wreck I'm sure was an accident. Or pretty sure, anyway. But that's not what I'm getting at. I'm just saying ... I mean, what if she actually *did* tell him the truth, whatever it was, and the shock was so bad my dad quit paying attention and that's when he drifted off the road?"

Sasha's the one doing the nodding now. "But why tell you any of it? I mean, if he's trying to protect you, or your mother, why say anything at all?"

"Well, actually, he didn't. He told Eva. Frankly, I don't know if my dad's ever wondered what I thought, or knew, about their behavior that week. But Eva knew. She was older, and too smart to fool, and he knew it. Plus, he was still this fairly idealistic guy at the time, one of those liberal Protestant guys from the seventies. Part of his *job* was counseling married couples about affairs and divorce. He was still committed to ideas like *openness* and *communication*. So Eva confronted him, and he told her that story, and then she told me."

"So what were they fighting about?"

"No clue. An affair, probably. Not even Eva knows."

Sasha considers all this, sliding her fingers across the base of her wineglass and staring into space. "Okay, he tells his daughter, and she tells you. But that doesn't explain why you think he didn't tell her the whole story."

"It's because of what followed. It's never really made any sense to me, and I've been thinking about it for twenty-three years. We had the funeral, which was awful, Dad on crutches, all of us completely wiped out. Then a month passes. Dad just hangs out at home in this depressed funk. Doesn't shave, barely manages dinner. The casseroles from the funeral are turning green in the fridge. Finally the day comes for Dad to return to work. That Sunday morning Eva and I are sitting alone in the pew while Dad stands up there in his robe and goes through all the motions— the Apostles' Creed, scripture reading, announcements. After the offertory, he takes the pulpit like he always did. The church is deathly silent. And without any preamble or explanation he reads aloud this Bertrand Russell essay called 'Why I Am Not a Christian,' the whole thing. Then he takes off his robe, walks down the aisle, stops so we can scoot out and join him, and the three of us exit the church. And he's never gone back. No more Jesus, no more openness and communication. Eventually he started selling real estate, then took early retirement." Gerald pushes aside his plate, crosses his arms, and, manners be damned, leans forward on the table, elbows and all. "So you can never be sure if what you're looking at is the whole story, or some massive misinterpretation. That's all I'm saying. Where's your bathroom, by the way?"

For a tense moment Sasha from across the table studies his face. He can't tell if she's shocked or concerned. Perhaps some combination of both. Then she shakes her head as if roused from a nap and gestures over her shoulder. "Down the hall, past the bedroom."

"Be back in a jiff." He tosses his napkin on his plate and gets up from the table. Against his back he feels her gaze follow him across the room, so he is genuinely relieved when he turns and treads down the darkened hallway, in solitude at last, his heart thumping in his chest. Here in the brown light of the hallway he feels himself pulling free from a net; something seems to be tugging at him, but what is it? Closing the door of the bathroom and sliding his hand up and down the wall in search of the switch, he finds himself breathing loudly through his mouth, his mind yanked from thoughts of Mom to images of Nora crying about being pregnant to Sasha telling him she can't have children. The bathroom instantly comes to life: mirrors in front and behind, furry purple mats on the floor, matching mat on the toilet lid. He sits down on the toilet, rests his elbows on his knees, and cradles his forehead in his hands. This has all become too complicated, too enmeshed. No wonder he preferred being alone. He opens his jaw wide to send blood to his head. A cigarette would be nice, but like an idiot he hid a fresh pack in a cluster of bushes four houses down from Sasha's in anticipation of his solo walk home. Hiding it from her still, and now hiding in here. He sits back on the toilet. Stupid, stupid. This is no way to live.

He goes to the mirror, one of those fashion-model jobs framed on all four sides by baseball-sized bulbs, and runs his hands through his shaggy brown hair, pulling the ends forward so that a curl appears like the toe of an elf's shoe beneath each ear. John

Lennon, circa 1968: that's the look he's been shooting for all these years. For some reason he's always associated the Beatles with his mother. It's a complex chain of association he's never fully traced. Now, after telling that story, he's struck by the fact that he's hiding in the bathroom and trying to be John Lennon. He's never once stepped foot in a psychiatrist's office—one thing he shares with the old man is a sneering distrust of the mental sciences—so he worries sometimes that he's never fully come to terms with her death. Sometimes he thinks it hasn't affected him at all, but if that's true then why is he such a fuck-up? Maybe it all comes down to a failure to grow up. Maybe he never had the opportunity to outgrow her, and hence remains that seven-year-old boy watching *Speed Racer* after school and waiting for her to come home and make him a plate of saltine-and-peanut-butter sandwiches. And aren't the Beatles essentially the sound of Lennon and McCartney deliberately, almost maniacally, manifesting in melody a childlike world of bright colors and love-soaked security? Particularly on the psychedelic albums, where LSD and pot unleashed the unconscious. Because, of course, both Lennon and McCartney lost their mothers at around the same age Gerald lost his: this thought sears through him like a suffusion of divine light. His image in the mirror wavers slightly. My God, *that's* the connection! And what were Yoko and Linda but grown-up mommies? The boys married their mothers, the Beatles broke up, and so commenced the long and winding road of solo albums.

A hollow knock sounds at the door. "Gerald?" Sasha whispers from the hall.

"Be right there," he calls, frantically flushing the toilet and running the water and mussing up a towel (purple like the mats, with a peach border and SM in peach cursive script along the bottom). After one last look in the mirror he opens the door. He expects to find Sasha standing there but the hallway is empty, so he starts toward the dining room, then abruptly turns back, cranks on the faucet one last time, and rubs water on the wine stain: this will be his alibi. Now happily bearing a big wet splotch on his shirt, he moves down the hallway again and turns right, into the dining room, when to his left he hears Sasha say, "I'm in here."

Here turns out to be the living room. She's sitting on the couch, her hands in her lap and a cordless phone propped up on the glass top of the coffee table. She's looking directly at him with a sad sort of apologetic look on her face. The expression diffuses some of the discomfort he's suddenly feeling (all over again). He leans against the doorway and tugs his shirt down to display his stain. "Sorry I was in there so long. You can't take me anywhere. You have any club soda or anything?"

"Come here, Gerald." Lightly, she pats the couch cushion.

He brushes the stain, releases the shirt, and walks toward her with the plucked-up courage of a ten-year-old at his first cotillion. He perches himself two feet away from her.

"You think you should check on your dad?"

"He's probably managing all right."

"There's the phone if you change your mind. He might appreciate it."

"Maybe you're right."

"You know, I'm not contagious."

"I realize that." He scoots a bit closer. He can see their reflection in the blank gray screen of Aaron's massive television set. They look for all the world like two terrified middle-school kids on their first date.

"Look," she says after a pause, "I'm sorry I asked you about Aaron. That isn't why I had you over tonight."

"No idea what you're talking about."

"Maybe you don't. Which is why I'm apologizing."

"For what? We were just talking, having a serious conversation. Then I spilled wine on my shirt."

"I just thought we could both use it. A night out, I mean.

Because we're both going through a tough time right now—or seem to be. I'm not presuming, am I?"

"No, that's probably accurate." He now feels stupid, sitting this far away from her. There's a blue-striped chair just to his left that he could have sat in, had he been thinking with a clear head, yet standing up now and taking the seat would be an asshole move of the first order. His specialty, in many respects, but you have to draw the line somewhere. "What with my dad and all."

"And Nora." She waits for this to sink in. "Or not? Again, I'm just asking. I mean, we can talk about something else if you'd like."

Or not talk at all? He has this crazy idea he's supposed to scoot closer and start making out with her. There's an unimaginable world on the other side of that act, a dark shadow world of guilt and responsibility, but right now he only hears the summons of his boiling blood. He could do it. The way she keeps throwing Nora's marriage in his face, he thinks maybe he's *supposed* to do it. "No," he finally says, his voice vibrating at the base of his throat, "this is fine. I mean, what's so, you know, why are you having such a hard time?" His voice accidentally trips over *hard* so that it comes out as a two-syllable word: rhymes with *petard*.

"Gerald, please. You don't have to keep acting like you don't know what I'm talking about." And at this precise moment the cordless phone emits its electronic cicada warble. She smiles in apology and, sweeping hair off her shoulder so that it coils like twisted drapery along her neck, stands up and clicks a button. "Hey," she says flatly, walking slowly toward the kitchen. He takes this as his cue to stand up as well. Waving silently at her, he starts stepping backward toward the front door. Since her back is to him, she doesn't wave back. Into the phone she chimes, "Oh, not much, just sitting here with Gerald," then turns the corner behind the breakfast nook, whereupon Gerald, now safely out of her line of vision, slowly turns the doorknob and steps out into the humid night air, cognizant not only that he's doing something utterly unforgivable but also that such a gesture might actually work in his favor—assuming, of course, that alienating himself from someone he cares about is in his favor, which, under current conditions, seems to be the case. Which doesn't say much for current conditions.

SIX

GERALD SHOWS up for his job interview twenty minutes late. Typical. He pushes through the glass doors and dashes into an elevator seconds before the doors close shut behind him. Only then does he realize he is covered in sweat. His shirt clings to the front of his chest, perspiration trickles down his cheek. God only knows what his hair looks like. Were he more in tune with the times, were he more in step with the era's particular modes of behavior, he might have called the receptionist on his cell phone and simply told her his plane was delayed. But of course he doesn't own a cell phone. And he left the magazine's phone number at home, along with an updated résumé and all the new clippings he had intended to pass on to his interviewer. He looks up at his fellow elevator passengers. Two men, both in jeans and T-shirts, confer quietly with each other. Gerald smiles at them both. They stop talking and regard him blankly. The elevator door opens. His floor. "Nice talking to you," he says, and sidles out.

Behind the front desk, which slopes up from the floor in a smooth, sumptuous curve of Formica, sits a young woman with

tightly braided cornrows and burgundy lipstick. With long pol-
ished nails—burgundy, to match the lipstick—she flips through a
Rolodex as she speaks quietly into the pencil-thin microphone of
her headset. It's like stepping onto the deck of the *Enterprise*.
When Gerald arrives at the desk and opens his mouth to say hello,
the receptionist, still staring at her Rolodex, raises a fingernail,
says, "Yes sir, that'll be fine, seven o'clock," and looks up. She
smiles as if in greeting. Gerald opens his mouth again, then up
goes the fingernail. "Well, then seven-thirty, how's that? No? I
see. The problem is . . . Well, yes, but unfortunately . . ." She nods
and rolls her eyes at Gerald. "Then *eight* o'clock sounds just, yes,
yes sir, we can do eight o'clock, that will be just fine. Yes I will, I'll
be sure to tell him." The smile disappears from her face the in-
stant she yanks the mouthpiece down. "What an ass."

"Excuse me?"

"Every morning he calls and every morning it's the same damn
thing, change this, change that."

"I see."

"And now we're gonna have to scrap the cover. Hold on a sec."
Still with the fingernail, she taps at a button on her desk phone
and pulls the mouthpiece back to its proper position. "Guess what.
Now it's eight o'clock . . . Yes, I know, I told him. I said . . . Look,
what am I supposed to do? What do you want? . . . Fine. I'll tell
him." She turns back to Gerald and smiles again. "Rock stars."

"Which one?"

"All of 'em, honey. Every last one of them."

"Who was that you were talking to on the phone?"

"A publicist. Rock stars don't call the receptionist. You kidding
me? Please. You're late, you know."

Gerald stares back in surprise. "You know who I am?"

"Well, you don't look like Snoop Doggy Dogg, and he's the
only other person I got on this roster, so I can only guess you're
Gerald Brinkman, interview scheduled for"—she flips through

her Rolodex again—"one o'clock in the P.M. Matt's waiting for you, third door to your left." She points down the hall and, with a free fingernail, taps another button on her phone. "Sorry, Trish. Where was I? Oh, right, so anyway, like I was saying, I don't need this from him, girl, I really don't, so I told him, I was like..."

Gerald readjusts his duffel bag and walks down the brightly lit hall, past framed replicas of famous magazine covers from the past. Pete Townshend in midleap. The Go-Go's in their underwear. Janet Jackson with hands cupping her breasts. The third door on the left stands open. Gerald stops in the hall, adjusts his shirt, mats down his hair, clears his throat, and looks inside.

His interviewer, a middle-aged guy named Matt Anthony, whom Gerald has thus far only dealt with via telephone, sits back on an easy chair, his sneakered feet crossed upon his cluttered desk, a telephone in his ear, a bottle of Evian water in his free hand. He looks to be about forty, give or take a presidential term, with nicotine-stained teeth, bulbous cheeks, and a thin mane of shoulder-length hair extending from a balding dome. He's also pushing about two-seventy, two-seventy-five, a physical detail Gerald had not anticipated from their phone conversations. Like the two guys on the elevator, Matt Anthony, too, wears a T-shirt, a tight-fitting black short-sleeved concert jersey with a lurid silk-screen illustration of a winged Icarus falling from the sky. Upon seeing Gerald, Matt swivels off his chair and drops his chubby elbows on his desk, all the while saying, "Look, I'm telling you, no, now you listen to me, we can *almost* promise you the cover, almost, but that's only if you ... What do you mean, why? Because that's how it *works*, honey—yes, I realize that, no, no, look, wait a second, you're not listening to me, I'm trying to tell you ..." Exasperated, he places the phone on his shoulder and jerks his head for Gerald to enter. He mouths the words *One minute* and puts the phone back in his ear. "Tell you what—no, wait, listen, you do the shot I talked about earlier and I *promise* you it'll be on the cover. No, only that shot. Take it or leave it. I'll be here. Yes, you think about it. I know, I realize that. Love you, too. And hey, honey: you won't regret it." He hangs up the phone. "Ever wondered what Debbie Gibson's ass looks like?"

"I'm sorry?"

"Debbie Gibson. 'Shake Your Love,' 'Electric Youth,' teen sensation, late eighties, youngest performer in Billboard history to produce a top-ten hit. Personalized line of perfume, short stint in *Les Mis*. C'mon. You remember Debbie Gibson."

"Sure, I guess so."

"Ever wondered?"

"That was Debbie Gibson on the phone just now?"

"No. Her mother."

"And you're putting her on the cover? Debbie Gibson, I mean."

"You trying to jerk me around?"

"No. I just—"

"The median age readership of this magazine is fifteen to twenty-eight years of age. The majority of said readers, let's say seventy percent, are male. Total number of fifteen to twenty-eight-year-old male record buyers who helped put Debbie Gibson into the top ten at the age of sixteen is, like, three. You follow me?"

"I think so."

"So what I'm saying to you is, no, we are not putting Debbie Gibson on the cover, particularly if you consider her last three LPs have gone straight to the cutout bins, sexy cover shot or no."

"But you just told me her mother—"

"Forget the mother. She has nothing do with Debbie Gibson. She hasn't managed Debbie Gibson's career in six, maybe eight years. Which maybe tells you something, I don't know."

"So why were you saying you'd put her daughter on the cover?"

"I meant her photograph. Debbie Gibson's mom's photograph.

She's a staff photographer for us, does concert shots now and again, movie openings, that type of thing."

"Debbie Gibson's mom, you mean."

"Debbie Gibson's mom, that's right. Her office is downstairs if you don't believe me."

"No, I believe you."

"Now guess who she's photographing. Go ahead. Guess."

Gerald is still standing in the doorway. His duffel bag strap cuts a sharp pain in his shoulder. All over the walls of Matt Anthony's office hang vintage concert posters from the Fillmore, from Madison Square Garden, from the Hammersmith Palais. Piles and piles of old magazines line the floor. Gerald thinks for a minute, shifts his duffel bag to his side, and enters the room. "Snoop Doggy Dogg," he says.

"Gimme a break. Debbie Gibson's mom does not photograph Snoop Doggy Dogg. You kidding me? Snoop Doggy Dogg is the biggest-selling rap artist alive today. He's got a second-degree murder charge hanging over his head. His debut album shipped double platinum. He's got parental warning stickers all over his CDs and CD singles. The biggest-selling rap artist alive today, especially one with a criminal record, does not get photographed by Debbie Gibson's mom. He gets photographed by the best visual artists this magazine can offer. The biggest-selling rap artist alive today gets Annie Leibovitz, Jim Marshall, Anton Corbijn. He sure as hell doesn't get Debbie Gibson's fucking mom. You understand what I'm saying to you?"

"Can I ask you something?" Tentatively, Gerald sits down in an empty seat in front of Matt Anthony's cluttered desk.

"Sure, anything." Matt tilts his head back to drink from his Evian bottle.

"Why did you ask me if I ever wondered what Debbie Gibson's butt looked like?"

"Just making conversation. It occurred to me, that's all."

"I see."

"What do you say about Winona Ryder?"

"I'm not sure, exactly. What do you want to know about her?"

"No first-degree murder charge, okay. No double-platinum debut album either. But a major box office draw. She's cover material, right?"

"Debbie Gibson's mom is taking Winona Ryder's photograph, is what you're telling me."

"Here's my vision. Tell me what you think: Winona Ryder, totally nude, on her side and wrapped in coils of motion-picture film. Like the Nastassja Kinski photo with the snake. Only without the snake. With film instead. Headline reads, 'Wrapping Up Winona.' Pun on wrap. What do you think?"

"She won't do it," Gerald declares.

"Good point. Ever seen a Winona Ryder nude scene? No, you have not. You have never seen a Winona Ryder nude scene. Know why? There isn't one. She doesn't do nudes. It's not her thing. Her thing is not doing nude scenes. She got to it first. The public only lets one female star at a time get enormously popular without a tit shot. Makes them feel virtuous. The public, I mean. The people. Makes the people feel good about themselves that they can love a chick actress without demanding to see her tits. Sells tickets, this feeling of virtuous self-worth. But they only need one actress at a time to feel this way. Winona Ryder is that actress right now. Which doesn't mean she wouldn't do the shot. We got her on the cover once wearing a pair of overalls and no top. You saw the outline of her tit, right there, if you were looking. And you probably looked, didn't you? Yeah, you looked. Admit it. Everyone looked. Well, that look sold lots of magazines. Some European fashion rag got her to pose nude in a bathtub wearing nothing but shiny CDs on her nipples. You probably missed it. Anyway, there's your evidence she's willing. The problem is she doesn't have anything to promote right now. No point in wasting a good tit shot, is what she's thinking. Wait till the next period-piece, contrast the costume corsets with a good dose of ultramodern decadent chic."

"I'm Gerald Brinkman, by the way."

"That's what I understand. Says here"—his chubby arms detonate an explosion of paper—"you've got this big hang-up about hip-hop music, about sampling and drum machines or something. Wait, here it is." With one hand he jerks open a pair of thick plastic glasses and fits them onto his face. With the other hand he holds up one of Gerald's press clippings and reads: " 'This album, like many of its *ilk*' "—he sneers this last word—" 'provides ample evidence that pop music has utterly lost its creative nerve. The whole form is exhausted. Creativity has been replaced by technology. Every single innovative idea in pop right now involves machines. Computers are the new Beatles, producers the new rock stars. Hip-hop is a producer's game, after all, as are dance music and rap. It is the producer who chooses the sample, programs the drum track, and arranges the edits. Once you take away all that, what have you got? Surely not a song. What you have is a personality to front a densely constructed backing track manufactured by machines and created by that producer. And that backing track consists of an old recording from the seventies, conceived years ago on analog tape, with real live musicians sitting in a real live room somewhere in L.A. playing intricately arranged parts over and over again until they got it right. But now this analog recording is just one more discrete component in the producer's elaborately constructed machine of sound.' " Matt looks up. "You ever worry someone might see this as a racist argument?"

"Some people did, I'm afraid."

"What'd they say?"

"I got a letter or two. One guy argued that rap was the new punk rock. Another said that inner-city kids can't afford piano lessons and that machines allow them to express themselves."

"You smoke?" Matt pushes a wadded-up pack of Marlboros across his desk.

"I do, but—"

"You can smoke in here. Unfortunately. I wouldn't smoke as much as I do if they outlawed it in the building, but the publisher smokes a pack a day, so it stays, the Please Smoke policy." He takes the pack from Gerald and pulls a cigarette loose, puts it to his lips, and lights it against his squinting right eye. "My thinking is, what the hell. Seven years off your life, right? Take 'em, I say. You know how my grandfather spent the last seven years of his life? In a hospital bed with a drool cup and an enema bag." He whips off his glasses and chews on his cigarette. "Drinking water's how you avoid all that trouble. Keep your system oiled. Don't let the rot clog up. So what's your response?"

"To what?"

"The letter-writer's argument. What would you tell him?"

"Oh, right. Well, first I'd say I agree with him that rap is the new punk. Then I'd say that punk, too, suffers from a dearth of imagination. It's simply a subcategory of rock, a particular sound of contemporary guitar-based music created by hotshot punk producers. Finally, I'd argue that the record companies subvert any real or imagined political impact rap might have by turning the music into a profitable commodity that, in the end, makes rap a sinister agent of decay in the very communities it is intended to benefit."

"You went to graduate school, didn't you, Gerald?"

"Excuse me?"

"Graduate school. Says here on your résumé you have an M.A. in English. Couldn't stick it out, could you? No cause for alarm: neither could I. Berkeley, early eighties, anthropology. Just like Greil Marcus. Fact is, half the writers here are ex-grad students. The place is crawling with them. But that's not why I asked you

that question. I could have figured that out without the résumé.
Know how? The clothes. Dead giveaway. Jeans and a sportscoat?
Classic grad wear. That was the first clue. Second clue was the
word *subvert*. Also *ilk*, *commodity*, and the phrase *real or imagined
political impact*. You speak like a grad student who's read some critical theory. Another dead giveaway."

Gerald seizes this pause in Matt Anthony's harangue to light
the cigarette he's been holding for the last three minutes. As he
brings the cigarette to his lips he notes his hands are shaking. He
has no idea how to respond. He has no idea if he's doing well or
horribly. He has no idea if the interview has even begun yet.
Placing Matt Anthony's lighter back on his desk, Gerald sits back,
takes a drag from his cigarette, and exhales. After a moment, he
asks, "Should I worry about this?"

"The grad school background? Not at all. Like I said, we're
sort of a clearing house for ex-grad students. Rock criticism is the
last refuge for the lazy intellectual. The less lazy ones write for *The
Village Voice* or *Spin*. The pretentious ones go to *The New Yorker*.
The rest, the ones who no longer have a theoretical ax to grind,
the ones who simply want to see Winona Ryder wrapped in motion picture film, they come here."

"I think I understand," Gerald says quietly, and exhales.

"You do, do you? You think you understand? You know what a
grad-school tone of voice is, Gerald?"

"I bet you'll tell me."

"There it is again, that tone. The tone is irony. A superior form
of irony. Like when you said, 'I bet you'll tell me.' What you
meant there was, 'Since you've got all the answers, why don't you
tell me?' That sound about right?"

"No, sir," Gerald whispers, his mouth suddenly dry as a catcher's
mitt. "I didn't mean anything of the sort."

"Hey, fuck it, you know? That's what *I* would have said if I were
you. Who is this blustery prick, is what you've been saying to

yourself from the moment you walked in here. Which is fine by me. Here's an ashtray." He slides a ceramic ashtray across the desk, upsetting a sheaf of papers in the process. Smashing out his own cigarette, which had been smoldering in his crummy teeth all this time, he continues: "I come off as a loud and obnoxious jerk to most people, I realize that. It's a part of my social identity I've learned to live with. Gotta live with yourself, after all. No one else is going to do it for you. Make friends with your demons is my feeling on the subject. To hell with all this processing and therapy crap. Just make your peace. Besides"—he takes the ashtray back just as Gerald drops his half-smoked cigarette into the pile of butts already crowding the side, then picks up the still-burning cigarette and places it between his lips—"I like this little conversation we're having. Gets kind of old talking about Winona Ryder's tits, if you get my drift. All anyone cares about round here is *Friends* and MTV's latest *Buzz Bin* clip. *Criticism* is dead—*that's* what you should have said in that article. Agree or disagree?"

"That criticism is dead?"

"Right."

"All criticism, you mean?"

"Sure, why not? Extend the idea, see where it goes. Ever read our album reviews? Nothing but promotion. It's pathetic. I'm the first to admit it, and I'm the senior record review editor. Eighty-one percent of the new albums we review get rated three-and-a-half stars. Five stars is the highest, and we give out roughly three of those a year. The occasional one- or two-star review we reserve for artists our readers generally don't care about anyway—Michael Bolton, Phil Collins, Céline Dion, crap like that. Otherwise, we just promote the albums. Name the last piece of real aesthetic analysis you read in our magazine, assuming you even read the thing."

"Offhand?"

"First piece that comes to mind, exactly."

"I'm not sure. The film criticism seems fairly pointed to me."

"Good answer. That's the only place where we flex any critical muscle, the film criticism. Know why? Because movie studios use credited blurbs in their film ads. 'Most satisfying movie of the year.' *Time* magazine. Free promo. You know you're going to see a dog if the only blurb on the ad is from, like, the WXJF Sixty Second Preview or something. Everyone knows this. It's one of the unspoken facts of our age. So blurbs are free ads for the magazine, and the magazine review promotes the movie. Everyone wins. Which doesn't mean there's no art to it. If you're going to let the film studios promote your magazine, you gotta make sure your magazine's name is associated with the right kind of movie. It's like putting a commercial on a certain television show: you have to know your audience. You want to sell your product to the right demographic. The marketing department depends on it."

"I never thought of it that way," Gerald murmurs, smiling. He is beginning to like Matt Anthony.

"As for pop records," Matt continues, crushing out Gerald's cigarette, "no one cares about reviews. You can blame Led Zeppelin for this. They were the first major group of the rock criticism era. Rock critics pilloried their first album, and it sold gangbusters. Ditto their second, third, and fourth albums. The rock press hated Led Zeppelin, and this fact only made Led Zeppelin bigger and bigger. Turns out Zeppelin fans relished those bad reviews. Made the group seem rebellious and independent. The rock press became the establishment Led Zeppelin rebelled against, and rock criticism became the enemy of the very people it was supposed to reach. And not much has changed much ever since."

"I see you're wearing a Led Zeppelin T-shirt right now."

"This? A collector's item. The 1975 tour, *Physical Graffiti*. I was eighteen, time of my life. Loved Led Zeppelin back then, and still do, matter of fact. Everyone loves Led Zeppelin. Don't you?"

"Sure," Gerald sheepishly admits.

"But you *didn't*, am I right? I bet you hated Led Zeppelin in high school. It's written all over that grad-school blazer you're wearing. And you know why? Because you let a bunch of grad-school rock critics tell you they were crap. And because all those mindless potheads in your high school loved Led Zeppelin. And now you love them. Hell, John Paul Jones did the string arrangements on R.E.M.'s last album, did you know that?"

"Yes, I did."

"Even R.E.M. loves Led Zeppelin. And what were rock critics telling you to listen to rather than Led Zeppelin?"

Gerald thinks for a minute. It occurs to him that this *is*, in fact, the interview. It began before Gerald had a chance to get ready for it. After a moment, he answers, "Springsteen?"

"That's right. Bruce Springsteen. The Boss. Mr. New Jersey. Last time I listened to Bruce Springsteen was in graduate school. How often do you wake up in the morning wanting to hear glockenspiels and saxophones? Never. And how often do you wake up in the morning wanting to hear 'Kashmir' at concert volume?"

"Okay," Gerald says, leaning forward, "I'll give you that. But I'd still take The Who over Zeppelin any day, and The Who got great reviews *and* sold tons of albums."

"The Who," Matt sneers. "Give me a break. Don't give me this baloney about The Who. Right now in garages all over the country hopped-up teenagers are making incredibly vital rock 'n' roll by copping riffs off *Led Zeppelin IV*. And where's Pete Townshend? Snorting cocaine with Andrew Lloyd Webber. Who else did they tell you to listen to? Talking Heads? Band of choice for yuppie art collectors. The Clash? Bad haircuts on MTV."

Gerald shrugs. "What about R.E.M.?"

"Like I said, kid, *Led Zeppelin*. Mellotrons and mandolins. Les Pauls and Marshall amps. By the way, you really think pop is exhausted?"

Gerald sits back in his chair. He can't seem to figure out where Matt Anthony stands on anything—Led Zeppelin, movie promotion, Debbie Gibson's butt. Nor does Gerald have the slightest clue how he's doing, interview-wise. But at least he isn't scared anymore. The only thing concerning Matt Anthony about which he is fairly certain is the fact that he, Gerald, can probably say pretty much whatever he wants to say and not concern himself too much about the consequences. Tossing his arm along the back of the chair, Gerald says, "Yes, as a matter of fact, I do. How else to explain the fact that Led Zeppelin is the current band of choice among punk-rock bands? Zeppelin used to represent everything punk rock was against."

"Maybe it means pop is developing."

"But how? Into what? It's nothing but pastiche, a pasting together of exhausted conventions. Sampling is just the most flagrant example of this development. There's nowhere else for it to go."

"I follow you," Matt Anthony says, nodding with enthusiasm. "I see what you mean. And I can buy it, up to a point. Sure, why not? But now let me ask you something else." He clasps his hands together and leans across the desk, staring Gerald directly in the eye. "What the fuck are you doing applying for this job?"

That's when it hits Gerald that he's been ambushed. Deliberately and with exquisite control, Matt Anthony has led him up to this very cliff only to see if he would make the leap. And he did. He jumped all by himself. Surrendering to his fate, Gerald sighs, "I honestly have no idea."

"Good answer," Matt says, and sits back in his chair. "Just the kind of thing I would have said. So listen, I'll call you next week and let you know what I think. Expect to hear no later than, I don't know, Thursday? Sound good? Close the door on your way out. And oh, Gerald?"

Gerald freezes midway through hoisting up his duffel bag. "Yes?"

"I was just kidding about Debbie Gibson's mom. Never met the woman in my life."

"How did the interview go?"

Gerald is smoking a cigarette out on the balcony of his sister's third-floor New York apartment. Below him an army of taxicabs honk and huddle. He watches the tops of people's heads as they pass, listens to the orchestra of city sound. Directly beneath the window a dreadlocked Rasta sits placidly at a table lined with pirated videotapes. People stop by and graze the titles as the Rasta salesman sits back in his chair and stares off into space, his hands shoved into the pockets of his army fatigues. On his way up to the apartment twenty minutes ago Gerald spied a pirated copy of *Let It Be*, the old Beatles movie that heretofore has never been released on video. He's been looking for a copy of this movie for seven years, at least, ever since he inherited his first VCR. And here, within five hours of arriving in New York, he finds it, right outside his sister's apartment. Incredible. Incredible city, New York. The guy wanted sixty-five dollars for it, but was willing to take sixty dollars. Gerald only had a twenty. Right now he's wondering how he can bring the subject up to his sister: really, what's a measly forty bucks to her? I get paid on Friday, he'll assure her. I'll mail it right back to you.

"I have no idea," he calls back, and drops his cigarette off the balcony. The coals skid across the sidewalk mere inches from a fast-moving pedestrian, who pays this celestial object no heed whatsoever. Ah, New York. This is the place to be.

"Surely you sensed something."

He pushes himself from the railing and enters the apartment, where his sister, Eva, is setting the table. She moves gracefully around the dining room in a checkered apron, wrapped with ironic domesticity around her tan office skirt and white silk blouse. Striking a match, she leans across the table and touches the flame to a cream-colored dinner candle. The gesture tugs at Gerald's heart. Eva has had her curly hair straightened and smoothed. It is shorter, as well, cut elaborately into several discrete sections—a sweep of bangs here, a curve of shag at the back. Jennifer Aniston, that's where he's seen that haircut. The girl from *Friends*. Yet to Gerald, Eva looks like a TV mom from the seventies, a perky and poised spokesperson for Lemon Fresh Joy. She is thirty-five now; in three years she'll be older than Mom ever got to be, the thought of which sends a tremor down his spine. Then it hits him: that's not a TV mom he's seeing; that's his *real mom*. All that shared identity stored in those DNA coils, a time-release capsule of familial repetition.

"Oh, I sensed something, I suppose. Hostility. Total uncategorical resistance. That type of thing."

"I'm sure it went fine," Eva smiles, and shakes out the match. "Can you get me a glass of wine, Pooko? It's on the counter in there, next to the fridge."

Pooko. His old childhood name. What was the origin? Something about number two, a toilet-name. Smiling at the memory, Gerald walks into the kitchen and all at once feels a hollow surge of envy. Over the central butcher-block island hangs a canopy of flat-black pots and pans, all of them arranged neatly in order according to size and circumference. The counters all support sleek black kitchen appliances of every sort imaginable—a microwave, an espresso machine, a bread maker, a blender, a toaster, a Cuisinart. Teenagers buy white plastic appliances; adults buy black. The whole room is saturated with the smell of freshly cut salmon, pink strips of which sit lined up next to the stove on soiled white butcher paper. It's Sasha's house all over again, he observes sourly as he pours red wine into a pair of crystal wineglasses, and here I am, the overgrown child overwhelmed by the grown-up kitchen. He hasn't spoken to Sasha since he slipped out of her house two nights ago, nor has she called him. His whole life sometimes feels like an endless succession of botched social encounters. He picks up the glasses by their stems and carries them precariously back into the dining room, the wine threatening to splash over the edge and onto the floor.

"Oh, Gerald," Eva says as he walks in, "you'll spill it that way. Don't you ever drink wine? You should carry a wineglass by the globe, like this." She slides her open palm under one of the globes, as per instruction, and holds it aloft. "See? No mess, no bother." She takes a sip and purses her lips. "It should have aired out a few more minutes."

"Tastes fine to me," he says, and takes a seat at the set table.

"No, not there. Wait until dinner. Follow me into the living room, I want to show you something."

Taking up his wine, Gerald joins her in the front room, another site of envy. The ceiling in this room is easily thirteen, fourteen feet high. Deep, fully stocked bookshelves recede into three of the four walls. On the low glass coffee table sit copies of *The New Yorker*, *The New York Review of Books*, *Architectural Digest*, *Town and Country*, *W*. Eva, still in her apron, sits at the couch thumbing through what looks to be an old college annual. He takes the easy chair to her left and sets his wineglass down on an accompanying side table. It, too, is stacked with books, several of which seem to be paperback galley proofs.

"What a crib," he says aloud. "I could die here, I really could."

"Why would you want to do a thing like that?" she answers without looking up. "Hold on a second, let me find what I'm looking for." She flips through the book some more, reaches out for her wineglass, sips, sets the glass back down on the coffee table, flipping furiously all the while. Gerald watches her in wonder.

Now that he's noticed it, he can't unsee Eva's resemblance to their mother. Though he and Eva talk on the phone maybe once every other month, if that, and only see each other once a year, on average, she remains for Gerald one of his absolute favorite people on earth. It was Eva who first turned him on to pop music. As a child of six or seven he would sneak into her girlish bedroom (basic color: yellow), flip through her vinyl carrying case of 45s, and sneak off to his own bedroom with his favorites, which he would play on his portable phonograph with the Mickey Mouse tone arm. He loved "Working on a Groovy Thing" by the Fifth Dimension, "Uncle Albert/Admiral Halsey" by Paul and Linda McCartney, "Puppy Love" by Donny Osmond, "Funky Worm" by the Ohio Players. He particularly loved "Funky Worm." On Christmas morning 1972, Eva presented him with that month's top-five singles, all of which he can still remember, even down to the color of the labels: "Good Time Charlie's Got the Blues," "Me and Mrs. Jones," "It Never Rains in Southern California," "Brandy (You're a Fine Girl)," "Baby Don't Get Hooked on Me." Maybe that's where the whole business started. Eva is still flipping through the annual, her mouth pursed in concentration. It's the mouth that recalls Mom so clearly, the way the corners curl up at the side in a perpetual smile, the way the teeth within seem a bit too large, thereby giving both Eva and Mom an aura of excessive happiness and high spirits.

"Hey, Eva," he begins, "remember that time back in Memphis when Mom bought you *Let It Be* at Sears?"

Eva nods briefly and runs her finger down the margin of the page on which she's concentrating.

"I was thinking about that today for some reason. Actually, I know why. You know that Rasta guy downstairs who sells the videotapes? Well, I was coming up here a while ago, and I looked through his titles, and—"

"Here it is!" she exclaims, and passes him the open book. He spreads it on his lap. The page she has selected features candid shots of young students from the late fifties, all of them male, and all of them in brown suits and skinny ties.

"What am I looking at?"

"Upper left corner. Holding a martini glass."

Gerald squints at the photo. For a moment he sees nothing he can recognize as pertinent to him—then stops. There in the picture's right-hand corner stands a young man of thirty or so in another brown suit and tie and, just as Eva said, holding a martini glass. The man looks uncannily familiar. "Weird," Gerald whispers, and looks up. "It looks like me."

"You bet it does." She pauses. "Don't you know who that is?"

He looks again. The young man smiles broadly, his narrow face beaming and his chin slightly cleft. The eyes stare directly at the camera lens and into Gerald's consciousness. His stomach flutters with a curious sense of déjà vu. This room, this book on his lap, Eva in front of him: he's seen all this before. The man in the picture continues to smile and stare. Gerald stares back.

"It's Dad, silly."

He glances at Eva, then returns his gaze to the book. He tries to imagine the young man in the picture ballooning to 240 pounds; he imagines the man's hair falling off, the glasses acquiring a strip of white athletic tape across the nose. But it doesn't quite work. Then he abruptly looks up. "Eva, that's not Dad. That's Dr. Torrent."

"No, it isn't."

"I'm pretty sure it is."

"It's Daddy, Gerald. Trust me. Walt showed it to me last night. He's got this thing where he insists you and Dad are the same person or something. He's obsessed with genetics these days, all because of this book he's editing. He thinks it's going to be a big deal, though I'm not so sure. Science books: name the last one you re-member."

"*Brief History of Time,*" Gerald replies, and hands the book back to her.

"Oh, right. Okay, well, that was a fluke. I mean, do you really think people are interested in genetics?"

"I don't know. After O.J. and all that DNA stuff, it seems pos-sible."

Eva gives him a noncommittal nod. "Well, anyway, the book is all about twins, which is apparently important in genetic research. They take these identical twins who've been separated since birth and study them as they grow up, often in dramatically different settings. One girl, say, grows up in a trailer in Illinois, the other grows up in a high-rise like this one, yet both end up depressed or whatever. So this is supposed to prove that—"

She breaks off at the sound of the front door opening. From the echo chamber of the foyer someone calls, "Eva, whose home-less shit is this in the hall?"

Gerald closes his eyes. The indomitable Walt.

When he looks up Walt, resplendent in a bright summery suit of cream-colored linen, a bow tie hanging unwound along his neck, towers over him. He wears a look of mock contrition, com-plete with a hand pressed tenderly against his chest. In a ridicu-lously feminized voice, he says, "Oh, *heavens*, I'm so *sorry*, Gerald, I didn't realize it was *you*."

"I'll bet." Gerald begins to stand but Walt thwarts him by dropping into the easy chair opposite the coffee table. He slumps low in the plush cushions, perhaps out of habit or self-consciousness, as Walt is somewhere around six-four, six-five, and has therefore probably grown accustomed to being the tallest person in any room he's in. Right now, as he sits hunched in the chair, his bent knees ride about level with his face—at least from Gerald's head-on perspective—while his shins and feet extend out so far, they end up under the glass coffee table. The feet are huge, as are the hands, which clutch the armrests like the oversized, minutely defined hands of Abe Lincoln in the Lincoln Memorial.

"Just riding your bohemian ass," Walt replies. His feet tap the floor, his knees pump up and down. Occasionally he reaches up and strokes his mustache and beard. His bald head sends off an ebony sheen in the living room's cool track lighting. Eva says he wakes up at six o'clock every morning without benefit of an alarm clock: just jolts upright and swings his long, heavy legs off the side of the bed. By six-thirty he's on the terrace with a manuscript and a red pencil and a frosted glass of vitamin-packed, high-sucrose fruit juice. He stays up till one almost every night and never drinks coffee, says he hates the stuff, makes him edgy. Gerald is in awe of Walt.

"I've always wondered about your preoccupation with my ass," Gerald murmurs. Eva is gone, he notices. She and Walt didn't even say hello. Marriage problems, or marriage comfort? "I meant to move that stuff before you got back."

"I like the way it looks in my foyer. Like found art." He steals a glance back at the kitchen, then leans forward, his elbows on his knees. He raises one eyebrow and lifts his right hand in a peace sign, wiggling the extended fingers in the air. "You got one?"

He means a cigarette. Back at Harvard, where he and Eva met, Walt used to smoke a pack and a half a day. He kept up this habit well into the first couple of years of his marriage, until Eva broke him. So he always bums from Gerald whenever they see each other. Perhaps Eva knows this and that's why she went to the kitchen. Gerald feels torn: should he refuse out of solidarity to Eva, or hand over the cigarette and bond with Walt? No one wants to smoke anymore, Gerald's noticed lately, but everyone wants to bum cigarettes—usually *his* cigarettes. There's something smug in all this surreptitious bumming, the way ex-smokers use smokers both to bolster their sense of healthy superiority and to provide them with cigarettes.

Gerald tosses his head back and calls into the air, "Eva, can I give Walter a cigarette?"

Walt is already up and wildly flailing his arms. But Eva solves the dilemma by yelling, "Just keep it on the balcony."

Gerald looks up—and up, and up—at Walt to register his triumph, and sees a strange thing: Walt is disappointed. "Forget it," he says.

"Well, *I'm* having one," Gerald tells him, and struggles from his seat. "Come out and tell me all about the latest in genetic research."

Of course Walt takes the cigarette anyway, sucking deeply at it like it's his last cigarette before execution. He says "Aaaahhh" when he exhales his first drag. Even the cigarette smoking Walt has under control. Gerald wonders if he should just quit and start bumming from people. Save him a lot of money. The problem is, he's the only person he knows who still buys smokes.

Leaning against the railing, Walt removes a piece of tobacco from his tongue and then asks, "Where'd you hear I'm into genetics?"

"Eva," Gerald replies, and instantly regrets it. He could have said nothing about Eva and then pretended to have been a mini-expert on twin research. "She said you're doing a book on the subject."

"That's right. British guy, popular science writer, like that dude, what's his name? Gould, Stephen Jay Gould, you've seen him on *MacNeil-Lehrer*." Of course, Walt knows perfectly well who Stephen Jay Gould is. Hell, Walt probably *knows* Stephen Jay Gould. "Science made easy, that type of thing. A bigger market share than you'd think. Popular science is taking over. The pop psychology of the next millennium, and I'll let you quote me on that. Your dad agrees with me."

"That figures" is Gerald's sullen reply. According to Eva, Walt and the old man sustain a regular and highly charged e-mail correspondence. The Harvard connection is part of it, for which

Gerald registers a bit of resentment. Gerald never even applied to his dad's beloved alma mater, partly because he wanted to be free of his father's weighty legacy, and mostly because he knew he wouldn't get in. The other part is, Dad adores Walt's bottomless interest in just about everything. Walt's like the son his father never had.

"The book's called *God's Software*," Walt continues, and takes a drag from his cigarette. "No one likes the title, though."

"I can see why."

"Basically"—Walt takes another drag and puffs out a perfect smoke ring, which drifts into the night air like a message from heaven, like part of the massive binary code comprising God's Software—"the guy argues that we're all hardwired from top to bottom—personality, prowess, illness, you name it. We're just machines with a DNA disc that determines everything."

"You believe that?"

"Not entirely. The findings are fairly sound, but the guy doesn't understand shit about creativity, or accident, or good old incorrigible human nature. It's like in that Dostoevsky book, where the guy insists two plus two equals five simply because he *can*. Plus, I think the book feeds a little too easily into that *Bell Curve* bullshit from a few years back. Another piece of right-wing eugenics ideology."

"Oh, so we've already arrived at the eugenics objection, have we?" Silently, as if on cat's paws, Eva has let herself out onto the balcony. She carries a stainless-steel tray on which sit arranged a tray of crackers and cheese and three wine goblets, the wine in all three globes tilting back and forth in perfect synchronization. "He's such a hopeless little lefty, Gerald. You have to take him with a grain of salt."

Walt has turned around now to face her. Once her hands are free of the tray—she's set it on the balcony's glass patio table—she goes to him, her forearms upright against his chest. She goes up on her tiptoes to kiss him but then rears back, her face puckered in an expression of distaste. "You smell like an ashtray."

"So kiss the ashtray," he whispers, and with an elaborate show of fortitude—she's performing for me, Gerald realizes—she plants a wet one on her husband's lips. Gerald turns away. So they're happy. They have even that. He thinks suddenly of his hopeless hovel back home, of Dad's belongings spread everywhere in those embarrassing beige shopping bags, of the pot seeds encrusted in the gaps between the hardwood floorboards, of his hollow and fleeting interpersonal connections, of his cat, of Nora and her secrets, of Sasha's mysterious maneuverings ... Then he returns his attention to the loving marital tableau displayed before him. He can't help it: even through the smoke screen of his envy he feels the clean airy element of their happiness and good fortune and finds himself floating right along with them. It's Eva, after all. It's Eva and Walt. They've earned their happiness. As he has not.

Eva, comfy in Walt's embrace, tilts her head against his chest and smiles at Gerald. "You're not a cheese eater, are you?"

"*Comme ci comme ça,*" he shrugs, and swallows back the glob of emotion in his throat.

"Well, it's not cheesy cheese, exactly. You'll like it."

"He doesn't have to eat it if he doesn't want to," Walt declares, and removes his arms from Eva's waist. Gerald smiles to see that all this time Walt has been secretly holding his cigarette off the edge of the balcony; it is tipped by an accumulation of ash half an inch long.

"I'm game to try new things," Gerald responds, and goes to the table. "I think it's about time to broaden my horizons."

"Oh, that's right," Walt says, and flicks away the butt. "You had a job interview or something. Wasn't that today?"

"Unfortunately, yes." Ceremoniously, Gerald holds aloft a Triscuit topped with a wedge of Eva's cheese and takes a big chomp.

"We'd love it if you moved up here," Eva tells him. She holds out the tray so that the two men—*her boys*, she is wont to say—can take their wine.

"You can stay here as long as you want," Walt adds. "And we know all sortsa people who own apartments for rent, co-ops, rent-controlled shit."

Gerald nods his thanks. "Just don't hold your breath."

"And Dad's *very* excited about it," Eva tells him with a motherly look on her face. Mom's old look, in fact. "You should hear him talk about it on the phone. You'd think Walt was publishing a book of yours."

"Well, that's good to hear and all, but still." Gerald sips his wine and smiles at both of them. All afternoon he's assiduously avoided dwelling on the job interview with Matt Anthony; as a result, he's been dwelling on it pretty much nonstop. The memory isn't very specific, just a lingering stomach flutter of regret that won't go away. And this little conversation isn't helping any. To Eva he says, "You know he's at my apartment right now, don't you? Dad, I mean."

"He's mentioned something along those lines," Eva says, glancing away.

"Mm-hmm." Gerald sips his wine and examines the night. The city sends back a complex orchestra of sound, the aural wallpaper of urban life. He tries to imagine this sound as part of his own life, wonders for a moment what it would be like to fall asleep nightly to this dissonant lullaby, and turns back around. "So you've talked to him lately."

Walt and Eva look at each other briefly, and then both sip at their wine.

"Which means you know something I don't."

"Perhaps," Eva says tentatively.

When Gerald does not respond, Walt leans back against the railing and nods his head. "Why don't you tell us what you know first."

[135]

"All right. Let me think for a minute." Gerald makes an elaborate business of scratching his head. "He told me he sold the house. He said he transferred his *Nation* subscription to my apartment. He informed me that the universe exploded into existence fourteen billion years ago in, what was it? Ten to the negative thirty-second of a second, I think was the figure he cited. And that was pretty much the extent of it. That's everything Dad's told me so far. Oh, and I took him to the emergency room last weekend."

Now Eva looks rattled. "What are you talking about?"

"The emergency room. Interns and gunshot wounds, just like that TV show. You could tell he didn't like it, but what the heck. Anything to make his boy happy. It was like a whole new Dad."

"My God, why didn't you *call*?"

"He told me not to."

Walt stares at Gerald for a moment. "Were you with him?"

"Of course I was with him. We were there about four hours. Why are you looking at me like that?"

Eva clenches a fist under her chin. "What did the doctor say?"

"It was an intern, hardly a doctor. A teenager to hear the old man describe it. He said Pop suffered a mild concussion and that's pretty much it."

"A concussion?" Now even Walt is confused. For once, Gerald feels comfortable.

"From the welt he took from the homeless guy who clobbered him." He waits for this news to settle in. "I took him out Saturday night and he started talking to this homeless guy in the parking lot, and as soon as I turned my back, the guy clobbered Dad in the head with a pipe or something." He realizes this isn't the whole truth and registers some shame on this account. "You know how it is. Standard Dad-type disaster."

"That's not good," Walt says to Eva.

"Look, can we stop with all the secrecy?"

Eva shakes her head in confusion. "You mean he's said *nothing* to you? That doesn't make any sense. How long has he been at your place?"

"Since Saturday, but that's not important. He keeps getting ready to tell me something and then stops."

"Well, Dad should tell you," Eva says.

"Tell me *what*? Maybe I should call him right now. It's my number, after all. We could call collect and I'd get the bill. How's that for convenient?"

Eva moves toward Gerald now, places a hand on his shoulder. "Gerald, sweetie." She pauses, tries to smile. "He's dying."

Of course. That's his first thought. *I knew that.* In the same moment Gerald realizes he really *has* known it. He's known it all weekend—probably before. He just hadn't let himself voice it as such. He was waiting for Dad to corroborate this hunch. Until Dad said something conclusive, the truth Gerald had been concealing in his heart could stay right where it was, concealed, an important letter the contents of which were already known but that would remain dormant so long as the letter stayed sealed. A moment later Gerald asks, "Of what?" Eva now looks warped, as if she's suddenly been submerged, and it takes a moment for him to realize his eyes are watering.

"Kidney disease," Walt says. "Late-stage kidney disease. Very late."

"You're shitting me." Rather than wait for an answer, Gerald pushes Eva away and leans over the balcony to get some air. On top of everything else he's feeling right now, he's also angry. The baby of the family, out of the loop once again. "Kidney disease. Christ, who the fuck's brilliant idea was it to spare me this news?"

"We've only known about it for a week or two," Eva tells him. "Honestly. He made me promise not to say anything."

"And how long has *he* known it?" But Gerald already knows

the answer to this one: too long. *Late stage.* So Dad's lifelong war against the medical profession has finally overtaken him. Or maybe the guy still thinks he's winning the battle. That idiot.

"Who knows?" Walt says, leaning over the balcony to get a better view of Gerald's face. But Gerald stares straight ahead. "He called us two weeks ago. We even flew down there, to Memphis. The house was empty. He was sleeping in a sleeping bag, drinking bottled water and popping ibuprofen for the pain. I had the old man in a headlock at one point I was so determined to get him to the hospital, but your dad's one stubborn son of a bitch." Walt tries a weak laugh. "Anyway, you know how he is. He'd rather lose a kidney than go on dialysis. Which, I'm afraid, is what happened."

"He lost a kidney," Gerald says flatly. "That's what you're telling me. He has one kidney right now."

"Basically, yeah."

"So, okay. He still has one left."

"But that one's going, too," Eva says. She settles down on the other side of him, leaning over the balcony. He is sandwiched between his conspirators.

A silence spreads. Gerald understands what they're doing. They're letting him come to his own conclusions. They want him to make this news his own, so he can give it a full and thorough reading. After a while, once he's sure his voice is steady and his eyes are dry, he says, "He wants to die, doesn't he?"

Beside him, Walt nods. "He's doing a pretty good job of it, yeah."

"But he doesn't have to," Eva says. She slides an arm around Gerald's shoulder. "All he needs to do is go on dialysis and he'll probably be fine. But he won't do it."

Gerald's heart, freighted with affection and frustration, lurches clumsily toward the old guy. He sniffs and laughs, both at the same time. "That fucker." Sooner murder an infant in its cradle than what? Eat healthy? Pray?

"But you could do something," Walt says quietly into the night.

Gerald turns to him. "You think so." The line comes out flat, in the form of a challenge.

"He *did* come to you," Eva joins in. They've become a team again, a sales team closing in. "He made us promise not to say anything. He wanted to be with you, to tell you in person."

Walt solidifies this observation with a heavy, paternal pat on the shoulder. "He chose you, kid. You're his boy. He wants to go with you there with him." Walt gently removes his arm. "But you can stop him."

"And how can I do that?"

"Give him a kidney," Walt suggests.

Gerald stares into the night. Shame assaults him. He shuts his eyes and gulps. There it is: the closer, the big sell. "Because I'm the one with his blood type."

"That's right."

"Well, fine, but he won't take it." Now Gerald looks at Walt, then at Eva. They both wear placid, patient expressions. They've made their pitch, and now everything else lies in Gerald's hands. "You know that as well as I do. I'd cut the thing out right now and hand it to him but he'll still refuse it."

"That's a possibility," Walt says, looking past him at Eva. Then, to Gerald he adds, "You gotta circumvent that possibility."

"I do."

"That's right, Holmes. You do."

"And how am I supposed to do that?"

Walt scratches his chin, hunches his shoulders, leans against Gerald, and says, almost in a whisper, "By being a good son."

SEVEN

"WE COULD really use you," Brent is saying.

Gerald nods, though in fact he's having trouble following this conversation, what with the two bong hits he took before showing up and now this martini Nora's father, Frank, made him: his first ever. The elegant wide-mouthed glass sits sweating beside him on the kitchen counter. Four sips of the thing dissolved all the density in his skull. Whew. Brent wavers a bit in his vision.

"I'm just really swamped right now," he demurs.

"What are you two powwowing about?" Nora wants to know, breezing into the kitchen with dirty plates stacked in her hands. For her first-ever dinner party postwedding she's elected for traditional-casual—jeans, blue T-shirt, zero makeup. Gerald actually tried to dress up a bit, donning his one and only golf shirt and even going so far as to iron his khakis. Then again, he's wearing his black Converse All Stars, so why even bother?

"He's coming around," Brent smiles back at her, and takes the plates from her. Brent's the only one here who seems to know how to dress. His black silk shirt, which he wears untucked, hugs his surprisingly shapely chest, while his tan slacks taper neatly at the ankles. Very much the dapper male. Gerald can't help it: he envies Brent's sense of style. Gerald doesn't have a sense of style; he has an attitude. An attitude used to be enough. When did it stop being enough? Turning on the faucet, Brent, with audible annoyance, asks, "Why isn't your mom helping you with this?"

"She just can't tear herself from the sparkling dinner conversation." Nora sidles beside Gerald perched on a wicker kitchen stool and takes a dainty sip from his drink. Licking her lips, she admits, "Gotta give it to old Frank: he sure knows his martinis."

At the sink, Brent gives Nora a warning look.

"Just a sip," she protests. Brent continues to stare at her, thus sustaining this weird, tense moment. What's up here, exactly? Is Brent worried she's revealed too much? Which would mean Gerald's knowledge of the pregnancy is still a secret. Would have been nice if Nora had let him in on this little fact. Unless, of course, it's not a secret, in which case he should have congratulated Brent already. "They've started on Clinton," Nora explains, her back to Brent. "Trust me, it is not pretty. I had to get out of there."

Gerald not only likes Clinton but is, somehow, virtually alone among his friends in doing so, despite the fact that all of them, save Aaron, are basically liberals. To them Clinton's an unfunny joke, a sell-out, a compromiser: Republican-lite, they call him. But he's the President, is the way Gerald sees it. And at least he got elected, which is more than Mondale or Dukakis managed to do.

"Anyway," Brent continues over the roar of the faucet, "I promise it won't be that big a commitment, Gerald. The Web site is graphics-based more than anything: the copy is pretty minimal, and you can write the stuff in your sleep."

"I said I'll think about it, Brent."

"Just come by tomorrow morning, like I said, and we'll work it all out. The pay's good, no question about that. The university's bankrolling the whole thing. Just think of it as Coca-Cola money."

"The only kind of money there is in this town." Nora waits a beat for Aaron to turn his back again, and when he does, she steals another sip from the martini, giving Gerald a conspiratorial wink.

To change the subject, Gerald announces, "Maybe I should get back in there. No telling what my dad's been going on about. Clinton's one of his more unseemly obsessions."

"Oh, I wouldn't worry about him. I don't think he's said a thing all night." When Gerald doesn't respond, Nora adds, "He doing okay?"

"He's fine. Just a little sore at me is all." Which is true enough. Gerald returned from New York earlier this afternoon, and within moments the two of them were going at it over the kidney transplant, among other things.

"Well, then, take these." Nora hands him the tray of coffee cups, each of which sits on a matching saucer, the whole set a marriage gift, he guesses. "Just set them at everyone's place. I'll follow behind in just a sec."

"And don't forget," Brent calls as Gerald heads into the dining room, "tomorrow morning, nine o'clock sharp!"

But this last remark is nearly drowned out by Frank Reynolds bellowing, "She's a lesbian, Libby, and everyone knows it."

"That is completely absurd," Nora's mother objects, shaking her head. Libby, decked out in a yellow sundress that nicely offsets her tan, sits in a tense upright position across from Frank, who leans back in his chair chewing on an unlit cigar with all the self-satisfied at-homeness of an Italian restaurateur. "You're getting that from Rush Limbaugh."

"The one and only."

"Rush Limbaugh," Kira breaks in, her voice wobbly with rage, "is the most vile, lying dirtbag on the planet. I wish him ill."

"Oh, well, he'd love you, honey," Frank shoots back.

All this time Gerald has been gingerly moving around the table placing the coffee cups and saucers at each place, his hands a tad unsteady from that martini that, it annoys him to realize, he left in the kitchen. Jeff Flibula, in a garish Hawaiian short-sleeved shirt and knee-length jams, leans back when Gerald arrives at his seat and asks, "What about you, Brinkman? You buy the Hillary-as-lesbian theory?"

"It's well documented," Frank assures everyone. "Those Arkansas troopers swear on it."

"Hillary's fine with me." Gerald continues his circuit of the table, passing Jeff's wife, Tanya, and stopping at his father, who sits slumped in a heap over the table, his chubby arms crossed before him and his tired eyes focused intently on Frank. Gerald senses trouble here. Republicans fascinate his father the way cigarette lighters fascinate four-year-olds.

"Hillary Clinton," Kira proclaims, her olive-green tank top and shapely bare arms making her seem even more combative than usual, "has been the most viciously maligned First Lady in the history of the United States. Conservatives just can't stand a strong woman, that's all there is to it."

"Her husband's a lying sleazeball," counters Frank, pointing at her with his cigar (and clearly enjoying himself), "and *she's* even worse. She was sleeping with Vince Foster, you know. That's the real story behind his suicide, in case you were wondering."

"Which sort of shoots a hole in your lesbian theory," Jeff murmurs.

As if to erase her husband's last remark, Tanya Flibula, in a bland one-piece dress of blue and white splotches, leans forward and declares, "It's not the philandering that gets me. That kind of stuff goes on in Washington all the time, everyone knows that. Just look at Kennedy."

"Or Roosevelt," Libby adds with a sisterly wink.

"All Democrats," interjects Frank.

"Right, which is my point. It's everywhere. Gennifer Flowers is so completely beside the point. What gets *me* is the welfare reform bill. They're now saying he's actually going to *sign* the next one that comes up, all just to win the election. That right there's enough to make me vote against him."

Frank gives her an approving nod. "Score one for Bob Dole."

Sasha squares her shoulders here and proclaims, "Personally, I think Gennifer Flowers matters." As usual, she's alone, Aaron presumably on call. Although she's been sitting across from Gerald all night, he's so far successfully managed to stay clear of a one-on-one encounter with her. In fact, they haven't really spoken since he sneaked out of her place Monday night. At the time he was relieved she didn't ring him up Tuesday morning for an explanation, but now he wonders if perhaps he should have called *her* with an explanation of his own. One more reason not to get involved with people. "Character does count," she insists. "Trust matters."

"Which is precisely what the Republicans want us to think," objects Flibula.

Beside Gerald his father stirs to action. "Perhaps we're all—"

"Whitewater," Frank declaims, apropos of nothing. "Now *that's* the thing that'll bring him down."

Libby glares at her husband before turning to Gerald's father. "Excuse him, Paul. You were going to say something?"

Dad gives her a brief nod of gratitude as the entire table falls silent: the strange lumbering man at the end of the table has finally decided to say something. Gerald's cheeks burn with worry. What brand of paranoid insanity is he going to unleash now? "I was just going to say, perhaps Clinton himself isn't the problem. Perhaps the problem lies with the whole process."

"You said it." Frank gives the old man an affirmative poke of his cigar.

"I'm saying that anyone who actually manages to become president has compromised himself so thoroughly that he's already disqualified to hold the office."

Sasha takes her accusing eyes off Gerald long enough to observe, "That's awfully cynical, Mr. Brinkman."

"Possibly, Sasha. You might be absolutely right about that. But just think: how do you get elected to the presidency in the first place? By selling your soul to the people with money and power, that's how. You can't help but become their pawn."

To the table writ large, Gerald explains, "You have to understand something about Dad. He pretty much subscribes to the idea that every elected official in the entire planet is in on some sort of mass conspiracy to regulate oil prices and wage war for profit."

Surprisingly, Dad concedes the point with a weak nod. "Oil prices are part of it, sure."

"Hell, oil makes the whole world go around." Frank tosses his arm over the back of his chair, twirling the cigar between his dangling fingers. "Even a dumb fuck like Clinton understands that. Far as I'm concerned, the Saudis can keep on using good old U.S. dollars to sell their bubbling crude. We'll all be sitting pretty, and the rest of the world can just stand in line."

"Now *that's* cynical," Kira says with disgust.

"Oh, hey, my dad wrote the book on cynicism." Nora has entered the room with a full carafe of coffee, Brent two steps behind her, his brow creased with concern—or is it anger? What *have* they been talking about in there? "Now who wants coffee? It's leaded, unfortunately: we're out of decaf."

"In this heat?" Libby objects, pushing away her empty coffee cup.

"Yes, in this heat, Mother. Some people like coffee after dinner."

"You know what I like in the summer?" Libby looks around

the table, her face beaming with hostesslike cheer, even though she's not the hostess. "A fresh sorbet. You know what I mean? Something cool and sweet."

"None for me," Flibula tells Nora, who is trying, despite the aura of anger she's directing at her mother, to make her way around the table. "You have any beer?"

Frank observes, "I'll tell you what sounds good: a gin and tonic. Which reminds me, Gerald, where's that martini I made you?"

"Left it in the kitchen." Gratefully, Gerald stands up. Solidarity with Nora notwithstanding, he has to admit the memory of that martini pretty much demolishes any desire for hot black coffee. He can almost taste that gin-soaked olive, which has been marinating in the martini glass all this time. And the room *is* hot as hell, as Libby pointed out. Is this a pregnant-woman thing, keeping the A/C low? Or are pregnant women already hot to begin with?

One look at Nora tells him he needs to sit down and help her out. But before he can do so, Sasha says, "I'll take some."

"Same here," Tanya agrees.

"Anybody mind if I excuse myself?" This from the old man, whereupon Gerald feels chastened for a whole new set of reasons. The night has been too much for him. Gerald should have made a stronger case for driving the car; he realizes this now. But the stubborn bastard had insisted on making the walk, partly, Gerald had assumed, to prove that he didn't need special treatment, let alone a new kidney, but also because so many of the streets are closed tonight to create a clean route for the official Olympic torch runner.

The moment his father begins standing up Nora's face crumbles in disappointment. Tears well in her eyes as her bottom lip quivers. Brent, who was beginning to sit down, immediately goes to her and puts a reassuring hand on her back. But Nora, either impatient or embarrassed, or both, brushes him off before retreating back to the kitchen, Brent following along behind.

Dad looks around in midstand, his eyes behind those wobbly glasses wide with worry. "I'm so sorry. I didn't mean to—"

"It wasn't you, Paul," Libby assures him, also standing up. In fact, only Jeff Flibula and Frank remain seated, the latter shaking his head.

"I don't know why you always have to ride that girl," Frank accuses her.

"I was just making an observation." Libby pauses to see if anyone wants to come to her support, but the whole room stands perfectly still, a circle of people all looking down, as if in preparation for grace—which, as it happens, Libby herself had delivered before the meal, over Nora's objections. "She's just under a lot of pressure right now. Anyone can see that." Now wearing a worried mother's expression, she releases the back of her chair and adds, "You all stay right here and finish your drinks. I'll go check to see if she's okay."

Gerald seizes this temporary lull in the tension to take his father's arm and steer him toward the living room. Dad, to his relief, consents.

"I didn't mean to upset her," his father observes against the disconsolate sound of Sasha and Tanya quietly picking up empty coffee cups.

"I'm pretty sure it wasn't you, Dad."

"I thought she did a lovely job tonight, didn't you?"

"Smashing. The perfect hostess."

"You think she noticed I didn't eat much of that pork?"

"Oh, I don't know. Your untouched plate might have given you away. Now just stretch out on this couch here."

"She didn't need to entertain all of us like this."

"You were the one who insisted on coming."

"I was invited, son." But the retort lacks force, so relieved is Dad to be relaxed and more or less supine again. With one ear cocked to the dining room Gerald shuffles about settling a pillow against the fat padded armrest of Brent's stylish black leather sofa. Thinking back, he can't quite determine who all among those present might know about the pregnancy. Libby and Frank, to be sure, but what about Sasha and Tanya? Tanya, possibly, but not Sasha. Which leaves Sasha and Flibula. Dad scoots toward the pillow and props it under his arm, his haphazard position equal parts collapse and languor.

"We need to get you home, old man."

"Just let me take five and I'll be fine." He removes his glasses and squeezes the bridge of his nose.

As if in symbiotic response, Gerald feels a surge of weariness course through his bones. The effervescent lightness of those bong hits has finally dissipated, leaving behind a heaviness he registers as a sharp pain in the center of his skull. Once again his thoughts turn to the by-now-lukewarm dregs of that martini and that inviting gin-soaked olive. For a fleeting moment he remembers being a boisterous boy, when his body's rhythms were governed entirely by adrenaline and hormones, nature's narcotics. How completely is his system dependent on willed chemical manipulation? When was his last night of pure, organically inspired sleep? "Feeling any better?"

"I'll be right as rain in about two shakes." Dad repositions his glasses and looks Gerald in the eye. "Go on, son, be with your friends. I promise you I'm fine. What time is it, by the way? We haven't missed the torch run, have we?"

Gerald checks his watch. According to the newspapers, the torch runner is scheduled to arrive in the neighborhood at around ten o'clock. It's now ten past that hour. But no one in the group seems too concerned: common consensus holds that the runner will be late. "We've got plenty of time. Seriously, let me take you home."

"Not on your life."

"We still need to talk, you know. Later, I mean."

"We've done enough talking, son."

"You think so."

"Go on. Help Nora in the kitchen."

"I'm not kidding."

"Honestly, Gerald, what else is there to say?"

"Oh, gee, Dad, I don't know. You mean besides everything?"

It is nearly eleven before Nora's ragtag party bursts from the front door and, drinks in hand and all differences apparently forgiven, marches loudly through the dark wooded streets of Virginia Highlands en route for Highland Avenue itself, the second-to-last leg of the official route of the Olympic torch run. True to his word, the old man has rallied. Gerald can see him up ahead conferencing with Libby, about God knows what. The night is splendid, muggy and thick in the manner of Atlanta June evenings but with a faint breeze threading its way through the leaves overhead. A fulsome summer moon dyes the sky a smooth cobalt blue. The rest of the party fans out about fifty yards in front of him, the guests walking in little clumps of animated banter, nearly everyone holding a plastic cup and their combined voices spiraling into the night air like embers in a bonfire. He feels isolated and alone back here, and rather likes the feeling. On either side the houses illuminate the way, lights glowing from every window and, in many cases, from open front doors. People sit gathered around open coolers on deck chairs set up on their front lawns as radios and stereos blast from upstairs windows. It's like being at one of those rocket launches in the sixties: the same air of happiness and anticipation.

Gerald tosses aside his cigarette. Way up ahead he can see the outermost layer of a huge crowd assembled at the Virginia-Highland intersection, from which throbs the sound of shouting, more music and thundering loudspeakers, squeals and laughter. A boy and his girl riding piggyback run past him like a monstrous hermaphroditic centaur, both of them whooping and hollering and the girl on top waving an American flag.

Nora stands about twenty yards away, waiting for him to catch up. With her hands jammed in the back pocket of her jeans and her left leg jauntily jutting out, she looks unexpectedly young and playful, more like someone's girlfriend than a wife. She was once his girlfriend, he ruefully reminds himself. What had he been thinking when he let her go?

"What's the matter?" she calls. "You too good to walk with the rest of us?"

"Just catching a smoke," he calls back, and jogs up to meet her.

"You're hiding it from Sasha, is what you're doing." She shakes her head in good-humored exasperation. "She knows you smoke, you doofus."

He smiles. In truth, he *was* hiding from Sasha. But not about the smoking. "Great party, by the way."

"It sucked, and you know it." He continues moving toward the crowd, but she stays him with her hand. "Wait here a minute. I need a breather before heading into all that."

By now her dinner party has been fully absorbed into the crowd. The only guest Gerald can still see is Flibula, who is holding one of Frank's lit cigars over his head to keep from burning someone. Gerald can't see his father, which worries him, but he stops where he is. He could use a breather, too, frankly. "Sorry my dad didn't eat anything."

"He wasn't the only one." When she turns away to look at the crowd, moonlight glows through the soft drapery of her blond hair. Another drunken college kid steps around them, shouting

"Whoo!" "So," she says, "be honest. Did I make an absolute fool of myself back there?"

"No idea what you mean."

"I shouldn't let her get to me. I realize that. It's what moms do, right? It's right there in the job description. Oh, and you should have been there beforehand, when we were setting the table. I finished laying out all the plates, then went off to dress, and when I came back she'd redone everything—different plates, new place mats, candles, the whole bit."

"The table did look pretty nice."

She gives him a playful little slap. "Traitor." She jerks her head toward the crowd and starts treading slowly up the street. Relieved finally to be on the move again, he matches her step by step. "The good news is, they're leaving tomorrow, thank God. And at least they aren't staying at the house."

"How's that working out? Living at Brent's."

"Oh, it's fine. I was basically living there anyway. And now I'm not paying rent on an apartment I never use."

Surreptitiously he scours the crowd for his father, but can't locate anyone he recognizes in the moiling mob; it's just this dense sea of milling, shouting people. And this is usually a busy street: on weeknights the party traffic crawls by at hometown-parade pace. But of course tonight's a special occasion, whole stretches of city traffic blocked off for the big event.

"Oh, and I told Brent."

He stops walking, his head tilted in uncertainty. "Told him what, exactly?"

"That you know about the pregnancy." When he doesn't respond, she adds, "That's what we were talking about back there in the kitchen, right after you left."

He isn't quite sure what this means. Is it more important that she's kept this news from Brent, or that she's now telling Gerald about the discussion in the kitchen? "That's good, I guess."

"You'd think so."

"Why keep it a secret in the first place, Nora? That's what I don't understand. You're going to have this kid in five months anyway."

"Try six and a half."

"The point is, I may be an old English major, but even I can do the math."

She crosses her arms across her chest and shakes hair from her face, surveying the crowd up ahead. In the front yard directly beside them two young mothers in lawn chairs quietly murmur back and forth, their babies sawing logs in their laps. "It's Brent," she finally says, and starts walking again. "No, that's not fair. It's both of us, really, but more Brent, I'd say." She turns back to him. "Actually, we *are* going to start telling people. Obviously. We just wanted to be married a little while before everyone starts snickering about why."

"But that's not the only reason you got married," he gently corrects her.

"I'll have you know, mister, we got engaged *before* we learned I was preggers."

This revelation throws him, no getting around it. "I didn't realize that."

"Nor will anyone else when they find out. The thing is," she goes on, choosing her words carefully, "he's sort of threatened by you."

Though the admission gives him a brief stomach flutter of satisfaction, he quickly objects, "That's ridiculous."

"Maybe." The crowd has begun to swallow them: they have to push their way through, it's so thick. So as not to lose him, Nora, who's in the lead, takes his hand and leads the two of them through the maze of shouting college kids, all of them holding beers, or numerous beers dangling from six-pack rings, or even twelve-pack boxes of Busch and Bud Ice. They work their way down Highland Avenue, past the fire station on their left and, on their right, the first of the little boutiques that run uninterrupted all the way to Virginia. This is the commercial hub of the whole neighborhood, the primary source of its charm as well as its high-rent scale, yet tonight everything is closed up, save the big white-and-blue Chevron station up ahead, which is lit to the skies, a line of customers snaking all the way to the street. Ergo, all this beer. Astoundingly there's not a cop in sight. They're as absent here as his dad. Where *is* the old man?

He is startled by the abrupt appearance of Nora's face inches from his own. He rears back slightly, afraid—absurd as it might be—that she's gone up on her tiptoes to plant a wet one on his mouth, but in fact she's shouting something in his ear. Her breasts, he can't help noticing, brush against the front of his golf shirt.

"Say again!" he shouts.

"I said," she repeats, her voice reedy and moist in his ear, "he didn't like that I told *you* before anyone else!"

But before he can respond, Sasha seizes the two of them, a shoulder in each hand. "God! I've been looking all over for you guys! Everyone's wondering what happened!"

"I know!" Nora faces Sasha now, all happiness and relief. "We turned around and you all disappeared!"

Which isn't true at all, Gerald realizes, but keeps this insight to himself, so liberated is he by the sight of his friends. Frank and Flibula stand on the sidewalk, yelling exuberantly at each other and puffing on their cigars, while Tanya and Libby huddle off to the side, deep in some sort of female tête-à-tête. Brent is two steps ahead, waving. Gerald's stomach drops with disappointment when he doesn't see his father.

"Hurry," Brent tells them when they finally force their way to the sidewalk, "they're saying the torch is nearly here."

"Oh, so we didn't miss it?" Nora is already snug under Brent's protective arm, leaving Gerald alone beside Sasha. One good thing: at least it's quieter here on the sidewalk, on the outskirts of all that chaos. "I was worried we were too late," she's telling Brent as she recedes from Gerald.

Sasha tugs his arm. Okay, here it comes. But actually Sasha wears a worried rather than accusing expression. "Your father," she says.

"Oh, can you see him? Where is he?"

"I'm not sure. I was keeping my eye on him, but just like that he completely disappeared. I was out looking for him, in fact, when I found you guys."

Though the news disappoints him, he assures her, "Don't worry about it. He does this shit all the time. You go back to the party, I'll go track him down."

"Let me come with you."

"Sasha, please, it's all right. Somehow or other we keep horning in on your fun."

"Why do you keep saying that? You know that's not true."

And he has to admit she's right. She isn't really all that close to this group anyway, as they're all Nora's friends. Again he's reminded of how the dynamic between them has changed—or how she's attempting to change it. By keeping her at a respectful distance these last two years, he could nurse his unrequitable little crush without guilt or fear of untoward consequences. But now she's trying to alter all that, for reasons that more and more make sense to him. It's *Nora* she's after, he suddenly realizes. How could he have missed it? The way she keeps enlisting him in Serious Business while Nora stands around with Brent, watching it all— it's as clear as day. All that stagy, effusive warmth Nora's lavished on Sasha these last two years has been a way for her to camouflage her closeness to Aaron, and now Sasha's returning fire. But Gerald's not ready to abandon Nora yet. Something about their last exchange has him on edge. So typical of Nora, keeping him on her payroll like this. "Look, you're just catching me at a bad time, that's all."

"Which is why you should let me help you."

"I need to explain to you about Monday night."

"I'm not *talking* about that," she shoots back, visibly angry.

"What's up, you two?" It's Nora, suddenly beside them, just like clockwork. Sasha looks at her briefly, then glowers at Gerald again.

Turning away, he tells Nora, "We're talking about my dad."

"Yeah, I heard he wasn't feeling well."

Gerald's heart jumps. "Who told you that?"

Nora blinks in surprise. "My father. Why?" She glances at Sasha, then turns back to Gerald. "Wait, I thought that's what you two were talking about."

Sasha asks, "*Frank* told you that? I don't understand. I had my eye on him almost the *whole* time."

Something has suddenly stirred the crowd. People begin to press in on Gerald from the back, pushing him into Nora.

He grabs her shoulder to steady himself. They tumble back onto the sidewalk, where they can stand upright again. With the crowd still pushing, he takes her shoulders in his hand and demands, "What *exactly* did your father say, Nora?"

Now it has apparently dawned on her what's up. "Just that your dad wasn't feeling up to it, and walked home."

"To my apartment? When was this?"

"Few minutes ago, I think. Is everything all right, Gerald? Is it that blow he took to the head, do you think?"

But Gerald's already pushing his way through the crowd, his stomach in his throat. Infuriatingly, he can't get through; people keep holding him back. After a moment he realizes why. The torch runner has arrived. Cutting a swath down the center of Highland Avenue is a trio of white pickup trucks with an Atlanta Olympics insignia stenciled on the drivers'-side doors and an assortment of city leaders in green Olympics blazers waving at the masses from the truck beds.

With great effort, Gerald finally bursts through the wall of partygoers and stumbles onto the street. Without looking back, he starts speed-walking against the slow-moving truck traffic, unencumbered, a bewildering matrix of anger and helplessness suffusing his chest. *Dad.* Nothing is ever easy with that son of a bitch. Behind him he hears Nora call his name, but he doesn't look back. Instead he starts jogging toward home, running past yet another pickup truck going the opposite way, people on the sidewalk patting him on the back and urging him on, as if he's part of the festivities.

And then, just up ahead, he sees her: the official torch runner. She's about twenty paces away and jogging right toward him, this attractive, smiling black woman in white shorts and a matching white Olympics T-shirt, a burning torch held aloft. A wave of cheers and confetti follows her as she proceeds down the street, toward Gerald, who, in a moment of panic, and to avoid a collision, dashes across the street, nearly cutting her off before he dives into the crowd on the opposite side, en route for home.

2

EIGHT

GERALD COMES to bright and early Friday morning—6:15, maybe earlier—his foot scissoring up and down against his ankle and his tongue Velcroed to the roof of his mouth. Sleeping Lester exerts a warm weight along his head. His mind continues to blather on and on in dream gibberish as he peels open his eyes. The disarray. The smell. The clothes on the floor. No doubt about it, he is dangling on the slippery edge of a steep and terrifying hangover. His brain feels as if it has been twisted like a wet towel. His eyes seem pressed against the back of his skull. Rolling over gently so as not to disrupt the precarious cliff-edge that supports him right now, he stares up at the ceiling and considers his next move: get up now and risk dizziness and a splitting headache, or remain in bladder discomfort a little while longer even though a good long piss and a gallon of water will make things much better in the end. Which is the better alternative? Which is the worse? A pressing dilemma. The Hangover Dilemma.

Normally he'd just stay in bed until he felt ready to rise, but unfortunately that's not possible. Last night at Nora's party Brent offered him a job as an Olympic Web writer or some such shit and Gerald, secretly stoned at the time, ironically accepted. But stoned nighttime irony always turns cold in the literal light of morning. Something else Brent said also presses down on him right now—a vague reference to "reporting for work" placed in fairly close proximity to the phrase "bright and early." What did it all mean, exactly? Eight o'clock? Nine? He vaguely remembers accepting from Brent a business card with a phone number embossed on the front, but where had he put it last night, this phantom card? Did he maybe dream the whole thing?

His bladder burns, his engorged penis poking from the open fly of his boxers. He decides he should just risk the quick headache and take the piss-and-water cure now so as to speed along his recovery. He swings his feet off the side of his bed and, as if one action were prelude to the other, simultaneously disturbs Lester and detonates a headache in his skull. Squinting his eyes against the pain, he massages his forehead and opens his mouth to admit more blood to his brain. A light burns in the living room, just beyond his open bedroom door. So Dad's awake. Always awake. And the only way to the bathroom is right past him. How to conceal this boner? Another dilemma.

To hell with it, he silently murmurs, and swivels back into bed and settles himself beneath the covers and grits his teeth against the pain. Whereupon he remembers, in sudden blinding detail, the nasty argument he got into last night with his father, the self-same argument that led directly to all that extra booze and all those additional cigarettes and hence to this stupendously bad hangover. Irony isn't the only thing that turns cold in morning light. No wonder the old man's awake.

"Dad!" Gerald calls.

No answer. Still sore, probably. Or embarrassed more like it. Maybe both. God knows there was enough anger and embarrassment last night to keep them both quiet for a good long while. What all had they said? Gerald tries to think. They said pretty much everything they needed to say. Plus a whole lot of other things they had no business saying, like, *ever*. And a little more besides. But how could he have avoided it? How could he have done it any differently? It was all going to come out sooner or later. And given the circumstances, better sooner than later.

For Gerald the argument began the minute he learned that his father had left the torch run without him. All the way home he nursed a nasty little embryo of grievances that had already gestated into something huge and hungry and living when he walked in the front door and realized his father wasn't home, after all. Pouring himself a stiff Scotch on the rocks, he settled down on the couch and waited, his little monster of resentment growing by leaps and bounds. Twenty minutes later he abruptly decided to go look for the guy—a big mistake, he now realizes. He took his watery drink with him into the dark, celebratory night, a full pack of smokes in one pocket and a set of Walkman headphones clamped to his ears, and furiously pounded the sidewalks. He didn't pay much attention to the music, so preoccupied was he with the beautifully articulate and fully justified monologue he was constructing in his head. The absent auditor of this monologue was, of course, his father, whose mysterious absence soon became yet another strike against him. When Gerald finally arrived back home well after midnight he was both exhausted from walking and exhilarated with all that unleashed anger, all at the same time. And it was in this state of mind that he greeted his living, breathing father, who was sitting at Gerald's still-malfunctioning computer, quietly repairing the damage he'd done last Saturday.

"Where were you?" Gerald barked the minute he opened the door.

His father swiveled around, his glasses perched low on his nose and his hair hanging in a greasy rope across his glossy forehead. The light from the computer screen gave his face a greenish, extraterrestrial glow. "I've been right here."

"You weren't here when I got home."

"Fine. Shoot me." Gerald opened his mouth to respond but then checked himself. His father was being smug, a sure sign of guilt: no response at all would score himself a point. After a moment, Dad returned his attention to the screen and said, "You got home before I did, that's all. I told you I wanted to see the torch run."

"I waited and waited."

"I was here."

"No, you weren't. *I* was here. I came straight home and waited here for like half an hour and you never showed. You should have said something. I've been out looking for you all fucking night." Gerald sat down to calm his rage. He realized how petty this sounded, how silly and childish, yet he couldn't drop it. In the last two hours his self-righteousness had grown omnipresent and unspecific. Everything was his father's fault.

"Well, stop looking for me. I didn't ask you to do that."

"You're *sick*, Dad. You flat-out told Frank you weren't feeling well. What was that all about?"

"I told Frank I wasn't up to it. I didn't say a word about not feeling well. There's a big difference." Dad swiveled back around to face him. "Did I ask you to come home? Huh? Did I tell you to walk all over town looking for me? No, Gerald, I did not. I didn't ask you to do any of those things." He returned to the screen.

"You don't *ask* someone to care about you, Dad. You don't *ask* someone to show a little concern."

"When I want you to show a little concern, I *will* ask for it. Till then, carry on with your life just as if I'm not here."

"But you *are* here!" Now Gerald stood up and grabbed the chair by its armrests and swiveled it around so that his father had to stare at him directly. "Why else did you come if not for my help?"

"You smell like a nightclub," his father said, rearing back.

"Don't change the subject."

Patiently, Dad took hold of Gerald's fingers and peeled them from the armrests of the chair. Gerald resisted. The two men were still clutching each other hand in hand, one standing and the other sitting, when his father said, "You have no idea what you're talking about."

"I know you're dying."

"Big news. So are you."

"Yeah, well, you're dying right now, and I'm not."

"So you say. Now I'm going to let go of your hands, Gerald, but you have to promise me you'll get a grip on yourself. You think you can do that?"

Gerald stared at him in mute amazement. What a completely bizarre moment. Taking a deep breath, he relaxed the tension in his hands and arms. His father released him. Only then did he register how wasted he was. The moment his father let go, Gerald's knees buckled slightly, the world within his head bobbed to the side like a compass globe, his lungs sort of emptied. With a shaky sense of defeat, he let himself fall backward onto his unmade bed. A pile of magazines bounced against his hip. Lester squealed and leapt to the floor with a thump.

Dropping his head onto the mattress, he looked up at the ceiling and asked, "What *do* you want from me, Dad?"

"Nothing" was the response. It arrived instantly, without hesitation.

"Well, I can't give you that."

"That's ridiculous, son." Now his father permitted himself a little laugh. "You can't refuse to give me nothing."

"Watch me."

"Don't start with this." Gerald sat up to see his father fishing around on the computer desk. With a sigh, he fell back on the bed and reached into the front pocket of his shorts for his cigarettes, withdrew the crumpled pack, and threw them at his father. The pack bounced off the old man's head and into his lap. Without comment, his father shook loose a cigarette, put it in his mouth, lit it with a lighter he found amid the papers and computer manuals arrayed before him, and threw the pack back at Gerald. Gerald caught the pack with both hands and brought it to his chest. "You smoke too many of these," Dad declared, exhaling.

"Don't start with *that*," Gerald shot back, and lit one for himself. He lay there on his back for the next couple of minutes, puffing and exhaling. The room gradually filled with smoke.

"You also drink too much," his father added. He formed his mouth into an O and puffed out a train of smoke rings. "And you smoke too much grass. I can't believe you smoke that junk at all, if you want to know the truth. That's kid's stuff, teenager crap. You're almost thirty."

"I *am* thirty."

"Well, there you go."

"What day is my birthday, Dad?"

"Now *you're* changing the subject."

"You don't even know, do you?" He took a deep, head-spinning drag on his cigarette and blew a long flume at the ceiling. "You realize you haven't sent me a birthday card in ten years?"

"When's *my* birthday?"

"July 26. A week from tomorrow."

"Today. It's past midnight."

"You know what I mean."

"Fine, then. You win. Congratulations."

"Look"—Gerald sat up and began looking about for something to tap his cigarette into—"Eva says you need a kidney transplant, we both know I have your blood type—wait, don't interrupt, let me finish. You say that isn't the reason you're here, so fine, we'll call it a happy coincidence. Live with it—no pun intended."

"You don't even have health insurance, Gerald."

"Wrong-o, Pops. I'm employed now, remember? No more grad school poverty for me."

"Which explains your opulent lifestyle."

"You don't know a damn thing about me, all right? You don't know how I feel right now, you don't know how stupid you're acting, you don't know how shitty it is to drop into my life like this so you can teach me some idiotic lesson about the majesty and finality of death. You have no idea what all this feels like, so don't sit there and act like you're some wise old Ward Cleaver or something."

"Who says I'm trying to teach you anything?"

"That's right, Dad. I forgot. You quit teaching me anything a long time ago. You got out of the daddy business way back when."

"You're drunk, son."

"And you're dying. We're even. Like father, like son."

"And incidentally"—now his father's voice was getting louder; Gerald had finally gotten a rise out of him, *finally*—"I've taught you plenty. You take that back."

"What did you teach me?" Gerald stamped out his cigarette on his hardwood floor. His head was spinning now, his eyes longed to close, and yet he was here now, wasn't he; he had finally arrived at his destination. That long monologue out on the street had found its audience. The monster of resentment was prying loose from its cage. "From the moment Mom died you clocked out. Before that, in fact. Eva and I haven't been able to reach you for decades, do you realize that? Do you have any idea what it's like to have this smiling void for a father? Do you?"

Dad stood up and declared, "I'm going to bed."

"No, you're not. I'm talking to you. We're finally having ourselves a father-and-son conversation, our first *ever*. You're not running out on me now. You're going to let me do this thing for you. You *have* to let me do it. You *owe* me."

"I *what*?" His father was standing over him now with his hands on his hips. Gerald almost longed for his father to strike him. He could even feel the solid impact of his father's fist on his face, the sweet and obdurate pain of skin on skin, of bone colliding with bone. "What do I *owe* you, Gerald? Tell me. What is it I owe you?"

"The chance to save your life."

"Wrong. I don't *owe* you that. I don't owe you that at all. You're confusing debt with fatherhood. *That's* the business I dropped out of—the saving business. I don't save people anymore. They can save themselves."

"You got that right." Now Gerald stood up to face his father head-on. Their noses nearly touched. "I know all about you and the saving business. Like the way you didn't save Mom."

"I'm not going to listen to this."

"Well, I'm not going to sit here and watch you die."

"So don't watch."

"How can I refuse? That's why you *came* here."

"Says who?"

"Then why is it? Why the fuck are you here?"

"Because I'm your father!"

"Then act like it!"

And that's when his father struck him. Gerald had moved closer and closer until he was squarely in his father's face, shouting, his hands clutched into fists above his own head and his neck stretched into cords, and that's when the blow fell. It was an open-handed slap across the head, just above the ear, and it wasn't gentle. The force of it caused Gerald's neck to snap back in pain. His knees buckled. The next thing he knew he was looking up at the ceiling again. The stained surface seemed to sag toward him. The world spun gently underneath. He blinked a couple of times and struggled up. His father was sitting in front of him on the swivel chair, his hands clutching his knees and his head lowered. The inside of Gerald's head echoed with a steady distant ringing sound.

A moment or two crawled by, a timeless little stretch of no-time.

Gerald could think of nothing to say. He had never been in this place before, this bleak terrain of father-son violence. Dad had never even spanked him, not once in all his life, not even when he was a snotty little towheaded boy. To break the silence, he said, "Wow."

His father looked up. He had been crying. Another new place, another entirely new event in Gerald's life. A dead wife, a destroyed career, and not a single tear: now this. "I've made a horrible mistake," his father said, his voice quivering. He grimaced once, to fight back more tears, presumably, and then turned away. "I shouldn't be here."

"I had it coming," Gerald replied, rubbing the side of his head.

"You wouldn't say that if you knew what I was talking about."

And that was pretty much the end of it. They didn't hug, they didn't apologize, they didn't try to laugh it off. They just became civil. Dad went into the kitchen and set up the coffeemaker for the next morning, and Gerald, after offering once again to give up his bed, respected his father's gentle refusals and put sheets on the couch. Then Gerald promptly passed out.

Now, in the searing clarity of the morning after, he touches the side of his head, as if expecting to feel some trace of his father's blow. But all evidence has been erased. Whatever head pain he's feeling now is wholly his own fault. At least that erection is gone. There's a plus. Nothing to do now but head to the bathroom.

When he passes through the front room he finds his father stretched out on the couch, his glasses perched on his forehead and a copy of *Spin* pressed to his nose. The rich, pungent smell of coffee hangs in the air. Gerald says nothing as he heads to the bathroom, and his father does not lower the magazine. Anxious to pee though he is, he first drinks three cups of water in straight succession. He even leaves the water running between cups. Standing over the toilet, he listens closely for some movement from the front room but doesn't hear a sound. He commences to pee. And pees and pees and pees. There seems to be no end to it, his bladder must be engorged to the size of a soccer ball. It just flows and flows. He starts feeling embarrassed, it's taking so long, and kicks the door shut behind him to muffle the sound, but out it pours, warm and acidic and foaming in the bowl like a draft of beer, while the skin along his neck bristles with relief. When the ordeal is finally over and he flushes it all away, his father calls, "You need a life preserver in there?"

"I called for you earlier," Gerald yells back, and enters the living room, the ambient white noise of the toilet trailing behind. But his father isn't there, the couch is empty. "Where are you?"

"In here." The call came from the kitchen, so that's where Gerald goes. Dad's standing at the sink counter, pouring him a mug of coffee. He hands him the cup but does not make eye contact. Gerald accepts it in his hands like the peace offering it apparently is. "I was reading," Dad says, still looking away.

"That's all right." Gerald sips the coffee: it tastes burnt and stale, as if it has been sitting on the burner for hours. "How long have you been up?"

"Couldn't say. Let me read you something. Follow me in here."

"Can I maybe wake up a little bit? I'm not feeling too steady right now."

"It won't kill you to listen," his father says over his shoulder, and moves into the front room.

The place is a wreck, of course. Has been ever since his father showed up. The guy is a chaos magnet: he attracts disorder the way a dog attracts fleas. Not that Gerald is any neater, not really, but at least he has specific places for things—books on the shelf, clothes behind the bed, CDs beside the stereo and against the wall and on the kitchen card table. But his father can disrupt even a manageable mess. Objects drift from the shelves, store receipts emerge from thin air and flutter to the floor, magazines fly right open and tug tenaciously at their staples. Gerald never even knew he owned this many coffee mugs: he counts at least seven on the coffee table, each mug stained inside with a dark, oily disk of day-old coffee. He kicks aside a carpet of old newspapers and sits down on the floor, leaning his back against the frame of the kitchen doorway. "Okay, shoot."

His father thumbs through the crumpled *Newsweek*. Television talk-show celebrity Rosie O'Donnell, jowly and jolly in a man's red suit jacket, beams from the cover. She wears an open-mouthed smile that does not extend past the bottom of her face, the same smile you use when your amusement at something has just turned to disgust, and for some reason she has her fingers crossed, both her hands raised prominently in the universal symbol for dishonesty and deceit. The headline reads, "The Queen of Nice." Lately *Newsweek* has been affecting a slick, postmodern sense of know-it-all irony, a *Letterman*-like approach to world events that's starting to grate, so Gerald isn't sure if this cover represents some sort of semiotic sleight of hand, a closed circuit of self-referencing ambiguity, or if it's just a bad photograph. But that's the way it is with postmodernism. It could go either way.

"Here it is." Dad pulls down his reading glasses, which have been riding on his forehead all this time. "According to this article here—it's about that Viper group out in Phoenix, you know what I'm talking about?"

"Not even faintly." Careful not to jar his head, Gerald leans forward and takes a scalding sip of his coffee.

"It's one of these militia groups, a bunch of suburbanites out in Arizona with a big yen for weaponry and homemade bombs, plus a pathological hatred for the U.S. government, that type of thing. It was in the news last week. Surely you heard about it. This is *your* magazine."

"Really? What do you know?" He scans the room. "You mean like these magazines on the floor there? Or those in the sink?"

"You should keep up, that's all I'm saying. You subscribe to these things, you should read them."

"I'll remember to do that, Dad, just as soon as you quit burying them under all my old newspapers. The Wiper conspiracy. You were saying."

"Viper," his father corrects him, and for the first time all morning he makes direct eye contact. Outside the sky glows with the first trace of morning light. Gerald hasn't been up this early in decades. "Anyway, this group apparently took home videos of their bomb-testing parties and the ATF nailed them for it. Hurrah."

"Keep talking," Gerald says, and forces himself upright. "I just need to drop an ice cube into this coffee."

"So this innocent bystander type gets quoted in here saying, let's see, here it is, he says—I'm quoting now—'A lot of people see us heading toward major civil unrest. It's not just this town—people are fed up with government taking more and more control of their lives.' End quote."

"Groovy." Gerald slides back down to his place on the floor, leans his head back against the wall, shuts his eyes. Maybe I should go get doughnuts, he thinks to himself. Seriously low blood sugar levels. "Another right-wing conspiracy nut, whoopty doo. Your point?"

"Actually, I've got three. First, what does this guy mean by the government taking more control of his life? What's his evidence? Second—"

"He's a conspiracy theorist, Dad. He doesn't need evidence."

"Right, fine. Second, that jet that got bombed the other night, the TWA thing. Hand me that paper there at your feet."

Gerald stretches out his leg and struggles to snag the corner of the newspaper between his big toe and the smaller toe next to it. Astoundingly, he succeeds. Feeling triumphant, he lifts his foot off the carpet and swings the unraveling paper onto the coffee table, bracing himself on the floor with his free hand. Coffee spills from his cup and lands with an angry pinch on his bare stomach.

"You could have just handed it to me."

"Please finish this, Dad. I've got a busy day ahead of me."

"It's not even seven o'clock. Here, look at this, you've messed up the whole first section, now all the pages are out of whack."

"And this would be whose fault, exactly?"

His father ruffles through the paper for a few minutes. Gerald's headache is now in full bloom. The pain, he notes, throbs just to the right of his sinus cavity. What side did Dad hit last night? Surreptitiously, so the old man won't notice, he turns his head left, then right, trying to remember how he was standing when the blow came. Dad's right-handed, so he must have hit me on the left. Could the pain have traveled across the inside of my skull? Did his sixty-seven-year-old father jar something loose?

"Here we are. Point number two. Pan Am 103 goes down in December eighty-eight in Lockerbie, Scotland. Libyan terrorists get the nod. That Air India bombing back in what? Eighty-five? Sikh extremists. Where was it supposed to land? Ireland. Nineteen eighty-nine, another bunch of Libyan terrorists take down a French DC-10 that goes down in the Sahara, I think. No, that's right: the Sahara. Look, they've got it all graphed and illustrated right here." He holds up the newspaper. Half the page is occupied by a full-color graph of airplanes exploding over a 3-D map of the world.

"There's no evidence that TWA explosion was a terrorist attack, Dad. The plane just went down."

"On American soil, exactly, and only two weeks after these Viper nutcases got nailed trying to destroy the U.S. government. A coincidence? I don't think so."

Gerald laughs. This isn't so bad, actually, sharing coffee with his father and listening to him spin his cockamamie conspiracy theories. It's not exactly *Leave it to Beaver*, but it's something. "You oughta think about joining that Viper group, Dad. I hear they're looking for a few good paranoids."

"Name the last act of Libyan terrorism directed at the U.S."

"Whew, got me there, Pop."

"Lockerbie. Now, what was the last act of terrorism enacted on U.S. soil?"

"Look, I don't know, all right? What's more, I don't really care. This is *your* big subject, remember? I'm just a lowly rock critic."

"Think, Gerald."

"Fine. That Trade Tower bombing. Ninety-three or whatever."

"Wrong. You're forgetting about Oklahoma. Timothy McVeigh, corn-fed farm boy with a bomb. Same-soil terrorism is still terrorism, Gerald: don't kid yourself on that account. We forget about Oklahoma because there were no radical Muslims involved, but a right-wing conspiracy is still a conspiracy any way you cut it. Allah or Ollie North: it still amounts to the same thing. Last question: what was McVeigh's big modus operandi?"

"Why don't you just tell me."

"The New World Order. That's what they're all clamoring about now, isn't it? No more bilateral control of the world's nuclear arsenal, no more mutually assured destruction. There's no monolithic enemy to make the U.S. government look virtuous and beyond reproach. So the new fear is the Tower of Babel. All the crackpots are terrified of a world without borders, without that comforting apocalyptic stasis. And now, my final question: what's getting ready to happen right here in Atlanta, this very week, in fact?"

"The Tower of Babel," Gerald says, and hoists himself up again. Boy, that coffee is running right through him: is it really possible he has to pee again? Where's he storing it all? "And this, I presume, is your big point?"

"More or less."

"Which was what, again? I'm sort of confused." He says this over his shoulder, from the bathroom. He has to speak loudly to be heard over the force of the stream pouring from him. Another deluge. *Man.*

"My point is we're heading for disaster," Dad calls back

enthusiastically, his voice buoyant with joy. "Atlanta is sitting on a keg of gunpowder, is what I'm telling you."

"Oh, and you'd love that, wouldn't you?" He returns to the living room to find his dad resplendent on the couch, a coffee mug resting on the deflated sag of his belly. How much weight *has* he lost in the last year? This was a guy with a boiler, with a real honest-to-God dome: now he looks like a sloppy and slightly out-of-shape granddad. Even beyond the current circumstances, Gerald kind of prefers the boiler. It was a testament to Dad's I-don't-give-a-shit attitude about contemporary trends of every sort, his categorical dismissal of the whole secular religion of physical fitness—Brent's religion, apparently, and now presumably Nora's as well. As far as Dad was concerned, the modern health industry was selling the same empty promise as Christianity—spurious virtue, self-righteousness, narcissism, sham immortality—and that's why he had that gut: it was an act of self-assertion, of cosmic defiance. But now that cosmos is coming to get him. "Is that why you're here? Is that what all this is really about? You know, I bet it is. I bet you want to be here when the New World Order explodes, don't you? You want to see the crackpots bomb the Tower of Babel. That's it, isn't it?"

"Wouldn't miss it for the world," Dad serenely admits. A tense and dangerous silence descends upon the room. Father and son are now sitting on their own keg of gunpowder. Even through the wreckage of his frayed nervous system Gerald realizes this is a perfect opportunity to address last night, to apologize for all that ill will and bad blood and to reiterate his offer, this time with gentleness and filial affection, to save his father's life. But something stays his tongue. For one thing, he and his father have already more or less made up. This conversation has been a testament to that fact. A voiced apology would betray their tacit forgiveness: the tacit assumption of an apology *is* the apology. For another thing, Gerald is beginning to sense, in some recalcitrant way, that he has been mistaken all these years in dismissing as harmless his father's growing paranoia. Perhaps the old guy isn't paranoid at all. How long has he known about his kidney problems? How long has he been courting his own death? To put it another way, what happens to paranoia when it gets validated? What's it called then?

"Well," Gerald finally says, realizing to his surprise that he must calm the quiver in his voice, "I can promise you no bomb is going off this week. Not if I can help it."

After a slight pause, his father replies, "We'll see about that."

Gerald shows up for work at nine forty-five. An astonishing coincidence: the headquarters for Brent's webcast is in the basement floor of the humanities building of Gerald's old, and Nora's current, university. At least that's what it said on the card Brent gave him last night and which he found an hour ago while fishing out money for his bag of Krispy Kremes. So that's where he goes. He parks his car on the street, just as he did back when he was a poor grad student, walks along the same campus route he followed on his way to all his old graduate seminars, and pushes through the same heavy door he pushed through every day for exactly one arduous and amorous and now-useless academic year. He wears cutoff army fatigues, Doc Martens, and a fading Mr. Bubble T-shirt he bought last month at a thrift store on Moreland Avenue. He almost hopes he'll get fired. No Proustian thrill overtakes him when he enters the humanities building lobby, no jolt of nostalgia races through his bloodstream. It's just the university, the English Department, the graduate school. He feels no regret about leaving this place—just the opposite, in fact. Plus, it's hard to be Proustian with a hangover.

He walks down the hallway, beneath the shadowless light, and pokes his head in each door, looking for Brent. Every room is identical. In the center stands a wide table buried in potato-chip bags and giant three-liter bottles of Coke and Diet Coke and Sprite and

Dr Pepper. Along the four walls loom the turned backs of busy programmers, all of whom hunch over keyboards and gaze silently into the screens of flickering monitors, their fingers dancing across the keys with all the robotic regularity of automatons at player pianos. Tap tap tap. Music plays faintly in only one of the four rooms he visits. The other rooms are eerily quiet. With a hollow sense of defeat, he notes that T-shirts and shorts are de rigueur.

A voice breaks the silence: "Man, I thought you'd forgotten."

He turns to see Brent racing his way. Even the boss sports a T-shirt, a crisp new shirt so fresh from the box Gerald can still see the fold creases. The front features a smiling cartoon character, a computer monitor from the looks of it, complete with Mickey Mouse feet and two bulbous, white-gloved hands. The character's face beams from the monitor screen, his eyes and nose formed from the five rings of the Olympic logo. In one gloved hand he holds aloft a torch; the other hand he keeps cocked along the side of his huge head/body/screen.

"Am I late?" Gerald asks.

Brent glances at his watch—a disposable digital affixed to a three-inch leather wristband—and murmurs, "A bit." Gently he takes Gerald's arm between his thumb and forefinger and guides him down the hall. "Not a concern right now. We're so far behind it hardly makes a difference. What can I get you? A Coke? Some fruit juice?"

"Coffee?"

"Sure, we got loads of it. This team really puts it back. Follow me."

Gerald is a bit taken aback here. Get started? Already? He figured he'd just drink some joe, talk about his duties, dork around on one of the machines, and head off to his all-but-abandoned desk at *Alternative Atlanta*. But Brent has other things in mind. He guides Gerald into one of those four rooms and walks him around that big central table to a tiny table in the corner, which houses the coffee machine. He pours Gerald a steaming mug, the side of which features the same cute cartoon computer from the T-shirt, and then leads him to an empty console and gestures for him to sit down. Taking the neighboring swivel chair, he hoists onto his knees a cumbersome duffel bag, talking a blue streak all the while, the most he's ever heard Brent say at a sitting. Gerald takes his coffee and follows along blindly, only half listening.

"So this is the main writing station where most of the content for the webcast is supposed to get written—though, as you can see, no one's writing any content. Not yet. Still designing the home page, if you can believe that. Still some glitches. You take it black? We got Sweet'n Low, Extra, even some, no? You're fine with black? Anyway, so, yeah, that's what's going on here. You can have this terminal if you want, just stick your name on it and no one should hassle you, here's a Post-it and some markers. Now, this is how it works: super simple. All these computers"—he waves around the room—"are hooked up to the mainframe in the other room next door, and every CPU in this room is networked with every other CPU on the floor, or will be by day's end. So when you come back here later today and file your stories, you just drop the files into the network box here"—he glides the mouse across the mouse pad; a little cluster of darkened icons floats across the screen and disappears into another dark icon—"and you do the same thing with your sound files and your GIFs and all that, there you go, and then one of the HTML guys will pluck it out and translate it. Got it? Now, first thing to remember—"

"What stories?" Gerald asks, and sips his coffee. It's hot as hell but seems to be premium stuff: Starbucks, from the taste of it. The coffee of the Pacific Northwest. Grunge rock, Microsoft, and mocha lattes.

"The ones you're going to write." Brent slyly smiles. "You don't remember anything from last night, do you?"

"Not really."

"That's all right. It's all pretty simple, like I said before. Think of this site as a daily news show devoted to the Olympics. Not to the games, you understand, which we can't touch. Copyright problems: NBC has the Web rights to the actual events. Very important. No game coverage. But the Atlanta street life, the daily goings-on out there at the Olympic Village, all that stuff is free game. And that's your beat." To emphasize his point, he punches Gerald lightly on the shoulder. Coffee spills onto Gerald's bare leg. "That's your job. You're our ace online reporter. People all over the world are going to read your stuff. All you do is head down to the Village, interview some people, take some photos. Then you come back here and we'll translate your stories and photos and sound clips into binary files and post them on the site. It'll be great, trust me. Now here." He zips open that big duffel bag and withdraws a sleek black laptop: it is smaller than a copy of *Vogue* magazine and about as thick. He drops it on Gerald's lap and keeps digging. "There's your text generator. Don't lose that, it's worth more than your car, probably. You can't even buy it commercially yet. And here's your tape recorder and your GIF camera." He digs deeper into the bag and pulls out a portable tape player and a curious plastic device the shape and weight of a Sony Discman and places these things on top of the laptop.

"What's a GIF camera?" Gerald stares mutely at all the hi-tech equipment on his lap, all of it hefty and sleek and molded in satin-coated graphite. Stroking the laptop, he feels a tug of boyish longing. He covets these things, these grown-up toys. What he really likes is the GIF camera, even though he has no idea what it is.

"You've never seen one of these? They're the next big thing. Look here." Brent takes the curious device, turns it toward Gerald, and slides open a little panel on the front, behind which lurks an ovoid camera lens. "There's your aperture, just like in a camera. The twist is there's no film in here. It stores the images as GIF files, which are graphic files your computer can read. When you fill up the memory in here—it can hold about ten shots at a time, I think—you just plug the device into your laptop here." He sets aside the GIF camera and locates one of the numerous cords dangling from the back of the computer on Gerald's lap. "This tiny one here goes right into the camera, there in the back. Just look for a camera icon on your desktop, click it, and you'll see all your pictures displayed as little thumbnails. Transfer them to your hard drive, drop them into the network folder, and we'll do the rest. Now how's that for simple?"

Rather than respond, Gerald uses this instructional lull to open the laptop. The lid exerts a satisfying hydraulic resistance as it swivels open. The screen is a creamy dark gray, velvety to the touch. The keys are flat as breath mints and responsive as flesh. He loves this thing. "What kind of stories am I writing?"

"Whatever you can think of. Just go down to the Village and walk around and interview people, find out where they're from, what events they're interested in, what they think of the U.S. or Atlanta, that type of junk. That should be enough for today's issue."

"Today? You want me to produce something *today*?"

"Of course." Brent laughs again, though without much conviction. His teeth are blindingly white, each one clearly defined against his healthy gums. This is one healthy boy. Gently, tenderly, he lifts the laptop off Gerald's ... well, his *lap*, and places it on the table beside the keyboard pad from Gerald's other work computer. Two computers, all his, and he's only been here ten minutes. Without the laptop, Gerald feels bereft, stripped of his toys. "We talked about all this last night," Brent says firmly. "I'm depending on you."

Gerald looks at the laptop, at the GIF camera, at the tape recorder. As it happens, he probably *should* head down to *Alternative Atlanta* to check in, if nothing else. He's been covering his basic weekly assignment so long now that his boss, Terry, more or less leaves him alone: as long as the pages turn up, he's basically on his own. But he's also way behind in his weekly duties for the first time since he started writing for the newspaper. At the same time he wants to see Centennial Park. And he absolutely loves that laptop. "I know, I'm not backing out. I just didn't realize—"

"Because if you can't do it I need to get someone else."

He waves Brent silent. Smiles at him. "What else do I need to know?"

Brent taps him on the shoulder and all tension dissolves. He even returns the little computer to Gerald's lap as a prize, as a piece of positive reinforcement. And, by God, it works. "Seriously, you have no idea what a big help this is. I'll get your paperwork later, it's somewhere around here, your, you know, your W-2 or whatever. Here's the big thing to remember. See these?" He reaches back into his duffel bag of goodies and Gerald's heart jumps: more toys! But all he withdraws is a no-tech pile of photocopies. "These are release forms. If you take anyone's picture, they have to sign one of these forms, otherwise we can't use that picture. Got it?"

Gerald takes the sheets and scans them. They look obsessively legal. They look official. They look, basically, like a pain in the ass. "Are you serious? Everybody I photograph?"

"Gotta do it, pal. Somebody sees his face on the Web page and doesn't like it, he can sue us."

"I thought the Web was this totally free space without copyright issues."

"Used to be, maybe, but not anymore. The lawyers have taken over. Now, let me go find you a bunch of T-shirts. I'll get you enough for the next two weeks. Just sit tight, fiddle around with the network software, get acquainted. If you need to call anyone, feel free. There's a phone right beside you. When I get back I'll introduce you around." As Brent swivels away and departs Gerald tries to overcome his surprise at Brent's unexpected energy, at his cool professional élan. The guy has success written all over him— a well-oiled, efficient machine devoted to efficient machinery.

Gerald looks around. None of the high school kids look at him, no one pays him the slightest bit of attention. He feels stupid here, way too old and far too low-tech. He has already forgotten everything Brent just told him.

The computer is still hooked up to the Web. There it is, waiting for him. Surf me, search me, log on and ride. Instead, he clicks onto Telnet to see if his old university e-mail account is still active. While waiting for his password to pass he looks down at the phone beside him and remembers he still hasn't properly dealt with Sasha. He should call her from here. She won't recognize the number on her caller ID, so if he chickens out he can just hang up. He's not sure why this idea has only occurred to him now. Maybe Brent's unexpected warmth has made him feel guilty. Or perhaps his hangover has simply burned through his defenses. Still, he hesitates as his in-box blinks onto the screen. No new messages; what else is new? In light of the outside world's blithe refusal to acknowledge his existence, he reaches for the phone after all and punches in the numbers.

She answers "Hello?" before the phone can ring a single time. He's so taken aback that he doesn't have time to decide whether or not to hang up. Instead he says, "Um, hey," and, just like that, the conversation's under way.

"Who is this?"

"Take a guess." Silence. "It's Gerald, Sasha."

"Oh," she whispers.

"You must have jumped at this thing," he blunders on. "How weird. It didn't even ring."

"I was waiting for another call."

"Oh, I'm sorry. I mean, I can—"

"*No,*" she cries, and then, praise be, laughs a little. "You're not sneaking away this time, buster. I've got a bone to pick with you."

"I can imagine." A small teenage girl—pallid, black-haired,

Asian—sits down at the computer terminal beside him and smiles. Gerald smiles back, nods. "I guess that's why I'm calling."

"You guess."

"I want to apologize," he continues, feeling all at once vulnerable here in the presence of this almost translucently delicate girl who, for whatever wigged-out teenage reason, has just extended her hand.

"I'm young," whispers the girl.

"For which time?" asks Sasha.

Gerald takes the girl's hand and gives her a tentative shake. "For Monday. Though last night couldn't be helped."

"I'll have to think about that," Sasha says. "How's your dad?"

"Oh, a little tired, maybe, but nothing to worry about. Thanks for asking. Can you hold on a second?" Cradling the phone against his shoulder, he withdraws his hand and raises a finger to the girl beside him.

"Young doe," she continues, unfazed. He has no idea what she's talking about.

"I see." Inanely, he smiles again. Returning the phone to his ear, he swivels away and, in a husky whisper, says, "I'm at work, so maybe I should call you back."

"Hey, you called *me*. We need to talk, you know."

"Which is why I called."

"We have plans tonight, but Aaron's on call tomorrow, so here's what I'm thinking."

"I don't know, Sasha."

"You haven't even heard what I'm going to say."

"The thing is, I've got this new job and everything."

"Right, I know. Brent told me all about it last night. He told me you have to go to Centennial Park tomorrow night."

Gerald swivels back around. The girl still faces him in her swivel chair, her thin hands resting between her bare legs. Her placid smile is adamant. For lack of a better response, he smiles back. The whole transaction has suddenly grown unbearably complicated: one phone call and he's back in that net. "That's news to me."

"What do you know, I'm full of surprises. So what I was thinking is, you can just take me along."

"Take you where?"

"To the park. Tomorrow night. I already covered it with Brent." She pauses, waiting for Gerald to answer. After a moment she says, "Look, you *owe* me."

He tries to think. What, exactly, does he owe her? When did he put himself in her debt? "Fine," he sighs. "Tomorrow it is."

"Don't sound so excited," she murmurs. So now he's hurt her again, on top of everything else. Ditto the girl beside him, this young doe, who has just turned away and stood up.

"I *am* excited," he assures her. "Look, can I call you later? I kind of need to go."

"Boy, doesn't *that* sound familiar." And she hangs up.

The girl is gone, of course. He feels terrible, ignoring her that way, but didn't she see he was on the phone? Then again, she was just being nice. A teenager making a social blunder, that's all it was. He looks around for her but she must have left the room—in tears, probably. No, that's ridiculous. He'll track her down later.

Then he looks at the computer monitor to his right, the one facing the chair the young woman had sat in, and notices a Post-it note hanging like a little flag off the side of the monitor's frame. The note reads *Nhung's Computer Don't Touch!!!* For Chrissakes, she was simply telling him her *name*. The poor girl's name is Nhung Do. A simple introduction between two people and Gerald had screwed it up. Another apology, another failed social encounter. Loneliness or regret: it seems to him there should be another option. Maybe there is for other people. Which is why he so often wishes he were some other person.

NINE

SATURDAY NIGHT. Gerald and his father step out of the Downtown MARTA station, onto Techwood Avenue, and into pandemonium. The mayhem crashes upon them like a tidal wave of amplified music and overheated bodies. It was nothing like this yesterday. There was a crowd, yes, but not this mob. He can't see more than three feet in front of him. The whole street glows like a sports stadium, with every inch of sidewalk supporting a decrepit kiosk or wobbly vendor stand, each selling the same repeated selection of cheap Olympic paraphernalia: T-shirts and pennants, pins and pincushions, hats and hologram posters. Massive red Coca-Cola banners thwap from the glass fronts of high-rise office buildings. Mimes and musicians create little openings in the crowd, each performer commanding a smiling, appreciative audience. Gerald's eyes dart back and forth and touch upon everything, but it's all too much, he can't sweep it all in.

"Just like I told you," his father shouts. "The Tower of Babel."

Sasha's also with them, somewhere in this throng. She clearly wanted Gerald to herself, but the old man was anxious to see the park, and Gerald felt his father's presence could serve as a buffer. He came pretty damn close to bagging this excursion entirely, particularly since he's already completed all the work Brent's assigned him thus far. He spent the day fighting the overheated hordes downtown, taking pictures with his nifty GIF camera, asking people to speak into his little tape recorder, bending over so they could use his sweaty back as a desk upon which to sign his release forms, and just generally feeling like an asshole. Most people when he stopped them—yesterday's story addressed the pressing matter "Which events are you most excited about?", bad grammar and all—registered real excitement, a genuine thrill. This was what they had come for, after all: to get on television, to be a part of the whole media event. But when they learned he was representing a "webcast," their excitement visibly ebbed. Most of them didn't have the foggiest idea what a "webcast" was, so he had to explain all of that, over and over again. By the time they read and then signed one of his release forms (a small suspicious handful refusing this last request), they were already tired of him, shaking him off like airport visitors ditching a Hare Krishna. The entire day was pretty demoralizing. Later that evening he and his father, in deference to Gerald's still-malfunctioning computer, opened the laptop and logged on to the site and there was his story, edited down to six paragraphs and two pulled quotes and three little GIF pictures.

"Sit tight," he tells his father. "I think we've lost Sasha." Though in fact the minute he says this, he spots her standing about twenty yards away and surveying the crowd, a look of gentle panic on her face. The vision stabs him: she's looking for *him*. Before this summer he would have welcomed such a display of desire from her, however circumstantial, and, in fact, he can't say he doesn't like it, a bit, even now. Equally nice is the warmth he feels when she finally plucks his face from the crowd and lets her shoulders sag with relief.

"I'm going to buy a leash for you two," she scolds when she finally sidles up. She's wearing a dark green Olympics cap and a soft aqua V-necked T-shirt so small its short sleeves extend no further than the ball joint of her shoulder. The edge of the shirttail fans out at her waist so that a provocative strip of bare midriff smiles at him each time she turns her torso to the right or to the left. "I can't take the stress of losing you guys every five minutes."

"We're already on a leash," Dad tells her. "That's our whole problem."

Huddled together now, they move as a trio through the crowd, past bearded folksingers and more rickety vendor stands and eventually a rabble of evangelical teens. The teenagers parade past in old-fashioned sandwich boards, they shout through amplified megaphones, they wave Bibles in the air and sweat through their T-shirts. He didn't notice them yesterday; now they're unavoidable. They're everywhere you look, an entire army of them, masses of teenage Christian soldiers marching up and down the streets in scattered ranks all afire with apocalyptic zeal. To Gerald's immediate left stands a buffed-up, charismatic youth leader with two male disciples, each holding one end of a giant red-ink-on-white signboard that reads: *Everything You Know Is WRONG! You have ONE option ONLY! REPENT!* To Gerald's right, a teenage mime troupe in black brings its latest performance to its climax as all ten members collapse to the ground in unison. And closing in from behind come a dozen or so clean-shaven teens dressed in matching stenciled T-shirts *(Jesus Rocks!)* and holding aloft piles of wallet-sized pamphlets. For the heck of it, Gerald takes one. The front asks, in block letters rimmed with flames, "Where will *you* be when the millennium ends?" Beneath this legend, a frightened stick figure peers into an open doorway, beyond which roars a hideous cartoon fire.

"Hey, Dad," he calls, brandishing the pamphlet. "Got something for you."

"Don't tempt me, son," Dad calls back, and laughs.

They keep walking in single file, down Techwood and past the beer stands manned by peroxide blonds in ribbed tank tops and blue silk running shorts, and before they know it the street opens up before them and just like that they're here: *at the Olympics!* The Olympics, in this case, being ... well, all of this— the AT&T Centennial Olympic Park, the crowds, the lights and excitement, the corporate pavilions and the paraphernalia, the street vendors and the Christian kids. Forget the games. *This* is the Olympics.

First up: the AT&T Centennial Olympic Park Fountain, the central feature of the broad, wide-open plaza just past the park's main entrance. Crisscrossing jets of water lit from below create a glittering candy-colored basket weave through which screaming children frolic and splash, just like in a commercial—as in a Coke commercial, or a McDonald's commercial, or a Sunny Delight commercial, all of which products are represented here at the AT&T Centennial Olympic Park. Beyond the fountain looms the Anheuser-Busch Bud World Pavilion, a mysterious twenty-one-and-over circus tent that at present commands the park's longest line. Bud World, red white and blue like the Budweiser logo, sports a self-consciously 1960s "sci-fi" look, complete with a Bat-Signal floodlight that rotates up top and casts onto the clouds an original insignia featuring the five Olympic rings stenciled over the Bud World logo. Behind Bud World, a bit toward the right and commanding a much smaller crowd, huddles the humble green-and-yellow Swatch Watch Pavilion, subtitled, *à la* Disney, the World of Time, while to the left looms the smooth chrome facade of the General Motors Century of Motion, which, Gerald learned yesterday after a thoroughly pointless forty-five-minute wait in line, consists of little more than a big theater without chairs in which visitors remain standing as they watch a twenty-minute short film of fast-paced helicopter footage that is supposed to convey the illusion of movement. Ergo: A Century of Motion.

Finally, at the farthest eastern extreme of the park, sandwiched between the World of Time and the World of Bud, rises the AT&T Global Olympic Village, the nucleus of the whole event and the flagship televisual icon for the entire Atlanta Olympic Games experience. The Eiffel Tower of this hybrid world's fair, the Space Needle of the Cellular South. As it happens, the AT&T Global Olympic Village isn't a village at all. It's just a facade for the village you're already in. Set far back in the park but commanding the most sky space, the Global Village facade is really just an enormous *television screen*, from which the terrifyingly huge face of Bob Costas keeps park visitors up-to-date on the sporting events going on elsewhere. His nostrils are as big as basketballs, his hair the size of a residential backyard. The television screen sits between the two halves of a subdivided gourd made of molded steel and white canvas, the two half-tunnels rising up toward the screen like bookends and leading the eye to the heart of things: the televised broadcast of Olympic events themselves. The mellifluent voice of Bob Costas permeates the air, pouring down from nowhere like Yahweh addressing Noah before the flood. Everything around them this hot and humid night looks as blue and clean as toilet disinfectant. The place really does take your breath away. Bob Costas waves down at the tiny people below him. The hordes wave back.

"Who's hungry?" Gerald asks.

"Count me out," his father responds, wearing that infuriating beatific smile.

"I'll bite," Sasha says, taking Gerald's hand. So as not to lose him, he tells himself. "My treat."

"Nothing doing." He smiles back. "Where are you going, Dad?"

"I think I'll go learn about the World of Time."

"You're going to be disappointed. I went to that stupid thing yesterday. It's just an elaborate commercial for Swatch watches."

"Then I'll buy a Swatch watch. You two have fun. Don't mind this old fogey."

"Just don't get lost," Gerald calls after him, watching with a pang in his chest as his father, smiling absently, shuffles alone through the crowd, the lining of his left back pocket hanging like a tail from his flat old-man's behind and the parade-confetti of his untied shoestrings bouncing happily about on the cement.

Alone at last. Or at least as alone as they'll get, what with the multitude around them. His stomach flutters. With one last worried search for his father, he turns to Sasha and jerks his head toward the food tents pitched behind the Global Village facade. "You ready to fight the crowd?"

"It's now or never," she replies.

The food tents pretty much replicate the standard American shopping-mall food court experience, with an international accent. Southern barbecue, Cajun catfish, Ethiopian wraps, gyros and Greek salads, pizza. The crowd mills about restless and overheated. Children run beneath adult legs, spilling sodas and slipping on unraveled gyros. A dank smell of fried food and body odor hangs oppressively in the heavy air—air that circulates somewhat better than it might otherwise thanks to a series of strategically placed jet-engine fans that rumble and blow, lifting people's hair from their scalps and scattering sweat and body odor into the atmosphere.

Standing in line—after some indecision, he and Sasha elected for Ethiopian grub, primarily because it had the shortest line—Gerald goes perfectly blank. Here he is, thirty years old and still suffering from the greatest of all adolescent afflictions: alone with a girl and *nothing to say*.

Sasha takes the lead. "You're really great with your father, you know. The way you look after him."

"Yeah, well." He swallows once and considers how much to tell her. So much has come out in the last three or four days. "He's the sort of guy who needs looking after."

"He just seems so ... I don't know. Serene."

"It just looks like that from the outside."

"Yet clearly something's up."

"It's nothing we can't handle, Sasha. We'll be fine."

"I see." She turns her attention to the front of the line. Silence descends on them again. Off in the distance, the fans rumble and blow. "You know," she says, still facing forward, "I don't want you to think I'm prying."

"I didn't say you were."

"But I mean, one day he gets clobbered in the head, then a week later he nearly collapses with exhaustion at Nora's."

"He wasn't that tired," he objects, worried now that perhaps Dad looked worse to everyone else than Gerald let himself admit.

"He looked tired to me." The line starts moving again, then abruptly comes to a halt. Another tense moment passes. "But, of course, if you don't want to talk about it, then I guess ... Well, that's your prerogative."

"Jesus loves you." It's a Christian teen, canvassing the food court. She's about sixteen, chubby and cheerful, her blushing cheeks pollinated with freckles, her teeth chained in braces, her enormous upper body wrapped in a *Jesus Rocks!* T-shirt patch-worked with sweat. In her hands she holds forth a pamphlet.

"I know you're concerned," Gerald tells Sasha. "It's compli-cated, that's all."

"Like I said, it's fine. Totally your prerogative."

"He died for your sins."

"But that's unfair to you, isn't it? You've been right there, from the beginning. You have a right to know."

"No, I don't."

"Yes, you do. You've been terrific these last couple of days, what with the casseroles and whatnot. I mean, if you really *are* that concerned, then you have a right to know what you're so concerned about."

"I said forget it, Gerald."

"He died on the cross so that you may live."

"No, but you deserve an explanation."

"But I'm not *forcing* you. If it's too difficult, we should drop it."

"Maybe I *want* to tell you."

"Now you make it sound like I *am* prying. I wish I hadn't said anything."

"That's not what I meant, Sasha."

"If you believe in Jesus, all blessings will flow."

"Because I honestly am concerned, Gerald."

"I know you are. It's just a lot to get involved in."

"I think I can handle it."

"I know, you're exactly right. You've been a real savior."

"His name is Emmanuel. He's the answer to all your—"

"Look," Gerald snaps, turning on the Christian teen, "can you go bother someone else? We're trying to have a private conversation here."

The girl blanches briefly but stands her ground. Beneath her huge T-shirt, which falls nearly to her knees, swells an enormous set of breasts. A sour smell drifts from her open mouth. Unfazed, she says, "Nothing is private from our Lord and Savior."

"That may be, but right now—"

"I mean, if he's dying, Gerald, if that's what you're telling me, then it might help if you talked about it."

"Talk to God. He can help you with all your problems."

"Look, would you kindly go fuck off?" The tent grows perfectly silent. Only the white noise of the fans remains. All eyes turn to him, Indians and Latinos and Midwesterners and Europeans, the whole tent now focused on Gerald and Sasha and their incorrigible Christian teen.

The girl gulps once, her eyes darting about in their sockets.

She seems unsure whom Gerald was addressing. "I'll say a prayer for you."

"Kiss my ass, and we'll call it even." And though they are nearly at the front of the line, Gerald grabs Sasha by the wrist and whisks her through the crowd, which parts for them verily like the Red Sea. Then it's back into the fray, back into the mob.

Not until the two of them have secured a bite to eat does Gerald finally turn to her and, as solemnly as possible, say, "Sorry about that."

"Oh, don't worry about me." The people flow by as Sasha bites into a corn dog, which they bought at a hog dog stand just outside Bud World. Swallowing with difficulty, she dabs a napkin to her lips before adding, "You're the one going to hell."

"I'll take my chances."

She chomps some more, swallows, and takes a sip from their shared Coke, a massive thing the size of a muffler. "How warm was I back there? About your dad, I mean."

"Tending toward balmy, I'd say." Now Gerald bites into his own corn dog. Geez Louise. The thing's so hot it's like a pissed-off scorpion on his tongue. Gesturing frantically for the Coke— which she passes, a gently disapproving smile on her face—he douses the diabolical dog before spitting the whole soggy masticated mess into a nearby trash can. That's another thing about Centennial Park: trash cans are fucking *omnipresent*.

"That's what you get for being so mean to that girl," she chides him.

"Ahh yes, the devil's own corn dog." He holds up his dinner and scowls at it, as if in reprimand. "Ever noticed how phallic these things are?"

"You're changing the subject."

"That's probably accurate."

"I mean, we can have this conversation or not. Totally up to you."

"What conversation?" And whatdyaknow, it's the man himself, fresh from the Swatch Watch World of Time and apparently walking on cat's paws.

"Speak of the devil," Gerald says with a happy hollow rising in his chest. "And I do mean literally."

"Wait, he was *here*?" His father looks around. "And I *missed* him?"

"Oh, he'll turn up again, old man. How was the World of Time?"

"Relative, mostly. But I got a nice watch." He proudly displays a brand-new lime-green plastic timepiece with a yellow peace sign on the face. There is neither a minute nor an hour hand. Just the peace sign.

"How much did you pay for that thing?"

"It was worth it. It's called the Swatch Watch Timeless Time Peace. Push this button and watch what happens." He holds his arm out to Sasha. Like a nurse taking a pulse, she takes his wrist between her thumb and forefinger and presses the tiny button on the side of the watch. The peace sign magically dissolves, giving way to a pixelled LED facsimile of an old-fashioned watch face, complete with Roman numerals along the outer dial. When Sasha releases the button, the peace sign returns.

"That's ridiculous," Gerald declares.

"It's ingenious," Dad counters.

"Why not just buy a regular watch?"

"You're missing the point," Sasha interrupts. "I think it's neat, Mr. Brinkman."

"Aw, maybe he's right. What's an old guy like me need a watch for anyway? I quit keeping time years ago. Speaking of which"— his father lowers his wrist—"this old fart's about had it. Think I'll just catch the next train home and call it a night."

Sasha, taking a careful bite of her corn dog, glances at Gerald, and then back at his father. "You feeling all right, Mr. Brinkman?"

"Just pooped is all."

"Then let's get you home," Gerald sighs, tossing his half-eaten corn dog into yet another trash can.

"Nonsense. You two stay here. I've seen all I need to see. You don't need me tagging along."

"You're not tagging along," Sasha pleads, though Gerald can detect a faint hint of relief in her voice.

"You're good sports to put up with this old bag of bones. But I'm done. You kids are on your own."

"But we don't *want* to be on our own," Gerald says sourly. Sasha furrows her brow, opens her mouth, but remains silent.

"Nothing I can do about that," his father concludes, patting Gerald on the shoulder. "Though maybe you should let this young woman talk for herself."

Looking away, Sasha takes a last noncommittal bite of her corn dog.

Despite the fact that it is nearly 11 P.M., they still have trouble on their way home securing a seat in the packed MARTA car, the atmosphere much more festive and loud than on their trip into the Village (all that Bud World beer), but after one or two stops they snag a bench near the back, Sasha pressed up against his thigh, Gerald's arm draped along the seat back. While exploring the park, they'd maintained a steady stream of stilted small talk; now, as the MARTA rattles along its tracks, he finally unloads on her everything there is to tell about his father. He feels like a kid unleashing his wish list to a fetching Hindu Santa Claus. And what does he want? Absolution, it surprises him to find. He wants to be free of the burden of his father's impending death, and he wants Sasha to free him. Throughout she keeps her gaze focused on the floor in front of her, her ear cocked toward him. The only time she responds directly is when he wonders aloud what a kidney transplant will cost him.

"Depends on your copay," she says. "What is it?"

"No idea."

"What did you pay the last time you went to the doctor?"

"The doctor? God, that was what, ten years ago."

"Not even for a checkup?"

He glares at her for a moment, recalling once again why he prefers to keep to himself. All these little things you're supposed to do, the whole apparatus of the grown-up world: fuck it. He's with the old man on that one. "When something goes awry, I'll go."

"What about your dad?"

"Regarding what?"

"What's his insurance situation?"

"Couldn't tell you," Gerald sheepishly replies. The car tugs to a stop. These MARTA machines are as smooth as jet planes, and nearly as comfortable, the white plastic interior and the pumped-in oxygen and the automatic sliding doors all lending the car a sort of sci-fi spaceship vibe, which Gerald kind of likes. He's starting to think he'll like the future, whenever it arrives. "Knowing him, it's probably not too pretty."

"And your deductible? How much is that?"

"No clue. What are deductibles generally?"

She surveys him almost in wonder. Yes, he wants to tell her, some people actually don't know this crap. "Five hundred, give or take. Depends on the provider. So a twenty percent copay—I'm guessing here—plus the deductible: that's easily fifteen hundred right there."

"Wow," Gerald replies, genuinely shocked: he doesn't have that kind of cash. "That's so expensive."

Gently, she touches him on the thigh. "It's your father, Gerald."

But he resents the gesture: he was just surprised by how far off

the mark he was in his own half-assed deductions; he wasn't balk-
ing at the price. Scooting away, he wraps up in one long but impatient sentence what else there is to tell—the argument Thursday
night, Dad's subsequent refusal to reopen the dialogue—and falls
silent. He feels worse than before, and on a variety of levels. He
feels worse than he's ever felt about his father, who, in his narrative
to Sasha, materialized before his eyes as a helpless creature in the
grip of something both malevolent and unimaginably huge: a
strange thing to feel about your dad. He feels worse than ever
about his relationship with his father and all the lost opportunities
he's let fall through his fingers. And he's disgusted at the botch he's
made of his own life. He wonders if it's too late to make amends,
another opportunity stupidly squandered. The world will make
you grow up whether you want to or not. They ride the rest of the
way in tense silence.

Walking home from the Midtown MARTA station, Sasha
breaks the stalemate by nudging him in the arm. "Whatcha thinking about?"

On Gerald's left Piedmont Park stretches out beneath its
canopy of lights and trees, pastoral and calm. On his right rises a
line of brand-new two-story apartment complexes that have gone
up in the last year or so, each individual unit painted a different
bright color—blue, then red, then yellow. A festive crowd weaves
a drunken web around them, the night air pulsating with excitement, yet he and Sasha remain quiet and calm, both of them
strolling at a leisurely rate. "It's weird, but for some reason I've
been thinking about an episode from my senior year in high
school."

"Let's hear it."

"Well, it involves my dad, obviously, so I guess it's not so
weird." He takes a breath, wondering where to begin. "He went to
Harvard, did you know that?"

"No."

"Hard to believe, but there you go. God, he's in love with that place. Obsessed with it. Maybe he sees those years as his best, I don't know. Everybody's got a favorite period of their lives, and maybe that's his. My sister went there, by the way. So did my brother-in-law. I'm getting off track, sorry."

"It's your story."

"True enough." He desperately wants a cigarette. His lungs gnaw at him, his head singing its desperate nicotine jingle, but he swallows back the urge. "So anyway, senior year I'm applying to colleges. My grades are fair to middling, A's and B's and a few C's, math classes mostly, while my test scores are totally average. Twenty-eight ACT, twelve-hundred SAT. Nothing terrible, but not Harvard material. Still, Dad's adamant. Harvard's the place for me. Every day when I come home from school he's waiting for me with Harvard brochures, Harvard videotapes. Then over dinner one night this friend of my dad's, Dr. Torrent, produces a brochure for this Princeton Review course, guarantees a two-hundred-point increase in your SAT scores."

"I took one of those courses."

"I probably should have. Anyway, to get Dad off my back, I agree to visit Harvard with him. If I like it, and I buy into his premise that his and my sister's legacy will work wonders with the admissions people, then, okay, I sign up for the course and take my chances. And that's what I've been thinking about. That trip to Harvard."

By now they've made it halfway to Monroe Avenue. Ahead of them a Blockbuster video franchise beams its soft blue glow to the sky. Cars push down Tenth Avenue, old Monte Carlos bouncing on their shocks, open-top Jeep Wranglers from which teenagers swing like children on a traveling jungle gym, Volkswagen Jettas cowering amid the chaos. The concrete throbs with rap and heavy metal. Sasha stays quiet, inviting him to continue.

"So we went. This was October 1983. What do I remember about Harvard? Let's see. I remember meeting the recruiter, this super dynamic black Young Republican type in a blue blazer and a yellow power tie. And I remember my tour through the dorms. I sat in on some enormous history class while Dad waited outside for me, though I couldn't tell you anything the professor said because I had my Walkman on. Here's something I recall. I know exactly what I was listening to on that tape player: Big Country, *The Crossing*. I can even tell you who produced that album: Steve Lillywhite. Remember Big Country?"

"No," she says with a nervous laugh.

"My point exactly. So after class, Dad cornered the professor— a grad student, I think—and asked him all sorts of questions, all of which the guy tried his level best to answer, and then Dad turns to me and says, 'Do you have any questions for this young man, Gerald?' And you know what I said? 'Are there any used-record stores around here?' The guy answered that question, as well. In fact, he directed me to about four used-record stores, all of them in Harvard Square. What else do I remember? There was a bridge leading away from the college, there were a bunch of rowboats somewhere or other, there was this pizza joint we ate at. And that's pretty much it. That's all I remember about Harvard University. Now, ask me what albums I bought at all those used-record stores."

"I think I see your point."

"*Wilder* by The Teardrop Explodes, the first three Style Council twelve-inch singles, an Aztec Camera 45, and *Power Corruption and Lies* by New Order."

"And now you regret this."

"Damn straight I regret it. Why do I remember those stupid albums when I can't remember anything my father wanted me to see? All I thought about the whole time I was there was 'Record stores, record stores.' Cambridge is a college town, college towns have great used-record stores—that's all Harvard meant to me. That's it, period."

"You were young, Gerald. All teenagers are like that."

"Sure. But there was something else going on there, too. I didn't *want* to go to Harvard, you see what I'm getting at? I mean, I wouldn't have gotten in anyway, but even if I had scored fifteen hundred on the SAT, I would have thumbed my nose at the idea. The whole time we were there, I kept thinking about those record stores, kept talking about them and asking about them, and every time I did, I could see Dad wince in pain. But he never jumped on me about it, even though I knew he couldn't stand it. He never said a single thing to me, not in all those years of my growing up, and yet I knew my obsession with rock music pissed him off. Disappointed him, even. But I kept it up, *because* it disappointed him. I liked it. In some way, I *wanted* him to lash out at me, wanted him to say, 'Enough with the record stores already,' so I could then feel wounded and misunderstood, I don't know. But he never did that. He just cut me loose after lunch and I went record shopping, and then we took a cab back to the airport and flew home that same night, and I went straight to my room to listen to all my new albums, and that was the end of Harvard. He never raised the subject again. I won. I went to the local liberal arts college."

"A pyrrhic victory."

"Sure, whatever that is." They've arrived at the Tenth Street and Monroe intersection. A quick left takes them to Gerald's apartment, while to get to Sasha's house they have to trudge up the hill and go right for about five blocks. If they're going to split up for the night, this is where they should do it. "We could go to my house and get my car if you want. Save you the walk home."

"I don't mind walking. It's nice out."

He shuffles here in indecision. "I hope Dad's all right."

"Should we check on him?"

"Oh, he's probably asleep by now," he lies, though not before noticing her use of the pronoun *we*. "If not, he's up reading."

She nods. "It's a long walk back to my house, so if you'd rather just—"

"No, not at all. I mean, you shouldn't walk alone."

"I'm not worried about that, but I could stand the company. I'll drive you back if you want."

No indication if she means right when they get there or sometime later tonight, though Gerald doesn't feel he's in any position to assume anything. After all, she's married. As is Nora, he suddenly recalls for no apparent reason. Nora's *married*. How had he let that happen? "After you," he says.

They stroll silently up Virginia Avenue, past the Philly steak shack and the apartment complexes, and then enter a brightly lit suburban strip. His doubts notwithstanding, he still wonders if he's up to anything erotic tonight, or if that's what's even in the cards. No, probably not. He and Sasha turn left off Virginia and head down a darkened residential street, placid beneath the moon, the green garbage bins standing sentry on the curbs. Dogs bark.

Into the silence blooming between them Sasha says, "If I ask you something, will you promise me you'll give an honest answer?"

He pauses. "Depends on the question."

"I thought you'd say that." She considers for a moment, then says, "Monday night, when you cut out: I think it was because of something I said."

He stops walking and takes a breath. At least this time his cigarettes are in his pocket. "That's what I wanted to tell you at the torch thing, Sasha. It wasn't you."

She's standing about three yards in front of him, illuminated from above by a streetlight. "I know it wasn't. I think it had something to do with Nora."

Blood rushes to his head; why does every road with this girl keep leading to Nora? He joins her at the streetlight, rams his hands in his pockets, and continues walking. "See, right there. I have no idea what you're talking about."

"Oh, I think you do."

They arrive at the bottom of the street, turn left again, and suddenly they're at her house. From the outside the house looks perfectly innocent, like a sleeping cat on its plush carpet of lawn. Silently they walk toward the house and proceed up her front walkway, Gerald all the while racking his brain trying to figure out what she's getting at. Once again, he can't be sure if she's needling him to spill what all he knows about Aaron, or if, as he suspected the other night, she's coming on to him to get even with Nora. Nora's certainly looming large in her mind. The complexity of the situation tightens around his heart like a set of bird claws.

He stops before her front door and lamely observes, "We're here."

"Am I right?"

"About what?"

"About Monday night. And what I just said about Nora."

"I don't understand what Nora has to do with this."

"She has everything to do with it, Gerald. That night, right before you slipped out, I asked you if you were going through a tough time. Remember that?"

"I *am* going through a tough time, Sasha."

"I know that, but I was talking about Nora."

"Nora's not my problem right now, okay? I left on Monday because ..." He pauses to figure out a response but comes up blank. "Like I said, I was worried about my dad."

"You're still in love with her, aren't you?"

"What does that have to do with anything?"

"So I'm *right*."

"Whoa, time-out here." He makes a T with his hands and steps away. Those bird's claws dig deeper into his heart. He runs his hands through his sweaty hair—it's easily eighty, eighty-five out tonight—balloons his cheeks, blows, collects his thoughts. "Look, I don't know where you're going with all this. I was worried about my dad, so I split. It was rude, I'm sorry, but that's the end of it."

"Why didn't you deny what I said about Nora?"

"Because it's not true," he snaps back.

"I think it is."

"This isn't about Nora, all right? It's about *Aaron*. That's what you're poking me about. You want me to tell you everything Nora knows about him."

She backs away, sort of takes this in. Her look of surprise, he realizes with a sinking feeling of defeat, appears to be genuine. "Wait: you're saying Nora keeps *tabs* on my husband?"

Panic floods his bloodstream. "That's not at all what I said," he hears himself telling her, his voice remote and faraway, as if his throat were located somewhere between his knees.

"Nora's *told* you things?"

"No, Sasha, I didn't mean that."

"I heard you, Gerald. You said Nora knows things about him."

"From college," he lies, though in fact he's impressed by the nimbleness of the response.

"Please, Gerald. Don't even try."

"I'm serious, Sasha. I thought you were talking about—"

"I mean, what does he do, exactly? Report to her? Write her e-mails? Give her a play-by-play?"

A door jerks open beside them. Aaron, shirtless, stands in the foyer in a pair of low-slung turquoise surgical scrubs. Silence slices the air as neatly as a scalpel. Gerald, still standing motionless on the walkway with his hands held before him in self-defense, lifts his arms in a show of exasperated surrender, though the gesture comes off as unconvincing, even to him. No doubt about it, Aaron's an imposing sight, lit up from behind so that the dark shadows articulate the finely hewn lines of his chest and arms.

Gerald feels a pounding in his chest that resonates all the way to his skull.

In a steady voice, Aaron says, "Having a little spat, are we?"

Sasha turns to him but says nothing. Calmly returning her gaze, Aaron crosses his arms across his bare chest and leans against the door frame. "You enjoy your dinner the other night, Brinkman?"

"We were just talking." Gerald wants to meet Sasha's eyes but can't figure out how.

"Yeah, that's pretty much what it sounded like. Two people having a conversation."

"Sasha misunderstood something I said."

"I gathered as much."

"And now we've cleared it up." Unexpectedly, Gerald's heart has already settled down a bit. After all, he's always hated this prick. Come to think of it, he doesn't really give a shit what happens from here on out. "Which means I should leave."

"I'm not listening to this," Sasha says, her voice without inflection, and angrily pushes Aaron aside before disappearing into the house. Her departure leaves behind a tense quivering wake. Gerald quietly begins backing down the walkway.

Aaron calls, "Hold on there, Brinkman," and closes the door behind him. As he advances toward Gerald he observes, "You were saying something about a misunderstanding?"

"I already told you, everything's cleared up." Aaron is now less than five paces away, and gaining. Gerald reaches in his pants pockets for his cigarettes and takes two more steps backward before adding, "Tell Sasha I'm sorry."

"You fucking tell her." Aaron is upon him now, his bare chest both a challenge and a threat. Menacingly, he starts circling Gerald, who keeps his eyes focused before him. "Thing is, Brinkman, I generally try to stay out of other people's business. Makes it a lot easier. Know what I'm getting at?"

"I have a pretty good idea."

"I mean, if you have something you need to say to my wife, you should say it yourself."

"I'll do that."

"Of course, then I'll have to smash your fucking face in."

"You're way off base here, man." Though it takes some doing, Gerald manages to stay right where he is, without flinching.

"You think so?" Aaron stops in front of him and stares Gerald in the eye. "Hell, maybe you're right, I don't know. By the way, how often *do* you and Nora talk about me? I'm just curious."

"Never, if I can help it," he lies.

"And you and Sasha?"

"About the same."

"Funny. That's not what I heard back there."

"I haven't the foggiest idea what you heard." Gerald finally withdraws the cigarettes from his pocket. His hands are trembling. "Nor do I give a shit."

"Yeah, see, but I do. I very much give a shit."

"Fact is, Aaron"—carefully, so as not to betray his fear, Gerald brings an unlit cigarette to his mouth—"I'd be perfectly happy right now if I never had to say another word about you ever again."

Unexpectedly, Aaron laughs—not with derision, either, but with relief. He knows he's cinched the deal; he's in the clear. "Dude, that right there is about the smartest thing you've said all night." Stroking his stomach, he shuffles backward up the walkway toward his house. Gerald finally turns away, his quivering hands rammed in his pocket, where he's having trouble finding his lighter. After about ten paces Aaron calls out, "Nice doing business with you, Brinkman."

"Just the man we've been waiting for."

His father is sitting on the stairs leading into Gerald's apartment and talking to Carol Radford, who, instead of her standard costume of baggy Wranglers and plaid work shirts, wears a sleeve-less dress of lime green and yellow. Another new note: her hair hangs free down her back, long stringy hair the color of a mouse's pelt. Fleetingly, Gerald wonders if she's been flirting with the old man. Then he looks at his father—the day-old razor stubble, the greasy unwashed hair, the ill-fitting T-shirt and baggy run-ning shorts, plus the sneakers-and-black-socks combination, his standard lounging-around-the-house uniform—and instantly aban-dons the idea. In direct defiance of Gerald's numerous admoni-tions to the contrary, the front door to the apartment once again stands wide open, the air-conditioning unit rumbling angrily in the window.

"I'm so glad we caught you," Carol adds by way of greeting, and clasps her hands together in a gesture of anticipation and delight. "I've been talking to your father here and we both think that . . . Well, we weren't sure when you were getting back." When Gerald does not respond—he can already feel what's coming—she smiles again, compressing her clasped palms. "I think your lottery number's just come up."

"You clearly have the wrong guy," Gerald tells her.

"Not so quick, son. Wait till you hear this."

Gerald glances at his father, then at Carol.

"We've got some great news for you," she beams.

"You don't say."

"Tell me how fifteen hundred dollars sounds."

"Depends on what it's for."

Unable to contain himself any longer, his father says, "For rent, son. This nice young lady has found someone who wants to rent your place. And for a king's ransom."

"I'm already renting my place," Gerald points out.

"Yes, I know," Carol quickly adds. "None of that will change."

"Says who?" Grinding his jaw, he steps past Carol and reaches into the house and slams the door shut. The sound echoes back to them from across the neighborhood.

Shaking his head, Dad says, "I wish you hadn't done that."

"It's locked, isn't it?"

"Yeah, I'm pretty sure it is."

Gerald's heart sinks at this news. All week he and his father have been sharing Gerald's one set of keys, as the spare set has been in Nora's possession for the last two years. Nora feeds Lester whenever Gerald is away, which isn't often. Only now does he recall that he gave his only set to his father back at the Olympic Village. But he doesn't say anything, since the man already knows this.

"Why was it locked, Dad?"

"No reason."

"I've got a spare," Carol interrupts, the woman with all the answers. "Now, Gerald, your father and I have already worked it out. It's a win-win situation for both of us, so hear me out." And though his mind is still nagged by his encounter with Aaron, Gerald sits down on the front step, leans back against the locked door, and listens to Carol's plan. Tonight, while rubbing elbows at a corporate banquet to honor the opening of the Olympic Games, Carol, who still apparently maintains tangential contact with her husband's local Atlanta circle, struck up a conversation with a board member from her husband's former company, a German guy who's been looking around for two weeks' lodging. The German man had just found out that the corporate suite downtown, the one he had reserved for the duration of the games, had accidentally been promised both to him and to another board member, so here he was, in Atlanta with no place to stay. Someone had directed him to Carol on the assumption that she might have something. The board member, who had brought along not only his wife but also his teenage daughter, was willing to shell out three thousand dollars for a decent place, provided he could move in as early as Sunday afternoon.

"Which is why this is so great for you," she concludes. "Since it's such short notice, I'm willing to split the fee with you and your father here, which is a better deal than you'd get anywhere else."

"Really?" Gerald looks her in the eye, wondering what all she's not telling him. "I have to move out for two weeks, and you get fifteen hundred bucks?"

"Think of it as a finder's fee." She doesn't add—because she does not have to—that she owns the place, or that he still owes her two months' rent—April and the current month.

"What if I choose not to leave?"

"Gerald, this is a wonderful opportunity."

"For you, yeah."

"Son, son," his father interrupts, "what are you doing here? This woman is doing you a favor."

"She is? Gosh, Dad, I thought she was throwing us out of our apartment."

"It's fifteen hundred dollars," Carol insists, showing more mettle than he would have expected. She's no longer stuttering or mangling her syntax. Perhaps she's already made the deal. For which he could sue her. Unfortunately, he'll need that fifteen hundred dollars to do so.

"And where are we supposed to go?" Gerald asks her. "Any ideas on that?"

"With fifteen hundred dollars, I'd think you could go anywhere you want."

"There's not an available hotel room in this entire city."

His father shrugs. "Call Nora."

Gerald turns on him and glares. Why's *he* so gung ho about all this? Because he's sick of living in this shithole, probably. Because he's seen Brent and Nora's place. Gerald opens his mouth to respond but stops cold as the evening's humiliations flood through him all over again, leaving in their wake a stillness of soul that surprises him. Of course: the deductible and the copay. His problems are solved. *If you believe in Jesus, all blessings will flow.* But Gerald doesn't believe in Jesus.

"What about Sasha?" his father is saying. "Or, what's his name, Jeff Flibula. His wife would take us in, I should think."

"Now you're talking," Carol says, buoyant with relief. "Plenty of people to take you in."

"There's also Kira," Dad continues. "Hell, we could live in the newspaper office."

"For fifteen hundred bucks, why not, right?"

"Forget the money, Carol," his father says, the woman's first name sliding off his tongue with (for Gerald) unsettling ease. "I see this as an adventure. I'd like to meet this German man, by the way. What's his name again?"

"Morris Grauffbaut." Carol laughs at the name, still riding on her excitement.

"Fascinating. You know, I used to speak German. Actually, I read more of it than I spoke, but I could definitely turn a phrase when I needed to."

"You should meet him. He's quite an imposing fellow."

"I'll take your word for it. So what do you say, Gerald? Does Ms. Radford here have a deal?"

But Gerald isn't listening to them anymore. He is staring at the sky, a deep slate sky smeared with eraser streaks. Stars twinkle weakly through the smog. A rim of light, a vast diffused halo spreads along the lower horizon: city light, nightlife. Or is it something else?

"Gerald?" His father gazes at him with a concerned expression on his face. Carol, too, seems a bit unnerved. "Did you hear me? Does Ms. Radford have a deal?"

Beyond this dome, endless space constantly expanding. Beyond that, nothing. In a voice that does not even seem to be his, he says, "What choice do I have?"

Inside the apartment sometime later—Carol had raced upstairs and returned with both a spare key and a postdated check that, given the brief amount of time she was gone, must have been written hours ago—Gerald calls out to his father, "You awake?"

Through the bedroom's open door his father calls back, "What's on your mind?"

The overworked AC hasn't managed to subdue all the uninvited heat from outside, so Gerald is lying shirtless on bare sheets, the covers in a wad at his feet, his bare chest lightly filmed in sweat. "I know what I'm doing with my fifteen hundred dollars."

"You don't say."

"Want to hear about it?"

"Shoot."

Gerald reaches back and makes a cradle for his head. "I'm using it as a deductible for a kidney transplant. Specifically yours."

As he might have predicted, his father does not respond immediately. Several minutes pass. In the kitchen the drowsy refrigerator shudders awake. "Save your money," his father finally calls back. "Get yourself a new computer."

"I'm serious, Pop."

"So am I. Buy a new computer, Gerald, top of the line, with a giant hard disk and huge megabytes of RAM and a lightning-fast CD-ROM."

"You're out of excuses here."

"And a laser printer. That's what you really need, a good laser printer. Maybe a scanner."

"The gods have spoken, Dad. The crooked path made straight."

"The path is always crooked, Gerald. Call Nora tomorrow. If

that doesn't work, call Flibula. Nora first, though. I'm not sure if I like that Jeff Flibula."

"It's a sign from above." Gerald swivels off the bed and enters the living room, smiling. "It's a gift from God."

"You're confusing God with a German member of the board of directors, son. Lots of people have made that mistake down through the ages. It's a common error."

Gerald leans against the door frame and cradles his chest against the blast of cold air from the AC rattling in the window just to his left. "You can't tell me this isn't uncanny."

"It isn't uncanny. There: I did it."

"Just tonight—I'm talking two, maybe three hours ago—Sasha was telling me I'd need at least a thousand bucks before I could even think about helping you out. A thousand bucks. And I was thinking, I'm doomed. Dad is doomed. Then I come home and there it is, a thousand dollars. That's no coincidence, Dad. Even you have to grant me that."

"Of course it's no coincidence. You've been waiting for your landlady to throw you out for a month now. It just worked out in your favor, that's all."

"It worked out *perfectly*, don't you see? It's too perfect to be a coincidence. Admit it: there's a design at work here."

Sitting up now, his father rests his elbows on his big cauliflowered knees, his entire body exuding an aura of profound, punishing fatigue, a weariness horrible to look at. "Let me just see if I understand you correctly. You're telling me God, or the Prime Mover, or whatever you want to call it, that this divine being has arranged all of this especially for you and me? That's your argument here?"

"Sort of."

"I'm not making fun of you, Gerald. I'm just trying to understand. Now, let's just examine what this elaborate design would involve. First"—he begins counting off with his fingers—"the

Prime Mover scheduled the 1996 Olympic Games to take place in Atlanta during this very week. Second, he arranged for this German fellow and his wife and his daughter to arrive here in Atlanta. Third, he arranged some protocol official to overbook the corporate suite. Last, he arranged for this fellow to offer Carol three thousand dollars, all so you could save your dear old dad. Is that about right?"

"You *are* making fun of me."

"I mean, if the Prime Mover went to all that trouble to give you your deductible so you could save me from dying, why didn't he just save me from dying and be done with it?"

"I'm just saying it's all too perfect. It feels like a sign, that's all."

"Son," he says wearily, "listen to yourself. You're talking nonsense."

"Explain it, then, Dad. Explain how all this worked out the way it did."

"It hasn't worked out," his father snaps back. Suddenly he looks at Gerald, his eyes tipped by tiny glints of light. "I haven't agreed to anything. Buy a computer, that's what I want you to do. I'm serious. That's what you really need around here. A good computer."

"Forget God, okay? Drop the Prime Mover theory. You can't explain it any better than I can, at least give me that."

"Sure I can. You're just confusing hindsight with destiny—a common mistake, but a mistake all the same."

"What makes you so sure?"

His father sits back in the couch and grips his head. "Because *every*thing looks planned in retrospect. Because the flutter of a hummingbird's wing outside our window affects the weather in China. Because divine intervention is inseparable from predestination. Either things occur as they occur, or everything happens according to plan. Drop it, Gerald. I'm tired and I want to go to sleep."

"So maybe it does happen according to plan. Why can't you even grant that possibility?"

"Because it's absurd. Every act of cellular division, every drop of rain, every single flutter of every single hummingbird wing from the beginning of time until now—you really think that's all been scripted in advance? But why? To what purpose? Why not have it all work out for the good? If you're an omnipotent God planning a universe in advance, why include Auschwitz? I'd rather believe in a plot without meaning, a design without design. Go read your quantum physics, son. Randomness rules."

"But you just said a hummingbird's wings affect the weather in China. So you admit everything's connected."

"Connected, yes, but not *directed*. There's a difference."

"And I'm connected to you. And you're connected to me and Eva and Walt. You're not free, Dad. Your own argument insists on that."

His father falls silent. Bluish light from the window behind his head darkens his face and shoulders so that all Gerald can see from the doorway is a blank amorphous silhouette. The AC gives a final furious rattle and then sputters to a rest. In a curiously disembodied voice, his father says, "You're making this awfully hard on me, Gerald."

"Can't help that, old man." Gerald can barely suppress the tumult in his chest, a bubbling over that feels, at the moment, like triumph. "Just trying to be a good son."

TEN

HERE AT Brent's place Gerald has to smoke outside, so that's where he's been spending a great deal of his time lately, standing just outside the front door and tossing the dead butts into a Folger's can he's hidden behind a big clump of bushes beneath the living room window. But today it's so hot out that even a hopeless hacker like Gerald can't bring himself to light up. The thought of smoking makes him kind of nauseated, actually. Maybe this is the time he stops for good. After all, he hasn't been high since he moved in—or not *really* high: he's sneaked a puff or two on the one-hitter, but that's it. Across the street one of Brent's neighbors drags a clattering lawn mower down his driveway; otherwise, nothing out here in this boiling cauldron moves. Gerald returns the cigarettes to the front pocket of his cutoffs and scans the street some more. Brent's place—Nora's, too: it's hard for him to re-member that—sits at the apex of a steep incline that curves off in the distance into a dark overgrowth of oaks in full bloom. All the houses on this street, Brent's included, are gray stone one-story bungalows, all of them nice enough but none of them with real honest-to-God porches, with swings and lawn furniture and what all, which absence is a strike against them, in Gerald's opinion. The shirtless neighbor across the street yanks the pull starter on his mower. The machine snarls to life. A few cars line the curb, but there's no traffic whatsoever. As of last night, Gerald's car also lined the curb, right outside Brent's place. After a half minute or so of fruitless watching, he sighs and heads back inside.

He finds Nora in the kitchen, cutting a bagel. She's in a pair of white shorts that may or may not be men's boxers (on women, boxers somehow become shorts) and a wrinkled white V-neck tee. She jumps back in alarm at his sudden appearance in the kitchen, grabbing the counter with one hand and clutching her chest with the other. "God, don't sneak up on me like that."

"Is that what I did?" He sidles beside her and fishes out his coffee cup from the little army of cups in the sink. He's not sure, but she appears to be braless.

She says, "I thought you were out."

"That's because I was."

"No, I mean *gone*. I looked out the bedroom window a few minutes ago and didn't see your car."

"Yeah, I need to talk to you about that." He rattles the full carafe from its canopied slot in the coffeemaker and fills his mug. Though this is the second pot he's made this morning he feels zero guilt on this account, since the coffee's his. He and the old man brought it with them last Sunday, along with milk, eggs, and ice cream. Dinner for the last couple of nights has been takeout, on the old man's tab.

"Is your dad out driving it?"

"That appears to be the case, yeah." Taking a seat at the kitchen table, he picks up the entertainment section of the morning paper, which he hasn't read, largely because he never reads the paper. He figures it's probably ironic that he works for a newspaper but does not read one. But what isn't ironic these days? Isn't this the Age of Irony?

"Well, I'm pretty free here. Where do you need to go?"

He sits back and thinks for a moment. "Not sure, actually. Depends on where he is."

She contemplates him from the counter, one hand on her hip. "I'm not quite following you, Gerald."

"Hey, there's a first."

Nora's bagel pops from the toaster. She plucks out the two halves, then starts running in place. "Oooh, oooh," she cries, the bagel halves bouncing about on her open palms, "Gerald, ouch, could you—" The bagel halves topple onto the table next to him. He gives them a bemused look before raising his eyebrows at her.

"Could I what?"

Giving him a sneer, she returns to the kitchen counter and starts opening cabinets. When she goes up on her tiptoes to peer into the upper shelves her T-shirt fans out, revealing for an insect's heartbeat the smooth underside of her left breast. Impatiently, she slams one cabinet door and opens another.

"It's the one beside the sink," he tells her.

"I think I can handle it."

"I'm just saying—"

"I got it, Gerald."

But she's all smiles when she joins him at the table. After carefully arranging the bagel halves on the plate she's brought with her, she begins daintily tearing off little chunks and popping them into her open mouth. Sipping occasionally from his coffee mug, he surreptitiously watches her eat. What he likes is her disheveled hair—pillow head, she calls it—and the way a creased strand accidentally echoes the line of her left cheekbone. Her skin gives off a moist morning smell that somehow consoles him. It's been a long time since he's sat comfortably with a woman still redolent of bed.

Abruptly, she stops eating. "What?"

"I didn't say anything."

"You were looking at me sort of weird."

"I was?" To hide his embarrassment, he brings his coffee cup to his mouth, takes a sip, and gently sets it down, all innocence. "Just thinking."

"You were trying to tell me about your dad."

"Right, that." He nods into his coffee cup, stalling for time. He's not sure how much to reveal just yet—about the illness, or about his own probably overblown suspicions regarding Dad's disappearance this morning. He'd much rather just sit here with her and shoot the breeze. How tired he is of keeping track of his father. "The main thing I need is a ride to campus. You planning on going to the library today?"

"I can take you to Brent, if that's what you're saying. What's up with your dad, Gerald?"

"Probably nothing."

"I can hear you guys talking at night. In case you're wondering." She scans his face to see how this registers. He returns his attention to his coffee mug. "Brent was asking me the other night why your dad's living with you—not that he minds or anything: he was just wondering—and I told him I had no idea. And that's the truth. I still don't."

So they're going to go into it anyway. He sits back in his chair and looks at her, trying to figure out where to start.

"I know he wandered off the other night."

He gives her a shrug.

"And he got that crack on the head. That can't be good. Does he have a concussion or something?"

"No. I mean, yes, he got cracked on the head, that's true, but that was, you know. That was nothing, really. I mean, it has nothing to do with why he's living with me." The point is, he still doesn't know what the old man's up to. Why he's here, exactly, or why he took off in the car this morning without a note or a warning. Gerald simply woke up and Dad was gone. Could mean nothing; could mean everything. The only evidence of his father's having been here at all is the read newspaper in the kitchen, though that was more than likely Brent's doing. "Here's a confession, if that's what you want. Two days ago I read my health insurance policy for the first time in my life. You realize I have a thousand-dollar deductible? Can they do that?"

Nora shrugs. "At least you have insurance. I didn't have any until this summer."

He knows what she means: he, too, didn't have insurance when he was in grad school. All he had to live on was his stipend, which barely covered his rent, so how could he afford insurance? "How are you paying for it?"

She tears off another chunk of her bagel and looks away. "I'm on Brent's policy, that's how."

"Typical."

She looks back at him, offended. "What's that supposed to mean?"

"Just that Brent has it, and you don't. He works for the same university as you, doesn't he?"

"Right, but I don't work for them. That's the whole problem."

"You teach for them."

"Yes, in exchange for this wonderful education I'm getting."

"They should give you health insurance. That's all I'm saying."

"Gosh, you're absolutely right." She gives him a playful pat on the shoulder. "I'll be sure to take that up in the next Graduate Student Union meeting."

"Oh, I can just see that: the Graduate Student Union. They'd love that, wouldn't they? All these egghead Ivy-League Marxists thinking they've finally achieved solidarity with the proletariat."

"Don't start up, Gerald. Smug superiority doesn't become you."

"Which is why I left grad school."

"Oh, that wasn't the only reason," she accuses, though he can't help but detect something almost flirtatious in the charge.

"Oh, yeah? Why else?"

She tears off another chunk of her bagel and chews on it meditatively. "Because you couldn't hack it."

"Wrong: I didn't *want* to hack it. There's a difference."

"And to get away from me."

He pauses here long enough to drink some more coffee. Already it's getting cold. He gets up to refill his cup. The summer sun streams through the window over the sink, dousing the kitchen in a snug warmth he wants to sustain for as long as possible. He has a premonition that this is the last comfortable moment he'll be able to enjoy for a long while. Turning back around, he admits, "I was confused back then."

"And you're not now?"

He laughs. "No. I'd say I'm still pretty bewildered."

She seems to like this answer. When she leans back in her chair to consider him more directly, he has to force himself to maintain eye contact, that vision of her left breast still sitting like a dollop of warmth in his gut. "You miss it?"

"Miss what?" For a crazy moment he thinks she means their relationship, but quickly catches his error. "You mean graduate school?"

"Sure." She pushes the plate away from her and asks, "Pour me a cup of that, will you?"

"It's pretty strong stuff."

"I think I can handle it."

He opens the cabinet in which Brent keeps all his coffee mugs, but unfortunately it looks like they're all in the sink. Which is his fault: he drinks coffee more or less all day, and so goes through coffee mugs as quickly as he goes through cigarettes. Lifting mugs from the sink, he asks, "Any of these yours?"

"Just rinse one out, Gerald."

"Suit yourself." As he runs water through a blue mug with the university's logo stenciled in gold on the side—Gerald himself has about three of these babies in his own apartment—he looks out the window and ponders her question. Brent's backyard isn't much bigger than the living room. There's a cement birdbath in the center of grass cut neatly to the stub, and that's about it. Though he would never tell Nora as much, he's found Brent's house to be a fairly cold and soulless place. Brent hardly owns a single book, for instance, and even fewer CDs. What does he do here all the time, besides work on his computer? Maybe that's the answer right there. "I miss the idea of it, I guess."

"The *idea* of it?" She's mocking him—but gently.

He slides the coffee mug in front of her and takes his own seat. "Something like that. I miss the thought of being an academic, or the idea of becoming a professor someday, with an office and a tweed blazer, all of that."

"The tweed blazer is key. They give you that at graduation, you know."

"Which in your case should happen when?"

She glares at him for a moment. He's overstepped. He'd meant to volley back at her, rib her a bit, but it seems he's hit a sore spot. But she maintains the genial mood by answering, "We don't talk about that subject around here."

"You have to be sick of it by now, Nora."

"You kidding?" She picks up her coffee mug, takes a sip, and raises her eyebrows in surprise. He tried to tell her: by his second pot of the day he shoots for Turkish mud. Squaring her shoulders, she tosses her disheveled hair aside in a show of mock bravura, whereupon he suddenly remembers she's pregnant. That's why her breasts seem so prominent. They're *bigger*—the realization of which thrills him inordinately. "That place would fall apart without me."

"Oh, I can believe that," he says seriously. "Everyone adored you up there, as I remember."

"As did you."

"That I did." The past tense verbs chastise them to silence. Nora takes another sip of coffee as Gerald, his heart in his throat, wonders frantically how to get the conversation back on track.

But Nora apparently has other things on her mind. "Speaking of adoration," she begins, her tone abruptly clinical and challenging, "what's up with you and Sasha all of a sudden?"

He's genuinely taken aback, though on quick reflection he accepts that he shouldn't be. Now that he thinks about it, her interest in this subject is even a little gratifying. "Nothing's up, exactly."

"I see." Nervously, she swivels her cup between her hands. "Well, humor me, then. What was she doing tracking you down the night of my wedding? And why did she show up at your house that day I swung by?"

"I don't know. Maybe she's just looking for a friend."

"Or maybe she's making a play for you."

He now recalls his mortifying performance Saturday night, since when he hasn't said a word to Sasha, largely because he moved in here the very next day, with no one the wiser. He wonders if she's been calling his apartment all week and bothering the Grauffbauts, whoever they are. More likely, she never wants to talk to him again. Which at least gets him off the hook, a state he generally prefers anyway. For some reason, though, he doesn't altogether like it now. How much longer can he spend his life trying to stay clear of everyone's hook? "Trust me, Nora, that's not even in the cards."

"If you say so."

"Look, why do you even care what Sasha's up to? She has nothing to do with you any longer."

For some reason, the remark unsettles her. She fidgets some more with her coffee cup and looks away. "Don't be so sure about that."

"Actually," he begins, treading lightly here, "I kind of need to confess something."

She turns back to him, her eyebrow cocked with concern. "Am I going to like this?"

"Probably not." He sits forward and settles his elbows on the table. A tense silence opens between them, during which Brent's black freezer dislodges a tiny avalanche of ice. This would be a good time for the old man to come bursting in, full of excuses and evasive bluster. But the silence, uncomfortable and unsettling, stretches on.

"Well?"

"Okay, here's what happened. Saturday night I was with Sasha—"

She interrupts him with a stagy cough.

"It wasn't like that, Nora. We were just hanging out." When she appears to accept this, he continues: "She went to Centennial Park with me and my dad. Perfectly innocent. Not a bad evening, as far as that part of it went." He pauses here with the realization that for this story to make any sense he probably needs to address Sasha's remarks about his lingering feelings for Nora. But he quickly dismisses this idea. "Later that night we started talking about Aaron and a bunch of other stuff, and I thought she wanted me to ... I don't know. Supply her with info, let's say."

"What kind of info?" The question comes swiftly, with more than a hint of anger.

"Take a guess." But Nora merely stares at him, her jaw firm. This was a bad idea. But better tell her himself than have Aaron rat him out. "About his fooling around, that type of thing. You saw what happened at the reception. Naturally, she wants me to reveal what I know. She'd already hinted as much earlier in the week. It's not too complicated, really." Nora gives him the briefest wisp of a nod. Her eyes, he now notices, are moist with concern. But he barrels ahead anyway. "The long and short of it is, I *might* have said something about you and Aaron."

Without warning, Nora emits a helpless little yelp. Wide-eyed and frightened, she covers her mouth with her hand and gets up from the table. It all happens so fast Gerald is more surprised than worried.

"Nora?" She's standing at the sink with her back to him. "Honestly, I didn't actually *say*—"

But before he can finish she whirls back around, her jaw quivering and her hands clutching the counter for support. Incongruously Gerald now realizes those aren't boxers she's wearing after all; they're just ratty old white running shorts with an elastic band.

"Who told you?" she demands.

"Told me what?"

"Stop it, Gerald. Please. This is painful enough as it is."

"Nora, wait. You're not listening to me. All I said to Sasha was . . ." He trails off again, unsure how to explain. What did he actually say? And what, precisely, is he guilty of? Nora's angry response has him so rattled he's starting to wonder if he even has anything to confess. "Look, she was asking about you, so I thought she wanted to know what you've told me about Aaron. That's all. I said—I don't know the exact words, it was something like, 'Do you want me to tell you what Nora knows?' That's the basic gist, anyway." To his relief, this explanation seems to have a calming effect on her: slowly, she releases the counter and relaxes her shoulders. But her eyes remain on full alert. "The point is," he continues, "I'm afraid Aaron overheard me."

And just like that, he's thrown her again. With a helpless whimper she buries her face in her hands and vigorously shakes her head. He can't figure out where the trip wire is. He keeps thinking he's in the clear, then *wham*.

"But we're cool," he assures her. "Aaron and me. Trust me. I'm never going to say another—"

He stops again. She's just mumbled something he didn't catch, muffled as it was by her hands.

Tentatively, he says, "Come again?"

She drops her arms in frustration and confronts him head-on. "I slept with him."

And though he thinks he understands what she's just admitted, he inanely concedes, "Right, in college. I knew that."

"I mean *recently*, Gerald." She hesitates here so that this can sink in. She even smiles a bit—the merest crooked edge of a smile, more self-damning than proud, though there's a touch of pride there, too. And it works. The news, now fully present in his imagination, sinks right in.

His voice trembling slightly, he asks, "How recently?"

She glances away in thought. Now he really does want that cigarette. He even thinks about lighting up right here in the kitchen, if only to assert his independence. But that would be tantamount to shouting an obscenity in church: the imp of the perverse, the old man called it, quoting E. A. Poe. All the more reason to do it. "Last spring," she whispers. Again, she pauses long enough for this piece of information to register, though this time, for a variety of reasons, he resists the opportunity to trace all the possible implications. "When Brent and I split up."

But of course. That's what Aaron was so angry about: he thought *this* was what Gerald was going to tell Sasha. And Nora's been sitting here thinking the exact same thing. So far this news doesn't make him feel anything in particular—how big a deal is this, really?—besides an unseemly desire to know more. Nevertheless, of all the questions he could ask right now, the first one that comes to mind is "Was this before or after you came by my apartment that day?"

Apparently it's the question Nora expected. "After," she quickly replies, with an air of accusation. All he can do is sit at the table and gently nod. He thinks he might be smiling, he's not sure. Part of him is sitting at this table talking to Nora, while another part of him has returned to that March afternoon when Nora sat on his couch with a beer ("I feel so *free*") and he sent her back to Brent. Though apparently he first sent her to Aaron. At least that seems to be what Nora is telling him.

"How soon after?"

"I don't even know why I'm telling you this."

But he knows why. In their back-and-forth about the old days they had opened up a place where the present didn't matter, where other people, even husbands, were secondary figures in the primary drama of their friendship. But he doesn't say this. What he says is, "At least you and Brent were broken up at the time."

"Oh, so that gets me off the hook?"

"Well, it's not exactly something June Cleaver would do, but I think you can be forgiven. Though, I have to say, I've never understood what you see in that son of a bitch."

"Oh," she sighs, "he's a college flame. Every woman loves a bastard, isn't that the line from Plath?"

"Fascist," he corrects her. "Every woman loves a *fascist*."

"Oh. Well, I don't think I agree with that. No wonder she killed herself."

"He is a bastard, though. You're right about that."

"Yes and no. Mostly yes, though." She emits a sniffled little laugh and rubs her nose with her wrist, very much the little girl now, bare-legged and pigeon-toed. "I was confused, that's all.

Brent was hinting around about marriage, and I panicked. I wasn't sure about him, so I ended it. Then I went by your place, and we got into that fight—"

"That wasn't a fight," he objects.

"Yes, it was, Gerald. It was a fight." She stares him down so that he has no choice but to concede the point. "Anyway," she goes on, "I left your place even more confused than when I showed up, and wanted to talk to someone, *anyone*. So I beeped Aaron, who called me back in like five minutes. Half hour later he was at my place. Lucky me, he was off rotation that day. Wouldn't you just know it? And Sasha was in Savannah, doing whatever she does."

"She's a drug rep," he reminds her.

"I know that, Gerald. She was in my fucking *wed*ding." She joins him at that table now. The day is advancing outside. It's getting so hot that Gerald can feel against the side of his cheek a faint nimbus of heat pressing through the kitchen window: shitty insulation, but of course these are all old houses, seventy years old at least. "I'd already had that one beer at your house," she continues, her voice quieter now, "and I had another while waiting for Aaron to come over. Soon we were doing tequila shots. A couple of hours later, I was drunk and bawling about something or other, and I more or less invited Aaron to take advantage of an emotionally distraught woman—his favorite kind, I'm pretty sure. *Quelle surprise*, he accepted the invitation."

"Boy, there's a shocker."

"So the next morning I woke up hungover and miserable, and before you could say 'Get thee to a nunnery,' I was betrothed to Brent."

"And then you found out you were pregnant."

"Yeah, well, that's the other part of all this I haven't told you about."

She's peering tentatively at him from beneath her blond bangs, both contrite and exceptionally alert. Which is when it hits him: Nora and her resistance to the Pill.

More fiercely than intended, he demands, "Tell me Aaron used a condom."

"Technically, yes."

"What does that mean?"

"It means we had one, but there was trouble with it." She narrows her eyes at him now. "You know how that can be."

But he resents the implication, however joshingly presented. A little too close to home. "This isn't horseshoes and hand grenades, Nora."

"It isn't?" She sits back in her chair and drops her arms helplessly at her side. "Kind of feels like a hand grenade to me."

To calm his heart, he decides to voice what they're stepping around anyway. "You really think it's his?"

"No," she quickly responds, even shakes her head for emphasis.

"How can you be so sure?"

"Well, I'm not. But I'm pretty close. It just so happens that he and Sasha have been trying to get pregnant for three years, and nothing's happened yet."

As Sasha confirmed last Monday night. So he'll give Nora that one. Plus, didn't Sasha say she'd already been to a fertility specialist? Which implies she isn't the problem. "Right, I knew that."

Nora looks hurt. "You did? How?"

"Sasha told me."

"Boy, you two *have* gotten chummy."

He decides to ignore this swipe. "You still can't rule it out."

"Maybe."

"You need to tell Brent."

"Hmm, I don't know about that."

He waits for her to elaborate. But she lasts him out. "Explain to me why not, Nora."

"Because it's more than likely Brent's baby, that's why. And if so, there's no reason he needs to know. It was a mistake, I admit it, but in the grand scheme of things it was a forgivable mistake, as you've just pointed out. And I did say yes to him before I found out. That considerably alters the dynamic, you have to admit. All I'm saying is, I see no reason to ruin my marriage before it even gets started."

"None of which applies if the baby's Aaron's."

"Which is unlikely."

"That's a pretty weak rationalization, Nora."

"Yeah, well, rationalizations are sort of weak by definition, aren't they? That's why they're rationalizations."

"You sound like my father," he laughs. An acidic discharge of dread hits his gut—his standard response to reminders of the old man, though this time the unease feels more directed and specific. Dad still hasn't returned from wherever he's run off to. Hours have passed, and not a word.

Though she appears reluctant to change the subject, Nora asks, "Wasn't I supposed to take you somewhere to meet up with him?"

"Not exactly."

"But I thought you said—"

"I was being ironic, Nora."

"Oh."

"In fact, I have no idea where he is. I woke up this morning and he was poof, gone, without a trace."

"So what? He's a grown-up. He can come and go as he pleases. Didn't he leave a note or anything?"

"No, which is what worries me. That and the fact that he seems to have taken all his stuff."

She pauses here. "Like what stuff?"

"You know, his stuff. His clothes and whatever."

"How do you know?"

"Because I've looked everywhere. His room is neat, the bed's made, and his clothes are missing. As is my green backpack." The one Nora bought him years ago for his birthday, he doesn't bother to add. The look on her face tells him the detail registers. For the last four nights Gerald's been sleeping on the cold leather couch in Brent's study while his father, after much arguing back and forth, has been camped out in the guest room, thereby securing him his first bed in weeks.

"So maybe he's out doing laundry."

"But you have a washer and dryer here," he objects.

"So? You know your dad. He probably doesn't want to presume. I bet he's sitting at a Laundromat right now, lounging through the rinse cycle."

He gives her a halfhearted nod. For although he has to concede that this explanation makes sense, it doesn't convince, somehow. After all, Gerald's endured these disappearances before. There's a crisp finality here that he recognizes from past experiences—the neatly made bed, the complete absence of any note, the dramatic timing. In the fall of 1983, for instance, on the weekend marking the tenth anniversary of Mom's death, his father unexpectedly disappeared for three days—again, no note, no explanation—and returned the following Monday with the cheerful news that he had been visiting friends and touring the White House, in Washington, D.C. The emptiness of Brent and Nora's house has the same eerie feel that his own home did that fall weekend, with Eva off at college and Gerald fending for himself with pizza and cable television and a bag of pot. How to explain all this to Nora?

"You were asking about him before," he begins.

"Yes," she whispers.

"You've noticed he's lost weight. I mean, he barely eats anything, you've seen that for yourself. And he's tired all the time, and so on. The long and short of it is, he needs a kidney transplant.

He's already lost one kidney, and the other's not far behind. The doctor says he has about two months and then he's, you know. He's whatever. He's . . . Anyway, that's what this doctor told my sister. Dad wouldn't know because he doesn't ever *go* to doctors. Simply refuses. It's like that story, the one by Melville. 'I would prefer not to.' Bartleby Brinkman: that's my dad."

"Gerald," she says gently, and reaches for his arm.

But he pulls away and continues. "But here's the big complication. He knows fully well I could give him a transplant—I'm young, I'm relatively healthy—but he refuses to let me do that. Instead, he apparently wants to sit here and die a painful, slow death. With me watching."

"My God."

"Already talked to God. No reply, as usual. Oh, and those discussions you keep hearing? Know what they're about? Here's the conversation in a nutshell. 'Dad, we have to go to the hospital tomorrow. I'm giving you my kidney.' 'No, son,' " Gerald continues in a deep-voiced imitation of his father, " 'that's quite all right. You're young, you keep that kidney of yours. You'll need it more than I.' 'No, Dad: *you* need it. I still have another one.' 'So have two. You never know when you might need an extra. Look at me.' 'Dad, you must let me do this for you. You can't die on me.' 'Of course I can, son. That's what fathers do: they die. They make room.' "

"Gerald, stop."

" 'But, Dad,' " he continues, alternating voices as appropriate, " 'I don't *want* you to die.' 'Oh, you're just saying that to be nice.' 'No, I'm not, Daddy: I really want to save your life.' 'Oh, now, you can't kid a kidder. I know how a son feels. Every son wants to kill his father. Read your Freud.' 'Oh, but Daddums, that's not true at all.' 'Sure it is. Killing your pop is the oldest archetype there is. You're in good company, good ancient company.' 'But I don't want to be in good company, Dad. I want *your* company.' 'No, you don't, Gerald. Stop jiving me.' 'Oh, how can you say that, Daddy? How can you believe that about me?' 'Easy, son: because I'm a stubborn bastard who's determined to ruin your fucking life.' " Here Gerald's voice catches. He stands up and turns from her, bracing himself on the counter.

"Gerald, sweetie." He hears her push her chair back; a moment later he feels her hand gently touch his back. "Honestly, I had no idea. That's so awful."

Her saying this releases a glob of grief in his throat. He's not sure what has him more upset—his father's predicament and his own helplessness to do anything about it, or the sudden sad realization that Nora, married, pregnant, and compromised by her own recklessness, is truly, irrevocably lost to him. He's known this for months, of course, but only now does he feel it in his bones. His father's disappearance has done that for him. Chalk up another victory for the old man.

"Gerald," she whispers, still stroking his back. When he releases the counter and stands upright she slides between him and the sink, and before he can pull away she has him firmly wrapped in her arms. Gratefully, he burrows his nose into the curve of her neck, where, he remembers from the old days, she smells most like herself, the maple scent of her morning skin tinged at the edge with a delicate dusting of dried flowers from whatever soap she uses. Her back is smooth beneath the T-shirt she's wearing. He can even feel her spine against the inside of his forearms. So conscious is he of these sensations that he barely registers the fact that he is whimpering like a baby into her neck. She continues to hold him, murmuring, "It's okay, just let it out," and tracing soothing ovals across his shoulder blades with her warm palms.

Embarrassed, he wipes his cheek against his shoulder and pulls back to get his bearings. But Nora refuses to release him. Instead, she takes his face in her hands and runs her thumbs across his cheekbones, drying them, her own eyes wet with concern. Her beauty here in the morning light stabs him in the chest. His mouth, which hovers inches from hers, hangs slack.

"Why didn't you tell me all this?" she asks, her moist breath bitter with coffee.

He fears that by saying anything he'll start crying again, so he closes his eyes and shakes his head, which isn't much of an answer. When he opens his eyes she's somehow inched even closer, her hands still cradling his face. She tilts her head to the side as if she's about to say something. At the same time—no getting around it— he notices that her eyelids are invitingly half closed. Before he can rethink what he's about to do, he leans in. Desire blooms within him as he presses his mouth against hers and backs her into the counter. To his relief, her soft lips respond, her breath mixing intoxicatingly with his own and the warm presence of her body at such intimate proximity causing his knees to tremble. He almost has her shoulders in his grip before she rears her head back and pushes him away.

But it's too late: she had received him: he'd *felt* it.

Blinking in surprise, he manages enough presence of mind to say, "God, I'm so sorry, Nora, I don't know what I was—"

"You cannot *do this to me*!" she cries, clutching her head.

"I know, I wasn't thinking. I was just—"

"Not after everything I just *told* you!"

"I realize that. Listen to me, Nora—"

She strikes him on the chest with her fist, a good solid blow that actually *hurts*. "You've fucked up my life once already," she hisses, and raises her fist again. "And I'll be damned if I'm going to let you—"

But before she can take another swing, the front doorbell rings.

ELEVEN

GERALD STANDS frozen in the kitchen, his heart bouncing off the inside of his rib cage. His first thought is *Brent*. Nothing more than that: just the name. In the last five minutes he has not even permitted himself to think the name *Brent*, let alone say it, but now the word pops right into his consciousness like a submerged bath toy released to the surface. There it is: the husband's name. And there, too, might be the actual husband, standing on the other side of that front door. Then it hits him: Brent wouldn't ring his own doorbell. The idea fills him with elation. Of course! It can't be Brent! Brent wouldn't ring his own bell!

"*Answer* it, Gerald." Nora's already backed herself halfway across the room, her eyes wide.

"But this is your house."

"I'm barely *dressed*," she explains, peering at him now from around the corner.

"Oh, Nora, come on—"

The doorbell rings again.

"Gerald!"

"Okay, calm down, I'm going."

Nevertheless, his heart's still pounding as he walks through the empty house and straightens his hair. All the objects he passes—the pictures on the wall, the furniture, the end tables and lamps—silently admonish him. I cannot stay here, he tells himself. But where can I go? How am I going to get there? Before turning the front doorknob he has to pause and collect himself, wipe all moisture from his cheeks, slow down his heart. The bell rings again.

When he opens the door, he is surprised to be staring not into the eyes of his AWOL dad, nor into the eyes of a smiling, brown-suited UPS carrier, but rather into the icy blue eyes of his mysterious benefactor, that errant friend of his father's, Dr. Stanley Torrent.

"My God."

"Oh, thank *goodness*," Dr. Torrent exclaims, and lightly touches his breastplate, and takes a deep breath. "You can't imagine how relieved I am to see you. I kept driving up and down the street because I wasn't sure if ... Well, you see, I saw that car outside and I heard some voices, but when no one answered I thought, perhaps ..." He consults a slip of paper in his other hand and, raising it, gives Gerald a hollow smile. "Well, in any case, I found you."

Gerald hasn't seen Torrent in seven—or is it eight?—years, at least not since his 1989 graduation from college (Gerald took a leisurely five years to finish). Though Torrent still looks as dapper as usual, the years have clearly caught up with him. His pinkish, delicate skin, as thin as cigarette paper and nearly as dry, now sports bright red gin blossoms, nature's price for decades of lunchtime martinis. The thin gray mustache that outlines his prissy lips has turned completely white, while the thinning hair on his head is now a sallow, nicotine yellow. The ordered symmetrical lines of his handsome face have shifted and sagged and warped: his mouth now seems lodged in a groove like a ventriloquist's doll, his ears now sprout little tufts of white hair, his neck is a tangle of creases and tendons. One thing that hasn't changed: he still dresses like the Northeastern WASP that he is. On this muggy day in July he wears pleated madras shorts, Italian Cole Haan slippers, and a pink Polo shirt, collar upturned. Gerald wouldn't be surprised if Torrent invited him for a quick game of squash at the club.

"Who is it?" Nora calls from the hallway.

Gerald turns around. Nora is tucking a sleeveless black shirt into a pair of pleated dress slacks.

"I'm sorry," Torrent calls from the doorway, "I didn't mean to interrupt. I know I should have called—"

"Please," Gerald cuts in, and finally extends a hand. "You're not interrupting a thing, Dr. Torrent. I'm glad to see you."

"Dr. Torrent?" Nora is beside him now. Hooking a strand of hair behind her ear, she extends her right hand. "So *you're* the mysterious Dr. Torrent?"

"Oh, I wouldn't know about that," he smiles, revealing a knife's edge of yellow yet still-perfect teeth. "Mysterious sounds rather grand, doesn't it? And you would be . . . ?"

"Nora," Gerald tells him, and ushers the gracious gentleman inside. "Nora Reynolds, an old friend. She's putting us up for the next couple of weeks."

"Putting up with them is more like it," she says dryly.

"Oh, yes, well, I can imagine."

They all file into the living room, which is dark and brooding, the pulled blinds admitting thin shafts of light that seem alive with flitting insects of dust. As he takes a seat on the couch, Gerald tries to steady the tremor in his chest. None of this makes sense. The miraculous appearance of this strange emissary from his past can only be the work of his father who, in his majestic absence, has been transformed into the deus ex machina of all these odd proceedings, even including that stupendously dumb moment of madness with Nora. He's visited by a vision of his father crouching outside one of these living room windows, a clipboard cradled in his arm and a set of binoculars fixed to his eyes.

"Splendid house," Torrent observes, looking around. He has perched himself uncomfortably on the edge of Brent's sleek leather easy chair—some sort of futuristic La-Z-Boy knockoff—his knees clasped together as if in anticipation of a saucer and cup of English tea. A rod of sunlight bisects his bony shins.

"Well," Nora sighs, depositing herself dramatically on the couch beside Gerald, "it's a start. Actually, this is my husband's place, so most of the stuff is his. Credit where it's due." Playfully, she extends her left hand and turns it in the murky light. Her wedding ring winks at the two bachelors in the room. "A newlywed, doncha know."

Torrent leans forward and adjusts his tortoiseshell spectacles to get a better view of the ring. "Congratulations. When did this happen?"

"Last week. We're staying here for now till my husband can finish this project he's overseeing, then we're off on our honeymoon. Gerald's working for him, in fact."

"You don't say?" He directs his smiling face at Gerald.

"Afraid so," Gerald responds. "We're one big happy family."

Stealing a warning glance at him, Nora slides her hands between her knees and turns back to Torrent. "Can I get you anything, Dr. Torrent? Something to eat, some breakfast? I think there's some coffee left."

"Oh, no, I don't wish to be a nuisance."

"It's no trouble," Gerald tells him. "I think I'll have a cup if there's any left."

"Oh, I'm sure I can squeeze out a drop or two. You sure I can't tempt you, Dr. Torrent?"

"Well, now that you mention it, that would be fine. I take it black."

"Don't we all," she says cryptically, and heads to the kitchen.

Silence descends upon the room, adding to the already gloomy atmosphere. A small chamber orchestra of domestic music issues from the kitchen: coffee cups clank on the counter, a faucet hisses, a carafe bumps the edge of a coffeemaker. As Torrent continues to drag an appreciative eye around the living room, Gerald sinks deeper into the couch and considers the possibilities. One, Torrent was scheduled to come on this day; two, Torrent raced here because he already knows something; three, Torrent was summoned here by his father; four, Torrent is here for no discernible reason. Gerald instantly dismisses possibility number four on the grounds that Torrent would have no way of knowing that Gerald was here rather than at his own apartment. Possibilities one and two are comforting since they suggest an explanation for his father's disappearance this morning, a disappearance that now appears to be preplanned and, hopefully, benign. Possibility number three, therefore, is the one Gerald fears most, since it suggests his father might be well on his way to doing something irreparably bad.

"Here we are," Nora calls as she reenters the room. She has arranged the coffee mugs, along with a pair of bagels, neatly on a silver platter. Gerald isn't sure what Nora is up to here: Dr. Torrent seems to have catalyzed in his friend some sort of dormant Martha Stewart gene. Nora has even picked up on Torrent's manner of speaking, with its royal we's and ironic WASPisms. Doncha know. Or is she just covering her agitation from that encounter back in the kitchen?

Torrent removes his mug and smiles up at her. "What a lovely tray. Is it a wedding gift?"

"That's a roger." She places the tray prominently on the coffee table and stands back to give it an appreciative look. "I've got reams of this stuff, half of it I'll never use in a million years. Now if you'll excuse me, I've got to run out for a moment."

Gerald looks up from his coffee. "You do?"

She scowls at him briefly before turning back to Torrent. "I'm trying to finish my dissertation, and I made a solemn vow to put in some library hours today."

"I don't wish to run you off."

She waves him quiet. "Don't give it another thought."

Gerald is about to ask *What about me?* but then stops. What's the point? There's no chance of his going into work today, not with this latest bombshell. If Torrent is in fact here to tell him about his father, Gerald will no doubt need the rest of the afternoon—the rest of his life, perhaps—to process the news, so work is pretty much out of the question for now. And anyway, he isn't sure he can face Brent today. Gerald tells her, "We'll lock up if we go anywhere."

Torrent stands up and extends his hand to Nora. "I certainly hope this hasn't been an imposition."

"Not in the slightest," she says, and hooks her hair behind her ear again before waving ta ta.

He listens as her car starts up and pulls away from the house. Not until the silence between them grows embarrassing does Torrent set down his coffee cup, rub his thin fingers along his knees, and clear his throat. "So."

"Dad must have sent you."

He bites his bottom lip Clinton-style and nods. "He called last night from a pay phone somewhere. I got the first flight in this morning. I don't have to tell you it wasn't easy. Flights into Atlanta are a mite full this week." He smiles gently, cradles his fingers between his knees, looks toward the window. "I don't suppose he told you I was coming."

"I haven't seen him all morning."

"That's what I thought."

"So you're right, he didn't tell me anything." Gerald waits for Torrent to add more. "Where is he?"

"I haven't the foggiest idea."

"But you knew he was taking off."

"I suspected as much, yes."

"And that's all you can tell me?"

"No, that's not all." He stands up in the middle of the room and paces around, stopping in front of a bookshelf, where he adjusts his glasses and leans forward to read the titles. As Brent apparently owns no books—not that Gerald knows of, anyway—these would be Nora's gender-theory and philosophy texts. Still with his back turned to him, Torrent says, "I'm in a difficult situation, Gerald. I don't know what all you know."

"About what?" Despite his own mounting impatience, Gerald does feel sort of sorry for the guy. He also feels sorry for Nora and Sasha and everyone else his father has dragged into this protracted performance. For two weeks now Gerald has been trying to keep the burden of his father solely poised on his own shoulders, yet his father keeps pulling new people in. It's as if he's trying to surround Gerald in advance with mourners so that he can slip out quietly while the wake is still swinging. "I know he sold the house. I know about the kidney disease and his plans to let it run its course. I know he came here to be with me, though for what I have no idea." He hesitates long enough for Torrent to break in. "And now I know he called you."

Torrent settles back in the La-Z-Boy and stares into the coffee mug cupped in his hands. Perhaps the thing he has come here to say is floating around in there. Perhaps he has nothing to say. "Your father and I," he begins, and waits. "We have a long history, as you already know."

Gerald stays silent.

"He was a brilliant theologian, your father. I hope you appreciate that. Maybe you don't, I don't know, but it bears repeating. He was spectacular. No one could touch him at Harvard. His knowledge of the writings, both ancient and modern, was encyclopedic, as was his grasp of continental philosophy—all of it. Nietzsche, Heidegger, Wittgenstein—none of this was too arcane, too secular, for him. It was he who first demonstrated to me how profoundly mystical Heidegger's philosophy of being really was, and he did so by reading and translating the original German texts for his own purposes. He was something, all right. Years ahead of the curve." Apparently having found in his coffee cup what he was looking for, Torrent shifts his gaze to Gerald. "He was a born theologian, Gerald, a born academic. He was so proud when you entered graduate school yourself. He told me once, 'Stanley, he's going to live the life I should have lived.' I'll never forget that as long as I live. It pretty much says everything that needs to be said about his life."

"But I quit graduate school," Gerald reminds him. Now he really is impatient. What does any of this have to do with the matter at hand? Where is Dad? "I'm sorry, Dr. Torrent, but I can't believe he sent you here to convince me he was a great theologian."

Torrent permits himself a brief, tentative laugh. "No, you're right. I apologize. I'm getting horribly off track." As if to make amends for his lack of focus, he sets the coffee mug on the stand beside him and, seizing the arms of the chair for support, settles back in the chair. "I feel wrong to be telling you this, Gerald, and at the same time I feel relieved that it is coming from me and not from him. I think I can set you straight in a way your father cannot. Or will not, whichever you choose."

"Just tell me if he's all right."

"You mean right now?" He peers over his glasses, then returns his gaze to the ceiling. "I can't tell you that. What I mean is, I don't know. I have no more idea where he is right now than you do."

"Then what did he say to you on the phone? I mean, with all due respect, Dr. Torrent, my father is dying. Please just tell me what he told you."

[238]

He takes a moment to collect himself. "Last night he called and asked me if I could come here to Atlanta and tell you what *he* originally came here to tell you. I asked him why, and he said he didn't think he could go through with it. So I told him I would do no such thing, and he insisted I must. Then he told me he was calling from a pay phone, gave me this address, and hung up. That was the whole conversation."

Gerald tries to process all this new information. He remembers his father stepping out for a walk last night, and then returning an hour or two later, so perhaps he made the call then. Perhaps that much is solved. But Torrent's explanation tells him precious little, otherwise. "I'm not sure I understand. I mean, he told me already. Actually, he didn't tell me, I found out. But it amounts to the same thing."

"You already know?" Torrent looks genuinely surprised.

"About the kidney disease? Sure."

"Oh, *that*." Torrent's chest sags with relief—or is it defeat? "I see what you mean. Yes. Well, I'm afraid that isn't what he came here to tell you. Not that it isn't important, Lord knows. But that's not what he sent me here to tell you."

And now Gerald begins to comprehend. All last week his father kept saying *I haven't told you why I'm here, I haven't explained to you why I've come all this way.* Once Gerald confronted him about his illness, he figured that was that: mystery solved. Yet his father continued to pause and prevaricate. During each of those long conversations about the transplant, Dad would reach a point where he would be rendered speechless, where his words seemed to dry up within him, and that would generally end the discussion. Gerald had assumed that his father was afraid to talk about his own death, but now he isn't so sure about this explanation. There's still something else. There was always something else.

"Is it about my mother?" The words fall from his lips before he has a chance to consider them in advance.

To his surprise, Torrent nods. "In a way, yes. Listen to me, Gerald. Your father is a curious man. He is both stubborn and passive at the same time. In a way, his passivity *is* his stubbornness. It's the one aspect of your father I've never understood. But it's always been there, even back at Harvard." He stops to collect his thoughts. "Earlier I was talking about his tremendous potential as a scholar, as a full-fledged theologian." After a moment, he says, "Bear with me, please. I've been going over this discussion all night, trying to figure out the best way to tell you what I have to tell you, and for better or worse, this is it."

When he doesn't offer any more, Gerald takes this as his cue to signal his approval. "Fine. However you want."

"I'll try to be brief. Where was I?"

"Theological promise."

"Exactly, yes. So you can imagine how surprised we all were when he chose the pulpit. By we, of course, I mean your mother and me. They were dating by this point—she was at Radcliffe—so the three of us were already inseparable. We were all in each other's back pockets, if you will. Your father's decision surprised us because, back then, *I* was the one slated for the ministry, while your father was the academic in training. That was how things originally stacked up. But at some point we exchanged roles. I'm not sure when this happened, exactly. It just did. It happened. For my part I realized early on I didn't have the ... What should I call it? The moral fortitude, let's say, to assume the pulpit. But your father did have it. So maybe that's why we traded ambitions. It's almost like he felt obligated to take up the call I rejected." Outside a lawn mower falls silent. Around them the house clicks and hums. Appliances quietly hold their own counsel. "I don't think your mother ever forgave him for that, Gerald. I'm sorry to be telling you this, but it's the truth. She was the daughter of academics herself, so it made sense, this desire for a comfortable, liberal, middle-class academic life. But she also loved your father, and that decided it. She accepted her fate and did not complain."

As it happens, Gerald did know this much. Although he'd never heard the whole story, he knew he had a disappointed woman as a mommy. Even as a child he was aware of how dissatisfied she was with her life. He had often heard her speak disparagingly of his father's congregation, referring to the wives collectively as "the schoolmarms" and the husbands as "the deacons." He remembers her disastrous attempts to update the church, particularly the youth ministry. One Christmas she arranged a youth choral presentation featuring both classic hymns and contemporary tunes like "You've Got a Friend" and "The Weight," a night Gerald can still remember as distinctly as any other event in his life. For the audience greeted the more recent tunes with scattered, grudging applause, and on the way home she lay hunched in the passenger seat crying miserably into a Kleenex. He also remembers his father saying nothing, not one single word, that entire drive.

"I know she didn't like the congregation much," Gerald says quietly. "I just never knew why."

"And now you do." Behind the glinting disks of his glasses Torrent's eyes seem to bob and sway. "I tell you all this to give you some background, Gerald, but that's all. I'm not trying to justify anything, or diffuse the blame, or make myself look good. I just want you to understand the context of what I must tell you now."

"You slept with my mother." Again, he speaks before he has a chance to think. He isn't even sure when this thought first came to him. Has it been dormant in his memory all these years, or has he only now realized it, what with his recent (near!) admission into the ranks of the adulterous? Is this an isolated moment of clarity, or is it the gradual focusing of a piece of foggy insight that has been lurking within him for two decades?

"Unfortunately, yes." Torrent lowers his head and collects himself. "We were lovers, your mother and I, for several years. Too long, in fact." Now he looks up. "I'm sorry, Gerald, but this is difficult for me. I know it must be difficult for you."

"You know something? I could really use a smoke right now. Would you mind if I stepped outside for a moment?"

Torrent closes his eyes and nods. "Of course not."

"Help yourself to more coffee." Gerald begins to stand up, then pauses. "Or whatever else you want."

"Don't worry about me. I'll join you shortly."

When Torrent steps out the front door ten minutes later—or at least long enough for Gerald to start a second cigarette—he's holding a Smucker's glass filled with ice and a clear liquid of some sort that Gerald, knowing Torrent's habits, takes to be gin. Frank's big bottle of Beefeater has been sitting on the kitchen counter since Nora's party last week, so it makes sense the old sot would have helped himself to some, even at this hour. The day is still punishingly bright, more so in contrast to the murk of the living room, the air so witheringly thick it seems alive. Torrent's rental car, a bulbous, pine-green Escort with plastic black fenders, sits crouched at the curb. The shirtless husband across the street has progressed to edging his lawn. Overhead, a cottony streak of jet exhaust curves across the flat blue emptiness of the sky.

"How miserable," Torrent remarks, and takes a dainty sip from the Smucker's jar, his pinkie extended. Gerald assumes he means the weather.

"It's okay, you know. About you and my mom."

"Oh, Gerald . . ."

"Don't feel so awful about it. It's actually one explanation among many that I've been entertaining through the years."

Torrent stops in mid-sip and peers at him over the rim of the jar. Slowly, he lowers the drink. "Explanation for what?"

"For why you and my dad are so weird around each other." He

tosses the cigarette butt into his Folger's can. "I saw you two, once. You and mom."

"Yes, I recall that."

"You were in the kitchen. I came downstairs for some reason—bad dream, loneliness, I don't know—and found you standing behind her with your arms around her waist."

He closes his eyes and nods. "Yes, well, that was long after everything had happened. We weren't lovers then. We'd dropped all that years before."

Gerald considers another cigarette, but decides against it: he would rather finish this discussion inside. Something about all this empty space gives Gerald the creeps. Private truths are being disclosed here, truths too intimate for the outdoors. "So why were you hugging her?"

Surprisingly, he laughs. "You know, I can't remember. Who knows? Probably in response to something your father said. We spent a great many evenings just sitting in your kitchen, hashing out old grievances. I'm sure you can remember that."

"I recall you being there a lot."

"Well, that's what we were doing, most likely. Knifing one another in the back, with tremendous grace and irony. Your father always set the right tone for those discussions. To an outsider, we might have seemed like three dear friends trying to out-compliment one another, while in fact we were cheerfully being perfect bastards, all three of us, like in Congreve."

"That week she died," Gerald begins, and hesitates. He's not sure he wants an answer to this question, though it's a question he's been asking for most of his adult life. "That whole week before the wreck they were fighting about something. Do you remember that?"

Torrent squints into the sun, considering. Then he purses his lips and shakes his head. "Not really."

"She was trying to tell him something when the car crashed."

He looks at Gerald now. Across the street, the neighbor's Weed Eater buzzes. "Where did you hear that?"

"Eva." The admission agitates him, as if he has just betrayed her confidence.

"How would she know?"

"Dad told her."

Torrent takes a moment to let this news sink in; when it does, he relaxes somewhat. "Told her what, exactly?"

"That Mom was on the verge of telling him something. Then they crashed before she could get it out."

"This is your father's story?"

"Yes," Gerald says impatiently, but then halts. "I mean, it's Eva's story. But she got it from Dad, I'm pretty sure."

"Have you ever asked your father about this?"

Not for the first time this morning, he senses the ground opening up beneath him. Because, of course, he's never asked his father a thing. Nor has he since raised the subject with Eva. Over the years, the story—really a mystery without origin or solution—has assumed the glacial gravitas of myth, but now he wonders if he simply made the whole thing up. Has he been nursing a lie all these years? He was only seven at the time, after all. How much does he really remember?

Torrent waits for an answer. But Gerald has no answer to give.

"Maybe we should go back inside," Torrent finally says.

Like schoolchildren staking out their claim to a classroom, Gerald and Torrent return to the living room and silently resume their self-appointed seats.

"So it ended years before she died," Gerald declares, as much to himself as to Torrent. Even more than the news about the affair itself, this is the detail he can't seem to absorb. "That's what you're telling me."

"In a nutshell, yes."

"And this is the big secret Dad came all this way to reveal? That my mom had an affair with you?"

After a pause, Torrent says, "The affair ended several months before you were born, Gerald." When this piece of news fails to get a response, he adds, "It ended *because* you were born."

Gerald can barely make out Torrent's expression. This is due in part to the dim lighting but mostly to the fact that Torrent is staring down at his drink again. "Yes. Okay. So my mom got pregnant and ended the affair." Gerald stops as a faint connection forms in his mind, amid all the other revelations he's trying to absorb here.

Torrent looks up and smiles. No, he grimaces. It is a pained grimace, emotional and physical, and it disappears the moment he swallows the gin he's been swishing around in his mouth. He settles back in the chair and rubs his face with his free hand. "Your father," he says flatly, "has always suspected that the child was not his."

"By 'the child' I take it you mean me."

"Precisely, yes."

Gerald's heart thunders in his ears. Like most people, he has only dimly understood the life he has inhabited all these years. Stuck as he is inside it, his existence is as intimate and yet as mysterious to him as the details of his own face. Whatever level of self-understanding he's achieved over the years has come to him obliquely, indirectly, the result of an ongoing collaboration between his various mirrored images and his own warped, foreshortened view of things. But now he is faced with an entirely new mirrored image, one that promises more self-understanding than he thinks he can bear. He does not need to run through the fat catalog of lifelong mysteries and enigmas that this new information seems to solve; he simply realizes, in a moment of clarity so blinding it gives him vertigo, that everything Torrent is telling him possesses perfect, almost preternatural plausibility. It's the fault line he's been standing upon his entire life. It explains why his father has never really fathered him, particularly after Mom's death. It explains his father's indomitable passivity in the face of every attempt on Gerald's part to get a reaction, whether he was rejecting Harvard or smoking pot in front of him or drifting out of graduate school and into his current life of shapeless indirection. "So," he finally says, "my father thinks you're my father."

"That's one way of putting it."

"And are you?"

"What do you think, Gerald?"

"I have no idea. I mean, either you are or you aren't. It seems a simple enough thing to tell me. Who cares what I think? You know the truth. Tell it to me."

"I'm afraid it's not that simple." The only sound is the angry buzz of the neighbor's Weed Eater. "It's true enough your mother and I were involved at the time that you were conceived, but it's equally true your father and she were also ... well, also involved."

"What kind of birth control did you use?"

"Well," Torrent replies after a delicate pause, "your mother used a diaphragm. Though the Pill was widely available, she didn't go on it in deference to your father, who found the very idea repellent. You've heard his views about the self-regulating body and so on."

"So it's possible, is what you're saying to me."

"But not likely," he insists, whereupon Gerald suddenly draws the connection that pricked at him earlier: Nora and Aaron. He had this same conversation less than twenty minutes ago: more evidence of the old man at work? No, that's absurd.

Again, as if repeating a script, he asks, "Why not? What's the proof?"

"You're the proof," Torrent smiles. "You're your father's son, Gerald. In more ways than you realize."

And that's when the phone rings. Like the doorbell a half hour ago, this latest interruption sends another seismic jolt of fear down his spine. The outside world keeps barging into Gerald's private disasters; he can't find a still moment in which to process everything that's happened to him this morning. Normally when the phone rings in this house he and his father leave it to Nora or to the answering machine, but now he feels compelled to pick it up. A premonition whispers to him that he's the target for this call. Is it Nora? Is it Brent, calling to inform him that he must leave the house immediately? Is it Sasha?

"Don't move," he tells Torrent, and dashes to the kitchen, where there's a wall unit. But he wants the cordless, since it will allow him to take the call outside, if need be. On the fourth ring he tracks it down on the night table beside Nora and Brent's unmade bed. With a weary sense of surrender, he sits down on the edge of the mattress, clicks on the phone, takes a deep breath, steadies his voice, and says hello.

"Bet you're wondering where I am," his father jovially remarks.

"You sonofabitch," Gerald replies, but joyfully. So he's alive. "Where are you?"

"Now now, none of that."

"None of what? You stole my car, in case you've forgotten."

"Borrowed, my boy. And don't be so possessive. Relax, go with the flow."

"Are you at the park? Are you in trouble or something?"

"Tut tut, Gerald. No guessing."

"Who's guessing? I'm asking you direct questions."

"That you are. Now," his father says portentously, "I understand you've had a visitor this morning."

That crazy image of his father crouched outside the living room window returns again, and then just as quickly dissolves. Of course: the old man called Torrent yesterday, so he'd know. "Yeah. Torrent's here."

"Excellent. He's a good man, Gerald. Don't you forget that. He's been wonderful to you all these years. How many people do you know who'd drop everything at a moment's notice and hop on a morning flight?"

"You would," he replies. "You'd do that for me."

"Well, sure. Of course I would. Now, have you two had a nice little visit?"

"Why are you doing this to me, Dad? What's this all about?"

For the first time, his father declines to respond. No false buoyancy, no sham cheeriness: just the sound of breath fanning onto plastic.

Afraid that his father will simply hang up and disappear forever, Gerald says, "He told me, Dad. He told me everything."

"Yes?"

"I mean, about Mom and him. And you. Now listen to me, please. Just listen. You're *wrong*. Everything you've been thinking is *wrong, wrong, wrong*."

"Gerald," he says quietly.

"No, now listen. Last week Eva showed me a picture of you at Harvard. You were about my age, I guess, late twenties or so, and even *she* was struck by the resemblance. You looked *exactly like me*."

"I need to go—"

"*No*, Dad! Don't you dare hang up this phone. Just hold on a second. Listen to me—"

"Someone's banging on the window, Gerald. I can't just—"

"I refuse to believe you've really thought this about me all these years. You must tell me I'm right. You absolutely *must* give me that!"

"Don't do this to me, Gerald."

"To *you*? What the hell am I doing to you?"

"I haven't told you why I called."

"Don't hang up, Dad. Do not fuck with me right now."

"Tomorrow," he instructs, "I need you to come to the park. You remember where we were last Saturday, with Sasha?"

"Of course I do. But I don't see—"

"Just listen for a minute. First, I'm sorry for borrowing your car, but I've got a lot of little errands to run and there wasn't anything else I could do. I'm sure Nora or Brent can get you from point A to point B, and if they can't, then hey, shoot me. Now here's what I need you to do. You work tomorrow, don't you?"

"Yes, but Dad—"

"Excellent. Now it's totally up to you, but if you want to see me one more time before I take off I'll be at that Swatch pavilion tomorrow night at, say, one o'clock. That's in the A.M. Remember that? Remember where I bought my watch?"

"Yes, of course."

"You'll find me there. Easy enough. I have something for you, and I'd like to give it to you in person. It's not crucial for you to show, but it'd sure mean a lot to me if you did."

"Dad, I don't understand."

"Oh, but you will, Gerald. You'll understand everything." Now another silence opens up between them. Gerald cannot bear to let his father off the phone. Yet how can he keep him there? How can he stop this stubborn, passive, indomitable disaster of a man from hanging up and severing their connection forever?

"Please," Gerald whispers. "Please don't hang up on me."

"Just do what I ask, son." Now his father's voice catches. That little sliver of a word—*son*—with its soft beginning and its solid, padded ending, its small middle gap into which an eternity of regret can fall. Gerald gets ready to respond but the connection rattles and goes dead.

He sits perfectly still on the bed, clutching the phone and staring at the bedroom floor. Moments pass before he realizes what he is doing: he is willing the phone to ring. He is holding his breath and chanting silently to himself. The word *ring* blips through his head like a ticker tape, over and over again. Nora and Brent have neither caller ID nor star 69. Hell, they don't even have call waiting. Even through the insistent mental clatter of his one-word mantra, he manages to remind himself of these facts.

"Was it him?"

Torrent stands forlorn and tipsy in the bedroom doorway. That face, that mottled drink-damaged face: is there a clue there to the mess that is Gerald's life? Is there some elusive hint of inheritance buried beneath all that patrician tidiness? He is still contemplating this question when, in answer to his most fervent hopes, the cordless telephone emits a tiny electronic warble. He punches the talk button and shouts, "Dad!"

"Um, no," a voice answers. "Sorry, but I'm not ... Is this the Einhorn residence?"

His heart still racing, Gerald closes his eyes and takes a breath. "Yes. Yes it is."

"Actually," the voice continues, "I'm looking for Gerald Brinkman." The accent is faintly European, with a liquid voluptuousness in the way the voice peels off the L in "looking," as if the man were talking while underwater.

"Speaking."

"Oh, well, good. This is Morris Grauffbaut." After a moment, he adds, "Your boarder."

Now Gerald remembers. Grauffbaut: rhymes with sauerkraut. "Right, right, of course."

"Is this a bad time?"

"Yes. I mean, no." He glances at Torrent, who takes this as his cue to return to the living room—not at all what Gerald intended. Now I've insulted Torrent. When is this morning going to end? "What can I do for you, Mr. Grauffbaut?"

"Well, I just got off the phone a few minutes ago with a Matt Anthony from New York. Something about a job. He called here looking for you and I promised him I would pass on the message."

New York. Debbie Gibson's butt. Anthony said he'd call with an answer by Thursday, and here it is: Thursday. Here's the answer. "Yes, sir," Gerald manages to say, "I know who you mean."

"So you were expecting his call?"

"More or less." For some reason, Grauffbaut chuckles. Another tense moment passes. "Did he say anything else?"

"He just left a phone number. Do you have a pen ready?"

"Yes, sir, just hold on a second." He rummages through the bedside table drawer and finds one of Nora's eyeliner pencils and a *New Yorker* subscription card. "Okay, shoot."

Grauffbaut relays the number and adds, "Best of luck to you. I hope everything works out."

"I doubt it," Gerald replies, "but thanks all the same," and signs off.

He places the phone on the bedside table and stares at the ten numbers he has just scribbled down. They mean nothing to him. How good can the news be, after all? Does he even want this job? Wouldn't he rather stay here with his father, assuming his father returns tomorrow night with his car? By the same token, what is keeping him in Atlanta, aside from his father? He can't stay in this house any longer, and he has no house of his own, and his love life is a shambles, as is his job at the newspaper, particularly since he hasn't been to the office since what, Tuesday? Who cares? That's the indispensable question of the morning. *Who cares?*

TWELVE

FRIDAY MORNING begins much as Thursday night concluded: on the phone. Although for the last twenty-four hours Gerald has successfully avoided calling Matt Anthony, he is resolved this morning to face the music. The magazine subscription card on which he'd scribbled the number sits propped against the phone, ready for action, so he doesn't have to search around for it, he can just pluck up the paper and dial away. He placed it there last night, just before going to sleep. Or, at any rate, before turning out the light and closing his eyes. He didn't sleep that much at all, truth be told, what with Torrent snoring away beside him and the light from downtown Atlanta glowing through the heavy hotel curtains. He was shocked and more than a little angry when he first learned that Torrent had a hotel room: he'd assumed everything was booked for the Olympics. But those reports of full citywide occupancy are apparently one more piece of hype. Torrent said he found a room after only three tries. His insomnia notwithstanding, Gerald did at least have an entire double bed to himself, and he certainly liked the big, puffy Best Western pillows, and after a week of sleeping on Brent's criminally uncomfortable sofa he had to admit that, on the surface anyway, electing to spend the night with Torrent was the first good decision he's made in months.

Not surprisingly, the worst call last night was to Nora. Yesterday, before leaving for the hotel with Torrent, he'd left a scrupulous and carefully worded note on the coffee table explaining the phone call with his father, the mystery of the missing car, their proposed meeting at the park on Friday night, and the reasons for his leaving that, in the note at least, hinged entirely on his fear of being "a burden." Because he knew that Brent was as likely to read the note first as Nora, he was very careful to keep his tone businesslike and unrevealing. But all day he had been nagged by the realization that the note wasn't enough. He needed to call Nora and talk to her directly. So she got the first call.

Brent answered and did not sound happy. Gerald immediately launched into an inept explanation for missing work, which Brent interrupted by saying, "Forget it. Nora told me everything. I just hope it all works out for you."

Gerald paused as the word *everything* rose before his eyes like the title of a film. Gently, he said, "I'm sure it will." A moment later he added, "Thanks for understanding. That means a lot." Brent's breath hissed against the mouthpiece. "You know, maybe I should . . . I mean, I can call back later if you're busy—"

"No, that's all right. We're pretty much done here." More hissing.

"I see. Well, that's good, I guess—"

"I'll get Nora." The phone clattered and fell silent. *We're pretty much done here.* Done with what? Done in what precise way? A good minute and a half passed before Nora picked up a second phone, shouted, "Got it!", and, after Brent hung up the original unit, announced, "Okay, I'm outside with the cordless. We can talk freely now."

"Sounds like you've already done a lot of talking."

Without emotion, she said, "Yes, I told him."

"Told him what, exactly?"

"Re*lax*. I didn't tell him about *us*. I mean, c'mon, give me a little credit." She hesitated here for effect, or maybe she was giving his heart a chance to return to his chest. "I told him," she added momentously, "about Aaron."

"Oh, Nora, tell me you didn't."

"Wait a second: *you* were the one who told me to. And then after what happened between us today, I thought—"

"Exactly. That's just my point. I can assure you this is nothing to—"

"Keep from your husband?"

"I was going to say it's nothing to take lightly."

"Oh."

" 'Oh' is right. Nora, honey, do you realize what you've just done?"

"When, Gerald? Tonight? Jesus, *tonight*'s the tip of the frigging iceberg." Here she sniffled, Gerald's first evidence that she'd been crying.

"Okay," he told her, "I wasn't thinking. Sorry."

"Hey, story of my life." Sniffle.

He glanced back at the hotel door. Ten minutes ago Torrent stepped out to get a "Coke," which Gerald understood to mean a stiff drink. He had no idea how long Torrent would be gone, and thus feared having to end this conversation prematurely. "How did he take it?"

"Who?"

"Brent, obviously."

"Terribly. He hates my guts. He wants a paternity test, like, yesterday." Sniffle. Sigh.

"Ouch."

"Which is just *fine* with me, incidentally. It's just what I deserve."

"He's just a little steamed, Nora. He'll cool off when—"

"But I don't *want* him to cool off. Don't you get it? I don't deserve him, Gerald. I don't. I should never have married him if I wasn't sure. And I wasn't, I just *wasn't*."

"Well, all right. Do the paternity test and—"

"Not about *that*. Christ, how obtuse *are* you? Haven't you heard a word I've said? Haven't you been listening? I mean about *him*, Gerald. I wasn't sure if I *loved* him."

"Brent, you mean."

"Of course I mean Brent! Who the hell did you think I—"

"No, I'm sorry. You're right. I knew that's who you meant." Behind him, the hotel door opened with a little pneumatic hiss of air. "I guess I just have a lot of shit on my mind right now."

"Oh, right. You and you alone."

Eyeing Torrent, who was moving unsteadily through the room with a full Coke can sloshing around in his fist, Gerald cleared his throat and said, "Well, okay then. Thanks a bundle. You've been a great help."

Nora stayed silent for a tad longer than was comfortable. On his end Gerald pursed his lips, performed a serious scowl, nodded once or twice. He wasn't quite sure if she was still on the line. If she was on the line, then he should stay quiet; if she wasn't on the line he should hang up. The tricky part was guessing correctly. He nodded again, whereupon she sniffled loudly and said, "He's there, isn't he? Torrent, I mean."

"That is correct, yes."

"Can't you call me from the hall or something? What about a pay phone? I really need to talk to you."

"No guarantees on that one, but we'll check on it."

She hung back a moment. "Okay, I get it. I know what's going on. This is the part where you pull back to save me from more trouble. I remember this one. You're worried about forcing your problems on someone else, so now you retreat. It's like the core of your whole ethical system, isn't it? No, I get it now. Because, I mean, hey, at *least* you didn't do *that*."

"Can we talk about this later?"

"You know what, Gerald? Don't even bother." And she hung up.

Next he called his editor, Terry, to explain why he didn't turn in a column, let alone a full-blown article, this week, but only got Branford McIntosh, the newspaper's film critic. "You're in pretty deep doggy doo," Branford informed him.

"I'll bet. Can you just tell him I called? And let him know I'll come by tomorrow and explain everything."

"Wow, wouldn't want to miss that. Hold on a sec." Deliberately short pause. "Okay. Gerald called, everything explained, love Branford. Anything else?"

"Yes. About this doggy doo. How deep are we talking, exactly?"

"Hmmm. Hard to say. Considering it's Terry I'd say no cause for alarm. Then again, I've worked here three years and I've never seen *anyone* in trouble with Terry. This is a first."

"Well, I'm glad I could make your day."

"We do appreciate it." And with an ironic *See ya*, Branford signed off.

On a roll now, Gerald called his apartment to see if Matt Anthony had tried the number again, but instead of Grauffbaut he got what he took to be Grauffbaut's teenage daughter. "So you're the guy who lives here?" she asked. Her voice came out slippery and bored; he could hear the excess saliva sliding around her gums, clear evidence of heavy orthodontia.

"That's right. The one and only."

"I like your cat. She sleeps with me every night."

"He," Gerald corrected her. "The cat's a he."

"He, she. What's her name?"

"Lester."

[256]

"That's a boy's name."

"Imagine that."

"Also, your computer doesn't work."

"Yes, I know that."

"And all these CDs. What, are you a musician or something?"

"Sort of," he said. "I'm a rock critic."

"Oh," she replied, crestfallen. "That's cool, I guess."

"Not really. So were there any messages?"

"For you?"

"Yes, for me. Has anyone called in the last five or six hours?"

"Only some girl. She's called about three times but never left her name. Is she your girlfriend?"

"I don't have a girlfriend," he told her, and instantly deduced it was Sasha, whom he hadn't spoken to since Saturday night. "Anyone else?"

"How should I know? Hey, how many of these CDs do you really want? I saw you had doubles of—"

"Any doubles you find you can keep."

"Seriously?"

"Yes. Just . . . look: if a *man* calls, any man, will you please give him this number?"

"Hey, I'm leaving. We're going out."

"I see. Well, have fun, and just make sure the machine—" But she hung up on him, too: Atlanta nightlife was calling.

Recalling all this, he now grabs the subscription slip, picks up the receiver, and punches in the numbers. He has to battle against an impulse to hang up and start over, but he succeeds. He completes the number. The phone rings once, twice, three times. On the fourth ring Matt Anthony shouts, "Yo."

"Um, Mr. Anthony?"

" 'Mr. Anthony' is my father. This is Matt. What can I do you for?"

[257]

"Oh, sorry. Matt, then." Deep breath: here goes. "It's Gerald Brinkman."

"What the hell? The mystery man. The elusive Gerald Brinkman. What happened to you yesterday? You were supposed to call me back."

"I know, I'm sorry. I just . . . It's complicated."

"Yeah, someone's living in your house."

"Right. The Olympics. Hell on the homeless."

"I hear you, man. So anyway"—Gerald hears Anthony shuffle some papers on his desk—"we talked it over here, me and the editors, and we kept looking at your clippings and all of that—you busy? You got a minute?"

"I guess so. I called you."

"That you did. What was I saying? Right, the editors. Anyway, they had their misgivings, you know. I'll tell you that up front. The magazine's committed to covering hip-hop. You'll just have to accept that."

"No, that's fine. I didn't mean to—"

"On the other hand," Anthony continues, after his fashion, "lots of folks secretly agree with you round here. We miss the grand old days of ass-kicking *rock 'n' roll*, if you get my drift."

"I think so."

"Then we bitched and squirmed and argued, standard modus operandi. Long and short of it is, the job's yours if you want it."

As of yesterday afternoon, he had firmly resolved to take a rejection in stride. Even if the magazine did elect to give him a job, he was still toying with the idea of turning it down. Yet now that he's heard the good news he finds he is elated. My God, *New York*! Big-time rock journalism! Movie stars and MTV! His blood races. Instantly he has a clear and detailed vision of himself walking the streets of the Big Apple, a professional writer making a go at it in the big bad City. Even better, he realizes he can escape all the bad blood that's brewing here in Atlanta. Bye-bye Nora, bye-bye

Sasha, bye-bye *everything*. Maybe he and Dad could get a rent-controlled apartment—

"Yo, hello in there. You still with me, buddy?"

"Gosh, sorry, I'm just ... Wow."

"It's a kick in the pants, isn't it? Now we're gonna have to go over some administrative hurly-burly, as you've probably guessed, and I should warn you—"

"Mr. Anthony?" He stops, backtracks, gets his bearings. "Listen, this is great news and all, but—"

"Right, like I was saying, we can't guarantee you a full-time position right off. That'll take a while. We thought we'd let you do a little reviewing, sort of freelance, and then if things pan out we can see about putting you on the roster. That's what I wanted to warn you about."

"I see."

"You don't sound too thrilled."

"No, it's not that. I mean, I'm grateful and all, but ... Actually, how much are we talking here? Money-wise?"

"Money-wise? Depends on how many reviews we buy. What I'm telling you is, don't pack your bags just yet."

The excitement in his breast slowly ebbs. So it's a mixed blessing. As all blessings seem to be. "I hear what you're saying."

"Give it the weekend, how's that? I can go ahead and send you some CDs and press releases, we were thinking of starting you off on the New Singles section, alternative stuff mostly, I can get it in the mail before the end of the day."

"That'll be fine."

"Contracts, guidelines, due dates, it'll all be included. You know the drill. Just listen to the records and dash off a column and we'll go from there."

"Yes."

"Gerald, don't sound so disappointed. This is standard procedure around here: trust me. It's how I started." When Gerald doesn't respond, Anthony adds, "I believe in you, pal. I really do. Went home last week and listened to The Who again. *Quadrophenia*—now *there's* a great fucking album."

Grateful for even this much encouragement, Gerald tries to laugh. It comes out hollow, but he gives himself credit for the effort. "Too many synthesizers," he argues.

"That's the best part. Townshend at his peak, no doubt about it. So I'll look to hear back from you, what? Late next week? You can e-mail it in, if you want. We're pretty technological these days. Whole place is overrun with computer geeks, God help us all."

"Good news?" Torrent calls from the bathroom, his voice laced in echo.

"I guess so." Gerald replaces the phone. "I just got a job."

"Ter*rif*ic!" Torrent emerges wearing a plush terry-cloth bathrobe with a Best Western logo emblazoned on the right breast. Rubbing a towel across his head, he asks, "With whom?"

"Some magazine. Listen, when do you need to go to the airport?"

"Not till six." He sits down on the bed beside Gerald. His skin is redder than usual, flush from the shower, while his old man's body gives off the moist warm scent of fruity shampoo. Gerald resists the impulse to scoot away. "Why?"

"Well, I've got a buttload of errands to run today, and I don't have a car."

Torrent takes the towel from his head, drapes it napkinlike along his lap, and places a damp hand on Gerald's bare thigh. "The car is yours, Gerald, if that's what you're asking."

"You're sure?"

"Absolutely. I planned to visit the Olympic Park anyway. This'll give me a perfect excuse."

"I'll bring it back before one. You won't even know I drove it."

"Pshaw," he says—without irony, it appears. Pshaw? "It's a rental. Bang it up all you want."

Little beads of moisture hang like Christmas lights off the end of his mustache. Wisps of white hair point every which way. Stanley Torrent, Gerald notes for the first time, is basically bald. All these years he's been quietly sporting a comb-over. And a pretty good one, as it happens: Gerald never noticed. Poor old guy: what kind of life has he made for himself? What must he think of me? Why did I say *buttload*?

"I promise I won't bang it up," he replies, and turns away, his face red with shame and, it surprises him to realize, resentment. Because of *this* guy, Gerald's relationship with his father is a bewildering mess. And yet he needs Torrent, all of a sudden. He really needs this old guy. When, and how, did that happen?

First, *Alternative Atlanta*. Although Gerald arrives sometime after 9 A.M., the offices of *AA* are basically empty this balmy Friday morning. It's been over a week since he's set foot in here, and he feels appropriately chastened. The glass front door, which opens out onto Cheshire Bridge Road—a winding, hodgepodge strip of psychic palm readers and topless bars and ethnic delicatessens— leads directly to the main newsroom, a wide-open space cluttered throughout by square brick columns around which sit heavy wooden desks, each supporting a flickering computer screen and piles and piles of paper. He moves through the maze of desks, grateful that no one is here. It is so quiet that Gerald wonders briefly if the paper has gone under, an eventuality that is always just around the corner anyway. Were it not for the insatiable demand in this sexually enlightened city for men-seeking-men personal ads, this free weekly would have folded years ago.

Terry is here, however. Terry is always here. Terry more or

less *lives* here. An ex-hippie with a degree in journalism from Georgetown University, Terry has neither wife nor children to keep him home. There was a wife, apparently, but that was decades ago. Nowadays, Terry lives in a rotting two-story house in Grant Park, the inside a clutter of books and journals and threadbare Oriental tapestries, the sagging front porch a pile of car parts and empty vodka bottles. Local teenagers in low-slung blue jeans and black Atlanta Falcon parkas patrol the street in front of his house and root through his garbage for leftover booze. He remains in this house for the same two reasons he sustains this newspaper: atrophied political idealism and spiritual indolence. Gerald knows nothing of Terry's sex life—he isn't even sure if there *is* a sex life— nor does he know much about Terry's financial situation, which can't be too terrific. The house itself is a family possession that Terry has let crumble for the same two reasons mentioned above. All Gerald really knows about Terry is, one, he lets Gerald do what he wants, and two, he can always be counted on for decent marijuana.

Terry is sitting behind his desk, marking up copy and sipping coffee from an enormous cereal bowl onto which he has ducttaped a wooden handle. From past experience Gerald knows this makeshift coffee mug contains more than black Colombian java. All he can see is the perfect vertical part of his boss's gray hair, which is parted down the middle and funneled into a ponytail that extends well below his shoulder blades. Gerald knocks on the door frame and waits. Raising a finger, Terry finishes up the paragraph he is reading and, marking a few things in the margin, looks up. The battleship gray of his beard is laced throughout with white powder from a Hostess doughnut, the staple of Terry's diet. He trains his bloodshot eyes at Gerald for a long, frozen moment. Gerald, smiling apologetically, stares back.

"Do I know you?"

"I can explain everything." Without waiting for further instruction Gerald enters the small, musty office—fake wood paneling on the walls, balls of crumpled fast-food bags on the floor—and takes the seat directly across from Terry's overloaded desk. "There have been, um ... extenuating circumstances, let's say."

"How extenuating, exactly?"

"Incredibly extenuating. Massively extenuating."

"You don't say. Extenuating enough for me not to fire you right here and now?"

"It's quite possible."

Throwing his hands behind his head and sitting back in his swivel chair, Terry unpeels a sinewy smile. "Let's hear it."

Gerald launches into a truncated account of his week, touching briefly on his father's illness, going into great detail about his father's disappearance (which he moves back to Tuesday, so as to cover the rest of the week), and concludes with a deliberately confusing explanation about why he failed to turn in his proposed review of last week's Sewer Pipe show.

"That's all well and good, Gerald, and I'm really sorry about your dad. No bullshitting here. But I'm still waiting for the Nightlife Roundup. Another responsibility you've shirked. What are the extenuating circumstances for that?"

Opting for humility now, Gerald explains, "None really. I just forgot to do it."

"Forgot? That's your big explanation—you forgot?" Terry looks at the ceiling, as if Gerald's answer were so complex and intricate, it required intense consideration. "Okay," he finally says, "you forgot."

"Like I said, extenuating circumstances."

Terry takes a sip of his coffee. Swallowing with difficulty, he smacks his lips, lowers the mug, and holds up a sheaf of papers. "Lucky for you, kid, the new girl saved your ass." He waves the papers in the air. "Did the roundup and the record reviews. Well done, too. She's quite the stylist. Of course you haven't met her yet since you haven't been here all week."

"New girl," Gerald says flatly.

"An intern, actually. College senior looking for résumé fodder. But she's good. Arrived here just in the nick of time. A gift from God, you might say."

"Look, Terry, I swear I'll make it up to you this week."

"Be still. I'm not through with you yet." Looking away as if to gather his thoughts, Terry makes a balloon of his cheeks, puckers his lips, and scratches his beard. "Fact is, Gerald, I'd fire you right now if I could afford it, college intern or not. Fortunately for you, I can't."

"I appreciate that."

Terry nods. "Now what's this I hear about another job in New York?"

Gerald is genuinely surprised. He's told no one on the newspaper about this—not one single person. Then again, the Lord works in mysterious ways—finding replacements, spreading rumors, causing earthquakes. "It was just an interview," he lies. "Nothing's happened yet."

"Really? Not what I heard." Terry leans across the desk and cups his hands together like a high school principal preparing to punch a few holes in some schoolkid's leaky alibi. "Look, Gerald, I've never hassled you about anything on this job, have I? You can grant me that, can't you? You can give me that much, at least. I treat you fair, you treat me fair. Only thing I ask from my employees: don't jerk me around. You thinking about taking a new job, fine. Just let me know in advance. Don't sneak around on me like I'm some asshole. You hear what I'm saying to you?"

"Loud and clear."

"This isn't the most lucrative gig around, I know that. But it's a family. I honestly believe that, corny as it sounds. That's the thing about getting older: corny stops sounding corny. It's a bitch, man. I don't recommend it, getting older. Avoid it at all costs. The thing is, if you're planning to jump ship, you gotta keep me informed. I can't go replacing you at the drop of a hat. I got a newspaper to run here. I got enough on my plate as it is."

And although he knows it is suicide to do so, Gerald can't help asking, "What about this new girl?"

"What about her?" Terry sits back and scrutinizes him.

"You thinking about hiring her full-time?"

"It's crossed my mind." He balloons his cheeks again, scratches his belly, smoothes his hand along his already-flat head of hair. "I'm feeling majorly jerked around here, Gerald, if you want to know the truth. That's the vibe I'm getting from you right now, and I don't like it. Any particular reason you're jerking me around like this?"

He looks down at his feet. "I'm not, Terry. I'm not jerking you around."

"If you say so." Terry swivels his coffee mug. "Listen. I know you've got some crap to deal with right now, like you said, your dad and all that. So what I'm saying is, try leveling with me for once. Just keep me informed on what's going on. No one is out to get you, not me and not this intern who saved your pathetic ass this week, so relax." He pauses to let this sink in, though Gerald keeps his gaze directed at the floor. "You know, I may not be the most successful yuppie in this city, but I'm one thing none of those people are: I'm honest. I'm a straight shooter who stands by his convictions. So I can't tell you how to run your professional life, and I'm no good at giving personal advice. But I do know two things. First, I know you've dicked me around for no good reason, and second, I know you're basically a good guy. So just remember that you won't get anywhere by hiding from people who've only got your best interests in mind. Which includes me. Or used to, anyway. Now I'm not so sure. See what I'm getting at? See how this works? Now don't come back here till you're ready to sit in that chair and look me in the eye."

Next stop, Web Central. Walking across campus, the sour memory of his encounter with Terry still burning in his stomach, Gerald is visited—belatedly—by a sudden unexpected bout of nostalgia. Graduate school. Nora. The early days of grunge. He is astonished that he once performed the duties of a student at this very institution, that he was once a young man dutifully engaged in the time-honored task of acquiring new knowledge. How proud his father was, Torrent told him yesterday. How proud and envious. Fulfilling the father's potential. And Gerald never knew. Yet how could he not? How could he not have known? The way his father pored over those critical texts, the way he tried so doggedly to engage Gerald in intellectual discussions—what were these but unequivocal clues? Wasn't this Dad's elusive way of reaching out, of making his wishes known? At the time Gerald had seen it all as his father's late attempt to reclaim a wayward son, the same surly and dissatisfied son he'd been disregarding for two decades. But it was pride. His father was proud of his boy. Or someone's boy.

He finds Brent in his usual spot in the main control room, hunched over a massive SunSystems machine. The place looks like the engine hub of the Millennium Falcon. Monitors lay stacked on top of monitors, the walls are plastered with butcher paper posters on which deadline dates and computer specs have been scrawled with Marks-A-Lot markers. The whole room hums and beeps like the nervous system of some massive, electronic leviathan.

"Sorry I'm late," he murmurs as he swoops into a seat next to Brent's overloaded desk.

Brent continues to rattle away at his keyboard, which, in true computer-geek fashion, sits nestled in his lap. Gerald surveys the room. Half the people lumbering about—a petite Asian woman in GAP shorts and a webcast T-shirt, two fat ponytailed technicians (Tweedle Dum, Tweedle Dee), a ponytailed teenager sipping on a Mr. Pibb—are brand-new to him. The place produces new employees like old bread produces mold. They just pop up and take over. Abruptly, the clitter-clatter beside him ceases. "Like I said, sorry I'm late."

Brent blinks as if he's just woken up, rubs his cheeks, and jangles his wrists. "Where've you been?"

"I had to go by my other job and sorta check in." Gerald smiles apologetically. "But I'm here now, ready for action. What are my marching orders?"

Brent freezes Gerald with his icy blue eyes. A nubbin of hard muscle tenses in Brent's jaws, a little bluish vein rises along his otherwise smooth forehead. This is the first time Gerald has looked at Brent since his tryst with Nora, and in a moment of pure, unadulterated panic, he wonders exactly how much guilt is written across his own face.

His voice calm and quiet, Brent asks, "Have you talked to Nora this morning?"

In fact, Gerald did try to call her. Once he was sure Brent was out of the house, and after he'd secured the rental car from Torrent, Gerald dialed her number from the hotel phone and began preparing his apology. But she never answered: all he got was her machine, with Brent's cheerful and unsuspicious outgoing message. He tried again from the newsroom, immediately following his encounter with Terry, but got the machine again. The device beeped nearly twelve times before activating the recording, which meant a full tape, so clearly he wasn't the only person looking for her. "I called this morning, but . . ." He trails off before he incriminates himself any further.

Pursing his lips, Brent closes his eyes and gives a quick nod.

Ruefully Gerald notes that Brent's doing his gerbil-like thumb-rub again—not a good sign. "I know you two talked last night," Brent says, and then lowers his voice, "so I wasn't sure if, you know, if she said anything to you."

Gerald glances quickly around the room as he scrolls through a quick list of possible answers, and, given the urgency, can devise only two: admit everything, deny everything. Neither seems very appealing right now. To buy time he asks, "Told me about what?"

For a blood-chilling moment, Brent gazes directly into Gerald's eyes and clenches his jaw again. He seems to be looking for some evidence of falsehood here—a twitch of the lip, a nervous blink. Gerald tries to freeze his facial expression only to realize that this is a fluttering red flag. Were Gerald truly confused, he'd show it by raising his eyebrows, shrugging his shoulders, dropping his jaw—something, anything but this stupid paralysis. Brent seems to get the message, because after a while his mouth slowly widens into a gentle smile. "So she did say something."

Gerald hasn't time to rehearse his next response. Only a quick, unhesitating reply will earn him the status of trusted confidant. "Well, she didn't say much. Just that you two had a long talk about Aaron. She said you were pretty steamed, which I can understand, and that's basically it. There wasn't much else."

He chances a look at Brent to see how this goes down. To his surprise, Brent's mouth drops open and hangs slack for a thundering heartbeat or two. "Aaron?" he says. "You're telling me it's *Aaron*?"

Instantly blood starts pounding in Gerald's ears. What has he done? What has he just revealed? Inanely, he adds, "Or whoever."

"It's *Aaron*? Sasha's Aaron? She *told* you this?"

"Actually, wait. Maybe I misunderstood what you were asking. See, I thought you wanted to know—"

"Fuck, I *knew* it! I totally called her on this. I mean, it makes perfect sense, doesn't it? She kept saying, No, no, you've never met him and all like that but I knew it, I *knew* it was that asshole. The wedding—that's when it hit me. You remember the wedding? Remember how he talked to her?"

He is pleading with Gerald now, enlisting his support. And Gerald realizes he can help. He can tell Brent everything he knows. He can tell him everything he knows about Aaron Vaughn and Nora Reynolds and thus accomplish two things at once: take the heat off himself *and* sever any further involvement with Nora, who will no doubt hate him for good when she learns who finally ratted her out. Problem solved: freedom gained. But now he finds that he doesn't want to end all involvement with Nora. He wants—can it be?—to take her away from Brent. That's really what he wants. The realization sears him like a brand. "Yeah," he nods, his thoughts darting every which way, "I remember the wedding. I mean, that's what I'm going on, same as you. Truth is, I don't know for sure if it's Aaron. I'm just guessing here."

"Yeah, right. I can tell by the look on your face, you know exactly who it is."

"But I didn't. I'm just saying—"

"Hell, who else *could* it be? It *had* to be Aaron." He looks to Gerald for confirmation, but Gerald remains perfectly still. "Anyway, this isn't your business, really, so forget you even talked to me this morning. I'll take it from here." He sits back clutching his narrow knees and takes several deep breaths, then begins nervously rubbing the razor stubble on his skull. Moments creep by—awful, unbearable moments. Finally he drops his elbows on his knees and leans forward, his hands resuming their gerbil finger-rub. Gerald leans toward him so that their skulls nearly bump. "So," Brent now wants to know, "I don't suppose she told you where she was going?"

"Going? When?"

"Last night. I'm just wondering if you know where she spent the night. I thought maybe she was with you, but then I remembered you were in the hotel with that other guy, Doctor Whatever."

"Why would she be with me?" Gerald's heart is racing again. This entire conversation has been like tiptoeing through a minefield, every step an unexpected explosion. He figures his best course of action is to answer every question with another question.

"Chill," Brent says. "I'm not suggesting anything." He pauses long enough for this to take hold. And it does, *literally:* Gerald can actually feel Brent's reassurance take hold of his stomach and give it a painful squeeze. "I was just asking. She took off last night and didn't tell me where she was going, so I'm just covering the bases. Calm down."

More news: more information he doesn't know how to process. "Did you try Kira's?"

"Sure. First place I checked. Kira, Tanya Flibula, Sasha, you name it. Even called her parents, which was a mistake. Now her mom is ringing me every five minutes wanting to know if she's turned up yet. Little friendly piece of advice: if you ever *do* get married, be sure to meet the mo—" As if on cue, his cell phone bleets. With a look that says, *See what I mean*, he extends his leg, reaches into his front pocket, and withdraws a tiny telephone device the exact shape and dimension of a *Star Trek* transmitter. He even shakes it once to pop open the tonguelike lid. "Yeah," he says into the mouthpiece. Nods, smiles. "No, nothing yet. Speak of the devil, though. I was just talking about you." Lowering the device, he mouths the word *Sasha*, rolls his eyes, and raises the mouthpiece. "No, I'm talking to Gerald . . . Yeah, he's right here. I was asking him— No, no, I haven't told him yet, but I'm sure he won't mind if you . . ." He looks at Gerald again with a sour expression that Gerald can't read. He nods once or twice and extends the little machine to him and shrugs. "She wants to talk to you."

Tentatively, like a child being handed a precious seashell, Gerald takes the phone and places it to his ear. "Yes?"

"Boy, I should wring your neck," Sasha tells him, right off the bat. "In fact, I almost decided to write you off for good, but for some inexplicable reason I'm giving you one more chance to redeem yourself. I've been calling your place all week, you know."

"That's what I hear."

"And you never called me back. Typical. Anyway, Brent's brought me up-to-date. I understand a little friend of ours has flown the coop."

Gerald looks at Brent. Brent smiles back. Abruptly he recalls Terry's parting piece of advice: *You won't get anywhere by hiding from people who've only got your best interests in mind.* "Actually, a couple of people have done that."

"Your dad, right. I heard about that, too. I've been a busy little bee. Aaron and I aren't talking, by the way, since you asked."

"I'm sorry to hear that."

"Oh, I'm sure you are. But that's not why I called. I *also* know you don't have a car right now, so I've magnanimously offered to drive you to the park. Or at least to the MARTA station. Brent's orders. We can talk then. And we *do* need to talk. Big time."

He looks at Brent again. But Brent is already back to business, the keyboard on his lap and the monitor before him pouring out numbers and commands. He gazes intently at the screen, as if cosmic deliverance from this mess were about to disclose itself via the secret cipher of hypertext meta-language. Burying his troubles in work. Perhaps Gerald should do the same thing. After all, he's nearly lost one job already, while his other job in New York is an iffy proposition. Besides, for all the tension throbbing between him and Sasha, he isn't sure he *wants* to be alone when he encounters his father. Of all the important things he's had to do in his life—and he's the first to admit he hasn't had to do very many—this is the one thing he should probably do alone. He should step up and field the ball, play the hand that's been dealt him, accept the baton, whatever. After all, this is the old man we're talking about here. The guy's dying, he's reaching out, he's liable to do anything given the state he's in. Gerald's got a lot of things to set right, and he might as well begin somewhere. He lifts the tiny phone to his mouth and sighs. "All right," he tells her, "that sounds like a plan."

Ten hours later, Gerald is sharing a table at Bud World with a very excited and voluble Sasha Mantrivadi. A surprising detail: Bud World has no chairs. This explains why they are standing rather than sitting at the table—less a table, really, than a round stainless-steel disk on a pole. But the tabletop comes to about midchest, so standing makes sense. In fact, everything in Bud World has been purposefully designed to discourage loitering. First, there's the atrocious line out front, which Gerald and Sasha endured for thirty minutes. Then there's the appalling cost of Bud World beer—six dollars per watery twelve-ounce serving. You do get to keep the cup, however. And it's a nice little cup, as these things go, sort of a miniature version of those fat sixteen-ounce plastic grain cups you got in college. Gerald's cup, a red one, bears the Bud World logo, while others boast various Olympic sports insignias.

The table's brushed-metal surface looks like some futuristic grade of Formica, this in keeping with Bud World's kitschy sci-fi decor. The ceiling rises twenty feet above your head, its cast-iron support beams visible to all, while the north and south walls each support a bank of television screens that interlock to produce a massive mosaic image. Right now, NBC is broadcasting highlights from that afternoon's team gymnastics competition. The shot they keep returning to over and over again, like a tape loop, is Kerri Strug's courageous third vault in the women's finals, the one that secured the American team the gold medal. Gerald knows the vault was courageous because the sports commentators keep saying it was. On-screen, the tiny four-foot-eight-inch athlete charges down the runway, somersaults through the air, and lands with a perfect thud on the mat, her face clenched in pain. The camera then cuts to her bandaged ankle, which should have disqualified her from competition. But it didn't. It didn't disqualify her one little bit. No mere sprained ankle was going to stop courageous Kerri Strug from fulfilling her Olympic Dream. Next the camera pans to her coach, a pudgy white-haired Eastern European man happily flapping the arms of his foppish, old-woman's warm-up suit. Then it cuts back to courageous Kerri Strug, her jaw still clenched in agonizing triumph, and before you know it the tape loop has started all over again.

"So you're telling me nothing happened between you two," Sasha concludes, her full beer sitting ignored between her cupped palms. "You move in and live there for three days, then Nora leaves. And that's all you know."

"Something *did* happen, Sasha, in case you've forgotten. My dad disappeared with my car."

"And that's why Nora left? You're not telling me something here, Gerald. I can read it on your face."

Tonight Sasha wears a tight cream-colored camisole top, a black miniskirt with matching belt, and black chunky-heeled shoes that force her shapely calves to flex when she walks. Each time she adjusts her stance the shimmering highlights of her shirt shift along the ample slope of her bosom. Her black hair, full and billowing, pulls into bold relief her maroon lips and glossy black eyes. As usual, she smells delicious—an odd mixture of patchouli and cinnamon, less a perfume than a pungent fragrance from some hothouse plant. When she came by campus earlier tonight to pick him up, she was surprisingly cheerful and warm, bubbling on and on about nothing at all. But the minute they secured this table, she opened the issue of Nora, and she doesn't seem anywhere close to closing it up. For his part, he's wearing shorts and a webcast T-shirt, a concession both to the heat and to his current homeless status. After work, and after eating a solo dinner in a Subway in Decatur, he walked back to campus, showered in the gym, and changed in the locker room. As of now, all his belongings—two changes of clothes, a toothbrush and a comb, his Sony Discman—lie hidden beneath his desk at Web Central, which stays open twenty-four-seven. Since Torrent took off, he's been out on the street, basically. He's decided not to think about where he's going to sleep until he gets his car back and finds out what his father has in store for him.

"Look," he says, "why do you automatically assume her leaving had anything to do with me? When was the last time you talked to Nora, anyway?"

"Hey, *you're* the one who does all the talking with Nora."

And here it was: Saturday night redux. Yet though he's known for days she was going to steer him back to this subject, all he says for now is, "Didn't we already have this conversation?"

"No. In fact, we somehow keep managing *not* to have it."

"What is it you want to know exactly, Sasha?"

"Depends on what you can tell me."

He lifts his hands in surrender. "Well, I got nothing."

"Liar."

Overhead, a gravel-voiced rock singer announces to all and sundry that he's travelin' down the road flirtin' with disaster. He is accompanied, two tables away, by a cluster of drunken males, all four of whom wear sleeveless black concert shirts and tight Wrangler flares. Not a single one has his tennis shoes tied. One of them is totally bald, while the other three sport fulsome mustaches and severe crew cuts that resolve themselves into majestic manes cascading along their fat necks. Amid the scrubbed suburban yuppies of Bud World, they look like visitants from the future, like time-traveling members of a postapocalyptic warrior tribe. "You're just going to have to believe me, Sasha."

Agitated, she slides her beer aside and places her palms flat on the table. "Fine. Then let me tell you what I *really* think. I think you're protecting your little ex-girlfriend because you're still hung up on her. And I think she got married because you were too chicken to commit. Oh, and she's been sleeping with Aaron."

The overhead stereo now blasts an old Journey tune from his high school days, something about a small-town girl living in a crazy world, takes the midnight train going anywhere. "You couldn't be more wrong," he murmurs into his beer mug.

"Yes, I thought you'd say that. The fact is, Gerald, I don't care what you're concealing from me any longer. I mean, I'm not *stupid*, okay? I know who Aaron is. I know what he's about. The thing is, when Nora got married, I thought you could use a friend. You sure looked like it back there at the wedding. And I thought, hey, so could I. But now I realize you're perfectly content being Nora's little lapdog, which—I'm sorry—could not be any more pathetic. Trust me: she's not worth the price."

"He generally sleeps with nurses," he tells her, to calm his pounding heart. "There was a thing last spring with another doctor on his rotation, but mostly it's the help."

"Ah yes: protect Nora at all costs." Above their heads Journey says, *Don't, stop, believing, hold on to your something something.* For the first time since they sat down Sasha takes a full drink of her beer, and when she slams down the cup a ring of foam lines her maroon lips. Then she grabs her purse and steps away from the table.

"Sasha," he calls, "wait a second. Don't run off like this."

"Like what?" she cries, whirling around. People turn to watch her, the whole crowd sort of opening around her so that she is left standing regal and tragic in the center of a sinister mob of rednecks and failed rock critics with zero social skills. "Like you? Like

Nora? Like your *father*? Everyone else is running away, why can't I?" She wipes her cheek against her wrist and scowls at her rapt audience. People on either side turn away in shame. She waits for him to respond, and he wants to, honestly he does. He could come clean with everything he knows and instantly regain her trust, yet in doing so he betrays another and ruins her life in the bargain. By saying nothing he can sacrifice himself and save her. Or damn her to an innocence that is less bliss than blind despair. Some choice.

"Just as I thought," she concludes, and slaps the tabletop. "I hope your father's all right. You can have the rest of my beer." And like a genie in a bottle she's gone.

Though it is already 1:03, Gerald is still standing in line outside the Swatch World of Time pavilion, an Olympic Park attraction that, according to the makeshift poster over the door, closed at one o'clock. What was his father thinking? Did he somehow know the place would shut down at 1 A.M.? He'd thought of everything else, so it's possible. As far as Gerald can figure it, the employees here plan to let people in until right up until closing time. He looks at his watch again: 1:04. The line has barely budged in ten minutes. His leg pumps up and down with impatience. He suddenly resents all these innocent, self-absorbed people, none of whom have the faintest idea how important it is that he get in there. Should he cut in line? Should he make something up—my wife's in there, I just stepped out to take a leak—and shove his way inside? Or is this all part of Dad's plan? A lesson in time, a demonstration in the tyranny of randomness and chance. He looks at his watch one more time, but there's no change.

An elbow pokes his rib. At first he doesn't give it much thought, chalks it up to the general bump and swarm of the queue, but when it comes again, with even greater force and urgency, he turns to look. His own name enters his ears. The voice is light, lilting, feminine. It is a voice to summon his blood. The voice is Nora's.

She's standing beside him, her thin blond hair barely obscuring the impish smile on her face. A burlap army surplus bag hangs off her left shoulder. In addition to a pair of heavy combat boots, she wears a matching pair of olive-drab army fatigues—her favorite pants, bar none—and a blank white T-shirt. She looks as if she began dressing for battle and changed her mind halfway through. He stares at her in amazement, but she continues to stare straight ahead. Taming his voice, he says, "Fancy seeing you here."

"Shhh." She juts her head forward. "I don't want Sasha to see me."

"She's not here."

"I thought I saw you with her, over in that line for Bud Planet or whatever."

"She's good and gone, trust me."

"You're absolutely positive?"

"Nora, my God. Relax."

Without further preamble, she turns her beatific face to him, her eyes wild with excitement, and seizes his arm. "You have no idea what I've been through today."

"Yeah, you and me both. Where the hell have you been? Everyone's been looking all over for you."

"Like who?"

"Well, your husband, for one. Sasha and Tanya. Oh, and your parents, particularly your mom."

"My mom? What the hell?"

"Apparently Brent called her. He was checking to see if you'd dashed back home."

"You talked to Brent?"

"Sure. Saw him at work. By the way, thanks for lying to me last night."

She glowers at him. "What are you talking about?"

"Didn't you say you told him *everything*?"

"Yeah, sure. I mean, I didn't tell him about *you*, but that's a different story."

"Nor did you make any specific reference to Aaron."

"*Obviously.*"

"Well, he knows about Aaron now."

She squints her eyes at him. "Come again?"

"I didn't tell him anything he didn't already know. Cross my heart. Ask him."

"Oh, God, Gerald, tell me you didn't."

"Well, Nora, fuck. What was I supposed to do? I had no idea you kept that little detail from him. It just kind of"—he steps back a bit to give himself enough dodging space in the event she decides to take a swing—"I don't know. It just slipped out."

But she doesn't punch him. She just rolls her head along her shoulders and whimpers a bit. "Jesus, I can't believe you—"

"Look, I'm sorry, all right? You gotta keep me better informed if you want me to help you fuck up your marriage." And that's when it hits him why she's here. The last two days have been so replete with coincidences and sudden reappearances that he hadn't stopped to wonder how she could have known where he would be at this exact moment. But then he remembers: he told her everything yesterday in a note he left her explaining why he was moving out of her place. Dad's phone call, his instructions to appear at this pavilion at 1 A.M., Torrent's hotel room—it was all in there. The line surges forward, and Gerald and Nora silently follow. He glances at his watch: 1:05. If he doesn't make it this round, he's done for. "Where have you been, by the way?"

"Out and about" is her preoccupied response. "I just couldn't fake it anymore, Gerald. I mean, it's over."

"Nora, listen—"

"Hell, it was never a real marriage to begin with. Basically, we

[278]

got into it again after I called you, and I just split. I spent the night at Kira's."

"That's not what she told Brent."

"Yes, well, apparently *some* people know how to keep a secret."

They are almost at the door now. Five more people and they're in. It occurs to Gerald that no one seems too concerned that Nora cut in line. This means he could have done the same thing. He could have charged to the front of the line and wormed his way inside, no problem. But had he done that he might have missed Nora, the realization of which gives him the jitters. But no, that's absurd: she could have found him when he walked out. "Look," he begins, just shy of the big glass entrance door, "why don't you wait out here. I'll only be a minute."

She grabs him just as the line stops moving forward. He's only three people away. Surely they're not going to bar him now, not after he's come this far. "This is it, isn't it?"

"I don't know what this is, Nora." Beyond the entrance the entire pavilion is packed. How are they going to fit him in?

"Are you nervous?"

He responds by nodding. And it's true. He's absolutely terrified. He hasn't felt this much trepidation since that day in August three years ago when he filed into the seminar room to take his Ph.D. qualifying exam.

Leaning into him, she takes his arm again and tugs. "I'll wait out here. But first I need to tell you something."

"Make it quick." He's not sure, but he thinks he feels the line inch forward ever so slightly.

"You have to look at me first."

Impatiently, he obeys, his foot tapping up and down as if to hurry her along.

A distant smile crawls across her face. How lovely she looks right now, frazzled though she is. Only now does he recall, with a puncture wound of emotion so strong it almost brings tears to his eyes, the events of yesterday morning. He suddenly sees a foggy yet provocative vision of Nora cradling his face in her hands and invitingly closing her eyes. "Yes?"

"I love you," she whispers.

A moment creeps by, a moment as big as the Olympic Park itself, but before he can conjure up a response he falls forward, and the next thing he knows he stumbles through the front foyer of the Swatch pavilion. He calls, "Nora!" but it is too late. The glass doors slide shut with a hiss and clack and he is suddenly alone among strangers, lost to all coherent thought.

Watches hang everywhere, each wall of the brightly lit foyer lined with glowing display cases. The watch faces glow like the buttons and dials of an ancient room-sized computer. Children run about, buzzed on the late hour and the vast emptiness of summer vacation.

He instantly spots his father slumped in the far corner, the green knapsack in his lap and a couple of days' worth of beard on his haggard, sallow face. Dad gazes serenely around the room, clutching the bag like it's a teddy bear; people walk past him and glance down and just keep walking. So he showed. As good as his word.

Gerald moves through the crowd and positions himself before his father. Dad's greasy hair lies slicked back along his mottled skull; his eyes seem sunken in their sockets, the irises ashen and dry. He wears black slacks and a black T-shirt with "The Church" written across the left breast.

"Nice shirt," Gerald says. "Been wondering where that was."

"Found it in my closet back home," his father replies, and pinches the shoulder, the fat of his chin bulging against his throat. "I take it The Church is a rock group."

"A very good rock group. Psychedelic guitar pop." Gerald settles down on the floor and leans back against the wall. "So now I know what you've been trying to tell me for two weeks. Can we go home now?"

His father squeezes the bag against his chest. "I had no idea it was going to be that hard to say."

"Particularly since it's not true."

"Gerald—"

"I mean, so Mom and Torrent slept together. So you wake up one day and realize your life has become a John Updike novel. Then you reevaluate some things. Fair enough." He shakes his head in disbelief. "But how in God's name could you go around thinking all these years that I was Torrent's son?"

"How do you know you're not?"

"Because I know."

"What's your proof?"

Gerald pauses. Somewhere in that crowd outside Nora is waiting to see what effect her confession has had. Or perhaps she was so distraught by his failure to respond in any meaningful way that she's disappeared. Poof, gone, never to be seen again. Meanwhile his father stares directly at him with a look that is part challenge and part fear. It is almost as if he seriously believes Gerald knows something decisive that will once and for all shatter the single great misconception that has governed most of his adult life. "A son just knows these things, Dad." He tries to smile here, to emphasize his little inside joke.

The old man remains placid for a moment. "Here's what kills me about all this. You may be right."

"Of course I'm right. It's a moot point, anyway, since we can verify it in about a week. They swab our cheeks and compare DNA and that's all there is to it. Costs about fifty bucks. I even found a Web site."

"Right, I know. Identigene dot com."

Gerald hesitates long enough to take this in. "So you've checked up on this."

"Of course I did. That was the whole reason I came here in the first place." He releases his hold on the bag and settles back against the wall so that his head is exactly parallel to Gerald's. His old body gives off a rank, stale odor. Probably forty-eight hours since his last bath. "That's what this trip was really about, if you must know. I wanted to get a paternity test, and I needed you to go with me. They need a sample from both the father and the child, so I needed you to participate. The problem was, I needed to tell you about Torrent and your mom, and I didn't want to do that."

"It wasn't exactly left-field information."

"I'm sure it wasn't." His father consents so quickly to this assessment that Gerald feels chastened somehow: after all these years, the wound is still fresh. "In any case, that's what I was trying to tell you all week."

"So why didn't you?"

"Still trying to figure that one out." His father gives a wan smile. He's really fading. An old guy in his condition has no business driving around on his own. Or sleeping on his own, for that matter. Where did he sleep last night? What kind of son am I that I haven't thought of this until now? "All these years I've been operating under the possibility that you were Torrent's boy. Crazy, huh? Even when you got older and started aping my mannerisms. Nurture versus nature, no way to know. So I maintained my doubt. Or maybe it was just the opposite."

"Opposite of what?"

"Of doubt. That's what I'm starting to realize. When it finally came time to tell you everything, when it finally came time to solve the great riddle, I realized I didn't want to know. I kept opening my mouth and each time the words wouldn't come. It was strange. Then I knew why. I genuinely didn't want to know. *Not* knowing all these years has been like an article of faith to me—my last and only." He chuckles, emitting a cloud of fetid breath. He's not just fading, he's dying. "To have faith in something, you gotta have doubt, so I decided not to know."

"So your last and final article of faith all these years has been the false assumption that I was Torrent's son and not your own?"

"Of course not. It was the faith that you were mine. The faith, not the proof. It was the fact that I brought you up as my own, even though there was still room for doubt."

"Can I ask you something?"

"Certainly," he smiles, and turns to face Gerald directly. "Ask me anything you want."

"Where the fuck have you been the last twenty-four hours?"

"Busy," he replies, and instantly the smile disappears. "Running errands, taking care of things. Which reminds me: I have something for you." He opens the bag on his lap and begins rummaging around.

"You're here because you're coming back home with me."

"It's right here, if you can give me a second."

"First thing, you and I have to figure out a place to stay. Nora's is out of the question for reasons I can't go into right now, and so is Sasha's, for equally complex reasons. But Torrent didn't have any trouble finding a hotel room, so I thought we could—"

"Voilà!" his father exclaims, and yanks aloft a thick white envelope, which he passes ceremoniously to Gerald. It bulges with the pressure of too many folded sheets resisting their crease; it has the heavy-lightness of a double album from the old LP era. "That's not all, folks." He rummages some more and produces another white envelope, this one with a Chrysler insignia along the top. He shakes this envelope once and out drops a car key attached to a black plastic alarm remote. He holds up this prize and waves it like a hypnotist before Gerald's disbelieving gaze. "Know what this is?"

"The key to your weird behavior?"

"In a manner of speaking, yes. And now it's all yours." He drops the key into Gerald's lap and leans back again. "Wait till you see it: blue exterior, leather interior, sunroof and CD player and this electronic cup holder, power windows, you name it. I'm telling you, this is a car to die in."

"You bought yourself a Jeep Cherokee is what you're telling me."

"No, stupid. *You*. I bought *you* a Jeep Cherokee."

"Why on earth did you do that?"

"Because you need it. Or will need it, eventually. That old heap of yours is fine for now, but someday soon you'll need a family car. Something big, with lots of storage space and room for little ones."

"You're making absolutely no sense."

"I'm talking about your future, son. The long term. You need to start looking down the road a little bit, and I thought this Jeep might start you in the right direction."

"But I have a car."

"Oh, that old thing? I'm taking that. Perfectly fine for what I need to do."

"Taking it where, Dad? Look at me: I'm serious now. Taking it where?"

"Eventually to the junk heap. Speaking of which, I should take off. I parked illegally when I got here, so I want to get to it before they ticket me. They're closing this place, anyway." It's true: the place is clearing out. Aside from a trio of attendants and two or three customers buying watches, Gerald and his father are the last people left. A chirpy female attendant commandeers the door, un-locking it for each departing customer and relocking it as the cus-tomer exits. Because the door opens to a tunnel that curves like an L, Gerald can't see out into the park, which means he still has no idea if Nora is out there or not. "Now, that envelope you have is very important," his dad continues, "so don't set it somewhere. Best to just shove it in your shorts and open it when you get home."

"Okay, time-out here."

"Everything's in the envelope. All will be explained. The Jeep is still at the dealership, but the receipt is in there, so you can pick it up whenever. There's lots of other very important documents plus full instructions, so again, be very careful not to misplace that anywhere." His father begins struggling to stand up.

Gerald opens his mouth to respond, but then stops. *Dad seriously thinks he's leaving. He honestly thinks he's walking out of here without me.* Roused to action, Gerald jumps to his feet and, taking his father's arm, yanks him upright and seizes his pudgy shoulders and pushes him back against the wall. His father barely resists; he's like dead weight in Gerald's hands. "Now you listen to me."

"Gerald."

"All this about the car and the documents—I know what this is about. I know how you think. This is your big dramatic way to—"

"Excuse me," says a female voice behind him, "but we're trying to close up."

"No, you're not," Gerald hisses, and stares her down.

The girl almost, but not quite, loses her friendly smile. She's actually rather attractive, in a chirpy television-commercial sort of way—perfect teeth, bouncy hair—so Gerald's threat slides right off her back like grease from Teflon. "Why don't I go get my manager."

"You do that," Gerald replies, and turns back to his father. "So here's what I'm saying—"

"The envelope."

"Right, I know. So you and I, we walk out of here together very slowly and then we head straight for my car."

"It's on the floor."

"Fine," he sighs, and bends to pick it up. Next thing he knows he's on his back and blinking in shock: only gradually does he realize that his father has just kneed him in the face. A black splotch gradually contracts in his field of vision, revealing along its border the blurry ceiling of the Swatch pavilion; the left side of his head throbs. Despite the pain, he struggles up and finds he is utterly alone, the envelope and Jeep keys arrayed on either side of him like murder weapons at a crime scene. God*damn* it. Shaking the pain from his head, he scoops up the envelope and the keys and scrambles to his feet and dashes to the door, which, surprise surprise, is not locked. The girl must have left it unlocked when she went for the manager. Even more frustrated than before—that *bitch*—he swings it open and dashes down the little hallway, the sides of which are painted with Leroy Neiman–like drawings of gymnasts and track stars, and bursts back outside, directly into a massive mob.

To his right the great blue beacon of the AT&T Global Village stage ascends against the horizon. On the facade's enormous television screen a rock group of some sort seems to be milling about. The real live rock group can be seen in miniature just below. The drums echo like gunshots across the assembled crowd, which is so large that Gerald, standing in a panic just feet from the pavilion exit, is already fully engulfed. Indecision overtakes him: look for his father, or look for Nora? Which is the easier task? Which is the more life-altering? When he looks down he notes with despair that he has already bent the envelope in half. He releases his grip and watches the envelope unfold in his two hands. The thing seems to be alive, writhing slowly like a small creature waking from a nap. He forces the envelope into one pocket and slides the key and its alarm device into the other. In passing he notes that the band is playing "Time Is on My Side."

"So where is he?"

His blood freezes, and then instantly warms again. Nora. So she waited for him. She's standing right at his elbow, clutching the strap of her backpack. He grabs her arm.

"Did you see him?"

"Who?"

"My dad. Which way did he go?"

"You mean he's not with you?"

"No. I mean, he was, but then he—" He breaks off here, too

frazzled to explain. "He just ran out of there ten seconds ago. You had to have seen him."

Nora shrugs, bobbing her head up and down in a vain attempt to make eye contact. "Hey, is everything okay? What happened in there?"

Amazing: he did it again. One minute he's there, the next, gone. Ascended into heaven. "He's got to be around here. There's no way he got far enough."

"I'm sorry, Gerald, I don't understand. You've got to calm down."

"Just stay here for a moment so I can track him—"

He is thrown from his feet before he can finish his thought. It's the only thing he registers at first—not the sound of the blast, not the heavy piece of flying shrapnel that skims off his head, not the sonic boom underfoot: only the gut-drop thrill of flight. If he registers anything it is the massive wallop he absorbs in his gut, the impact of which is powerful enough to hurtle him several yards from where he is standing. In the initial aftermath of the blast he hears nothing but a hollow oceanic roar of no-sound, a seashell whoosh of total emptiness laced at its edge by the hermetic hiss of his own breathing and the steady throb and thump of his heart. A sharp smell of sulfur fills the air, while in his head the tide of silence slowly subsides. He now hears the thunk-a-thump of drums, the roar of applause, and the frayed reverberation of distant thunder. Slowly the truth blooms within him. An explosion of some sort. For the second time in three minutes, he struggles upright and shakes his head.

He surveys an extraordinary scene. The crowd around him, extending beyond his legs in a wide twenty-yard radius, spreads flat along the ground, elbows and arms poking up and waving for attention. A cirrus cloud of gunpowder smoke hangs low overhead. The screams have grown louder, this owing to the fact that the live band has stopped playing "Time Is on My Side." Scattered faces, many of them painted in blood, detach themselves from the carpet of bodies and rise toward the gun smoke. As others drag themselves from the ground and move about, another new sound emerges—that of shattered glass crunching beneath rubber-soled shoes. The entire event, from initial blast to aftermath, is over within a minute. Gerald realizes, in a flash of clarity borne of adrenaline and fear, that he has slightly less time than that before panic takes hold of everyone. He cups his hands to his mouth and begins calling Nora's name.

He finally locates her—or, at any rate, her combat boots—just inches away from where he was originally standing. With her legs splayed out behind her and her hands flat on the ground, she looks like someone trying, and failing, to perform a push-up. Shoving aside a cluster of concerned onlookers, he drops to his knees and touches her arm.

"Stay where you are. Don't move. Can you hear me? Nora?"

She nods. He slides his arms under her shoulders and hoists her up. She is as limp and heavy in his embrace as a canvas sack of sand. More dead weight.

"Tell me you're all right." When she doesn't whisper back, he takes her head in his hands and carefully searches for blood. He finds only dry hair dusted with powder. "Talk to me, Nora. Please, say something."

People crash by as the shouting gets louder, yet she manages to stand her ground, so okay: she's all right. A booming voice issues instructions from the stage but the specific words get submerged beneath a wash of amplified echo and crowd panic. The tide surges left, the entire crowd now stampeding toward the Swatch pavilion and beyond, where the park exit awaits like the gates to paradise.

THIRTEEN

As GERALD leads Nora through the Centennial Park exit, he detects a gentle resistance in the crowd's forward flow. People disperse and open their arms to the world they've just reentered. News of the explosion hasn't reached this far: perhaps it didn't really happen. Around him families regroup. Fathers count heads, tearful mothers lick napkins and wipe bloodstained cheeks. He steps around a group of young people huddled in a sobbing embrace. Everyone else wears a vacant look of dazed amazement.

"Stop here," he commands, and Nora obeys without protest. She bends over, hands on knees, and takes a number of deep breaths, as he gently touches her back and rubs her there: hard bump of spine, clasp of bra strap. "Where's it hurt?"

"My left hip."

He registers a sigh of relief: at least it isn't the stomach. "Did someone smash into you?"

She breathes some more and stands up. The crowd creams past her. Voices buzz. "I'm not sure. I was just standing there, then bam."

"I know. I felt the same thing."

"Then I blacked out. It was like I was being walked all over by a herd of elephants."

He suddenly remembers that Sasha may still be in the park. Not to mention his dad. He watches the people pour through the exit gate. Behind him the ambulance siren grows even louder, the street crowd peeling back onto both sidewalks, creating a narrow valley down the center of Techwood. Gerald and Nora force their way into a pack of onlookers gathered before a Coke stand. Everyone is talking about the blast. "Do you think you can drive your car?" he asks.

"I think so." Wincing, she touches her hip and arches her back. "But it's not here."

"Where'd you leave it?"

"At Lindberg and Piedmont. I took the MARTA."

The complications heralded by this news tighten along his spine. He can't leave her standing here like this, yet he doesn't have a car, either. His dad has his car. What's more, he came here with Sasha, who, rather than pay for downtown parking, picked him up at the university and then drove the two of them to the Midtown station, all of which means he can't leave until he locates Sasha. He can't just take off and let her wander around this place looking in vain for him—assuming she gives a damn about him in the first place. Police on horseback, their megaphones blaring with clipped instructions to disperse, move in a zigzag down the lane created by that last ambulance.

"All right, listen," he tells Nora, pulling her deeper into the crowd, "we'll take the MARTA, but we have to find Sasha first."

"Oh, Christ. I totally forgot about her."

"Yeah, well, we should probably head back in there and find her."

"They won't let you."

"They have to. Now I want you to stay right here and—"

"No way."

"Nora, listen to me. You might be injured. And, given the circumstances, you might be in serious trouble."

"No," she snaps. "Don't even go there. I'm *fine*. You take off now and I'll never find you again. They'll just round me up in a herd and shove me on a train." After a moment she says, "We have to stick together."

This last line recalls two things, both of them related in his mind: the night Sasha helped him with his father at the Star Bar and Nora's recent confession, to which he has not yet responded. "All right," he relents, "you win." They walk arm in arm across the street, picking their way through the flow of people moving in the opposite direction and ducking the security guards who reprimand them. At the entrance they meet a regiment of Atlanta city police officers, three enormous white males the size and build of pro wrestlers and a busty black woman wielding a billy club. The woman steps forward to confront them.

"No one goes back in," she tells Gerald sternly, spreading her legs and tapping the stick in her left palm. "The park's closed for the evening."

"I know. I was in there."

"Then you understand what I'm talking about." She jerks her head at the road behind him, the road he's just traversed. "The trains are thataway. Best you should start walking toward them."

"We've got friends in there," Nora pleads.

"Not for long you don't. They'll be out shortly."

"She," Gerald corrects her. "We need to find her before we leave. She's my ride home."

"Take the MARTA. It's free of charge tonight."

"But she won't know we've left," Nora explains.

"Call her when you get home." To register her impatience,

the officer slaps her billy club again and smiles. "She'll figure it out soon enough."

All this time the crowd has continued to pour out of the park. Each of the cops blocking the entrance is engaged with a similar situation—worried people wanting back inside to search for lost companions—and each cop is shaking his head and patiently pointing north, up Techwood and toward the MARTA station. The situation seems hopeless—in more ways than one—yet Gerald decides to give it one more try. "Listen, I realize this isn't your fault, but we really need—"

And just then—another random miracle—Gerald hears someone call his name. Nora looks back first and is already waving toward the voice when Gerald turns to see Sasha wobbling their way in her clunky shoes. Without speaking, the two women fall into an intense embrace that instantly renders Gerald nonexistent. He looks back at the policewoman to let her know all is well, but the poor woman is already engaged with another anguished couple, this time a set of concerned parents from the suburbs, trapped in the jaws of their own awful crisis.

"I can't believe I *found* you," Sasha cries into Nora's shoulder. She avoids looking at Gerald, though Gerald does his best to catch her eye. "All day I've been calling your place and Brent wouldn't tell me—"

Nora releases her and steps back. "Are you okay? Are you hurt?"

"I'm *fine*. I mean, I was way over by the stage, so I didn't even hear it, really. I thought it was, you know, the light show or whatever."

"I think it was a bomb."

"I *know*. I just called Aaron with my cell phone and he hadn't heard anything yet. He was sitting around in the break room watching Conan O'Brien and while I'm talking to him, right at that moment, they break in with a special report or something.

Then someone pokes his head in and says he has to hightail it to the admitting room because the ambulances were bringing them in any moment."

"Bringing who?" Gerald interrupts.

"The injured." Still avoiding his eye, she keeps her attention on Nora. "It's madness in there. They've got like five ambulances on the grass. Bodies are everywhere."

"Is anyone dead?" Nora asks.

"I don't know. I don't think so, but, you know, anything could happen. I mean, they herded us out of there pretty quick." Now she turns to Gerald, a look of surrender on her face, and he understands what has happened. Disaster simplifies things: there will be time for anger in the morning. "You all right?" she finally asks him.

"I'll survive." He smiles apologetically. All at once weariness overtakes him. The flimsy edifice that is his life keeps crumbling down, and yet there's still so much left to fall. Faintly, he hears Nora ask, "What about your father?" But he's too distracted right now to answer her. Instead he listens as Sasha explains how she and Gerald left her car at the Midtown station and how she can probably just pick it up tomorrow, Aaron can drive her in his car, he gets off first thing in the morning, the important thing right now is for all of us to stick together, don't you think?

Standing at her front door and rattling her keys, Sasha waves back to let them know all is well. Nora's dashboard clock reads 2:42. From behind her steering wheel Nora waves back, and then turns to Gerald, who's still slumped in the backseat. The car rumbles quietly, the radio playing softly in the background. In the dim light of the car's interior Nora's face conveys soft, velvety vulnerability. She arches an eyebrow. "So?"

"Interesting dilemma we're in."

"You could say that."

The whole MARTA ride home Gerald had stood clutching a pole and wondering if the faces assembled around him were the last ones he'd see before annihilation. Meanwhile the train sped smoothly along its tracks, the lights overhead wobbling once or twice as if in tasteless jest. No one uttered a sound, the entire compartment as silent and still as a tomb. Only when the doors opened and people disembarked did anyone speak, and even then the only people talking were those who had made it out of the train. The poor souls still stuck inside looked out the window in silent apprehension. Safely back at the Lindberg station, Gerald followed Sasha and Nora up the escalator, through the turnstile, out into the night air, and across the emptying parking lot. Beyond the mesh fence surrounding the lot, cars moved slowly along Piedmont Avenue in orderly columns of green and blue. The glossy chrome facade of the Gold Club, a locally famous strip joint, glimmered in the night air like a postmodern cathedral. All the way home he sat quietly in the backseat fingering the envelope and staring out the window. Up front, Sasha and Nora listened attentively to the radio, every station crackling with hyperventilated reports of the bombing. No deaths yet, was the repeated phrase, emphasis on *yet*. Stay tuned for details.

"Well," Gerald says, "we should probably think about driving away."

"You're not sitting back there."

"Seems as good a place to be as any."

"I'd much prefer it if you climbed up front." She pats the empty passenger-side seat. "There's a seat belt and everything."

Once he's settled in beside her she rattles the car back into gear. In silence, they lurch away from the curb. One last look back at Sasha's house reveals an unnerving sight: all this time Sasha has been peering at them from behind the curtains of her living room.

"Please observe that I'm driving away, as per your instructions."

"I see that."

"Any requests for a destination?"

"No, but I'm open to whatever you have in mind."

"Okay," Nora says, and pulls to a stop. They've arrived at the Virginia-Highlands intersection, catercorner from the big Chevron station and two blocks from both Brent's place (don't even think about it) and his own (occupied). "Tijuana's out of the question, but we have to go somewhere. Unless you want to drive west. Hey: we could just hit the road and keep going. Like a Brad Pitt movie or something."

He glances down an empty Virginia Street and thinks for a moment. This is absurd: it's still his place. And all his stuff's in there. What is the law in a situation like this? Is there even such a law? What exactly is the situation? How do you define it?

"The light's about to change, Gerald."

"Take a left."

"You're sure?"

"Are you?"

She answers by taking the left anyway. A smile tugs at the edge of her mouth. She goes to second gear, then third. The houses flash past in a blur. Before she can really get her momentum she comes to an intersection and takes a sharp right, accelerating into the turn. The car lists to the right.

"Nora—"

She ratchets down to third gear, the clutch grinding in protest, and takes another hairpin turn, this one to the left. They hit an upswell in the street and lift, momentarily, off the ground, Gerald's stomach rising like a balloon into his mouth. He grabs the dashboard and holds his breath. They bounce back to earth, whereupon Nora shifts to neutral and skids to a stop at the next intersection, directly beyond which looms Gerald's street.

Nora sits rigid in her seat, one hand clutching the steering wheel and the other locked around the gearshift. Her jaw muscle throbs.

"You want to calm down a little bit?"

"I am calm."

"We just survived a bomb blast, you know."

"I'm just *driving*."

"Right, but maybe this a good time to be a little extra careful."

"You said turn left—"

"Yes, I know that."

"—and I turned left, just like you said."

"That's fine, Nora."

"I mean, Christ"—and now a little quiver enters her voice—"what just happened to us?"

"You mean before or after the bomb went off?"

At this, she drops her head onto her arms, which cradle the steering wheel. Her shoulders gently shake. Is she crying? Or laughing? Could be a number of things. No way for him to know for sure, which is probably just as well. Presently she sits up, runs her hands through her hair, and jangles her wrists in the air. "Okay."

"Feeling better?"

"Not particularly." She shoves the car back into gear. Quietly they float across the intersection and onto his cobblestoned street, the houses on either side dark and complacent. How many of these people slept through the whole event? What a morning they'll all have. After a bit she pulls to a stop, yanks the parking brake, hugs the steering wheel, and, leaning forward, cradles her chin on her arms. The radio, turned so low as to be almost inaudible, continues its staticky symphony of panic. "So now what?"

All the lights in his building are out, both downstairs and up. Or at least the ones facing the front. There's a fairly good chance someone is still up watching the news right now, perhaps even in his very own Batcave, but who? Grauffbaut? His surly daughter? Does he want to stay in his place with someone he's never met or stay at someone else's place with someone he knows? He has a mild interest in seeing the daughter ("I like your cat, by the way. She sleeps with me every night") but represses this curiosity easily enough. "What all's in that backpack of yours?"

"The usual," she replies. "Underwear, toothbrush, hair dryer. Why?"

"Just wondering." He sits back against the car door and, crossing his arms, examines her face, trying to figure out where they are right now—where in their relationship, where in the world, where and on what sort of trajectory. "As I see it, our options are as follows. We can kick this family of very wealthy and powerful Germans out of my apartment, or we can flip for the backseat and crash here in your car. Or go to Kira's."

"That's a possibility." Smiling now, she settles back against her own door. They face each other now, their torsos turned and the parking brake jutting between. "But I'd just as soon not bother Kira. Last night didn't go too well, truth be told."

"Should I wake up the Germans?"

In response she shoves her hand into the pocket of her army fatigues. Producing a nickel, she turns it once or twice in the faint light. The nickel winks. "Heads or tails?"

"Aw, to hell with that. You're a pregnant woman: you get the backseat. How's that hip by the way?"

"Still throbbing, sort of. Or maybe I'm just imagining it. I can never tell anymore."

"Are you worried?"

"About the baby? Not really. It'll take more than a thump to cause a miscarriage, if that's what you're asking."

"I see you've done your research."

"Best chunk of research I've done in three years."

"And you're sure about this? Having the kid, I mean."

"Absolutely." Abruptly, he is struck by an embarrassing realization: he's never asked about the baby. He's known this news for a little under two weeks, and yet he's never asked her a single question about pregnancy or motherhood or how she feels right now or any of it. This is a pregnant woman he's talking to here. There's a human being gestating inside her.

"I never doubted that," he says after a pause. "I'm talking about now, after that fight with Brent. The terrain has changed somewhat."

"I realize that," she whispers, and looks out the windshield.

"So I guess what I'm asking is, Are you sure about leaving him?"

"He kicked me out, Gerald."

"That's not how I understood it."

"Well, it amounts to the same thing."

"What if it's his kid?"

"Then we have a problem."

"I thought the problem worked the other way around."

"Then that shows how little you know."

"I wonder if you realize what you're saying."

"Gerald, look at me." Since he's already doing that, she leans forward to give him a better view of her face. Her shoulder presses against the steering wheel. "I don't. Love. Him."

As I explained to you, in another context, earlier tonight. He should say something now, out loud and with unwavering conviction. He should do this despite the fact that she's married. And pregnant. And unsure who the father is. He should say what he feels, and say it with an even voice. He opens his mouth. And says, "I understand that."

"What do you understand?"

"What you said before. About Brent."

"You're not getting out of this, you know."

"Look, I hear what you're asking me, okay? I heard you back there at the park. I understand the subtext."

"Subtext? Who said anything about a subtext?"

"Or whatever. I'm just saying—"

"Wait a minute: you think there's a *subtext*?"

"No, Nora, listen to me—"

"It was three words, Gerald. Three very clear and unpretentious Anglo-Saxon words."

"I know that, Nora."

"So which ones constituted the *subtext*? Actually, you know, this is very fascinating, that you would think—"

"Nora, please. Hold on a second."

"Hold *on*?"

"I just mean, let me—"

"I *have* been holding on, buster. *Three years.* Do you understand *that*? The whole time you've been sitting in your apartment getting stoned and suffering from insomnia, I was holding on, waiting until you got a clue. But you never got it. You never got the clue. I mean, what is *wrong* with you? Am I really this much of a schmuck?" She slaps him once, not very gently, on the chest, and drops back against her door, wiping her wrist along her cheek. Sniffling, she draws her knees to her chest and hugs herself into a little ball.

"You're not a schmuck," he whispers. And although she does not respond, she does smile a bit, which is a start. "But you're right. I'm pretty clueless."

She manages a laugh—really just a soggy little snort, but, like that smile, it's still something. He's not sure but he thinks they might be getting back together, right here, right now, in Nora's car, her trusty blue early-nineties Honda Accord, the same car she drove way back when—same tapes in the glove compartment, same muffin crumbs in the seat cushions. Now's the time they've chosen to do this astonishing and reckless thing. Which just goes to show how much choice you have in these sorts of things. Randomness rules.

"In my defense," he declares, clearing his throat, "you did get married to someone else."

"I know. Sorry about that."

"You're apologizing for getting married?"

"Yeah," she concedes, looking him in the eye, her face aglow with disbelief. "I guess I am."

"Then we're even."

"You think so, huh?"

"We'll call it a truce, right here and now. Clean the slate."

She squints an eye at him. "You're not saying what I think you're saying?"

"I think I might be."

"Because I know this might be as good as I'll get from you. Assuming, of course, I understand the subtext."

"You can interpret it any way you want."

"Oh, so *I* have to do the work here?"

"Well, interpretation is one of your strong suits."

"Correction: it's a job skill. Don't think you're getting out of this one, Brinkman. Eventually you're gonna have to give me something solid, something I can really hold on to."

He sinks lower into his seat and stretches out his leg so that their feet touch. She sinks lower as well, thereby increasing the pressure of her foot on his. A foot kiss, then. He's not complaining. "Man, if I had a nickel for every time a woman asked me that."

"Hey," she shoots back, and kicks at him with her customary bravura. "Watch it, pal. I'm a married woman."

He awakes to the sound of someone tapping at the passenger-side window, just above his head. Voices murmur outside. A feeble morning sun streams through the windshield, while inside the car the air is suffused with the moist but not unpleasant smell of his and Nora's sweating flesh. Nora lies asleep on his chest, her mouth hanging open and a string of saliva adhering to his T-shirt. He takes a moment to orient himself and then twists around as carefully as possible so as not to wake her.

Peering at him through the window is a rock-faced policeman, his blond hair slicked back off his forehead in a smooth corn-colored sheen and his broad shoulders blocking the morning sun. Nora stirs, smacks her lips. The cop steps back and makes a two-finger gesture at Gerald.

"Nora," he whispers, but she's already up, staring wild-eyed out the windshield. Another officer, this one short and female, stands guard just beyond the hood.

As Gerald reaches behind himself to open the car door he realizes he's sporting a stiff boner, against which something narrow and sharp presses. What to do? Well, he has to get out, so that pretty much eliminates his other options. Once the door is open he forces out his legs and bends over long enough to make sure his T-shirt is untucked. Then he stands up to face the male cop head-on, the front of his shorts making a little pup tent beneath the shirt. The air hangs about him heavy and humid: all night it had rained, the sound of which had lulled him and Nora right to sleep.

"State your name, please."

"Gerald Brinkman."

The male cop nods and turns to his partner, who gently touches the firearm on her belt. "Mr. Brinkman, please step away from the vehicle."

Nora's head pops up from the other side of the car. Her hair is a sweaty, windblown mess, her left cheek bearing the phantom imprint of a wrinkled shirt.

Mindful that this is one of the most banal and clichéd lines in all of moviedom, he nevertheless asks, "There a problem, Officer?" and subsequently realizes what that is in his pocket: the envelope. He fell asleep last night with Nora in his arms and forgot all about it. His stomach clenches with guilt. Dad. Somehow this is all going to be about Dad.

Just as the cop prepares to answer, he is interrupted by a crackling beeper. He holds up a finger and steps back, tilts his head, and punches a button on his holster. Though Gerald can't pluck a single word from the rainstorm of radio static that erupts from the little device, the blond cop nods right along, a native fully versed in the local dialect. Pursing his lips, he looks across the car at his partner and calls, "They found it."

"Found what?" Nora wants to know, and takes Gerald's arm in her hand. He didn't even hear her approach.

"Mr. Brinkman's car," the female cop explains. To Gerald, she says, "A car registered in your name was issued a parking ticket last night outside Centennial Park."

"That was my dad." It is all he can do to resist pulling out that envelope. His arm tingles with temptation. Chief among the reasons he doesn't do anything of the sort is the fact that he will have to lift his T-shirt to do so.

"Your father was driving your car?" the blond cop asks, each enormous hand clutching one of the many bulky objects strapped to his belt.

"That's right."

"Where is he now?"

"I have no idea."

"You mean you don't know where your father is?"

"That's what I mean, yes."

"So you can't tell me where your car is?"

"No, but I bet you can."

The cop gives Gerald an even, unfathomable stare, and then jerks his head back to the police cruiser that, Gerald now realizes, has been parked behind them all this time. Acknowledging her partner, the woman tentatively steps forward, eyeing Gerald with gentle suspicion. Her hair, which is the brownish yellow of a Bit-O-Honey, forms a helmet around her head, only to resolve itself along her neck in a wavy shag. When she doesn't say anything for longer than seems accidental, Gerald remarks, "Pretty intense treatment for a parking ticket."

"Not under the circumstances," she replies, her face expressionless.

"I take it this is about the bombing last night."

"That's right. We're checking on every car that got issued a ticket in the vicinity of the park. Your car was one of those listed. We checked the registration and located this address, and that's why we're here. This is your address, isn't it?"

Wearily, he admits, "I live in the apartment out back. But my landlord rented my place to someone else." As if this explained anything.

"So is that why you're sleeping outside in this car?" Still poker-faced.

"You know, I honestly can't remember anymore."

"I need you to understand you're not in trouble, Mr. Brinkman," she continues. "We're just following leads. You shouldn't feel that you're in any trouble at the present time."

"That's a comfort."

The blond cop waves to his partner, who nods back, and then turns back to Gerald. "Would you mind coming with us, Mr. Brinkman?"

Gerald rides in back, Nora fidgeting beside him. The whole ride the female cop keeps a nervous eye on them from the front seat. The radio hisses and crackles. Thank Christ that erection's gone: there's a small blessing. Without uttering a word, Nora took his hand the moment they settled in, so between her anxious hold on him and the female cop's watchful eye, Gerald can't bring himself to open that envelope. Not that he really wants to. Whatever information it contains will either be validated or overturned by the events of the next five minutes, so he figures he can wait a little longer. The world around him, for all its disorder, is still an Eden compared to the world inside that envelope. But he has to open it, eventually. He realizes that. He must eat of that fruit.

The police car glides to a stop. So preoccupied has he been that he hasn't paid any attention to the drive itself. Now he notes that all this time they've been heading toward Little Five Points, specifically to the parking lot of the Star Bar, the very same Star Bar where, exactly two weeks ago today, he was watching Sewer Pipe perform, running into Sasha, and administering first-aid to his father. So the old man *has* been in charge all this time.

"We're here," Nora says in an ironically singsongy voice.

And there's his car—the crack in the back windshield, the idiotic bumper stickers: *Mean People Suck*; *The Moral Majority Is Neither*; *The Who—Maximum R&B*. Another police car squats beside it. A black officer, portly and mustachioed, stands in the open car door speaking into a radio mouthpiece. Gerald releases Nora's hand.

"Stay here," the female cop tells them through the plastic window separating the front from the back seats. She and her partner get out and approach the other cop. All these police officers: the state has taken over.

After a moment or two, Nora clears her throat and asks, "So what are you thinking?"

By way of an answer, he withdraws the envelope from his pocket and sets it on his lap. It forms a little teepee on his thigh. He spreads it as flat as he can and inserts his thumb in the corner of the flap and slides his nail along the edge. Inside sits a sheaf of paper, ten or twenty pages in all. Bank statements, a Jeep

Cherokee sales receipt, some sort of legal document that begins *Whereas*. The top page is what catches his eye. It is a letter, composed in laser-printed, single-spaced, ten-point Times New Roman font. *Dear Gerald*, it begins. *By the time you read this, I will be gone. Obviously, there are loftier and more eloquent ways—*

Beside him his door opens. The female cop, her face softened for the first time this morning, leans forward and says, "Would you step outside, Mr. Brinkman?"

Air leaves but does not enter his lungs. He opens his mouth but then sits back against the seat, breathing slowly and steadily.

"Gerald?" Nora asks. "What is it, honey?"

So here we go. Passing her the pile of papers, he looks at the cop, smiles against the emotion welling in his throat, and steps out into the moist morning. He follows her to his car and steels himself to look through that cracked windshield. But the car is empty.

"You Gerald Brinkman?" the fat cop wants to know. Gerald nods. "This look like your vehicle?" Another nod. The cop turns to the woman, jerks his head at the empty expanse behind the parking lot, and returns to his mouthpiece.

The woman touches Gerald's arm. "Why don't we walk this way, just over here? I apologize about the rain."

"Not your fault."

"I guess that's true." She sends him a wan smile as they start off across the empty parking lot, which descends down a steep embankment. After about thirty yards the parking lot ends, giving way to a flat plain of mud and wild grass. Trees jut up here and there, while scattered all over this desolate stretch of urban waste are garbage bags, foggy plastic tarpaulins, beer bottles, yellow milk jugs: the abandoned remains of a dispersed homeless community. "You should know we've found your father," she's telling him, her hand still gently touching his arm, "but I'm afraid he's not in the best condition."

"So he's alive?"

She pauses. "Well, yes, but he—"

"Where is he?"

They stop at the edge of the parking lot. That's when he sees the old man. He's on his back beneath a tree, being examined by another cop, the fourth of the morning. As far as Gerald can discern, this fourth cop—white and wiry, with a chocolate-milk mustache beneath his nose—is speaking into a mouthpiece attached to his breast.

"Mr. Brinkman," the woman calls, but Gerald is already running across the mud. The skinny cop stands and squares his shoulders like a punt returner preparing for a form tackle. Gerald lifts his hands to show he means no harm and approaches more deliberately.

"Dad, it's me," he calls.

The cop widens his stance and clutches his belt but just as quickly relents when he sees the female officer, who has just joined Gerald, signal an okay.

Dad's eyes are closed, his hands cupped into a little church steeple along his chest. His face radiates peace and well-being. Gerald crouches down and touches his father on the cheek. The eyes shoot open.

He gazes at Gerald with all the innocence and incomprehension of a newborn. Then he opens his pale pink lips, which are as dry and delicate as crepe paper. "I thought I ditched you last night."

"No such luck," Gerald replies, and crouches down to get a closer look at his father. The mist has resolved itself into a needle-sharp downpour. "You're not getting rid of me that easy."

"Apparently not." The old man winces. Behind Gerald the two officers confer quietly amid the sound of radio static and the soft hiss of rain. "Some night, huh?"

"And to think you predicted it."

"Hey, I can do better than that: they think I did it."

"Did what?"

"Ignited that bomb."

Gerald's heart tightens into a fist. Of all the impossible things he's thought during the last two weeks—and surely this is a fortnight in which the impossible suddenly seemed possible—this was the one thing that never once occurred to him. And yet it is occurring to him now. His mind reels. What else is in that letter? Is Nora reading it right now, and if not, has she turned it over to the other officers? "That's ridiculous," he says, his voice cracking slightly.

"Of course it is. But that's what you get for parking illegally in this country." He winces again. With difficulty he adds, "Maybe. Those Vipers. Are on to something."

Again, air leaves but does not enter Gerald's lungs. With difficulty, he asks, "How are you feeling?"

"Like complete. Shit." The old guy laughs. "It's your fault, you know."

"If you say so."

"That green knapsack. That's the whole case. That and my parking ticket."

"I don't understand."

The eyes close again. "Some witness says the bomber carried a green knapsack. I'm carrying a green knapsack. A perfect match."

"Dad," Gerald whispers, both of them basically drenched now, "why are you out here? What's this all about?"

"You know how a dog dies?"

"You're not a dog."

"Too bad for me."

"And you're not dying."

"There's where you're wrong, my boy."

Gerald stands up and looks at the two police officers. The woman, seeing him, stops talking to her partner and steps forward. "We've got an ambulance coming."

"You honestly think he blew that bomb?"

"We don't think anything," she says evenly.

"Gerald," his father whispers. "Sit back down. I don't feel like yelling at you."

He looks at his father and grits his teeth. That peaceful expression is still there, but now Gerald sees that it conveys something more complicated than mere contentment. It is a look of surrender. He crouches back down beside his father and wipes the moisture from his face.

"You need to know something," his father begins. A thin glaze of white paste lines his dry lips. "When I came here last week. I was a lot worse off. Than I let on."

"I can see that."

"So there was really nothing. You could have done."

"I don't buy that, Dad."

"Not asking you to buy it. Just accept it. Another thing." He closes his eyes again, perhaps to gear himself up for another assault of words. "That letter. I gave you. Have you read it?"

"I started to."

"Well, ignore one paragraph. I wrote it before seeing you. Last night. But don't ignore all of it."

"I won't."

"I made a botch of this, didn't I?"

"A botch of what, Dad? What were you trying to do?"

"Die like a dog." Now that air of contentment and surrender is edged with terror, the old man's eyes trembling slightly in their sockets. "Boy, am I tired. Didn't think it would feel like this. Dying. But it does. That's about all I can say about it. Don't know what I thought it would feel like, but not this. One more of life's big disappointments. The last one." Suddenly he jolts up like someone absorbing an electrical charge, and then collapses back onto the ground. Silently, Gerald takes his father's heavy head in his hands and scoots forward in the mud. "One more thing. You still listening?"

"I'm right here."

"I wanted to get out of your way. But I botched it. I couldn't shove off without seeing you, so I came here. To tell you some big secret. That I don't believe anymore. Who believes in anything? You believe in anything?"

Gerald feels his chest heave with grief. All this past tense: all this air of finality. "I'm glad you came," he struggles to say. "I believe in that."

"Yeah? Well, here we are, then." His father closes his eyes. Gerald leans over to get a better look, taking one of the dying man's trembling hands in his. They sit there, father and son, in silence. An ambulance siren, the second or third in two weeks, approaches from the west.

"Though not for long," Gerald tells him, referring to the ambulance. On his lap his father smiles peacefully. His chest moves slowly up and down. His grip tightens.

Thursday, July 26, 1996

Dear Gerald,

By the time you read this, I will be gone. Obviously, there are loftier and more eloquent ways to say this—I have shaken this mortal coil, met my great reward, joined the choir eternal—but the longer I sit here running through these alternatives the more I sound like John Cleese in the Dead Parrot sketch. So gone it is.

I'm sitting at a computer console at a Kinko's somewhere in Buckhead. They let you rent these things by the hour, and my hour is ticking away. Some practical matters. Your new Jeep is waiting for you at the dealership: they know who you are. The bank account contains exactly half the total amount I received from the sale of the house and its belongings two weeks ago. The other half I've placed in a parallel account for Eva. There's also my estate, plus an insurance policy. You are free to do with this money as you see fit, though let me suggest you consider putting a solid down payment on a house of your own, preferably in Nora's neighborhood. Apparently you can pick up a nice two-bedroom home for under $200,000. Given current projections, that house will appreciate by $20,000 a year, so it's a no-brainer. You can easily manage the mortgage payment with a solid $60,000 down payment, though you should consider putting down a bit more, to lower your monthly payment. Talk to Walt about all this: he can explain the specifics. The main point is, stop renting. You're just burning your money every month, whereas a mortgage is rent money you pay to yourself.

I apologize for leaving you this morning without so much as a note. I'm in the middle of some complicated arrangements right now, and I'd just as soon not involve you in any way. Though perhaps it's a little late for that.

I don't know what Stanley told you, but here's what I know. He and your mother were involved right around the time of your conception. I never determined if you were his or mine, of course, but the proximity of their affair was enough, in those days anyway, and given the kind of man I was back then, to plant a nasty little seed of doubt. That's what I came here to tell you this week. In any case, I apologize. If you wish, you and Stanley can solve this matter to your own satisfaction, however you deem fit.

One last thing: Stop sleeping through your life. Stop doing work you don't like and avoiding people who only want to love you. I should know. I'm the poster child for avoidance. In that respect, you're my son right down the line. But you can be better than that.

I cannot bring myself to end this letter. Dying is harder than I thought. Take solace in the fact that each life begets another. Drive your cart and plow over the bones of the dead. Understand that no matter what you might be thinking right now, you'll still never appreciate how ruinously I loved you, and in a way I don't really expect you to. But please, in spite of everything I've written here, in spite of everything I've told you all these years, believe that much.

FOURTEEN

SUNDAY MORNING. A precocious July sun sidles up to the kitchen window and spills a bucket of yellow light into the cluttered sink and onto Gerald's shirtless back. Sitting hunched at the tiny kitchen table of his new house, he sips a tepid cup of coffee and scans the front page of today's newspaper. Like every other newspaper in the country, the *Atlanta Journal-Constitution* has gone full-color, the front page as busy and bursting with blues and greens as a page on the World Wide Web. Movie stars and baseball players lounge along the top banner next to a smiling cartoon sun in Wayfarer sunglasses. Just beneath the fold a headline reads, "One Year After the Bomb: Investigation and Reassessment: 3 Incidents' Connection Strengthens." His tongue trips over the awkward possessive noun in the headline's third tier. Some layout hack. Since his brief stint last summer as an Internet copywriter, he's pretty much given up on newspapers, at least local ones. He gets his news from the Web—abcnews.com, cnn.com, msnbc.com. He sips some more coffee, squeezes goo from the corner of his eyes, and begins reading.

The three bombings that shocked Atlanta out of its complacency earlier this year might be linked, say investigators.

Jack Killorin, head of the Atlanta office of the federal Bureau of Alcohol, Tobacco and Firearms, told reporters recently that the basic components of the two most recent bombs—from their design to their targets—all match up, thereby linking the three separate incidents. Killorin argued that it was highly unlikely that all three bombings were committed by more than one person or by one small, closely knit group.

This latest theory marks a sharp reversal from earlier assumptions made by bomb investigators and law enforcement officials, all of whom refused for months to link the Centennial Park bombing and two subsequent explosions at an abortion clinic and a gay nightclub, respectively.

"One city, seven months, three bombings that share a general technology—to have three bombings and they not be related seems incredible," Killorin said.

The bomb that went off last summer in Centennial Park was a nail-studded pipe bomb packed with black powder. Conversely, the bombs that rocked a Sandy Springs abortion clinic last January, injuring seven, and a gay nightclub later that February, injuring four, were made of dynamite. Killorin was not fazed by this small discrepancy.

"Experimentation is not uncommon, but the technology is the same," he affirmed. "How is the person trying to use this bomb? He is trying to fire shrapnel into people."

Gerald sets the paper down. So it's been a year. A year since his father died in an ambulance, still holding Gerald's hand. A year since the people of Atlanta woke up to the news that their mass orgy of worldwide marketing had become an opulent desolation. A year in which two more bombs went off in Atlanta while a fat, bewildered, and totally innocent security guard named Richard Jewell became the obsessive focus of half-wit journalists suddenly confident that they'd found a "loner" and a "crank" who "fit the profile" of a "terrorist." A year in which Gerald, reading all those accounts of poor Richard Jewell, couldn't help but think they were talking about his own father, another bewildered loner who— for that brief two-hour respite between being discovered unconscious in Grant Park and surrendering to a peaceful death en route to Grady Hospital—was the Bureau of Alcohol, Tobacco and Firearms' prime suspect. Amazing. The years just keep going faster. Further proof that time is relative to motion, that memory and desire are at least as important as the second law of thermodynamics, Dad's own unlikely god.

He turns to little Paul, sound asleep in his swing. The swing stands about four feet high on its triangular base, weighs about four pounds total, and can be picked up and transported just about anywhere. Paul can sit in it for hours, and often does. Lately he's learned that if he kicks his legs back and forth he can increase the momentum, so that's the latest noise in the house—not the rhythmic swoosh of the swing so much as the unnerving sound of Paul's little knees banging violently against the tote tray. But he doesn't seem to mind the pain. Seems to like it, rather. All that padding, all that flesh.

At the moment, though, he's perfectly still. His mouth hangs open like a little bulb coming to bloom, while his head sits perched on his left shoulder at what looks like a very painful angle. Fortunately, Paul's soft spine is still mostly cartilage; after nine months spent curled inside Nora, this is nothing. He prefers to have his spine bent, anyway. His favorite sleeping position is to be curled into a comma on Gerald's chest, his knees bent against his belly and his little hands folded prayerlike beneath his chin. He's pretty good about holding up his head, which is startlingly heavy for so little a creature, balancing atop his tiny shoulders like a precious porcelain vase filled with rich gelatinous liquid. Gerald has heart-stopping nightmares of dropping the boy on the street and cracking that skull. The nightmares are so awful, they jolt him awake, his blood racing, whereupon he finds Paul sound asleep beside him, his skull in one piece and burrowing into Gerald's rib cage.

Still staring at the child, Gerald looks—as he generally does, with morbid regularity—for evidence of the boy's absent father. The only tip-off is the hair, what little there is of it. When you tilt Paul's head a certain way in the light, a faint dark-gray widow's peak appears like a buried image in a hologram, and that's where you can see Aaron's influence the most. Otherwise he's his mama's boy through and through. He's got his mother's big olive-green eyes, and her small, petite nose, and even her prominent philtrum cleft just above the top lip. Everything is perfect—the finely articulated fingers and toes, the lovely round head with its faint tracery of blue veins, the smooth unblemished skin. So Gerald doesn't think about Aaron all that much. There are even times—like now, for instance, as he watches Paul sleep, or when he changes a diaper, the child smiling back coquettishly and pedaling his little feet in the air, or at night when he rocks the boy to sleep between nocturnal feedings, his lips pressed against Paul's head with its warm biscuity smell and its diaphanous coat of celestial dust—Gerald can almost feel his resentment dissolving into an airy mist above him. Which doesn't mean the resentment isn't there.

He stops the swing with his fingertips. Paul remains motionless, his eyes closed and his little fists balled. The toes are icy cold—Gerald should have put socks on him before letting him swing like that—while the crotch of the jumper he's wearing is damp to the touch. Sweat or pee? Delicately, Gerald unhooks the tote tray, lifts the child from the seat, and sniffs the diaper. Good, just sweat. Last feeding was what? 5 A.M.? Roughly. He looks at his watch: 8:47. Should be hungry by now.

Paul barely stirs as Gerald cradles him against his chest and locks that lolling head beneath his chin. Swaying there in the kitchen he wonders, briefly, if his own father ever did this with him. But of course he did: nothing more universal in human existence. In animal existence, for that matter. People always talk about the miracle of birth and so on, but for Gerald it's been just the opposite, not an instance of divine intervention but a pure and unambiguous triumph for Mother Nature. Watching Nora push this gray, slick, bloodstained thing from between her legs, then witnessing the uncanny instinct with which the boy, twenty minutes after arrival, latched on to his mother's engorged breast, Gerald truly understood what it meant to be a member of the animal kingdom. This was how living creatures entered the world; this was the primal ground upon which we all stood. As for Paul, he still languishes in all the animal amenities. He eats when he's hungry, sleeps when he's sleepy, soaks up affection like a sunbather. He positively basks in contact with other human bodies. When Gerald cradles Paul to sleep he feels sometimes as if he is transmitting nourishment to the boy, an illusion made all the more believable by the air of sated contentment Paul displays upon waking.

Contentment is another thing Gerald's felt these last six months. There was that awful period after the funeral, to be sure, then that terrible time after Brent and Nora received the negative result from their paternity test. And for several months there last fall Nora and Gerald were so isolated from their friends that they were reluctant to leave the house. That solitude, however, became their healing balm. There was a baby coming, after all. And despite all the crying and the boredom and the daily seclusion of parenting a newborn, despite the searing moments of doubt he sometimes experiences when he watches Nora coo to this child she made with someone else, despite the grief he's felt all year about his father, not to mention the belated wellspring of grief for his own mother that this experience with parenthood has mysteriously tapped, Gerald has been, on the whole, more content than he's ever been in his life. A surprising discovery: he's good at this. He's a natural father. Paul fits quite comfortably in his arm, a perfect fit. The child lights up when Gerald tugs at his little toes and cries when Gerald sets him down. So he's found a new skill.

He looks around the kitchen—*his* kitchen, the very first kitchen he's ever owned, however contingently, given the terms of his thirty-year mortgage. He's been in this house nearly a year. In which short space of time the property has appreciated over ten thousand dollars. Eighteen-hundred square feet, three bedrooms and one-and-a-half baths, central heat and air, new roof. The living room still emits the dusty art-studio smell of new paint: during those lonely early months here, he and Nora tried to displace the haunting silence of their shared isolation by repainting the front of the house, a two-week stretch of covered furniture and newspaper carpet that brought them closer together. So a full year of lucrative residency. Yet the place still feels haunted to him. It was his father's idea, after all. His and Eva's, actually.

Eva: how awful it was when he called her last year, and how delicately she tiptoed around the issue of blame and negligence. Could he have done more than he did? Probably not. Could he have tried harder, however fruitlessly? Definitely. But to what end? What difference would it have made? Some. He could have searched harder for the guy. He could have sent the cops after his car. He could have loved him more, reached out to him more, been more of a loving son.

Paul stirs. Whispering endearments and encouragement, Gerald sways through the sunbathed living room and dining room, shuffles barefoot down the hallway, and swings the smiling boy into the bedroom, Paul's arms frantically grabbing the air and his green eyes open wide. Amazing: he always wakes up in a great mood. It's going to sleep that's the bitch. A sour, earthy morning smell clings to the bedroom air. Lester lies in a comfy coil amid a crest of blankets. Gerald goes to the edge of the bed and peels back the covers with one hand, Paul still cradled in the other, and lowers the child onto the smooth white sheet. The boy flops down into the slight declivity formed by Nora's sleeping body, bumping to a stop directly in front of her blue nursing nightie. Without even opening her eyes, she fishes free a fat breast and scoots forward, the boy grabbing anxiously at the areola with his tiny fingers and whimpering as he fits his lips around the wobbly nipple. In seconds he's attached, and grows still, and starts sucking. Gently, Gerald steps around the bed and crawls in behind her. With his foot he nudges Lester, who, apparently getting the message, slowly stands, stretches his heavy body, and jumps with a little annoyed thud to the floor. Free now to stretch out, Gerald slides his hands along Nora's waist and cups her free breast from behind and presses his lips against the crook of her neck. He hears the gummy sound of a sleepy mouth opening in surprise. Then a dreamy whimper. Her body relaxes in his hand, nestling itself in the crook of his waist.

"Go away," she murmurs. "I don't want him to get flustered."

"He's starving. He won't mind."

"Plus, I'm trying to sleep." She nestles deeper into him, rolling her head along the pillow to give him more flesh to kiss. "How long have you been up? You smell like coffee."

He nibbles her cheek, eliciting a breathy sigh. Her hips wiggle against his waist. "I thought you hated it in the morning," she whispers.

"Shhhh."

"No complaints here."

He breathes in the sleepy smell of her skin. Paul sucks away, oblivious. July was the month Nora planned to wean him, but when the time finally arrived she found she wasn't ready yet to wean *herself*, so they're still at it, mother and child, a self-contained unit. Aside from the rice cereal he's started eating lately, Paul has so far subsisted entirely on Nora's milk. He knows nothing else. If Nora falls back asleep Gerald will leave her alone, but if she wakes up he'll tell her about the news story. In addition to the standard new-mother duties, her primary burden this last year has been to help him through his grief; his burden has been to help her through her guilt and her increasing alienation from her friends. She and Brent officially filed for divorce last August. She moved in with Gerald a month later. They combined her guilt and his grief and thereby sealed their commitment.

Fortunately or unfortunately (Gerald can't decide which), hers wasn't the only marriage destroyed by that bomb. Because Brent was never really part of their inner circle to begin with, and because the baby wasn't his in the bargain, he excised them all from his daily life without leaving so much as a scar. Not so Aaron and Sasha, the latter of whom moved back to Michigan last November, following her own divorce. They see absolutely nothing of Aaron, and that's probably all to the good, relatively speaking. All good, his father would say, is basically relative. Nor does Gerald see much of that old crowd from the newspaper, whose employ he quit last fall to reenroll in the graduate program at the university. Things go wrong, but things work out as well.

Nora's neck twitches against his nose. Paul continues to nurse, loudly and with self-absorbed satisfaction. "What's made you so affectionate all of a sudden?"

"It's been a year."

"Calm down, Boo," she tells Paul, who just whimpered. "It's right here, sweetie."

"It was in the newspaper," he goes on. "Today's the twenty-seventh—July 27." Releasing her, he rolls onto his back and stares at the ceiling. "They're calling it the anniversary of the blast or something. A new local holiday."

She shifts her position somewhat and whispers encouragement to Paul, who's still whimpering. Must be changing breasts. When all is still again, she says, "I guess I hadn't thought of that."

"I was reading the paper and there it was, this story. It kind of threw me."

"It's just a day, honey."

"I know."

"It doesn't mean anything. It's just a day on a calendar."

"Hoo, but what a day." When she stirs again, he touches her hip. "Don't go anywhere."

"Where would I go? I'm not even wearing pants."

"Let's just lie here all day," he proposes, though in fact he's got a ton of reading to do. With their combined student stipends, Gerald's occasional freelance record review, and the rare but sometimes necessary dip into Gerald's savings, they manage to make their monthly mortgage payment without too much trouble.

"Sounds wonderful," she replies, and reaches for his hand.

"We'll order in pizza, take the phone off the hook, lock the doors."

"Whatever, baby. You're the boss."

He slides off his boxers and nestles into the groove of her behind. Death dissolves in his thoughts. He must marry this girl. He must ask her officially, someday soon. Just pop the question, as they say. Be resolute. Who else can stand you, Brinkman? Who else could possibly put up with your shit?

"So," she murmurs, her attention still focused on Paul but her thighs also relaxing against his hips, "you have any suggestions for the meantime?"

"One or two. Just as soon as that kid falls into a milk coma."

"We're out of condoms, you know."

"No problem. You're still nursing."

"I don't think so, Captain. This is *me* we're talking about. The original Fertile Myrtle."

"I can think of worse things to happen."

After a brief pause, she carefully turns toward him. Apparently Paul is already deep into that milk coma because she manages this shift without hazard. That's what the whimpering was about: he was full. Both of her big breasts hang loose from the nursing flaps at the front of her nightgown. Her morning breath fans across his face. "You wanna back up there for a second?"

"I know what I'm saying."

"I'm not implying you don't." Her mouth hangs open in a smile of mild disbelief, her teeth chalky and yellow from sleep. He looks back and nods. Turning back to the sleeping baby, she touches him delicately on the cheek. "Let me get used to this one first."

"Fair enough."

"Also, there's the little matter of stretch marks, plus the ten pounds of lard on my hips, plus the episiotomy, which I don't relish experiencing again anytime soon. Not to mention the basic wear and tear on the boobs."

"Then don't mention it," he replies, and reaches for her left shoulder so that she must face him again. Sinking deeper into his own pillow he aligns his face with hers, their lips barely touching. "Or mention it but don't *say* you're not going to mention it."

"That's a tricky double negative there, Professor Brinkman."

"I realize that."

"And you with an ABD degree in English Literature and everything."

"Exactly," he tells her, and slides his knee between her legs. Along the top of his thigh he detects a dollop of dewy warmth. Behind her back Paul begins breathing loudly through his open mouth. "Which means it's a positive."

ACKNOWLEDGMENTS

In deepest gratitude I raise a foamy tankard to the following: Jim Rutman, my agent; Danielle Perez, my editor; Robert Cohen, my writing coach at Bread Loaf; Damaris Rowland, early champion; Mark Trainer, friend for life; Tom Bissell, boy wonder; Herman Carrillo, the Next Big Thing; Michael Collier, Phyllis Aleshia Perry, Lara JK Wilson, Will Clarke, Carol Burrage, Steve Almond, and everyone else at Bread Loaf; Tod Marshall, Kip Soteres, Liz Griff, Melanie-Conroy Goldman, Nathan Ragain, indispensable early readers; Bill Nelson, soundtrack composer; and most of all my wife, Rebecca, editor-in-chief and soul of my soul.

ABOUT THE AUTHOR

MARSHALL BOSWELL grew up in Tennessee and spent some of his grad school years in Atlanta. His short stories have appeared in a range of magazines, from *Missouri Review* to *Playboy*, and in *New Stories from the South, 2001*. His books include the story collection *Trouble with Girls*, as well as critical studies of John Updike and David Foster Wallace. He and his wife and their two sons live in Memphis, where he teaches American literature at Rhodes College.